KU-341-739

Georgina Newbery's abiding passion for fashion was nurtured during five years working for American *Vogue* and John Galliano in Paris. Eventually, exhausted, she turned her hand to the less demanding (she thought) task of novel writing. Surprised by the success of her first two novels *Catwalk* and *Think Pink*, and drawing on her extensive knowledge of the fashion industry, she now writes full time. She divides her time between London and Paris and travels as much of the world as she can on her journeys between the two.

Sand and Slingbacks

Georgina Newbery

WARNER BOOKS

A *Warner* Book

First published in Great Britain by Warner Books in 1999

Copyright © Georgina Newbery 1999

The moral right of the author has been asserted.

A CIP catalogue record for this book
is available from the British Library.

ISBN 0 7515 2821 8

Typeset in Perpetua by M Rules
Printed and bound in Great Britain by
Clays Ltd, St Ives plc

Warner Books
A Division of
Little, Brown and Company (UK)
Brettenham House
Lancaster Place
London WC2E 7EN

www.littlebrown.co.uk

for Christopher, David and Ian

with so many thanks to Alice and Alice
for mad frogs, cross porpoises and handbags, to
Benedict for helping me think, and of course to
Geoff Richards and Mike Pohling for their
continuing help and support.

Chapter 1

PANDORA Williams, chipper in threadbare jeans cut into hot pants and a worn Petit Bateau T-shirt, was draped across from her favourite editor's desk. Her legs were slung carelessly over the arm of her chair. She stroked them in a sort of fond but absent-minded way and blew a long stream of Marlboro smoke at the ceiling.

'You've got to get me out of this, Mimi.'

'Pandora, this shoot won't happen without you. I don't understand why you don't want to go. Imagine the pictures!'

'Imagine the amoebic dysentery more like.' Pandora snorted at the idea.

'That's India.'

'I don't care. How about the danger factor?'

'And Manhattan's so safe.'

'Imagine the fleas, the smell, the lack of air-conditioning. Nina actually expects us to spend three days in tents in the desert at a camel fair, where I expect we'll all get stampeded over in the night. There won't even be running water!'

'I'm sure I can negotiate that into your contract if you really want it.'

'What? Are you mad? You may be Nina's golden girl at the moment – as well as the absolute *dernier cri* in up and happening fashion stylists – but I doubt even you could achieve the installation of a pipeline for little old me.' Pandora's eyebrows did a sarcastic little dance. 'Or were you planning on running a hose over the desert from the Euphrates with a handy chlorination plant on the way?' She laughed.

'Other girls'd give their eye teeth to be going on this trip.'

1

'So, let them all make dental appointments! Plan this one without me.'

'But don't you see the romance in it? It's a fairy story place.'

'Fairy story! Romance! Dirty towns, dirty roads . . . I'd rather read a French nineteenth-century novel . . . in French!'

'Still no different from Manhattan . . .'

'A tour bus that belches fumes and breaks down miles from anywhere, loony Baghdadi truck drivers killing us whenever they get the opportunity and . . .' Pandora ran out of steam.

'And Richard the Lionheart's castle, the biggest bazaar in the world, the oldest constantly inhabited capital city in the world . . .' Mimi wouldn't be thwarted.

'You sound like a history book.'

'Stop interrupting; I'm trying to persuade you to go. Welcoming people who'll love you, bigger landscapes than even you can imagine,' said Mimi as she warmed to her task, pushing her halo of thick black curls out of her eyes and switching her phone off. Pandora sighed pointedly, lit another cigarette and let Mimi talk. 'Just think, you'll be going in the footsteps of all those incredibly brave and intrepid Englishwomen who took Syria by storm in the nineteenth century. They weren't frightened of a bit of a stomach upset; they mounted their camels and galloped off into the sunset, with the wind in their hair and thousands of admiring Bedouins following in their wake, tribesmen so loyal that they'd lay down their lives for them.' Mimi hoped Pandora wouldn't ask too many specific questions after this rather general account of the facts; she was still researching the trip herself. She drew breath and looked at Pandora, who was still smoking and staring at the ceiling. 'Well?'

Pandora swung her legs off the arm of the chair. She switched on her professional ravishing smile and laced it with just a threat of black cloud for the benefit of her favourite fashion editor.

'Watch my lips, Mimi. I don't want to go.'

Mimi looked as if she were about to cry, but Pandora, with a merciless swirl of bum-length, inky black hair, blew her a kiss, sped out of the building and jumped into the back of a big black Merc. This supermodel was off to a warehouse in the meat packing district where, amid the carcasses of a thousand cattle, the French designer Cristo had decided to photograph her in Audrey-Hepburn-inspired white organza fairy dresses for his spring–summer cosmetics campaign to be launched the following year.

Sheikh Faisal bin Ali al Mez'al, carelessly elegant in dress and attitude, lounged cross-legged on cushions in the outside drawing room of his house in Damascus. His mobile phone was tucked under his ear; he picked absent-mindedly at a loose thread hanging from the hem of velvety old Levi's.

'Yes, Nina, of course I'll be there.'

'Where are you staying, darling?' Nina's voice was tinny after its journey via satellite all the way from New York.

'I'll be at the Carlyle. I leave in an hour.'

'I am flattered that you're coming for the sale. You could have bought the emeralds over the phone.'

'Ah well, I'll do anything to get to a party . . . And I've got business in New York that I should really attend to in person.'

'I hope it won't take all day. Why don't you join us for lunch before the sale?'

'Thank you, Nina. I'd love to.'

'Great. Pandora's being a little backwards in coming forward about shooting in Syria. I'm sure she'll change her mind once she's met you.'

'Can't wait.'

'Four Seasons at one then?'

'See you there.' Faisal put the phone down and rubbed his hands involuntarily. 'Ha!' he said.

'Ali must be sick with envy,' Faisal's cousin Faraj said from where he sat cross-legged on the rim of the courtyard's central fountain. He dipped his fingers in the water and shook his head. 'You don't try and make his life any easier, do you?'

'I don't know what you mean,' said Faisal, his voice rich with false indignation.

'I'm only half joking.'

'So'm I.'

'I mean, here he is, feeling terminally hard done by already and you swan off to New York, where you plan on consorting with the star of all his dreams and spending what he considers to be his money on emeralds.'

'But you know as well as I do that there's nothing I could possibly do to make Ali feel less hard done by. I've tried, I really have. But every time I think I might have made one more step towards atoning for the sins visited on him by my parents he brings up yet another grudge which he's been secretly nurturing for years and years.'

'I know it's not your fault you got all the good stuff . . .'

'Good stuff! At the age of eight I was packed off to school in a cold, miserable country where I hardly spoke the language let alone understood the religion. A trunk full of things off the school list and nothing that I really needed. And I was only allowed home when I'd got a degree . . .'

'Rubbish. You and I spent all our holidays together in the desert. You're exaggerating.'

'No, I'm not. I was with you in the desert, not at home in the warm embrace of my mother like that spoilt little Ali, who spent his youth practically getting away with murder and was never denied a single thing.'

'Except an education.'

'Be sensible, Faraj. The English public-school system would have chewed up Ali and spat him out in no time. He wouldn't have got in anywhere for a start.'

'All right, all right.' Faraj raised his hands in defeat. 'I don't know why we're arguing. We both know that he only uses his grudges as an excuse for the many rather frightening flaws in his character . . .'

'And that I deserve nothing less than a trip to New York as a reward for putting up with the snotty little toe rag without chucking him out of the house.'

'Car's here, sir,' Faisal's secretary called from the front door.

'Thanks, Ahmed.' Faisal slipped on brown suede, snaffle-free Gucci loafers, slung a monogrammed Louis Vuitton suit carrier onto his shoulder and hurried to the door, carrying about him an air of carefully reined excitement.

'You can't fool me,' said Faraj. 'I know you're nervous as hell.'

'So long as you don't tell anybody, Faraj, then I don't care what you know.' Faisal slapped his cousin on his back. 'I'll see you in a couple of days. Ahmed, you know where to get me if there's a crisis.'

'Good luck with the bank,' Faraj called in parting.

'Stuff the bank! It's the emeralds I'm after. And tell Ali I'm bringing him back a supermodel!' Laughing, Faisal ducked through the low door in the wall, oblivious to the lead weight of the afternoon heat, and was gone. Once out of sight of the house, gone too was his air of jocular excitement. Faisal's driver, glancing back, saw only a rock hard expression on his face, tinged perhaps with melancholy.

A little later another figure slipped out of Faisal's house. Hugging the walls for shade rather than cover, this man slipped down side streets until he came to a halt at the terrace of a large café on the outskirts of the bazaar. He scanned the crowd of café patrons impatiently.

Finding the face he was looking for, he made his way to a shaded corner table, gloomy in contrast with the sharp, bleaching light of the mid-afternoon sun. He called for a water pipe and coffee and sat down.

'Ali!' The new arrival's hand was shaken heartily. 'So? What says the pawn in our little game, eh?'

'He's gone. He'll sign.'

'You're sure?'

'He doesn't care where the money comes from so long as he gets his emeralds.'

'I'll call Pictikhov and let him know.' Oily in a too-tight, sweat-stained, shiny grey suit, Ali's companion stubbed out his cigarette – contraband red Marlboro from the Lebanon – and hurried back to his rented house.

Inside the café a storyteller, hunched over a battered little

5

book, began to tell a tale as old as the Crusades featuring two brothers who loathed one another to the point of madness.

Ali spat neatly into a cross between cobbles.

'*Plus ça change*,' he said aloud to no one in particular and pulled on his water pipe, watching the bubbles rise busily to the surface.

Chapter 2

COURTENEY was late as usual. Swept along with the crowds pushing down Seventh Avenue, she fought her way across the sidewalk to the twenty-foot-high glass doors of the building that housed the magazine. She slid across the marble floor of the lobby, ignoring the flower stall, the newspaper stand and the sandwich shop which did business outside the security cordon protecting the rest of the building from the general public. Rooting around for her magnetic pass in the murky depths of her fake Gucci backpack, she found enough money for a toasted cinnamon and raisin bagel and turned back, scrabbling about for an extra couple of dollars for a cappuccino. She was in luck; she found enough for two and having bought breakfast and discovered her security pass jammed between the pages of her thick work diary she headed to the bank of elevators which would take her to Mimi's office on the 14th floor.

She arrived to find George, Mimi's other assistant, already ensconced at his desk, staring thoughtfully out of the window and not doing any work.

'Hey!' Courteney gave him a cappuccino before balancing her breakfast on one of the piles of paper that littered her desk and dropping her bag and coat on the floor. 'She in yet?'

''Course she is. She's with Nina and may be for some time.'

'So you're on strike till she gets back?'

'No – I'm gathering energy before I make my first onslaught on the day. And it's gonna be a long one.'

'No shit. So we're going to Syria after all?'

'I'd put money on it. Pandora can huff and puff all she likes but if Nina Charles says, "Get your pretty ass over to Damascus," she'll go. I think Pandora likes making all the fuss 'cos then we have to be extra grateful that she's come with us when she does.'

'What if the sheikh says no?' said Courteney through a mouthful of bagel.

'Yeah, likely. Why's he sitting on Nina's table tonight if he's gonna say no?'

'Maybe he's a cheapskate and'll do anything for a freebie?'

'Freebie! He's paying a thousand dollars for the honour and Nina's got all night to work her charm on him.'

'And when did anybody, ever, in the history of the world, hold out longer than about thirty seconds against Nina Charles's charm?' Courteney flicked bagel crumbs off her T-shirt and pinned her straggling hair out of her eyes with a Slim Barrett feather clip left behind after a long-forgotten sitting in the studio upstairs. 'So, what is there to do today? Do we hold fire on the Syria stuff till it's all confirmed or what?'

''Course we don't hold fire, sweetie. I've made you a list. Can you get onto Flash and check his and his assistant's details for the visas? I don't know which of his boys he's planning on taking but can you just make sure none of them have Israeli stamps in their passports? And whatever you do, don't let him start making difficult demands.'

'Yes sir!' Courteney saluted George and, pushing aside a pile of paper made mostly of empty envelopes and curling Post-it notes covered in unintelligible scrawl, she reached for two freelancer booking forms. It didn't matter how grand the photographer was, his assistant still had to fill in the details every time they were booked for a shoot. In the spaces provided she put Flash Harry and Joey Tranq's names and question marks beside them. Were they their real names? She then checked that there was room for passport numbers as well as nationalities and scribbled at the bottom of each page: 'If either of you have Israeli stamps in your passports we'll have to get you new ones – please let me know. Fax me back quickly Joey, I'm filling in the same forms for Saul and his current beau.'

She spun round to the fax machine that sat equidistant between hers and George's desks and, straining to reach without having to stand up, sent them on their way before pulling her phone forward and dialling Flash Harry's number.

'Hey Joey!' she said to the person on the other end of the line as she drew pictures of daisies on the back of an invitation to a private view she'd missed the previous May.

'Hey,' replied Flash Harry's assistant.

'I need to talk to you about Syria.'

'Fine. Got firm dates yet?'

'Nope. But can we confirm the option for Flash and one assistant for the middle two weeks of September?'

'Bit close to the shows. Flash wants to know if we can make it earlier.'

'The fair's around the eighteenth I think. If we go we'll definitely be there for that day.'

'Can't the sheikh move the fair?'

'Doubt it.'

'Well, I mean, if he wants Flash to be there then he'd better arrange things round Flash, no?'

'Honey he couldn't care less if we were there or not, let alone who takes the pictures.'

'Not sure Flash is gonna want to go somewhere where the host doesn't want him more than anyone else.'

'God, Joey, he's not going to get all superior on us is he? That's why Mimi's chosen him instead of Saul. Saul'd be impossible on a trip like this. Nina and Mimi love that Flash cares more about the pictures than whether he gets the best room or the best car or the best anything for that matter.'

'Nice schmoozing but it won't work. You and I both know it's my job to make sure he still gets über everything so that he doesn't have to make a fuss himself.'

'My heart bleeds for you.'

'Come on, Courteney – my life's tough enough as it is.'

'I thought you loved working for Flash.'

'Yeah – if he ever notices I'm actually there.'

'Honey pie, we know how hard you work. We appreciate you.'

'Fuck off, Courteney.'

'OK, OK, cut the crap. Fill in the gaps on the fax I just sent you and get it back to me like pronto right?'

'I'm rushed off my feet here.'

'Well if you're that busy then I'll hedge my bets and send the same questions over to Saul Smytheson's office just in case Flash really doesn't want to do it.'

Joey couldn't risk another minute. 'How dare you?' he snapped down the phone. 'I'll fax you back in five.'

Courteney grinned from ear to ear. 'Knew you wouldn't let me down, honey.' She put her phone down with a satisfied 'Right' and stood up, checking her appearance in the long mirror on the back of the office door. 'I'm off to get my daily fix of the cute new boy in the art department. Back in a minute.' And off she went almost crashing into Mimi in the doorway.

'Where's Courteney going in such a hurry?' Mimi asked as she sat down at her own desk, always clear but for a phone, a bottle of Evian, a tall blue water glass, and the large pad she now opened and began to write in.

'Checking the equipment we'll need to take with us.' George lied glibly.

'Good. So, where are we? Flash and Joey optioned?'

'Fax coming through now.' The machine began to whirr and the option forms Courteney had sent Joey started to come back covered in spidery handwriting. George grabbed them before Courteney could come back and lose them for him.

'Pandora's practically confirmed. How are you doing on the flights?'

'Fine. There's plenty of room for us on any flight we like. We can leave that part till the last moment if the dates are still a bit up in the air.'

'I expect they can always make room for us,' said Mimi with the blithe assurance born of working for the biggest fashion magazine in the world. 'Clothes?'

'We've got most of the list, but that new London magazine whose name is not to be mentioned in this office want the Dior just before us so I'm trying to arrange a carnet to go straight from them to Syria and we'll pick it up there and then send it back to Paris from Damascus.'

Mimi shook her head.

'It'll never work. All the clothes'll get lost and those that don't will certainly get stuck in somebody's customs along the way. They'll just have to live without the dresses. Can't they have something else?'

'They don't seem to care that we're us and therefore a million times more valuable to Dior than they are. If you're worried about losing things in customs then send someone to collect it all and accompany it.'

Mimi didn't get George's hint. 'But I want all the clothes here to check before we go. Don't tell me that if we get sent something dirty we'll be able to drop the dress into a specialist dry cleaners in Damascus. They simply won't be equipped for all that beading on the waffle wool.'

'They might. I could go to London and collect the stuff and have it cleaned there if needs be.' George was all innocence and eyelashes.

'Give me a break, sweetling – I'm hardly going to take that kind of a risk. Besides, you can't go to London, I need you here. Get me Dior on the phone. We'll see who gets those dresses when they want them.'

'Yes, ma'am!' George tried to hide his disappointment and failed.

'And I hope you don't plan on adopting that Eeyore expression on a permanent basis. Why don't you go and get us both a cappuccino to cheer yourself up? On me.' Mimi threw her purse across the room to George who failed to catch it. He sighed noisily, dialled the Dior press office in Paris, put them through to Mimi, picked up the money from the floor and escaped towards the elevators blinking away his tears.

Faisal limbered up for his meeting with the bank by practising finance speak in his head as he walked down town. His destination this morning was the real reason for his trip to New York; it was convenient that the bank had called and suggested that he come on the same day as the Sotheby's jewellery sale at the Met. His father had died six months ago now and the banker, a man called Sykes, had evidently decided that it was time Faisal assumed his familial responsibilities along with his inheritance. Faisal thought Ali extremely fortunate in that not only was he free of obligations as far as making sure that their extended family was provided for, but he didn't even have to know anything about the work which making these provisions entailed. A little pulse of nerves beat in Faisal's temples; he hoped it wouldn't show.

Heat simmered above the pavements. Faisal didn't notice it; his concern was with his fear of being discovered, being exposed as a fraud, fear of being taken for a ride, treated like an ignorant dilettante – all of which he believed himself to be. Buttoning his navy alpaca single-breasted herringbone suit jacket and shooting gold-linked cuffs, he turned right at Pine and William and strode towards his bank where, inside a set of leaden doors, a girl sat at a fine, reproduction Chippendale desk.

She smiled at him encouragingly and asked, 'Yes sir? Can I help you?'

Basalt eyes twinkled in reply. 'I hope so.'

The receptionist blushed and cleared her throat. 'Who was it you were here to see?'

He took a deep breath. 'A man called Sykes. Tell him Faisal al Mez'al's here, will you?'

Fourteen stories up, looking out over Times Square and Seventh Avenue, the heart of a huge media organisation beat strongly in an office housing Nina Charles, editor-in-chief of the biggest fashion magazine in the world. It was ten o'clock in the morning on the first Wednesday in September. Midweek apathy had settled on her staff and Nina was using Mimi Ytuarte – one of her up-and-coming, bright young thing, it-girl sort of editors – as a medium for putting enough oxygen into her team to last till Friday.

'Look, Mimi, it's more or less in the bag. I hope you've got Courteney and George onto the flights already.'

'Don't worry, Nina – everything'll be fine.'

'Good, 'cos I'm lunching with the sheikh and I want to be sure of everything.'

'He's here already?'

'He's got business to do first before he starts splashing out on jewellery tonight.'

'Who's he buying for?'

'Himself apparently. Seems he's rich enough to indulge this passion.'

'And no lady to display them on? Which are the ones he has his eye on?'

'The emeralds.'

'No kidding! Just the thing for a dusty desert town. You should get him to lend them to you for the shoot. I mean, if he doesn't mind us invading his desert then he probably won't mind us borrowing his rocks too, will he?'

'I don't like your tone, Mimi. I know none of you are that keen to go on this trip.'

'Well . . . Pandora seems determined to get out of it one way or another.'

'Are you all under the impression that you're going to a land of ancient barbarity where people rape and pillage and murder on a whim or what?'

'I'll make sure everyone does a bit of research.'

'It's the Middle East, Mimi – not the moon.'

'I know. But . . . I've always heard that the Middle East made the rougher parts of Bogata look relatively secure.'

'You've been listening to your mother again. If you must know, I'm more concerned about Rory. I'm not going to let him go. Pandora'll be persuaded, you'll do as you're told, but Rory, too fiery a canon to let loose in Syria, don't you think?'

'Nina, if he wants to go he'll just go. There'll be no stopping him.'

'Watch me. I've been keeping that man out of trouble for more than twenty years. And beautiful Bedouins straight from the desert are the kind of trouble I really think he doesn't need.

13

I took him to Morocco once and in spite of a personal nervous crisis he still managed to chase half the house servants around until they threatened to resign en masse – and that was before he started on the farm boys. Amazing really, they all had the most terrible teeth.'

'Perhaps he'll take hundreds of toothbrushes with him as bribes.'

'Don't be suggestive, Mimi – and don't you dare mention this to him.'

'Panic not, Nina.'

'I think I'll send him to Vegas to do that bikini shoot I've been putting off. I'll let him take anyone he likes and give him an unlimited budget. That should keep him out of the way for a while.' Nina crossed her immaculate, black silk, grosgrain Chanel capri-pant-clad legs and looked reflectively at her comfortable black patent J P Tod's. 'So, I've had lunch booked for us and the sheikh. Ideal opportunity for everyone to persuade everyone else that we're all perfectly civilised and will have a ball dancing about taking pictures together in Syria.'

'What time?'

'One o'clock sharp. Four Seasons.'

'Yes ma'am!' And in a flash of crisp white cotton Ralph Lauren and tailored Gaultier pants Mimi was off to put plans into action.

'Wait!' Mimi stopped in the doorway and turned to face her boss, pen and paper ready to take down more instructions. 'I left a message telling Pandora to come too. She never called me back. You'd better check she hasn't had a better idea. Tell her if she lets me down I'll have her hung, drawn and quartered before the day is out.'

The banker, protected from the world by the armour of bespoke double-breasted pin stripes softened by the fey detail of a watch chain, held himself safe from Faisal's reaction to his news behind a huge leather-topped desk.

'I don't understand.' Faisal hated having to make this admission; he felt as if the words the banker had so recently spoken

14

must have been meaningless, not only to himself, but to the other two suits present at the meeting.

'It's really very simple. Your father sold everything.'

Faisal struggled to hide a sudden feeling of vertigo. His knuckles were white as he grasped the arms of his chair. 'When you say everything, you aren't including the house?'

'Oh, no. Not the house, nor the desert. And, of course, you still have title to your personal belongings: cars, jewellery and so on.' The banker flashed an envious glance at Faisal's lapis lazuli lighter. 'French, about nineteen ten I should think?' he said, wistfully.

'My father left it to me.' Faisal had begun to breathe more easily. He put the lighter in his pocket, irritated at having been caught fiddling with it. 'And the cash he got from selling everything, how much of that is there?'

'Very little.'

Faisal held on tight while the green and red paisley carpet began to swirl again beneath his feet. 'I don't under——?'

'He spent it, Mr al Mez'al.'

'On what?'

'That I wouldn't know.'

'But what am I going to do?' The question escaped from Faisal before he had time to reign it in. He kicked himself for giving away his confusion.

'Well, there are always the mineral rights.' The banker smiled at Faisal through polished teeth.

'There aren't any mineral deposits to buy the rights for, not in my patch of desert anyway.'

Sykes picked up a document which had been sitting in solitary glory at the centre of an expensively tooled green leather blotter.

'Someone thinks there are . . .'

'Flash Harry for you. Do you want to take it?' Nina's long-suffering assistant called through the door to her boss's office.

'Put him through. Hello? Darling, how are you? Are you very excited about Syria?'

'Nina, what is this you're threatening me with?'

Nina knew that it wasn't the vast, echoing space of Flash's TriBeCa studio that was putting the hollow fury into his voice. 'Threats? I'm not threatening anything. What are you talking about?'

'Oh, so optioning me and Saul Smytheson for the same shoot isn't a threat. I'm sorry. I misunderstood. For a moment there I thought you were having your minions play us off against each other.'

'Flash, how could you think such a thing? There must be some misunderstanding.'

'Oh no, babe.' Nina could hear Flash Harry grinding his teeth down the phone at her. 'I have a little faxlet here in my own fair hand. It's signed by a girl called Courteney, who, if my mind doesn't deceive me, you lured away from Saul's employ yourself not so long ago. In it she asks all sorts of extremely personal questions, like is Flash Harry my real name, and if not what is it, followed by a warning to Joey that if she doesn't get an answer in five she'll option your favourite ageing queen and his current boyfriend for Syria.'

'Well, I think it's fair enough for her to ask if Flash Harry is your real name – after all, she's the one dealing with the visas and the plane tickets and things. And are you called Flash Harry on your passport, precious? If so then I apologise. But if *my* memory doesn't deceive *me* then your name is actually something very *vin ordinaire* which you insist on hiding from the general public due to some strange idiosyncrasy that I'm sure your shrink finds fascinating.'

Flash Harry spluttered. 'But what about the Saul bit, Nina? I'm not supposed to actually go into competition with that clown, am I? You're not seriously suggesting that he who answers some minion's questions first gets to go on this trip are you? Have you asked him whether his wigs travel under separate passports? And as for Israeli stamps – you talk about my hiding my origins, ever asked him about the nose job?'

'Stop it, Flash, or you'll say something you'll regret.' Nina's voice was arctic chill. 'I take it from all the fuss you're making that you really want to go on this shoot.' Nina's assistant came into the office making a 'It's one o'clock and you've got lunch with Faisal' face at Nina, who nodded and waved the girl to go and fetch her jacket. 'Listen, I will have words with the over-enthusiastic Courteney, but, with the greatest respect, I expect she was simply trying to encourage your assistant to get a move on. You know how all these children vie with one another to have the most important, busy and un-pin-down-able boss. Have Joey call Courteney and confirm everything and I'll make sure Saul doesn't even hear about the shoot, all right?'

'Fine. Don't you dare go giving this job to somebody else, Nina.'

'My we are using tough tones with someone who can make or break your career in a lunch date, Flash.' Nina stood and shrugged on the jacket which was being held out for her. She grabbed her bag, slipped the shoes she'd kicked off back on again and moved round her desk ready for her escape. 'Speak to you later, darling.' She smiled down the phone. 'And if you've got a minute, do make sure that Joey's given Courteney all the details she asked for in her fax. We don't want to have too many more of these conversations, do we?' And without waiting for Flash to reply she put down the phone.

'Where does that man get off?' Her assistant shrugged and Nina hurried off to her waiting car, checking her watch, hating the fact that she might now be late.

'Pandora? I'm on my way . . .' Mimi's car headed across Central Park to pick up the supermodel and take her to lunch with Faisal the Sheikh. She was trying unsuccessfully to imagine a sheikh who liked to buy jewellery when the driver stopped for Pandora, who leapt into the car, all bum-length raven hair, fantastic eyelashes and never-ending legs.

'What do you think?' Pandora asked. She'd have given Mimi a twirl if the confines of the back seat had permitted it. The driver almost crashed when he saw her in the rear-view mirror.

'Pandora! It's a bit obvious, isn't it?'

'Nina rang and told me to behave properly, so I thought I'd give her the last word in supermodeldom. Besides, I thought Faisal the Sheikh would appreciate a bit of flesh baring while he was here. Must be awful being surrounded by women wearing black sacks over their heads and down to their feet all the time.'

'Pandora! You'd get shot if anyone but me heard you talk like that.'

'Admit – I have a point.'

'No. I won't. Don't you think you could have worn something over your underwear?'

'This is an outfit, sweetheart. It's Julien Macdonald silk knitted lace, and you know how unbelievably chic that is. Besides, if I feel under-dressed I can always arrange my hair to cover me up a bit.'

'Still, there's revealing and then there's downright naked, don't you think?'

'Mimi – you're going to have to be careful. You're sounding more and more like Nina every day. You're only a year older than me. As one of the hippest fashion editors this side of the Atlantic, you should be wearing Macdonald as well.' Pandora looked critically at Mimi's immaculate navy Gaultier suit and its jacket, which only just held her exuberant breasts at bay. 'All right – I give in. You look lovely. And I wish I could force myself to wear navy – it's so smart but I can't help but think I should wait until I'm a grandmother.'

'You bitch! Oops – we're here. Now, Pandora, promise me you'll be good.'

'I won't promise a thing, Mimi. I don't want to go to Syria so I have no need to suck up to Nina's new pet favourite.'

'Pandora, please.'

'Oh don't panic, Mimi. I know my job. I play dumb and lovely, and you and Nina and your steely brains negotiate the deal. We all go to Syria, you shoot thousands of lovely pages for Christmas and I collapse with exhaustion while struggling down the runway at Chanel in a month.'

'I promise to get you a holiday in between. Come on. Let's hit the fray.'

'I do have a brain, Mimi.'

'I know you do, sweetling.'

'I can be more than just charming.'

'Of course you can.'

The dining room of the Four Seasons was low-season empty. Far from the door, cut off from the girls by the central marble pool, Pandora saw Nina point them out to the sheikh. Faisal stood to greet the supermodel his brother couldn't stop talking about. She was magnificent; her proportions could have been a little Amazonian were it not for the china fragile quality of her bone structure, flawless satin skin and ebony hair which hung in a straight river to a point where it danced, innocently suggestive, a generous hand-span lower than her waist. Faisal clocked all of these things automatically and was not overwhelmed. Her body fulfilled all the conventional demands of late-twentieth-century beauty but it was to her eyes that Faisal found himself drawn. They refused to conform; in their watery green depths he saw her daring him to look at her, daring him to see behind the supermodel mask. And when she recognised that he'd seen all that she'd dared him to, there was a shift in their light; now they reflected a barely tamed animal fear, thinly veiled by glaring bravado. Under different circumstances he might have found her fascinating.

'Hello,' she said. 'I'm the pretty girl with the legs and this is Mimi with the brains.' Pandora's voice was acid as they arrived at the table. She kissed Faisal on both cheeks and sat down. 'You are a chic sheikh. Where's your tablecloth and party dress?' There was a stunned silence. 'Well?' Faisal didn't answer. Nobody else thought she was funny. She leant over to the guest of honour and in a stage whisper told him, 'I'm supposed to bat my eyelashes and play dumb.' Faisal simply raised his chin as if he understood this scantily clad giraffe. 'You'll have to excuse the concrete-booted comments.' Faisal raised an eyebrow a quarter of an inch instead of answering. 'Don't you speak at all?'

'Shall we order?' Nina sliced through the atmosphere with the edge of her smart English voice.

19

'I'll bet this makes a change from sheeps' eyes and rice doesn't it?' Pandora just couldn't help herself. Faisal stared at her, unsmiling. It was time for Nina to take control.

'You'll have to excuse Pandora.' Nina turned the full force of her charm onto Faisal. 'She may seem *mondaine* but in fact her experiences are somewhat limited.'

'Manhattan, flight, car, hotel, location, shoot, hotel, car, flight, Manhattan.' Pandora's voice was brittle. 'Nina does have a point. I'm sorry, Faisal, but I really did expect you to turn up wearing a tablecloth on your head.' She tried to be gracious, recognising that Nina's tone of voice meant the assembled company should get in line and stay there. Faisal, however, did not speak fluent Nina; he hardly seemed to be taking in anything at all.

'Faisal?' Nina was worried now.

He blinked, shook his head, and without warning stood up, dropping his napkin and smoothing his jacket with the palms of his hands; Pandora noticed they were shaking. He smiled vaguely at his lunch dates and said, 'I'm sorry. You'll have to excuse me.'

And before Mimi'd finished saying, 'But what's the . . . ?' he was gone.

'Now look what you've done!' Nina was horrified.

'Don't blame me.' Pandora defended herself with a determined mouth and firmly crossed arms.

'You don't think his marching off like that might have had something to do with your asking him about sheep's eyes and rice? Pandora, how could you?'

'You mean how could *you*, don't you?' Pandora felt tears of fury burning her eyes. She blinked them back, determined not to cry. 'All you wanted me to give him were legs and hair. So legs and hair I gave and he ignored them! If I shut my brain down like I'm supposed to then that kind of comment comes out. And if you hadn't got all schoolmarmy on us then it wouldn't have been so bad. It was just when you sounded so disapproving that it made me look worse. I'd have got myself out of it. I promise I would. Anyway, it wasn't me that made him

20

shake; he was all pale and nervous before we arrived, you know.'

'Pandora, I don't think you understand quite what's at stake here.'

'Oh patronise me some more, why don't you? I was trying to make a point there but you're obviously not interested. You just want to blame me because the sheikh didn't behave according to your rules. I'm not hungry either.' It was Pandora's turn to drop her napkin and stand up ready to march out of the restaurant.

'Pandora! Wait.'

'Why?'

'I didn't ask you to shut your brain down, I just asked you to do what you do best which, let's face it, is to look lovely. That's your job, darling, that's what we pay you for. If I wanted a rocket scientist I'd go out and get one. And you're right, Faisal obviously did have other things on his mind or he'd have reacted with proper horror to your comments about the tablecloth and the sheep's eyes.'

'Nina, you do realise that if you'd ever let me finish school then I might not be such an embarrassment to you in public. If you want a pretty me with nothing much to say for herself then why don't you just get a cardboard cut-out and have that put on the chair? Eh? Eh?'

'Don't be so tetchy. You've never wanted to be anything but the most beautiful woman in the world and I think we can agree that you've achieved that ambition. You are the ideal woman, you are what women all round the world aspire to.'

'On the outside.'

'What?'

'On the outside. Inside I'm a mess.'

'Oh well, if we're going to get all self-indulgent and intro-spective . . . Come on,' Nina's tone was cajoling. 'We know what you're up to so you can stop pretending, Pandora. You're still trying to get out of going to Syria. I have to tell you you're as transparent as this water and I'm afraid all this posturing just won't wash.'

'Fuck you, Nina!'

*

21

Faisal folded his wiry six-foot-plus frame into a series of angles onto the edge of a chair. Static crackled from Damascus and the sheikh leant far forward over the desk in his hotel room, as if the act of getting closer to the phone would automatically clear the line.

'I don't understand, Faisal.'

'I have to admit, Ahmed, neither do I.'

'But there's no rush to sign these papers. Bring them home and I'll look them over for you.'

'I signed them already.'

'You did what?!'

'What else was I supposed to do? I mean, seriously Ahmed, my father left us with about two pounds fifty sterling. I didn't have any choice.'

'You sold your birthright and with the money you're going to buy emeralds. I'm shocked.'

'Birthright! I've sold the Devil's Kitchen, not the title or the house or . . . Don't be like that. I wouldn't have skipped lunch to tell you if I thought you'd be angry. I thought you ought to know. I didn't expect this reaction at all.'

'You called me hoping that I'd salve your guilty conscience, you mean. Even you couldn't sit and chat up a supermodel when you knew you'd done something so fundamentally wrong.'

'I thought you'd be pleased. Twenty million dollars, Ahmed! Just think. It'll shore up what's left after my father sold everything. Besides, he was the one who negotiated the sale. He must have wanted me to do this. If he'd lived then he'd have signed the documents months ago and this wouldn't have been anything to do with me. I'd be innocently dancing about in a speedboat somewhere off Monte Carlo at this time of year, not sweating it out on Wall Street with a selection of suits who speak a language I don't understand.'

'But—'

'So don't take it out on me, Ahmed. Never mind the emeralds; now there's money to pay your salary, Ali's allowance; I've got overheads that I can't ignore.'

22

'If only you'd had the patience to bring this all home so that we could have made the decision together. I can't trust people who want to drill for mineral rights that everybody knows don't exist.'

'Perhaps there's a new system that means they can go deeper or can find things they couldn't find before.'

'Don't you think we'd have heard about it?'

'Not necessarily. I'm going to call Faraj.'

'Well you'll get even shorter shrift from him. Faisal, at least admit you might have been hasty.'

'I did what I felt I had no other choice but to do. I was cornered. Anyway, thanks for your support, Ahmed. I'm really glad I rang you.' Faisal humphed as he heard the line go dead in Damascus before he'd had time to slam the phone down himself.

He didn't call Faraj, or anyone else for that matter. Instead he sat and drew sharply pointed triangles on the empty legal pad he'd taken from his briefcase. Bored of triangles, he started on boxes, carefully colouring them in. The Cartier travel clock beside his bed ticked away the hours and Faisal didn't move. The chill of loneliness enveloped him. If he'd thought to eat something then he might have felt better, but he was too confused to remember that an increase in blood sugar always helps with depression, and there was nobody who cared enough to remember for him. The phone broke his reverie. Long-fingered hands pushed dark, unruly hair away from his deep-set basalt-black eyes. He checked the clock, ignored the phone and went to shower. Ahmed could go jump; Faisal had emeralds to buy and supermodels to flirt with and nothing, not even this sudden unfamiliar sense of alienation, was going to make him stop and consider the gravity of what he'd done.

New York sweltered; even the buildings seemed to sag under the weight of the relentless heat. Pandora, bored, listless, hiding from the burning weather, lay in the cool gloom of her silver drawing room kicking her legs like an upside-down ballerina doing grandes échappes in the air. She was surrounded by the trappings of her success: her Gucci holdall; her mobile phone, the sound switched off, flashing at her with a constant stream of new messages; a monogrammed, pigskin, Hermés diary, bursting with social and professional engagements. Discarded on the floor beside her was her bank statement, one more reminder of how the world loved her enough to pay her handsomely for doing nothing but look lovely, day in, day out, for ever and ever . . . She kicked the bank statement away and then, inspired, threw the rest of these trappings into a corner.

Rory heard the noise from the elevator down the hall. He found Pandora dancing naked, head back, arms stretched wide, whirling, feral, howling her ennui.

'Pandora! What the hell do you think you're doing?' She stopped short, holding on to the arm of the sofa while the room still spun around her. She focused: Rory stood at the drawing room door, his face flushed with a mixture of confusion and embarrassment.

'Had a lovely lunch, precious? Aren't you back a little early?' Rory filled the silence left by the death of her howls. Pandora cast herself back onto the sofa and threw an arm over her eyes achieving total desperation in her appearance.

'Oh, darling, is that all it is? Are we having a tiny little crisis? For just a second I thought you'd gone stark staring mad.' He leant against the door jamb and folded his arms. 'Don't tell me – Mimi wants you to wear something nasty from the woodshed for her next shoot. No – Nina thinks you're too old to model and wants you to get a job as an assistant at the magazine.' Rory's eyes were wide at the thought of this possibility.

'Don't be ridiculous – as if Mimi would try to make me wear something I don't like. You know she knows I have impeccable taste. And how dare you suggest I'm over the hill – I'm barely twenty-seven!'

'So, what's the matter, my precious? You were playing wild wolf there, darling. I was worried for a moment that I was going to have to call for an ambulance. Let me help you work it

24

out. You know other people's problems are my speciality.' Rory perched on the arm of the sofa and looked down at the pure perfection of his niece's body.

'I'm not supposed to tell you about it. But Nina's just been so horrible to me that I might get my own back.'

'Oh that Nina, nothing but secrets. She really should know by now that if there is one I'll find out about it sooner or later, even if I have to pump people full of truth serum while they sleep to make them tell all.'

Pandora sighed, sat up, crossed her legs and leant forward. 'All right, I'll tell you. But there is one condition.'

'What, darling? That I make us both a mid-afternoon gin and tonic? No problem.'

'No – not drink.'

'What then? Come on, spit it out or we'll be here all night.'

'Give me a chance to get a word in and I might be able to.' Rory mimed zipping his lips. 'You mustn't breathe a word of this to Nina or Mimi. If they find out I've told you they'll never photograph me again.'

Rory unzipped his lips. 'Don't be ridiculous.'

'Promise, Rory!'

'Ah, the seriousness of youth! Yes, darling, I promise.'

'You've crossed your fingers.'

'All right, Pandora – look, uncrossed fingers and toes and legs,' he said, waving them all about doing an unlikely impression of a dying fly. 'Satisfied?'

'Fine. Now shut up and listen.' Pandora lit a red Marlboro preparatory to telling her tale. 'It's like this: Nina wants to shoot the central story for the Christmas edition in Syria.'

'How fabulous! When do we leave?'

'That's just it. I'm leaving. You're going to shoot bikinis in Las Vegas.'

'Over my dead body.'

'Seriously! Nina doesn't trust you with the Bedouin boys. She thinks you'll make trouble and ruin everything.'

'As if . . .'

'Well . . . Admit it, Rory, you do have a penchant for a

25

born-with-it tan. And look at all the trouble you caused in Morocco!'

'I only did—'

'Stop interrupting.'

'Sorry.' Rory stuck his bottom lip out in unconvincing contrition.

'The point is she's asked this sheikh if we can go and shoot at his camel fair in the desert. She really wants to do it. She's convinced it'll put all the other Christmas issues to shame and we'll come out with something really special.'

'So what's the problem apart from the fact that I'm simply going to have to turn up and save the day anyway? You can't go to the Middle East without me.'

'Rory – can we talk about me first?'

Rory sighed. 'I'm sorry, precious. You first and me in a minute, I promise.'

'The thing is that I just don't want to go to Syria!'

'Oh, Pandora, you didn't?'

'Didn't what? I'm talking about what I'm going to be made to do in the future, not what I've done already.'

'You don't want to go because you fell madly in love with the sheikh and then you were absolutely horrible to him and now you're embarrassed.'

'Fall in love with him! He wasn't there long enough to fall in love with. Nina and Mimi told me to sit still and act stupid so I sat still and got my own back.'

'Oh, darling . . .'

'All I did was say a couple of relatively risqué things but I swear he didn't even notice. I might as well have been a brick wall. And before we'd even ordered he marched off saying he'd forgotten he had something very important to do.'

'Oh dear.'

'Don't raise your eyebrows at me like that, Rory Williams. You've never seen anything like it. Can you believe it?'

'And has he said you can't go and shoot his camel fair?'

'No.'

'Then what's the problem?'

'I don't want to go to his stupid camel fair. I . . .' Pandora dried.

'Yes?'

Pandora sat straight now, pulling her mane of hair back from her face and tying it in a loose knot. 'I don't know . . .'

'Well . . . Was he more beautiful than you?'

'That's not the—'

Rory bulldozed through Pandora's attempt to explain herself. 'Don't be upset about that, my lovely. I'm not surprised. You're always quite rightly stunned when people don't fall at your feet and beg you to grind the heels of your sharp little Manolo's into their willing behinds, because it happens so seldom. And just because you measure your eyelashes to cheer yourself up when you're miserable doesn't mean that everyone else should have a fixation about them too, darling. Besides, if he's a desert Arab then his eyelashes are probably long enough to make yours look as if they'd had an over-enthusiastic trip to the lash dressers.'

'Thanks, Rory. You've made me feel a whole lot better . . . Not! Watch my lips. I am not in love with him! He is not my problem.' Pandora, still naked, stormed out of the room, frustration fighting with fury in the swinging of her bum-length hair. 'I just don't want to go.'

In her bedroom, Pandora sat and looked at herself in the mirror; the void she saw behind her eyes filled her with such a vertiginous terror that she was forced to shut them and catch her breath.

There was a tentative knock.

'Permission to ask forgiveness, darling?' Rory poked his head round the door and smiled winningly. Pandora couldn't resist him; he was her uncle, her father figure, her best friend. Ultimately she could refuse him nothing. He pushed the door wider and carried in a tray loaded with a plate of thickly buttered toast and Marmite soldiers and an ice-cold carton of milk. 'Comfort food, precious,' he said, setting it down on her dressing table before standing back and looking at her, his hands on his hips, his head cocked to one side, an eyebrow raised in ruthless appraisal. 'Now, if you'll take some advice from your Uncle Rory, who wants nothing but what's good for you and only things which'll make you happy, I think you'll find that the cause of all this bolshy nervous thoroughbred behaviour is a tiny touch of hypoglycaemia, so I should eat up if I were you before you start changing for the sale tonight.'

'What sale?'

'Darling, Sotheby's have moved into the Met remember?'

'Oh my God!'

'And we've got to be there in our best bib and tucker and all glittery and shiny for the paparazzi, haven't we?'

'Shit!'

'So I'm off to start squeezing myself into my Mr Pearl corset so that my Saint Laurent doesn't catch me about the waist. And you, baby, why don't you take courage from your Marmite soldiers and drink your milk and then we'll go to the party together, eh?'

Rory whistled as he danced back down the hall. Perhaps he was right; Pandora picked up a soldier and after a bite or two couldn't help wishing he'd boiled her an egg to dip it into.

The crowd for the gala Sotheby's sale at the Costume Institute at the Met was herbaceous-border luxuriant in colour and design. Society, money and beauty had all rushed back from their holiday retreats for the night to make pure glamour for the photographers jammed behind barriers, jostling for the defining picture of the night. Nina paused for them and gave them a view of some very expensive dentistry. She and Pandora, frosty with each other but performing well for their public, were framed tonight by Rory on one side and Nina's husband, the famous architect Sam McAllistair, on the other.

They made a magnificent foursome: Rory in a vintage Saint Laurent, *haute-couture* 'smoking', Sam in a white dinner jacket, Pandora in gun-metal grey satin Donna Karan, and Nina in floor-length white beaded Dior. They'd tried to pick up the sheikh at his hotel but he hadn't been there. He hadn't answered

Nina's calls either. She bared her teeth in a professional smile to cover her concern and headed up the steps of the Met.

Downstairs, in the Costume Institute, tables for three hundred guests had been set up in one room; drinks before dinner were to be served in another under a roof of suspended arrangements of Nina's favourite flower combination, white dog roses and copper beech; in a third chamber the auction of the year was ready to be started. The jewels to be auctioned were laid out on purple velvet cushions. Each lot was the centrepiece of an arrangement including pictures of past owners wearing the jewellery as well as the documentation that came with it to prove provenance. Nina was justifiably proud, she'd had everything to do with the display – even if her assistant had done all the dirty work and even now was manning the doors and would be working her fingers to the bone until long after midnight.

The emeralds that the sheikh wanted were in front of a portrait, borrowed from the Hermitage, of them being worn by the last Tsarina of Russia. Nina found him there looking at them.

'They are mesmerising.'

'Indeed.'

Nina was surprised; she'd thought him hard-featured but the sheikh was beautiful when he smiled.

'I'm afraid that set out like that and with so much interest in their story they'll fetch a much higher price than their reserve.'

'They deserve a high price. How can one put a value on something so beautiful?' Faisal seemed overwhelmed by them. Nina turned to look over the room of potential buyers.

'So, you'll fight off other bidders?'

'Whatever it takes.'

'I'm glad to see you're so determined. Oh no . . .' Nina's face fell. Pandora was bearing down on them.

'Pandora.' The sheikh kissed Pandora's hand.

'Aren't they lovely?' Pandora hardly acknowledged him; she pressed her nose against the glass case. 'Nothing can be more beautiful than emeralds,' she breathed.

'Do you think so?' asked Faisal. Nina backed off, having

given a critical retreating glance at the emeralds. Pandora would look magnificent in them if Faisal would lend them to be photographed.

'Oh yes,' she heard Pandora say as she moved away. 'If you buy them who'll wear them?'

'No one. I'll keep them in Damascus and look at them every now and then.'

'How awful! They'll die if nobody wears them.'

'They're not pearls, Pandora.'

'Why do you want them so badly?'

The sheikh didn't answer her question. 'Excuse me. The sale's about to begin. I must find my seat.' He disappeared into the crowd. Pandora didn't follow him. Instead she perched on a tiny gilt and purple velvet chair, legs crossed, and pared her nails with the sharp end of a jet Victorian crucifix while the voice of the auctioneer rang out announcing the first lot.

The audience was made up of a mixture of buyers and voyeurs. There was no way of telling these two groups apart, except, perhaps, that those who were determined to avoid spending more than the $1000 they'd already laid out for cocktails and dinner were more relaxed than the buyers. They spent the sale searching the room, checking that they were as well dressed, well coiffed, well manicured as the next person. Faisal, intent on buying, ignored the spectacle provided by the audience and made his way to the seat Nina had arranged for him. Once the sale had begun, only the sound of Sotheby's reps manning the phones, whispering occasional 'The bid is with you sir's down a hundred long-distance phone lines, broke the sale room silence until the gavel fell on each 'Sold!', after which the rounds of applause grew. Ten per cent of the proceeds were going to the Costume Institute and the governors' smiles stretched wide as their cut of the profits ballooned. Nina was pleased too; the evening would be the success of the season, and she and her magazine would glow in the papers in the morning with a great big slice of reflected glory.

Then it was time for the sale of the emeralds. Somewhere down the line, a telephone bidder was pushing up the price.

Faisal didn't bat an eyelid. The bidding went from fifty thousand dollars, to one hundred, one hundred and ten, twenty, thirty. Only when the price reached four hundred and eighty thousand dollars for a necklace, earrings and a bracelet did he suddenly blanch. He turned and stared at the rep looking after the telephone bidder. The rep stared back, impassive; he whispered something into the receiver. The auctioneer raised his hammer to sell to the telephone bidder. Faisal sighed. Nina saw him make fists, frown deeply, breathe in and look up. With a split second to spare he topped the telephone bid. The emeralds were his for the outrageous price of half a million US dollars.

As the applause for Faisal's gritty determination shook the room, the sheikh disappeared through the nearest exit. He paid for his jewellery with a draft drawn on his American bank and slipped the emeralds out of their case and into his inside breast pocket. He hurried out of the building and found himself on the steps of the great old museum struggling for air. The surge of adrenalin he'd felt as he bid for his emeralds had drained away; now his legs shook and a cold sweat sprang uncontrolled along his hair line. He sat down on the sun-warmed steps, closed his eyes and dropped his head, resting his elbows on his knees. The hair he'd oiled back in an attempt to tame it rebelled over his hands.

'What have I done?'

Across the steps Pandora perched on the balustrade, the thick grey of her dress the exact colour of the sky, the green of her eyes flashing fire in the burning light of the setting sun. 'Is that a rhetorical question or should I answer it?' she asked him. Looking round, Faisal caught her staring at him and leapt to his feet, blushing furiously.

'Cigarette?' she asked. He didn't even answer her. Turning on his heel, he headed purposely into the maze of the Upper East side. A corner took him out of her sight before he tore at his black tie as if it were strangling him and opened the top buttons of his shirt, gulping in the New York air – a mixture of stale petrol fumes, frying onions and hot dogs – like it was pure oxygen. Pandora shrugged, threw away her half-smoked cigarette and ground it out under the perspex heel of her silver-satin-strapped Manolo Blahnik sandals.

'And fuck you too then,' she shouted in Faisal's general direction. 'It's time for dinner so I'll go eat.'

Faisal's disappearance did nothing to take away from the success of the evening. Nina filled his place at dinner by moving a couple of celebs around and seating Leonardo di Caprio next to Pandora to cheer her up. This ploy didn't work; Leo may have been charming but Pandora was in no mood to chat up someone as beautiful, as famous and even more in demand than she was herself.

'Cheer up, precious.' Rory glittered at her. 'Didn't my Marmite ploy work?'

'No. So I suggest you don't dare talk to me, Rory. Why don't you give in to temptation and just be really cross because I'm behaving like a bad-tempered child?'

'Hmm, darling . . .' Rory, not listening to Pandora, started to clap. 'Sshh . . . Nina's going to make her speech.'

'But I wanted to tell you . . . I'm clear why I can't go to Syria now.'

'Not now, Pandora!'

'Why not?'

'You want me to be cross, precious? Well there's a time and a place. We'll talk about this later.'

'But Nina's going to make me go.'

'Quite right too.'

'But I told you I can't.' The clear tones of Pandora's voice rose above the post-applauding quiet. Everyone turned to stare at her. She glared back but was silenced when, after only one murderous look, Nina began her speech.

Chapter 3

Faisal, chain-smoking, restless, disoriented, walked the streets of New York all night, weaving between the fountains of purple fumes which wound up from between paving stones, lacing the air. He watched the people who lived on the streets practise survival – panhandling, searching through trash cans, whining for attention from those who might afford the time to help them. He threw a pocketful of change at three old men who sat on the steps of up-town Barneys; they were laughing and telling jokes for cash. The word 'birthright' echoed round his mind like a doleful refrain; he would have given his newly acquired $20 million not to have heard Ahmed say it.

He kept on walking, the rhythm of his footsteps almost enough to empty his mind. It never occurred to him that carrying half a million dollars' worth of emeralds might have put him at risk on the Manhattan streets. Muggers passed him by on the other side of the street; nobody wants to tangle with a man exuding such an air of pure animal frustration.

Eventually, as the blush of the early dawn pushed the electric-edged night westwards from across the East River, Faisal turned back towards the Carlyle. There he threw himself, fully dressed, onto his bed. His dreams were evident only in the curl of his eyelashes, butterfly fluttering on the sharp lines of his cheeks. He remembered nothing of them when he woke up.

'Pandora?'

'Hm?'

'Darling, wake up, it's me.'

'What?' Pandora pulled herself to a sitting position and pushed her hair out of her eyes. 'What time is it?'

'Darling, it's eight-thirty. I know this is a little early for you . . .'

'A little!'

'I need to talk about Syria with you.'

'Won't you ever give up, Nina? Besides, I can't go. Faisal hates me.'

'No he doesn't, darling. I saw the way he looked at you last night.'

'Yeah, right.'

'Darling, I can tell you now. He wants you to go.'

'Nina, stop it. I don't care what he wants. The only times I've met him he's done nothing but be rude to me. I made all sorts of efforts to be nice to him last night just to please you and Rory and he practically spat at me before he disappeared.'

'I'm sure you're overreacting. You're just not used to people being so subtle with you.'

'Subtle! He couldn't have made himself clearer. And I don't care what efforts you make, Nina. I don't want to go.'

'What are you so frightened of, precious?'

'I'm not frightened of anything. I just don't happen to like trading in five-star comfort for sand in my slingbacks.'

'You've been to sandy locations before.'

'St Barts! It's hardly the desert, Nina. And even the desert locations I've been shot in have been within spitting distance of trustworthy air-conditioning and a cool drink when I want one. Surely there's some other desperate girl who'd like to do this.'

'You really don't care do you?'

'About what?'

'Me, or Rory, that we might need you to do this for us.'

'Oh don't start on a guilt trip, Nina. It won't kill you to shoot with somebody else for once. And you didn't even want Rory to know about it so don't bring him into the equation.'

'All right, you force my hand,' Nina said pointedly.

'What?'

'I'm going to have to tell you the real reason I need you to go.'

'Entertain me.'

34

'I'm frightened that without you Mimi won't be up to it. If you go then you can help her control the rabble. Without you she'll be putty in Flash Harry's hands.'

'So send Rory as stylist or Saul as photographer. You can't pin the success of the team on the doubtful talents of the model as an administrator of people. Remember it's me who's supposed to be allowed to do the spoilt brat thing while everyone else makes the concrete team to protect my fragile sensibilities from the rough and tumble of the rest of the world.'

'But I know that if you and Mimi go together then the pictures will be magnificent. They'll be works of art. You'll get all the credit.'

'Bullshit, Nina. Flash and Mimi'll get the credit. I'll just get "we expected nothing less of you Pandora" as if all I did was stand there and look lovely and didn't perform at all.'

'How can I persuade you?'

'Nina, you can't. I'm sorry.'

'I'm not giving up.'

'You'll have to eventually.'

'We'll see, darling.'

Pandora put the phone down and began to chew the skin round her left thumb. She slapped her hand away from her mouth. If she did go to Syria no one would thank her for turning up with mangled fingers. Pulling on pale blue cotton men's pyjamas, she padded down the hall. She needed to talk to Rory.

Fogged with sleep, Faisal paid his bill and left a note of apology and an explanation for the Carlyle to send over to Nina's office. He took a cab to JFK. It seemed to be held together with bits of string and old suitcase belts, and the journey in the rattling old yellow machine with stuffing bursting out of the hot brown plastic seats soon burnt the mist off his brain. He smiled at the driver, whose English was mostly Korean, and tipped him well and, slinging his suit carrier over his shoulder, he headed into the airport with a spring in his step. For the next twelve hours or so there was strictly nothing he could do about his situation; birthrights, deserts, cash flow, brothers, disapproving old retainer secretaries – all of them would just have to wait while time took charge until Faisal made it home. He bought the *New Yorker* and the *Economist*, *Esquire* and the *New York Times*. The front page of the *Times* featured a photograph of Pandora and Nina not smiling at one another on the steps outside the Metropolitan Museum of Art. Faisal ordered coffee in the First Class lounge and scanned the report of the jewellery sale to see if there was anything about the frosty air between the great editor-in-chief and her protégée, the supermodel. Even his mobile phone was switched off. Nobody could get him here, he was cocooned from the world and he loved it.

Chapter 4

Aᴺʸ lingering post-sale hangovers were to be left at the door when Nina drew the final planning meeting for the Syria trip to attention. Light-hearted laughter lit the room on this last afternoon before the Labor Day weekend. Next week the team would work; today it was still summer, and talk of budgets and steamers, make-up and film, let alone the cost of carrying Flash Harry's colossal quantity of equipment as excess baggage, could not distract from the fun to be had going through *Women's Wear Daily* and the other reports of the jewellery sale. The ice in the *New York Times* picture of Nina and Pandora was noticed by everybody but mentioned by no one; Nina didn't like her disagreements being made public and would deal sharply with anyone she suspected of having an opinion on the matter.

At Nina's editorial planning meetings the team involved in the shoot is called to a conference room, the focus of which is a large table covered in cardboard folders filled with Polaroids of the clothes that are to be shot. Next to each clothes folder is another containing location shots. The narrative of fashion shoots is usually told by the clothes, but the focus of the photographic tale this time was Syria itself. As far as the clothes were concerned, Mimi had let both her imagination and her budget run riot. There were Gucci, Pucci, Prada and Armani for the Nizam House in Damascus; Calvin Klein, Donna Karan, Ralph Lauren and Anna Sui for Richard the Lionheart's bedroom at Crac des Chevaliers; Jil Sander, Yohji, Helmut Lang and Ann Demeulemeester for St Simeon Stylite and the bazaar at Aleppo; Alexander McQueen, Chanel and Allaïa for the ruined desert city of Palmyra; and finally, there were the hard-won Dior party dresses to be photographed at Mimi's favourite location, the camel fair.

Other lists were jealously guarded by the assistants who'd made them. Joey held six typed pages detailing the equipment without which Flash Harry simply could not travel, and another six describing the things that could be used as tools for negotiating purposes. George had the confirmations of flights and hotels ready with everyone's passports and long-queued-for visas in another folder. Courteney held an empty pad simply in order to look efficient; she was, in fact, much more interested in poking Joey sharply in the ribs as revenge for his showing her fax to Flash.

Mimi was there, nervous but proud of Nina's trust in her, and so was Flash Harry, whose real name was still a secret between Nina and himself. Joey Tranq, Flash's assistant, whose real name was Joey Tranq, sat between George and Courteney on one side of the table, the three of them appearing to be cool but secretly keen as puppies. Rory, who might have been banned from travelling to Syria but refused point blank to be kept from the meeting, sat with his back turned to Gavin Cheveux the hairdresser and Frankie Paris the make-up artist. Nina sat at the head of the table with her trusty assistant who always stayed at home and held the fort while everyone else rushed round the world being glamorous. Pandora wasn't there. Supermodels are simply expected to turn up on the day of the shoot and look magnificent; their opinions – artistic, or otherwise – are not required. Besides, she still hadn't agreed to go to Syria; this was a drawback which Nina had every intention of dealing with at some point during the afternoon.

'So, Mimi . . .' Nina smiled and nodded at the stylist for the shoot to start.

'Right. Umm . . . well, Faisal sent Nina a note this morning confirming his invitation and promising that we can shoot the emeralds too which might help in persuading Pandora. As you all know, this means we leave on Tuesday. George has all the travel and hotel accommodation confirmed . . . Umm.' Mimi read from her block.

'Do you have to take two assistants with you?' Nina interrupted.

'Yes.' Mimi was dreaming about spending the coming long weekend with her boyfriend and forgot to argue the point.

'Try persuading me, darling. A simple yes is just not going to get you a budget for both of them.'

Mimi pulled herself together and forced her mind back to the present. 'Right. Well . . .' She took a deep breath and began to concentrate. 'We'll have over a quarter of a million dollars' worth of clothes with us. Even if we don't manage to shoot all the pieces we take with us I'll need both these two just for steaming them let alone packing and unpacking the coffins as we go along. Besides, the clothes will need guarding twenty-four hours a day. If I'm really truthful, one assistant for the clothes and one to help with the styling's hardly going to be enough. If I thought for a moment you'd let me take your girl with me I'd ask for her too.'

'Don't be ridiculous, Mimi. You've got half the staff of the magazine going with you. I'm hardly going to let you take my own assistant along as well.'

'Darling, if you need someone to help with the styling then surely I should be the one to go.' Rory's eyes were wide in a sort of 'there you are, I told you I'd be needed somewhere' sort of way while he exercised his right eyebrow in a persuasive manner. Nina wasn't impressed.

'Rory, I've made your position on this shoot perfectly clear: there isn't one. And I'm not going to waste everyone else's valuable time explaining again why you can't go. If it hadn't been for a certain somebody's inevitable indiscretion you'd still be in the dark about it and I wouldn't be wasting half my days banning you repeatedly from getting involved.'

'I could take a holiday and go to Syria and find them.'

'Don't be childish, Rory. You're going to Vegas with an unlimited budget. Now just shut up and live with it.'

'Yes, ma'am.'

The conference room phone rang.

'Oh for God's sake!' said Nina, irritated. 'I thought I said no calls except in dire emergency. Get that and tell whoever it is to go away.'

Her assistant had already picked up the phone. 'It's Pandora.'

'What does she want?' Nina, exasperated, leant back in her chair and stared at her assistant as if it were her fault that Pandora was disturbing the meeting.

'She says she can't do the Syria shoot. Her booker got her diary wrong and Cristo needs her for those ten days . . . What? Oh, and she can't find her passport.' Nina flicked the hands free facility on the phone so that Pandora could hear her.

'George has her passport already for the visas. And tell her it's just too convenient about the Cristo sitting. I know she's lying and she's going to Syria whether she likes Faisal or not,' she said, still addressing herself to her assistant.

'It's not going to work, Pandora.'

'I'm serious! I'm not Nina's in-house model. I can't let Cristo down.' Pandora's voice reverberated round the conference room.

'Pandora, Nina looks as if she's about to detonate. Can you call back later and explain? This meeting shouldn't last more than another twenty minutes or so.'

'Honestly, that girl will be the death of me. Go and put the cauldron of oil on to boil so I can poach her in it later.' Nina shouted loudly enough for Pandora to hear and, not waiting for her response, she turned back to business.

'I could always go in her place.' Rory batted his eyelashes at Nina. 'I've always wanted to be a supermodel.'

'Have you no pride?' Nina picked up her pen. 'Right, let's get on shall we?'

'Nina?'

'Mimi. Good. Right. What are we going to do about Pandora?'

'I think I've found some hope at the bottom of the Syria box.'

'Well?' Nina's voice was razor sharp; Mimi took a deep breath and tried to blunt it.

'Nina, with respect, I don't think this bad mood you're in is going to achieve anything.'

'I thought we were talking about Pandora.'

'We are. I just thought I'd take my life in my hands and let you know that slicing through people with your voice will just leave a pile of bloody pieces and no work done.'

'I hardly think you're in a position to make this *genre d'observation*.' Nina's voice was still a sharpened icicle. 'Tell me your brilliant idea and perhaps the cumulous thundering on my horizon will back off a bit.'

'Right. I'll need your help.'

'Well, as long as you don't need my time.'

'I wouldn't dare to ask for that.'

'That's enough of your lip, my girl.'

'Well, if your beloved assistant could help.'

'Oh well, she's got plenty of time – what do you need her to do?'

'Get Pandora books about famous romantic women travelling in Syria. I'm sure there are some, but I can't remember any of the names and haven't got the first idea where I'd go for books about them even if I did. Send them over to the Cristo shoot so she can mug up on them and think about it while they photograph her.'

'Mimi, really. I would've expected more from you. Pandora's never going to sit about and read all afternoon. You know what she's like – I'm not sure when she last read a book, but it certainly wasn't some erudite biography of a dry Victorian spinster using a camel for lack of a husband to satisfy her needs.'

'Nina!'

'Admit it, darling, she's hardly going to wade through the travel journals of Gertrude Bell in an afternoon.'

'But wasn't there another one? One who fell in love with a sheikh and went on raids and kept leopards in her garden in Damascus? Come on, Nina, this is why you're editor-in-chief of this magazine. You know everything.'

'Shh . . . I'm thinking.'

'Shall I call you back?'

'Nope . . . I know, I've got it. You are brilliant, darling. I can't believe I didn't think of this myself. All bad moods banished, precious. She'll love the Digby story and I'll have it sent over there myself.' The line went dead before Mimi had time to ask who it was that Nina had just remembered.

Pandora, wrapped in an old Galliano sheerling to ward off the refrigerated air, was having her hair pinned into a pile of loo-roll-sized rollers in a back room of the New Jersey Beef Distribution warehouse. *The Wilder Shores of Love* lay, spine broken, on a tray of eyeshadows at the place where Jane Digby made her first trip to the ruined city of Palmyra. Pandora's phone kept ringing, deep in her ancient Kelly bag; she ignored it. Her hair was a disaster and had to be started again; she was patient with the hairdresser. Even the clothes, carried in and hung on rails by a bevy of excited assistants, failed to distract her as she ploughed through Lesley Blanch's gripping account of the romantic saga which was Jane Digby's life.

Late in the afternoon, blue with cold and with chattering teeth and cheeks pink as she defrosted after a day being photographed in cold storage, Pandora shivered her way out of the building and into the car which waited for her. She massaged her cheeks in an effort to encourage circulation.

'Take me home,' she said flatly to her driver. Her phone rang; the screen said 'Mimi home'. Taking a deep breath and focusing, Pandora smiled as she pressed the button and answered it.

'Mimi . . .'

'It's Labor Day weekend,' Mimi yelled across the airwaves. 'Coming out to Sagaponack with us? It's your last chance before we give up the lease for the winter.'

'You've got to be joking.'

'Why? I thought you said you didn't have any plans.'

'And I'm not making any neither.'

'Why not? Last chance to play in fresh green American country before we go sand blasting in the desert.'

Pandora sighed. 'You're still counting chickens, Marianita . . .'

'Don't you Marianita me.'

42

'I'll do anything I like.'

'Pandora, only my mother gets to Marianita me, and only when she's cross, so don't try and act her age or her dress size.'

'Don't see why you hate it so much. I think it's a lovely name. If ever I have a daughter I might call her Marianita.' Pandora's car sat on Broadway, stuck in the treacle of Friday night traffic. She had all the time in the world to argue with Mimi.

'All right, call me anything you like. And tell me why you won't go bush with us for the weekend.'

'I'm shagged.'

'Really? Who by?'

'Don't be coarse, Mimi. And I think you'll find it's by whom.'

'Get on with it and stop being pedantic.'

'Ouch! Such a long word for this time on a Friday afternoon.'

'Answer the question, Pandora.'

'All right, all right. I'm shagged, by which I mean I'm shattered, *crevée*, *nazze*, *épuisée*, pooped, had it . . . anything else I can say to make myself clearer?'

'I don't believe you. Come to Sagaponack and read if you like, I won't tell anyone. I know Nina had a whole Middle Eastern library delivered to the Cristo shoot this afternoon which is why I'm so confidently counting chooks. You should have seen Nina's poor assistant's face when she was sent off to trawl around the city to find them for you. She has a great "as if I had nothing better to do" expression that Courteney's trying to learn to copy.'

'Don't be ridiculous. If you honestly think I'm going to strain my eyes and make them puffy before a big shoot by reading then you've got another think coming. I'm going home to Uncle Rory. We're both shooting next week and obviously need our beauty sleep. I'm going to get a manicure, a pedicure, a brushing, a waxing, a pummelling and a massaging and I might just take in lunch and a movie if there's time along the way. Then, in spite of my loudly voiced objections to this whole Syrian trip, I will meet you at the airport on Tuesday morning bright and early and all ready for an adventure. And if you dare crow I won't turn up, all right? And I make no promises about good behaviour so I should get some sleep if I were you. You'll need to be very relaxed if the stress of this shoot isn't going to give you a heart attack, let alone eczema, asthma, a scattering of boils, a dose of the runs and any other stress-related complaints that you can think of.'

'Well, I'm glad Jane Digby persuaded you. You know we're all pawns in Nina's greater plan but if nineteenth-century real life heroines can help the inspiration then that can't be a bad thing.'

'Fuck off, Mimi, and remember what I said about crowing.'

Faisal's brother Ali lay on cushions counting the stripes of sunlight that struggled through gaps in the cheap bamboo awning stretched across the courtyard of Ivan's rented Damascene house. He checked his watch, an oyster Rolex, and stood up.

'I've got to go. Thanks for the good news.'

Ivan laughed and coughed and hawked phlegm into the dusty oleander fighting for survival in a corner which it shared with a cracked and leaking drain.

'Pleasure. Nothing like a pocket banker to help get a job done. Apparently he shook like a leaf at the thought of abject poverty and didn't even ask who the investors were when Sykes offered him the twenty million dollars for a few measly holes in the ground. When's he back?'

'In an hour or so.'

'Can I trust you?'

'What do you think?' Ali grinned and slapped the rancid butterball Russian on the back. 'How could I let myself down at this precious stage?'

'Just so we're clear.'

'Don't worry, Ivan. We're clear all right. He's so convinced of my profound stupidity that it would never occur to him I might have the imagination to betray him. It's time to make that self-satisfied brother of mine take stock. I can't wait to see him howl when he realises what he's done.' Ivan watched, disinterested, as Ali capered about the courtyard, dancing with excitement. 'And the best bit is that he did it all himself. He made all the decisions. He signed all the papers. Oh, it's so perfect it gives me goose bumps.' Ivan waited, bored, for this bout of mania to subside. Ali stopped to catch his breath.

'You'd better go and play devoted sibling then,' said Ivan. 'Wouldn't do for you to miss the great and glorious homecoming.'

Ivan e-mailed his boss in T'bilisi.

Pictikhov,
    Situation as follows: Faisal signed. Hard-done-by brother promising anything we ask. Fashion shoot will go ahead. Faisal therefore occupied from Tuesday 8 Sept till after camel racing on 18th. Should not start shipping in till after 18th. Too much traffic.

The instant reply to this missive read:

Start shipping 8th. Have to move merchandise. Keep Faisal covered – use brother. Warn in advance if there's to be any interference. Personnel moving into place. Will hold you responsible if anything goes wrong.

In spite of the heat it was Ivan's turn to shiver; Pictikhov never made threats lightly.

Faisal made it all the way to his room before anyone noticed he was home. He kicked his shoes off, threw himself onto the bed and buried his head face down into the pillows, desperate for a few hours of oblivion.

'Hey brother.' Ali stood at the door.

Faisal turned over, and kept his arm over his hot, tired eyes. 'Hey.'

Ali took this as an invitation to sit down. Faisal tried not to flinch; Ali made his skin crawl. He forced himself to relax and smile properly, eyes included. Ali wasn't taken in for a second; he cocked his head to one side and it occurred to him that if Faisal were to be genuine with him just once, even if it involved admitting quite how much he loathed him, then he might not be so helpful with the Russians.

'How was New York?'

'Fine.' Faisal swung his feet to the floor and headed downstairs barefoot where he slumped onto the cushions on the long, low seat in the liwan, the alcove drawing room which opened on its fourth side onto the main courtyard of the house. 'Where's Ahmed?'

'It's Friday.'

'So it is. I forgot. I'm a bit confused after all that travelling.'

'I can't say I feel sorry for you.' The business of having tea served filled another uncomfortable couple of minutes.

'Pandora's everything you said she would be.' Faisal felt impelled to try and make conversation.

'And she's coming over here?'

'Not sure. I think I might have put her off a bit.' This was safe ground to cover. Faisal would avoid talking about the sale of the desert until he'd convinced himself that it had been a good idea; he couldn't have his little brother thinking him weak.

'No . . . Don't tell me that the famous, the gorgeous, dare I say overwhelming, Faisal al Mez'al charm didn't work? She must be quite something if she didn't instantly fall at your feet and swear undying love for you like every other woman you've ever met.' Ali poured himself a whisky and waved the decanter in a friendly manner; Faisal shook his head.

'Well . . . she seems to be fairly under the thumb of a whole list of people who are determined that she comes over so you might get a chance to have a bite at the cherry after all.'

'Unless you get there first.'

'I wouldn't do that to you. Fair's fair. And anyway, fortunately for you, I was a little distracted in New York so she never saw any of the famous charm you talk about. I wish you luck with her.'

'Very magnanimous of you.' Ali's turn to bare his teeth. 'So . . . pleased with your precious emeralds?'

'Enough.' Faisal could see them where he'd packed them, nestling in his luggage with the document which detailed the sale of the mineral rights.

'And how was the bank?' All whimsy was banished now; Ali's tone was wicked.

'Fine.'

'Fine?'

'Yeah – fine. It was bankly – you know, full of suits and secretaries.' Faisal flushed furious.

'Anything to report?'

'Your allowance is safe if that's what you're asking.'

'Oh yes, because I'm too dumb and too selfish to ever think about anything more complicated.'

'I didn't say that.'

'That's what you meant.'

'I don't want to fight with you, Ali.'

'No, of course you don't. You wouldn't lower yourself to my level.'

'We'd just say things we'd regret.'

'Might clear the air.'

'I don't think so. I'm going to see Faraj.'

'That's it, Faisal, run away again.'

Faisal turned on Ali, his eyes blazing, his hands clenched firmly by his sides. 'I'm not running away. I'm saving you from embarrassing yourself.'

'No, you're not, you're avoiding the issue.' Ali's words echoed round the empty courtyard. He slugged back his whisky, poured another couple of inches from the decanter in the sideboard and slumped onto the sofa fighting back tears of frustration, anger and a jealousy which put his teeth on edge.

Pandora sat on Rory's bed and shared a joint with him.

'You've done the right thing, darling.' Rory smiled at her. 'I know you hate the idea of all that dust and donkey dung and I think it's noble of you to go and help Mimi out.'

'I still haven't forgiven Nina for appealing to my better nature.'

'She's right though. This is all about team work and so it's fundamental to have the right team. With you it's perfect. Without you the whole thing falls apart.'

'You know Mimi's under the impression that I'm going because of Jane Digby.'

'Well, read the book and perhaps you will be by the end of the weekend.'

'I don't think so. I can't believe I'm going to a place that holds no interest for me, to stay with a man who evidently loathes me, just so that Mimi can keep climbing her ladder to inevitable stardom. It's not very realistic, is it? I mean, sooner or later I'm going to be too fat and ugly to be a model and she's going to have to go on difficult trips on her own.'

'I shouldn't think any trip'll feel difficult after this one. And as if you'll ever be fat or ugly.'

'What if I got bored?'

'You, bored of modelling? Don't be ridiculous. And I might give up wearing lilac silk pyjamas . . . And while we're on the subject, did you see that flock of flying pigs go by?' Rory threw away the dead roach and started rolling another joint. 'You're a good girl, Pandora. Your heart's in the right place. I'm proud of you.'

'You're not going to get maudlin on me, Rory, are you?'

'No . . .' He blinked back tears.

'Here we go again.' She put her arms round his suddenly shuddering shoulders.

'It's just that sometimes you remind me so much of your mother.'

Pandora reached for a handkerchief and let her mind wander to a place where there was a confusion of camels and kindly men in dusty white dresses who cleared a space for her on a tattered old rug and gave her sheep's eyes to eat; her stomach lurched in anticipation.

Chapter 5

FAISAL lapped his cousin Faraj for the sixth time. The two men were forced to shout at each other to make themselves heard above the noise of the extravagant fountain Faraj had had installed at one side of his pool. It was four thirty in the afternoon but there was no sun to disturb the steamy dark and loucheness that Faraj had adopted in the pool room of his modern Damascene house. Faisal swam a whole length under water, and when he could hold his breath no longer he surfaced, spluttering, and blurted out the fact that he'd sold the family desert for US $20 million.

'How much?' Faraj stopped mid-length as Faisal lapped him again, this time on the surface, ploughing down the pool, expressing nothing but a concentrated nonchalance in the regular pump of his powerful shoulders.

'Twenty million dollars.' Faisal executed a perfect racing turn and, surfacing again, turned on his back and floated, his face thoughtful in the shimmering lights around the grey slate pool. Faraj still hadn't moved; his jaw grazed the surface of the water.

'Not all at once.'

'Don't look so amazed. No, not all at once, over five years. But I reckon I can do enough with that to keep us safe for the moment.'

'Yeah, I'm sure you can live quite happily on that for a month or two.'

'No need for sarcasm.'

'And who bought?'

'Georgian conglomerate.'

'Conglomerate of what?'

'I don't know . . . investors. The bank said it was a safe deal so I signed it.'

'When you say Georgian . . .'

'Exactly – Americans.'

'Oh, Americans. I had visions of a band of hooligans from the Caucasus asset-stripping our beloved desert and leaving it a complete disaster zone.'

'Mafia?'

'Still Americans are all right – unless they're mafia too. But you didn't check?'

'Faraj, I'd just been kicked in the solar plexus with the information that my dear departed father had been quietly siphoning off my inheritance just to pay for rubbish . . .'

'Like your education, your flat in London, your allowance.'

'I didn't ask to be sent away to England.'

'Oh yes, you'd have loved the opportunities your little brother had in Damascus. Too much mother love and not enough schooling has made Ali a fool, Faisal, and you know it.'

'If we'd been given the same upbringing then we might not loathe each other so much, don't you think?'

'Oh my heart bleeds for you. Get over it, Faisal. Ali doesn't care about you. Just because you're related to each other doesn't mean you have to look out for one another. I bet he'd stab you in the back at the first opportunity if he weren't such a coward.'

'I shouldn't dislike him though. He's my brother. He's all that's left of my immediate family.'

'So what?'

'You're a cold-hearted bastard sometimes, Faraj.'

'But you love me, don't you?' Faraj made kissing noises in the direction of his cousin.

Faisal ignored him. He stopped at the shallow end and stood up, shaking the water from his abundant curls. 'One hundred,' he said and pulled himself out of the pool in one smooth movement before reaching for the heavy navy bathrobe which lay ready for him on a nearby chair.

'Wait, I've got another fifteen to go.'

'Get fitter, Faraj. You'll lose the racing if you don't watch out.'

'Different muscle group needed for that and they are primed and ready. I've won the camel racing every year since my eighteenth birthday. I don't intend to let myself down this time.'

'I'm not convinced.' Faisal laughed at his cousin's breathlessness.

'Well if you didn't drop bombshells while I'm innocently trying to get some exercise then I might get my hundred done faster.'

'I'll wait.' Faisal lay back on a planter's chair and closed his eyes.

Seven minutes later Faraj heaved himself from the pool and shook himself like a dog, showering the dozing Faisal and reaching for an identical navy blue bathrobe. He threw himself down on the pair to the planter's chair.

'You disapprove, don't you?' said Faisal without opening his eyes.

'What's to disapprove? Why should I be supportive when you've given my desert to who knows who to do God knows what with it? Eh? Eh?'

'Don't be like that. It's too late to do anything anyway. The deal's done. And it's not your desert, it's mine, and I've only sold the mineral rights in the Devil's Kitchen. The fair site's safe.'

'Is it just? Aren't you even interested in finding out more?'

'I'll be interested when the fair's over. For the moment I'm taking a holiday on this year's four million. And when Pandora and her acolytes come to take pictures of my beautiful country I'm going to have the time of my life showing them round.'

'Except it's not yours any more. Besides, I thought you said you were leaving Pandora to your brother.'

'I'm not going to jump on her.'

'You're just going to crowd her till she falls at your feet and worships you just because she can't help herself.'

'I think you'll find that her innate racism will stop her from having anything more to do with us than she absolutely has to.'

'What makes her anti-Arab?'

'Not so much anti as ruthlessly stereotypical – she asked me where my tablecloth was and if I missed the sheep's eyes.'

'Sounds interesting. So why won't you let Ali have a go if you're so disinterested?'

Faisal snorted. 'Ali's got about as much chance of getting into her pants as he has of getting into mine.'

'I thought you were trying to be nice to him in spite of your unnatural antipathy.'

'In this case it's better to be cruel to be kind – if I keep him away from her I save him from being let down in public. You know how hard he tries and how pathetic it is when he so consistently fails. Let him have his dreams.'

'And you call me a cold-hearted bastard.'

'Just do me a favour.'

'What?'

'Back me up when I tell him he's got to be in charge of the fair.'

'Oh great . . . Ruin it for everybody, why don't you?'

'Ali won't ruin it. Khaled will do all the work. You can get there early and make sure my beloved brother doesn't fuck up too seriously. It'll be fine. Don't think for a moment that Ali'll actually do anything. It'll run like clockwork. But I want him to feel he's got some responsibility.'

'Fine responsibility if he's just going to sit there while somebody else does all the work.'

'He'll be very pleased with himself.'

'I'll believe it when I see it. So, what do you want me to do this evening?'

'I knew you wouldn't let me down. First you've got to ask all the questions everyone else might be nervous about, specially the ones Khaled and Walid will want answering about the fashion stuff. I know those two, they're curious but too proud to ask questions in case they look ignorant.'

The meeting called by Faisal that evening had an air of informality which in Nina's office would lead to outright anarchy.

Faisal sat on the central banquette in the main liwan of the Mez'al House flanked by Ali and Ahmed. The other participants were the people traditionally involved in the camel fair.

Faraj lounged in a corner of the liwan in a long white shirt, washed thin with age, smiling wickedly at Faisal and smoking the red Marlboros he helped himself to from a tortoiseshell box on a tray in front of him. He was planning a pleasant evening indulging in his favourite occupation after sex and making money – teasing Ali, a pastime at which he excelled. His relaxed appearance hid not only a mind like a steel trap but also an absolute loyalty to Faisal.

Sitting to one side, chewing a never-ending supply of sun-flower seeds, his right fingernail long and pointed and ideal for picking bits out of his teeth, sat Khaled, Faisal's land agent. A middle-aged, silent, efficient man, with an ear for the unsaid and a talent for administration which Nina Charles would appreciate in her office full of noisy, creative prima donnas in New York: his only extravagance was an exuberant mous-tache.

His assistant, Walid, busily took notes. He was new to the job and terrified of letting Khaled down. For Walid the idea of an American fashion magazine coming to photograph the fair was simply terrifying. He was convinced that he'd install their loos in the wrong place and that the overflow would run into their tents, or, worse, that the boy he'd employ specially to look after the loos would lose his concentration for a minute and that the mess would overwhelm the whole camp, and then that everyone would get dysentery and die and that he'd have his throat cut by the formidable Faisal and be left to be torn apart by wild dogs . . .

Khaled watched his assistant's shaking hands with amuse-ment; he knew Walid's fears and chose not to remind him that under no circumstances would he countenance anything so dis-astrous as the misplacing of specially imported plastic loos.

The sun had long since set and the cool of the evening was prettily accessorised by a lantern-lit fountain playing a quiet game of musical diamonds. A selection of beaten brass trays was piled high with food and a houseboy served cardamom-scented coffee in tiny, handleless cups.

Under a layer of pungent cigarette smoke Faisal drew the meeting to order.

'Thank you all for coming.' The sheikh smiled at the answering laughter; as if anyone would think of not turning up to such a party. 'We've got two things on the agenda tonight: the fair which Khaled will tell us about in a minute, and the people from the fashion magazine who are coming to take pictures at it.'

'Tell us about the fashion people.' Faraj waggled his eyebrows leerily and laughed.

'This is the magazine.' And there was Pandora glowing on the cover, beautiful as a sunrise on sand.

'What do they want with a camel fair?' Faraj asked, on the dumbstruck Walid's behalf.

'They'll just take pictures of that girl in expensive dresses with tents and camels in the background.'

'Do we get paid for the extra work involved?'

'No.'

'So what's in it for us?' asked Faraj. It was Faisal's turn to laugh.

'Don't you think it'll be entertaining watching these people trying to take glossy pictures when there's not going to be any hot running water?'

'We could make hot running water for them,' offered Khaled, solemnly beginning to calculate the cost of such an exercise.

'I don't think so,' Faisal answered. 'Walid'll suffer heart seizure if we give him much more responsibility, and I wouldn't want to do that to his mother. The camel fair will go on as normal. You can have the fashion people's tents set up between mine and Ali's. I'll leave a list of furnishings I'll lend them from this house and Ahmed'll have them sent out for you and Khaled to arrange. I'm not having some poor boy spend the whole fair stoking a fire so they can have hot baths whenever they like. You can find someone to get some loos going for them and set up a water tank for those and I'll make sure there's enough drinking

54

water. They should be all right.' Walid wrote all this down avidly, pale with anxiety. Faisal continued. 'They're only staying a night or two with us and then they'll be off and I've explained in fairly graphic detail how basic the amenities will be for a bunch of New Yorkers at our little rural event.'

'Where else are they going in Syria?' Faraj asked.

'All over. They'll shoot here, Aleppo, Palmyra. I'll take them into the desert myself, slowly, so they can get acclimatised to it. Don't want to shock the poor things with too many empty spaces not surrounded by buildings at once, do we?'

Faraj laughed. 'You'll be with them all the time?'

'Well, they are my guests. I can hardly have them swanning around the country making fools of themselves, can I? They'll probably be arrested for lewd behaviour before they get off the plane anyway. They definitely need looking after.'

'But what about the fair?' Ali whined.

'Ah, Ali. That's where you come in.' Faisal grinned wickedly at his brother. Ali cringed as if he expected the sheikh to suddenly lay about him with a camel stick. 'Don't look so frightened, little brother mine. You're going to love this. For once I'm giving you some responsibility. I know how fond you are of the fair,' Faisal smiled at Ali through shining white teeth. 'So I thought you could be in charge of it this year.'

'What?' Ali was furious.

'You're' welcome.' Faisal was triumphant.

'You thought wrong. I'm not slaving away on your behalf while you traipse about the country playing tour guide to these Americans.'

'Save your breath, Ali. Work hard and I might give you a pay rise.' Faisal stood up.

'But I thought you said I could have a bite at Pan—'

'Later, Ali. You've got a meeting to run. And here you are, I've brought you your very own pad so you can make notes too. Good night everyone.' And lighting the surrounding darkness with an impressive smile, Faisal disappeared to his private courtyard where he settled down to listen to the mess his brother might make of the meeting next door. As Ali began to talk it wasn't exactly a malicious smile on Faisal's face, but there wasn't much kindness in it either.

Faisal let the lamp go out and sat, a thicker shadow in an already ink black place, only the glowing butt of his cigar giving away his presence. The sound of the chat in the next door courtyard receded behind the curtain of the dark. He lay back and listened to the sound of the fountain playing and stared, mesmerised by the stars dancing attendance on a week old moon. His mind whirled.

Instinct inspired Faraj to accompany Ali on a binge that night. In an Ottoman merchant's house turned elegant drinking den, Faraj had poured arak into his cousin until there'd been room for no more. Ali hadn't quite spilled the beans about Ivan and Pictikhov, but in his desperation to remain discreet he'd slammed his hands over his mouth to stop the words flowing out once too often for Faraj to ignore.

'What are you hiding from me?' was answered by only high-pitched, drunken giggles dissolving into a senseless tirade of jealous fury against Faisal, first born, favourite.

Eventually, when Ali smashed his water pipe by physically throwing one too many insults aimed at his brother in the air, Faraj took his arm.

'I'll take you home.'

Ali turned instantly into a truculent little boy. 'I'm not going home.'

'It's late, you're tired, and you've been showing off for hours now. Let me get you back.'

'I'm not going home!'

'Fine. I'll leave you here then, and they can throw you out with the rubbish in the morning. See if I care.'

'No. I don't mean that.'

'What then?'

'Take me somewhere else.'

'It's too late.'

'Not somewhere you can stay. Just take me there and go away. It's a secret.'

'You're making about as much sense as a baby.' Faraj hauled his cousin to his feet and shouldered his slurping weight. 'All right, you show me the way.'

Having stumbled up the steps leading out of the old house, Ali stood at the top blinking in the glare of the street lamp. He pointed a wavering finger vaguely in Faraj's general direction and then slumped against the wall. Faraj put his cousin's arm around his neck and prepared to act as a crutch.

'Which way?'

'Follow me.' Ali lurched forward and Faraj shook his head in disbelief.

'I can't believe I'm doing this.'

Five minutes later they'd arrived at the mouth of an alley, at the end of which Faraj could vaguely see the outline of a door. Ali turned to him grinning.

'This is where the fun really starts,' he said, pointing himself with the concentration of the falling-down inebriate towards the entrance to the Russian's house. 'I go in there and you go home. This is for grown-up fun and I know you're frightened of that.' Faraj watched as Ali felt his way down the dark, unpaved alley and through the wooden door which he'd pushed open and forgotten to slam. Faraj followed. At the door he sank to his haunches and prepared to wait, invisible in his gloomy corner. He listened.

Inside the house Ivan lay with his head in the lap of an over-weight Lebanese woman. Draped in a grubby cream nylon outfit, decorated with an unlikely pattern of birds of paradise made out of a rainbow collection of sequins, she stroked his oily hair and smoothed his forehead and held the mouthpiece of his water pipe for him until he was ready to use it.

Ali fell through the door and collapsed in a corner, breathless with concentration and trying not to be sick. Ivan stared at him with distaste. Ali lost the battle against nausea and in a mis-guided attempt at damage limitation threw up into a jug standing on a nearby table; unfortunately the jug was full of water, so that the sickly mixture overflowed onto the floor. Ivan closed his eyes and grimaced. The woman sighed and stood up; somebody had to clear up after Ali and it was practically always her. Ali sat back, exhausted, a film of sweat shining on his grey green forehead.

'Sorry,' he said insincerely, careless of the fact that Ivan's whore was on her hands and knees with a grey dishcloth mopping up the remains of his dinner and a lot of sicky arak.

'I wish you wouldn't do that.' Ivan kept his eyes closed, waiting for the clearing up process to be finished.

'It wasn't my fault. Faraj kept pouring alcohol down my throat.' Ali carefully cupped his fragile head in his hands and groaned. 'Do you have to smoke that disgusting thing? I'll be sick again,' he warned as Ivan puffed on the mouthpiece abandoned by his woman.

'What did Faraj want?'

'He's just jealous and now he has to get into my good books.'

'What makes him suddenly so keen on you?'

'Because my brother's put me in charge of the fair . . . Just so he can keep Pandora for himself, the selfish bastard.'

Ivan sat up and dropped the water pipe. 'He's given you the fair, has he?'

'Give me another reason why Faraj would take me out and entertain me like he just has for a whole evening and pay for everything including the girls? He knows he's got to be nice to me if he's going to get the prime site for his tents and be allowed to win the camel racing like he's always done.' Ali steadied his gaze on the sudden alert figure of Ivan, perched now on the edge of his sofa, pink spots of excitement decorating his rotten apple cheeks.

'But this is wonderful news. Why? Where's Faisal going? Away again?'

'No. He's going to have a ball with the fashion people and I'm supposed to high tail it out into the Badiyyat right now and start drawing lines in the sand for the tents to go up on.'

Ivan stared at Ali in disbelief.

'Fantastic. Don't you see?'

'Don't tell me anything too complicated now, Ivan. I won't understand and it'll make my head hurt and I'll be sick again.

Where's Faraj? He would disappear when I need carrying home. I'll teach him. I'll make him put his tents downwind of the loos. Hah!' A new wave of nausea silenced Ali's spate of spite. He groaned and lay down, flat on his back, covering his eyes with his arms. 'Ivan, I don't care what you do. Just make your plans and I'll fall in with them. I'm glad you think my being in charge of the fair's wonderful. Lend me a couple of thousand sterling then I'll even think about letting you come along to do all the work for me. But right now I have other things on my mind. Get that woman of yours to get me a blanket. It's . . .' Ali's speech ran out of steam and now he lay comatose, stretched flat on the sofa, his head to one side, a small dribble of saliva ruining the pallor of his spoilt thoroughbred face. Ivan got up and left him uncovered and went to the study where his collection of high-tech equipment sat buzzing, ready for use. He began typing furiously, a smile spread wide across his great round face.

And, while the whore whistled up mint tea in the kitchen and Ali began to snore out of tune with her, Faraj listened from behind the street door, his eyes closed, his face screwed up in concentration as he tried to hear what was going on. It was hopeless; since Ali'd stopped talking he hadn't been able to hear a thing. He'd have to wait until the house was empty before he could have a look around; he wanted to know the meaning of Ali and this other man's conversation and, having nothing better to do, he was prepared to wait until he could.

Ivan's speedily typed message read:

Pictikhov,
    FYI – The sheikh plays into our hands. He's put our man in charge of his fair. Any arrangements that must be made can therefore be made through him. He asks me for money in return for which we can have any advantage we care to take.

Chapter 6

THE cold, damp dawn was a vague memory and lead-weight heat had begun to sear the paint off the buildings before Faraj felt it safe to explore the house he'd watched since delivering Ali there in the dead of night. Ali himself had left early, holding his head and blinking in the acid sunlight. The other man left much later. Faraj waited till he'd turned a corner before trying the door and finding that nothing more than a few sharp kicks were all it needed to make it swing wide before him. Ignoring the squalid living quarters, he made a beeline for the computer equipment he could hear buzzing behind a door. The communications room was impressive. An Inmarsat phone was incorporated into a computer system which had been left switched on; Cyrillic script wove across the screen saver. Faraj tried pressing return and was rewarded with an advertisement for American porn featuring a pneumatic blonde equipped with a frightening collection of whips and leather contraptions and calling herself Queen Tyra, which flashed on the screen as the saver disappeared.

Faraj sat down and swung his feet up onto the desk, examining the preposterous proportions of Queen Tyra as if she might reveal something more interesting than the obvious. Dismissing her, he shuffled through the papers which were scattered about the desk; none of them were in a script he understood. He picked up a matchbook, examined it idly, and dropped it where it had previously lain in an overflowing ashtray. He flicked through an address book; the writing in it was meaningless to him. He thought about stealing things and having them translated, but the office was too small and too empty; anything he took away with him would be missed. He rolled his head about on his tired shoulders and stood to leave. Only then did he notice that the door to the main room of the house was covered in a map of the Eastern Syrian desert, and circled on it was the traditional site of the Mez'al family camel fair. He looked more carefully. Further to the east, well on the way to the western bank of the Euphrates, another site was marked. Faraj cocked his head and squinted a little as if this would make the Russian writing clearer; it didn't. He checked his watch. It was time for his daily swimming contest with Faisal, and now it looked as though he had information which might slow his cousin down.

George loved going on fashion shoots. He loved them even more when they involved long journeys with an impressive quantity of baggage; the opportunity the travelling provided for making lists – while martyring himself at the altar of his own, not inconsiderable, administrative skills – was his idea of heaven. And he always pretended to be nervous so that he could put on his false eyelashes as armour-plating against recalcitrant airline officials and potential fights with photographers. He stood at the Royal Jordanian Airways desk at JFK bursting with efficiency and eyelashed up to the hilt. Not long ago he'd been a nervous youth who'd never been much further than Brighton. Now the world was his oyster and he relished every opportunity of reminding it that nothing fazed him; not even a quarter of a million dollars' worth of clothes, a desert, and Pandora Williams all rolled into one.

Courteney, on the other hand, was not much use when it came to getting people on and off aeroplanes with their Kelly bags and bottles of Evian intact. She lounged on a black plastic chair gossiping with Joey, a man whose relaxed demeanour – legs outstretched over the mountain of equipment he'd brought for Flash – was misleading; he had the luggage covered, his eyes sizing up any stranger who came within ten feet of it.

Gavin Cheveux and Frankie Paris arrived together, having had a limo sent for them and their bags. Cooler than a back-stage pass to a Galliano show, they nodded to George,

Courteney and Joey before choosing other plastic chairs, a little apart from the assistants, and striking up a quietly competitive conversation about their respective careers.

The flight left in one hour. George tapped his black patent Birkenstock-sandalled feet impatiently; there wasn't a protagonist in sight. He fingered his mobile, longing to call Mimi and find out whether at least she was going to turn up. He didn't dare; she'd shout at him for being a fusspot. He breathed deeply, resenting Courteney's ability to remain calm, and forced himself to stay cool.

'Hey guys . . .' Mimi, breathless, flushed and dressed from head to foot in unironed navy Nicole Farhi linen, skidded to a halt beside George and smiled at the assembled company. 'Where's Flash? Where's Pandora?'

'I expect they're on their way.' George chewed nonchalantly on his right thumbnail, refusing to get excited.

'Well ring them and check, sweetling – don't you think? I mean, aren't we all supposed to be checking in about an hour ago?' She smiled at the girl holding the fort of the otherwise deserted first-class section of the check-in desk. 'Can we all book in together? I know these children are only flying steerage but it would be easier. You see George here has all the tickets and the passports.'

'Are you all here?'

'Not quite. But George, why don't you check us all in anyway?'

'I'm afraid I need all the passengers to be present in order to check you all in.'

'Oh. Well, can you do the steerage children, you're all here, aren't you?' Mimi looked round brightly. George sighed. Did she have to keep talking about them flying steerage when he'd been planning on trying for an upgrade? Why else would he wear a suit for a twelve-hour flight? 'George, come on darling . . . stop standing around like a stranded palm tree. Call Pandora, will you? And Joey . . .' Joey looked at Mimi vaguely. 'Wake up, darling, and call your boss and find out whether he's on a bridge or in a tunnel? It would be nice if we could all start together rather than leave half the company behind.' She turned back to George, her brightness already tarnished at the edges. 'Carnet?'

'Done.'

'At last, one thing done right. Where are the papers?'

'Here.'

'Are they safe with you, Georgie?'

'Mimi!' George looked crestfallen.

'Oh, sweetling – don't look so downhearted. I had to check. All right I'll leave them with you. Joey, that all Flash's kit?'

'Hmm . . .' he agreed.

'And where's your luggage?'

'Here.' He picked up an orange backpack so small it couldn't have held much more than a toothbrush and a change of underwear. 'I wasn't allowed to bring anything else because then I can have Flash's luggage as my own and not let it out of my sight.'

'What? As hand luggage! Don't be ridiculous. You can't carry all that on to the plane.' Mimi puffed with annoyance. 'You're just going to have to put it in the hold.'

'I don't think so, Mimi. Flash wants everyone to take some of it on as hand luggage. He's terrified that if one single thing's lost he won't be able to take any pictures at all.'

'Tell me, Joey, has he got his all-singing, all-dancing Sure Shot and some of that Kodak Ultra film that'll do whatever you want it to at anytime of the day or night?'

'He always does.'

'Good. I'll carry that for him and then we'll have something to use in case of emergency. The rest of it goes in the hold.' Mimi checked her watch. 'Now George . . .'

'Yes, Mimi?'

'Have you got Pandora yet?'

'No, Mimi.'

'Why not?'

'She's not picking up land or mobile. I've left messages.'

'Joey?'

The photographer's assistant looked up from his telephone

63

conversation in which he was frantically describing the fate Mimi'd chosen for his kit if Flash didn't turn up pronto.

'He's on his way. Give him ten minutes.'

Mimi turned to the girl behind the desk and gave her a shot of pure charm. 'I'm sorry about this. Ten minutes tops and we'll all be assembled.' Mimi fingered the drawstring of her navy linen pants and tried to pull herself, and therefore everyone else, together. She caught George staring at her fiddling with her trousers and stopped. Suddenly everyone was nervous. One by one they all put on practically identical Gucci sunglasses and felt a little better, armoured now against defeat should anything go wrong this early in the trip.

Flash appeared, grumpy and dressed like a safari-suited adventurer, his multi-pocketed khaki waistcoat bulging with paraphernalia.

'What the hell time of day do you call this for making a man get on a plane? Where's Pandora? Why did you make me get here before she does? And what's this about chucking my kit in the hold to be broken? You do want me to take some pictures, don't you?'

'Darling.' Mimi kissed him hello. 'Thank God you're here. It's just because I know you're not the precious sort of fusspot, demanding photographer that we're giving you this opportunity to practise your art with such a huge guaranteed audience. Now all we need is our star performer and we can all jump into a little comfort in the first-class lounge and relax.'

'Can't we check in without her?' Flash stood, hands on pear-shaped hips, bottom lip stuck out in petulant annoyance.

'Nope.'

'Then I hope you kill her when she arrives. She might be the ultimate babe but that doesn't mean I'm prepared to be kept waiting by her.' He humphed in disapproval and shrugged his heavily laden waistcoat into a more comfortable position.

'I know, darling.' Mimi was all conciliatory gestures and breathy calm.

'She's here!' With a yelp, George's voice sang out over the busy crowds of JFK on a Tuesday morning. 'Pandora! Pandora's here.' He began to dance attendance on her as if she were a princess. Fortunately the two hundred and fifty thousand dollars' worth of clothes, packed in the long, black reinforced tin boxes known as coffins, had already been carefully stowed by MSAS cargo in the hold of the plane, or this would have been the ideal opportunity for anybody who felt like it to help themselves to a little light Dior. Relieved, the fashion team pushed their dark glasses onto their heads or tucked them into their shirt fronts as they were swept along into a little bout of supermodel worship. Joey was the first to draw back; after all, he still had the precious responsibility for his boss's cameras and film. He didn't have all day to spend attending to Pandora's feathers.

And Pandora was making the best of being forced for Mimi's sake to spend a fortnight with the only man who'd ever seen behind the model mask; she gave back as good as she got. 'Nice toenails, Georgie. Look, we're wearing the same colour.' She flashed him scarlet Saint Laurent fingernails and he blushed with the pleasure of being noticed. Then she turned her charm onto the airport officials; she tossed her river of hair and sashayed up to the girl at the Royal Jordanian Airways desk, where she slammed her keys, phone, Evian and cigarettes onto the counter.

'Hi.' She blinded the check-in girl with her most electric smile. 'Any chance of getting everyone upgraded?' Her laugh was like a shower of tinkling diamonds and the girl behind the desk was smitten.

'Let me see what I can do . . .'

Pandora turned and winked at George, Courteney and Joey and thereby won their eternal devotion. Even if they didn't get an upgrade, at least the most famous supermodel in the world had tried to get one for them.

At twenty-nine years old, Faisal's terror of confronting his responsibilities was oddly contrasted with a consistent commitment to physical fitness; while his mind drifted in a sea of excuses and what ifs and maybes and buts, his body was primed in case he should ever ask anything serious of it. It wasn't that

Faisal was not an intelligent man; rather that his brain wasted its energy on making life complicated instead of beating a clear path towards the answers to the many problems he posed himself each day. He still beat Faraj at their hundred lengths of the pool game and then sat with his feet dangling in the water, sucking the salty skins off sunflower seeds, while Faraj swam up and down his aubergine, black lacquer and slate decorated pool room, no longer competitive, simply counting. Faisal had his thinking face on, one that drew the great overhang of brows far down over his nose, hiding his eyes.

Faraj gave up swimming at seventy-five lengths and climbed out of the pool, wrapped himself in his thick blue bathrobe and sat paddling his feet opposite his cousin. Faraj chewed on all his fingernails one by one. Then he kicked his heels in the water for a bit. Then he couldn't bear the silence any longer.

'Can I say something?' Faisal nodded. 'I could be out there in a day.'

'Hmm . . .'

'Well, a day and a bit. And I'd be discreet.'

'I'm sure you would.'

'So?'

'I don't see the point. I've sold it, Faraj; it's not ours to fuss about.'

'So what are you looking so worried about?'

'I'm not.'

'Give-away eyebrows. You should learn to control them.'

'Thanks for the tip.'

'I don't understand how you can be so relentlessly incurious about this.'

'I've taken the money and I'm running. Who wants to go to the Devil's Kitchen anyway? At this time of the year it'll be a death trap.'

'But what's a shady Russian doing with a map of your desert on the back of his door with odd little markings on it?'

'How should I know?'

'Will you get that head of yours out of the sand, Faisal! Ali makes me drag him there in the middle of the night, has a conversation with this Russian about you, about the fair, about Pandora — don't you at least want to know what Ali's doing there?'

'He's entitled to have his friends.'

'Of course he is, specially the sort of friends who let him pass out drunk.'

'And who got him drunk in the first place?'

'In the hope that he'd tell me what he was being so secretive about.'

'Faraj, to say you were making a mountain out of a mole hill would be a major understatement. There wasn't anything to stop you getting into this house so this man, whoever he is, obviously has nothing to hide.'

'I didn't say that. The door was locked but the wood's got dry rot so it fell open easily with the help of a little shove.'

'Tell you what, if it'll make you feel better then let's go and ask Ali direct questions. What do you think about that as an approach?'

'He won't tell us anything. He's like a child with a nasty secret, all festering and malicious.'

'If he's so childlike then it shouldn't be too difficult to get information out of him, should it?'

'We're all going on a summer holiday,' sang Pandora again, her tinny, tuneless singing voice reverberating round the first-class cabin. She got away with this kind of behaviour because she was a supermodel and because the only people travelling first class to Damascus that day were the team going to photograph her in Syria. Her demand for an upgrade for everyone had worked and Gavin, Frankie, George, Courteney and Joey were too grateful to complain. Mimi checked Flash's reaction to Pandora's performance; he was staring at her hard through thinly sliced eyes, looking as if he were sizing up a side of beef in a butcher's shop. Mimi sighed loudly and turned the page of her book. Pandora took another slug of her gin and tonic and breathed in, ready for another rendition of the same song.

'Pandora, please!'

'Why don't you join in, Mimi? We could all sing along. Good for team spirit, don't you think?'

'What's got into you? I thought you were going to spend all weekend relaxing and getting ready for this trip – you should be massaged into a state of nirvana by now.'

'Didn't work unfortunately. Rory spent all weekend whinge-ing about going to Vegas and I spent all weekend whingeing about coming here so we ended up getting rat-assed in his bed-room and not relaxing at all, so this,' she waved her gin at Mimi, 'is simply hair of the dog.'

'If I didn't know you better I'd say you were trying to hide something.'

'Oh yes, pickle – I'm hiding the pure terror the idea of spending a fortnight with that rude sheikh inspires in me. Ha ha.'

'I thought you'd decided not to worry about him.'

'I'm a supermodel – wouldn't you be disappointed in me if I just sat all quiet like a good little girl? I'm supposed to be a bit of a lunatic. You should thank your lucky stars I don't have a rock star or a footballer for a boyfriend who I might've insisted came along too. I'm just doing my job, darling, and I'm enough of a professional to perform for your delectation at all times of the day and night and not just when I'm in front of the camera.'

'Carry on like this and you'll be shattered by the time we get there.'

'As if, Mimi. You know what they say about me – I'm inex-haustible.'

'Great.'

'Ah, pickle, you could be too if you'd only take life a little less seriously.'

'I'm not a natural. I have to work hard to keep up with people like you.'

'Don't put yourself down, Mimi. Nina wouldn't have sent you on this mission if she didn't think you were up to it. Look, she's given you all of us to manage, and so far everyone except me's been good as gold.'

'I s'pose so.'

'And the reason they're good is that they're so mesmerised by my performance that they'll forget to do anything but get on with their jobs while I do all the mucking around.'

'Pandora, you're a joke.'

'Thank you, darling. Now, will you sing with me?'

'Please, Pandora, NO!'

'So, Ali,' Faisal paused. Ali sat at an uncomfortable angle from his brother in the outdoor office; the corner of Faisal's mother-of-pearl and ebony inlaid desk jutted out at him like an accusing finger. Faisal sat back and squinted at his brother as if he were trying to bring him into focus. Faraj simply leant against the wall, looked genial and chewed on a silver toothpick. 'Bit hungover?' Faisal asked.

'What do you care?'

'No need to be horrible. I'm always concerned for your welfare.'

'Enough to send me away to the desert so you can keep all the fun to yourself.' Ali stuck his bottom lip out and screwed up his eyebrows in a sulk.

'I thought you were keen on the desert.'

'You thought wrong.'

'Your friend's keen though.'

'What friend?'

'The one you spent the night with last night.'

'And what makes you think he's interested in the desert?'

'Might be something to do with the map he has on the back of his office door with the site of your special responsibility marked on it, not far from a big "X marks the spot" on the Devil's Kitchen and the catacombs too.'

Ali didn't answer. He could feel the sweat running down his sides from his armpits. His pale blue lawn shirt was soon stained with dark giveaway marks.

Faisal watched his brother melt. The silence thickened. Faisal raised a questioning eyebrow. Ali shrugged. Faraj kept his genial expression firmly in place, in spite of an almost overpowering desire to shake information out of Ali. Before he could make his move Ali made a desperate crash into the conversation in his own defence.

'What is this? You two playing good cop bad cop or something? Faisal all nice and friendly while Faraj does his dirty work for him as usual?' Faraj's mouth hardened. Ali's knuckles were white where they held the edge of the desk.

'Don't be stupid, Ali.' Faisal instantly regretted what he'd said. They wouldn't get anything out of his brother now. He watched Ali, who sat, unblinking, waves of jealous hatred forcing the blood to his head which he felt must soon explode. How dare Faisal, with all his undeserved and expensively educated privilege, patronise him? Ali screwed his courage to the sticking post and made a mute oath to protect the Russian's interests at all costs.

Faisal, innocent of the frightening, whirring, grinding fury which was housed behind the elegant, cosmopolitan exterior of his brother, saw only the new determined line of Ali's jaw. There was no point in carrying on the conversation. He planted both his hands on the table and stood up. Ali shrank as if he expected to be hit. Faisal looked at his brother and thought him nothing but pathetic. 'Right,' he said.

'Interview over, is it?' Ali asked, sneering to cover up the frightful grin fear would draw across his face.

'Well, I expect you've got things to do.' Faisal bared his teeth at his brother in a semblance of a smile. Ali bolted from the house before Faisal could change his mind.

Hardly had the door to the courtyard closed than Faisal gave in to spluttering laughter. 'If he didn't look so like me I'd be convinced he was a changeling.'

'I don't believe you just did that. We nearly had him. You two do try and keep up a veneer of civility so he would have had to tell us something sooner or later. Even if he'd lied we'd have had something to disprove but no, you had to go and ruin it.'

'Rub it in a bit more, why don't you?'

'Just making a point. Now I suppose I'd better just go out there and have a look.'

'What?'

'Go . . . To the desert.'

'Haven't you got anything else to do? I thought you'd like to come along with the fashion people.'

'How much less could you care about this whole thing? First you go and sell the desert, your birthright, my birthright, to a bunch of *soi-disant* Americans . . .'

'They are . . . and don't use the word birthright. Come on, Faraj, this is the late twentieth century, what are we really going to do with a hundred square miles of desert?'

'I can't believe you said that.' Faraj took a deep breath and carried on where he'd left off. 'Besides, you and I both know there's no more oil out there than there is in my kitchen.'

'So? More fool them.'

'Then, for some reason, a Russian friend of your brother's suddenly pops up with this very spot marked on his office door. And the possibility of your Americans turning into Caucasian Russians, maybe mafia – I only say maybe, but it is an option you will agree – is still not enough to get your stubborn old head out from in the sand.'

'Mafia!'

'All Russians from the Caucasus are mafia – it's a well-known fact.'

'And I thought Pandora was the only person I knew who was into racial stereotyping. This is just make believe. You've got no—'

'Evidence. No, not the tiniest piece. And why?'

'OK, calm down . . .'

'Because you couldn't even be civil to your brother for long enough to get anything about his Russian friend from him. He might have proved your point for you. The investors might be innocent Americans. But at the moment the option still exists that they might not be.'

'I can always ring the bank.'

'I could go out there and have a look.'

'Why bother?'

'Because whatever the bank tells you we've still got a bunch of free-spending fools looking for oil in a place which officially doesn't have a drop of the stuff. American or T'bilisi bad guys, I want to know what they're doing there.'

'All right, go. I know you're longing to sneak out there incognito and mount some kind of covert spy mission. You'll persuade that poor Said to leave his wife and his family and to come with you . . .'

'You don't want to come with me?'

'You must be joking. You honestly think I'd like to come and play 007 in the desert? How little do you know me?'

'The gentleman's protesting a lot, Faisal.' Faraj didn't look convinced.

'Besides, how can I when I've got the fiery Pandora Williams and all her hangers-on arriving?' Faisal checked at the Tag his father had given him for his eighteenth birthday. 'Shit! I'm supposed to be at the airport to meet them.'

'When?'

'Two hours ago.'

'Your priorities are so wrong, Faisal.' The sheikh ignored his cousin, pocketing his car keys and his father's lapis lazuli lighter before looking under the desk for his shoes.

'So I'll call you from Palmyra?'

'When you've taken your disguise off and booked yourself in at the Zenobia.'

'Well, there's no need to make life more difficult than is absolutely necessary.'

Faisal shook his head. 'Fine. But you won't have anything to tell me, I promise.'

'Where will you be?'

'I don't know. Call here. Ahmed always knows where to find me and I'll have the mobile. If we're not in the desert yet, it might just work.'

'Wish me luck at least.'

Faisal grinned and shook his cousin's hand. 'Of course I wish you luck. Come on, I've got to get to the airport.'

'You should be coming with me.'

'Change the record, why don't you?'

72

'Fine.'

'And don't go all pinched and cross on me.'

'Fuck off yourself.' Faraj left, laughing to show he held no hard feelings, and Faisal roared round the Damascus ring road in his shiny white Merc, bent on saving the fashion circus from hell on earth trying to get through customs and immigration without him there to oil the wheels of Syrian officialdom.

Pandora, infamous for her lack of patience, stamped her feet and tossed her hair, and was stared at by a crowd of guards whiling away their military service on either side of the airport immigration gates. She wasn't the only team member to snap with nervous energy. Nobody liked the bullet holes in the airport windows nor the way the apparently pre-pubescent soldiers slung their semi-automatic rifles about themselves as if they were handling pop guns in a school playground; there was something much too reminiscent about New York in this scenario which made the fashion folk feel uncomfortable. Usually their status as style icons shielded them from the armed side of keeping the peace. Here in Damascus involvement in high fashion meant strictly nothing. Everybody started getting tetchy and Pandora gave an Oscar-winning, spoilt-princess performance in the vain hope that someone might recognise her behaviour and get her a limo quick.

'I'm bored.'

'I'll bore her if she doesn't shut up and stop whingeing,' Flash Harry said to Mimi in a voice directed at Pandora.

'Flash, don't be so mean. I will make beautiful pictures for you, I promise. Don't tell me I have to behave myself as well.' Pandora twirled for the guards, inadvertently kicking over a pile of Flash's kit with her dance.

'Oops.'

'Just sorting out these few minor problems.' Mimi's voice had a fragile quality which might soon shatter into tears. 'I can see you're all getting frustrated. Pandora, why don't you let Frankie do your nails or something to pass the time?'

Frankie looked up from her conversation with Gavin about

their respective experiences of truly terrible airports and blinked at Mimi. 'What?'

Gavin simply carried on talking. 'Of course I remember going to do the hair from hell for Candy and being stuck at Zanzibar airport for a whole day, darling . . . Darling, are you listening?'

Pandora ignored Mimi's suggestion and had a better idea. 'Why don't you just call our pet sheikh on your handy mobile and get him to come and get us out of this mess? We've been here for over two hours. I thought George was supposed to have sorted out all the visa applications and things beforehand.'

'For some reason my not so handy mobile doesn't seem to want to work. And George does have all the forms ready. I'm sure we'll get out of here in a minute.'

Mimi turned away from the star of her Syrian show and went back to the immigration desk, where she joined her assistant in explaining to the fifteenth official in a row why this circus of American fashion types had turned up and what they planned to do on their camping trip near the Euphrates. There was no sign of Faisal who, Mimi was sure, could have solved all these problems in a trice. With slightly shaking hands, she wiped a fine film of perspiration from her brow and peeled her lips back to smile at this fresh inquisitor.

'Why are you here?'

'We're taking pictures for this American magazine.'

'Where are you staying?'

'We are the guests of Sheikh Faisal bin Ali al Mez'al.'

'And if you are his guests, why is he not here now to collect you?'

'If only I knew!' Mimi wailed.

'Mimi!'

'Faisal!' Mimi was like a prisoner reunited with her true love after a long and undeserved incarceration. Faisal grabbed the hand of Mimi's current recalcitrant official and slapped the man on the back before speaking quietly into his ear for a moment. The man's moustache twitched in Pandora's general direction before he began to laugh out loud, a big belly laugh that continued while Mimi and her precious charges were ushered through the immigration control, where Faisal conducted a bevy of helping hands who struggled with the luggage.

'Where've you been?' Mimi couldn't help asking.

'I'm sorry. Everything that could possibly go wrong with my coming to collect you did, from my secretary telling me your flight would be four hours instead of two hours delayed to a cousin of mine taking up valuable time making up stories from the *Thousand and One Nights*. Come on. Let's get you home.'

Pandora leant far out of the window in her bedroom at Faisal's house. She'd opened the perfectly turned lattice shutters, and beyond them the moon, an elegant crescent, hung in partnership with the man-made impression which topped the minaret of the great Umayyad Mosque nearby. She stared hard; if she didn't know any better she'd have said the moons were in competition with one another.

She should have gone to bed. They were shooting early the next morning and Pandora was so handsomely paid only to be beautiful. And she lied when she claimed that she didn't tire; without sleep her eyes would be puffy, her skin would have a dull grey sheen to it and the energy that sparkled so regularly for the cameras would refuse to be summoned. But her blood was pumping too fast for sleep. She felt transported. Faisal's house was like nothing she could ever have imagined.

Stepping through the low door in the wall, bending almost double to protect her head from the carved lintel, she'd found herself in a man-made Garden of Eden. Perhaps it was the long journey that made her feel like this; or perhaps the fact that she'd so dreaded coming to Syria in the first place made the impact of the marble oasis garden of the Mez'al House all the more impressive. Outside, the street was crowded, dusty, scattered with rubbish and donkeys, all of whom seemed determined to crowd her out of their way. Inside, the velvety dark of the courtyard was lit only by a series of little brass lamps hanging from archways and in a circle around the singing fountain. Pandora was overwhelmed by a series of sensory satisfactions; she drowned in the scents of jasmine and oranges, she'd never seen such bougainvillaea, the colours glowing in the gentle darkness, warm against the cool marble walls, striped, she noticed, like the outside of a Tuscan duomo.

She'd stood, bewitched, entranced, unable to move; this was a garden out of a fairy tale. Realising that her own beauty paled into insignificance beside this place, she felt at once bereft and somehow liberated as she stood, under a jasmine-covered trellis, stupid with impressions and waiting to be told what to do.

It was Faisal who'd shown her to where she would sleep. Terse but polite, he'd led her up worn stone stairs to the first floor, where her room lay behind a sandalwood door. She had waited while he'd made a cursory check that everything had been prepared for her to his satisfaction; he'd touched the flowers by her bed as if by feeling them he'd know how fresh they were. And then he'd left her to open the little latticed windows and look out over the night.

Mimi and the others didn't have time to be overwhelmed by the fairy-tale aura of Faisal's old house. George and Courteney had set up shop in a dusty downstairs drawing room, closed for the summer and opened up now for them. An hour after they'd arrived, everything they'd brought for the shoot was hanging in strict order on the portable rails which Mimi had shipped over with the coffins full of clothes. The accessories, still half-wrapped in crisp white tissue paper, were laid out in order on a table, under which the shoes were lined up in strict rows waiting to be ticked off on one of George's lists. Courteney wasn't so busy; collapsed in an old leather chair, her legs slung over the side, she'd fallen asleep without even remembering to take her dragonfly hair-grips out or remove what remained of the mascara she'd applied a lifetime ago in New York. George looked at her, half fond, half disapproving, and went on with his lists. Her lack of enthusiasm for the job in hand gave him the perfect excuse to get ready for overwork martyrdom, an opportunity he took up with alacrity.

Next door Flash, legs crossed Buddha-style, sat in the middle of a great sturdy table, while he had Joey lay out the cameras, lenses, filters and lights around him. He looked like an oversized ornament in a shop selling an odd assortment of photographic equipment.

Gavin Cheveux and Frankie Paris had little unpacking or arranging to do. The tools of their trade fitted respectively in specially made Louis Vuitton and Pickett's cases. They'd retired to their adjoining rooms and continued their quiet competition about the hardships they'd faced in their careers by comparing their given spaces unfavourably.

'Frankie, I do believe you are the lucky one, don't you have an *en suite*?'

'*En suite* schmon suite! Darling, there's only a shower, and I hardly dare turn it on to see if there's any power.'

Gavin smoothed his forehead in a dramatic gesture.

'Frankie, how can you be so ungrateful? Look, I have a sink and a pitcher full of water. And Lord only knows where these towels came from.'

'Didn't you bring your own?'

'You know I'm as weak as a cat. I couldn't carry a single extra thing. Besides, I learnt to my cost that travelling heavy in countries like this God forsaken sandpit only means that the help help themselves and one's still left with nothing to dry one's face with after a good wet shave.'

'Oh God, do you have to be so explicit? I remember the time we were halfway up the Zambezi in a fucking canoe! We were shooting a story about what to wear for work . . .'

Mimi was on the phone to Nina.

'Got here at last!'

'And no casualties along the way?'

'In spite of a personal longing to strangle Pandora on the plane, no.'

'Be nice now, Mimi. She'll come up trumps tomorrow. She always does.'

'She and Flash are getting a bit atmospheric together.'

'That's a good thing. The pictures will be full of antagonistic energy. I know you'll keep them under control. And you will remember to make Pandora wear a hat, won't you?'

'I can't promise she'll take a blind bit of notice of me, but I promise I'll do my best to keep her covered in factor fifty-five and a wide-brimmed hat at all times.'

'And don't let her make any trouble by being revealing.'

'Wouldn't dream of it. She might get some sun on her skin.'

'Well, there's no need to disrespect the traditions of the country in which you're travelling either. After all, I don't want to have to come and pull you out of some gaol.'

'Promise I won't get stuck in any gaols, Nina.' The editor-in-chief's sigh carried via satellite all the way from Manhattan.

'Good, so take me some lovely pictures and you'll be back in the land of the living before you can say Ali Baba and the Forty Thieves.'

'It'll be more like being back in the land of the living dead we'll be so shattered. Mind you, I love the fact that your girl's in charge of my seats for the shows. I'll get to sit with you and Rory and everyone'll think I'm a really big cheese.'

'Darling, you are a *légume* of the greatest proportions already. Now tell me, apart from with Flash, is Pandora behaving herself or are she and the chic sheikh still pointing sharp knives at each other?'

'Last I saw of them Faisal was taking Pandora off to her bedroom and they both seemed a bit subdued.'

'Really? Keep me informed. If I'm not very much mistaken those two will fall directly from the heights of their respective pedestals and into each other's arms.'

'Nina, I wouldn't have had you down as such an incurable romantic. Mind you, is that what you really want for Pandora? A Syrian sheikh?'

'Couldn't care less so long as she's happy and we get the exclusive on the wedding and I get to help design the wedding dress.'

'I'd better go and make sure that our priceless supermodel is sleeping like a baby or I'll have more to worry about than her potential love life.'

'Quite. Your precious shoot will go horribly wrong when she turns up tomorrow with steamer trunks under her eyes and skin the colour of dirty parchment.'

'Exactly.'

'Call tomorrow, darling, and tell me how the first day went.'

'Night, Nina.'

'Good night, Mimi . . . And good luck.'

The end of Faisal's cigar glowed in the gloom of his courtyard. He sat cross-legged on the cushions of the liwan and stared through slightly unfocused eyes at the flashing jet on black of his still playing fountain. He shivered. It was as if the cloak of loneliness – his constant companion since he'd put his signature to the document selling the desert – prevented him from taking any action. He looked up and his vision cleared at the spectacle of star-studded velvet darkness surrounding a little silver crescent moon. He smiled at it; he thought it lovely.

'Pandora!' Mimi stage-whispered through the sandalwood door: silence. Mimi tried the handle and pushed the door wide. Silhouetted against the open casement, she saw her friend staring out, mesmerised, at a Christmas decoration of a crescent-shaped moon.

'Isn't it beautiful?' Pandora asked.

'Shouldn't you be in bed?' Mimi replied.

'I can't sleep with this hook hanging above me, it might come in in the night and carry me off.'

'Don't be ridiculous. Come on, you haven't even unpacked. Where's your nightie?'

'Nightie?' Pandora was brought suddenly back to earth by talk of such pedestrian matters. 'I haven't got a nightie.'

'Well what do you sleep in?'

Pandora began to undress. 'Nothing of course.'

'Natch. That'll be great in the desert when we're all in tents.'

'Well, I didn't think I'd be sharing with anybody.' Pandora, naked now, her skin polished by moonlight to a pale, sugary alabaster, lay diagonally across the bed and threw her arms over her head, stretching every muscle in her body. Mimi began to unpack Pandora's things, laying them carefully in the little low chest of drawers at the end of the bed.

'Here's your wash bag. Don't you want to clean your teeth?'

'You've been on the phone to Nina, haven't you?' Pandora sat up and plumped the old, down-filled, starched linen-covered pillows into a comfortable nest against the head of the bed.

'Of course I've been on the phone to Nina. I had to tell her we got here all right.'

'You're so responsible.'

'It's my job.'

'I know, don't get tetchy. I was being nice.'

'Hmph.'

'And she told you to come and check on me.'

'She's as concerned for the potential bags under your eyes as I am.'

'You're both worry warts.'

Mimi snapped shut the clasp of the oversized antique Kelly bag Pandora'd brought as luggage and put the empty bag down. She perched at the end of Pandora's bed. 'You've got even less luggage than poor old Joey.'

'Didn't see the point of bringing much. George and Courteney are carefully steaming all those lovely Dior dresses for me to wear and Frankie's brought the whole of Space NK with her so I can just go to her if I need anything.' Pandora rubbed her bare skin reflectively. 'Besides, if I'd had much more luggage I'd have bruised my shoulders and that wouldn't have done for the spaghetti strap shots would it?'

'Pandora, put something on. You make me uncomfortable.'

'Really? Why?'

'You just do. Here, wear a shirt.' Mimi threw Pandora an old Hilditch and Key dress shirt Pandora'd swiped out of her Uncle Rory's wardrobe and then began to pick up the discarded clothes from the floor and fold them carefully.

'Mimi, what are you doing?'

'Looking after you.'

'Well go and look after yourself for once. It must be forever since you last slept and it won't do if neither of us is on form in the morning.' Pandora ignored the shirt she'd been offered, rolled onto her stomach, cupped her chin in her hands and stared out at the stars. 'The view's better from here,' she said.

'What?'

'There aren't any man-made things to distract you from the moon.'

Mimi looked down at Pandora's perfect proportions outlined by her river of thick, black hair. 'Go to sleep,' she said quietly, leaving Pandora to lie awake for hours, watching the stars dance and feeling the desert breeze gentling over her cool, pale skin.

Chapter 7

FARAJ began his undercover journey by hitching east from Damascus with a Baghdadi truck driver who took him as far as Palmyra and dropped him there at three in the morning outside the great Temple of Baal. The promise of a late summer dawn traced the sky between the date palms silver; Faraj sat on a fallen Corinthian column, loosened his tightly wrapped head cloth and kicked off his sandals, enjoying the best part of the day in the desert, when the light looks fragile enough to shatter and the air is dust-free, clear and cool.

It wasn't long before the man he was waiting for arrived and set up camp for the day in a hollow surrounded by fallen pillars. Said nodded at Faraj, wished him welcome and fell silent while he built a little fire and began to stew thick, sugary tea flavoured with desert sage. Faraj waited patiently for the ritual of making tea to take its course; when in Damascus he liked to speed through life doing a Playboy of the Western World routine, but each time he returned to the east it took no time for him to shed his urban disguise and cloak himself in the instincts and traditions bred from desert living since the dawn of time.

Said gave Faraj a grubby glass of tea and one of his fat, generous smiles. He lit a huge, paper bag of a hand-rolled cigarette and leant back into the armchair he'd made out of two-thousand-year-old fallen masonry. His moustache twitched with curiosity.

'What brings you all the way out here when you could be bathing in asses' milk in your modern house in Damascus?'

'Nice to see you too, Said.'

'On the way to the fair already?'

'Eventually. It's kind of a round trip. I don't suppose you'd like to come with me?'

Said looked round at the deserted ruins of the ancient city bathed in gold reflected from the flat orb of the early morning sun. 'Why not? There've been about four tourists this summer so I'm not just broke, I'm fed up of sitting here watching very little of the world pass by.'

'Good.' Faraj nodded at Said's pride and joy, his two camels, Sammy and Hassala. 'We'll take your friends.'

'Where are we going that we can't take a car?'

Faraj leant back and let the sun bathe his face and felt the breeze from across the salt flats tousle his hair. 'Let's just say I feel like a bit of fresh air and exercise.'

'Fine. We'll have to be careful with Sammy though. He's never been further than that.' Said pointed up the hill at the seventeenth-century Arab fort which guarded the city's ancient ruins from long dead marauders.

'We'll just have to watch his poor feet then.'

Said sipped his tea. He stubbed out the end of his gigantic cigarette, examining the remains carefully for stray bits of useful tobacco, and changed the subject.

'You racing this year?'

'Of course.'

'Bet you five hundred American dollars that I beat you. Where are your beasts?'

'Being taken care of. I've detailed Khaled to get them to the fair and keep them keen.'

'Hah! In that case you'll definitely lose to my superior camel power. They'll be angry with you for leaving them with an administrator with other fish to fry than keeping racing camels fit. And they'll be furious that you went for a jaunt with Sammy and Hassala instead of taking them.'

'Maybe, but Sammy and Hassala will be exhausted.'

'In that case we don't go.'

'I'll give you five hundred dollars just to come with me.'

'Don't insult me! I'm your friend. I was joking. And I've got nothing else to do. And if it means I lose a camel race, at least I'll have had an adventure.'

'Who says this trip is going to be exciting?'

'If it isn't then what are you doing here? Face it, Faraj, you never leave your beloved swimming pool unless it's for a very good reason. And, racing aside, you're hardly the type to sneak about the desert disguised as a camel-riding Bedu.' Said's eyes were thoughtful. 'You didn't drive yourself here or I'd have seen your car. You need a guide, you need to take a look at something, and you need to do it incognito.'

Faraj stood up and looked down at his newly engaged travelling companion. 'And I need to get a move on. Have these two eaten?' He pointed at the camels.

'Enough to last them a week.'

'Then let's give them something to drink and get out of here. There are miles to go before we sleep.'

Said climbed onto Sammy's back using the camel's neck for a leg up. 'You up to this, Faraj, or do I need to couch Hassala for you?'

Faraj looked at Said through narrowed eyes. 'That's enough of your lip.' Faraj pulled himself up onto Hassala's back and, laughing into the newly born sun, set off along a mud-packed path through the date palms. 'I'll have you flogged for impertinence later.'

Standing on the roof of his house, Faisal sniffed a hint of autumn cool in the clear dawn air. Downstairs he could hear the bustle of the servants laying breakfast in the courtyard and the noise of George and Courteney and Joey fighting for their particular crises to take priority. Faisal had already seen Mimi, hurrying to wake Pandora; but of the supermodel so far there had been no sign.

He stood, facing the rising sun and, beyond the pollution, far to the east, the desert. If all went well then Faraj would reach the spot marked by Ali's Russian friend on his map today, or at least tonight. 'Why stir it all up?' Faisal asked the distance, as if Faraj might be able to hear him.

'Stir what up?'

He started at being caught apparently talking to himself. Wearing nothing but an old dress shirt, Pandora stood before him rubbing sleep from her eyes and then tying her hair back with a strip of pale pink ribbon. He thought he'd never seen anything so beautiful.

'Morning.' He smiled at her, avoiding her question. She didn't seem to mind.

'Can I look?' she asked.

'Sure.' She stepped barefoot onto the dusty surface of the roof and turned instinctively to where, pale as a full moon, the sun was rising over the hills surrounding the city.

'Wow!'

'It's better in the desert. The pollution blankets the sun here. Save your amazement till we go east.'

'Right.' Pandora jumped as the Moslem call to prayer began to reverberate from a thousand minarets over the roofs of the city.

'What's that?'

'This is a religious place.'

'Oh, it's the m . . . mue . . . what's the word?'

'Muezzin.'

'You don't?'

'Pray? They're a little late for me. I've been up too long.'

Pandora looked out over the mass of roof gardens and minarets and Faisal watched her pull herself together for the day. Her hair was firmly tied, the sleep was rubbed out of her eyes, and in taking a deep breath she seemed to grow an inch or two. She turned to face him and smiled, and the exquisite beauty who'd surprised him a moment ago was gone; she'd been replaced by the public Pandora as she was when paid to perform. She frowned.

'Stop doing that.'

'What?'

'Looking straight through me all the time.'

'I don't.'

'Yes you do. You've got that piercing black stare that sort of strips away the bits that everyone else is always interested in and then searches for something else.' She laughed bitterly. 'I wouldn't bother if I were you. Beyond my legs and eyelashes you won't find anything.'

'Won't I?'

Her eyes flashed a warning before emerald shutters hid their expression and she stared back across the roof to the stairs. 'Gotta go. I'm here to glitter and shine, not perform sun-worshipping rituals at this time of the morning.'

Her voice was unnecessarily sharp. Faisal stepped back to let her pass. She tossed her hair at him. She didn't like strangers seeing the unvarnished private side of her character; they might see what she did when she looked there, and what she saw gave her vertigo. She held tight to the rail as she headed down the stairs.

'Pandora, do hurry up.'

'I'm ready!'

'What? You're going out like that?'

'Why not?'

'You can't just wear a sarong and a T-shirt.'

'It's perfectly decent. You're not going to photograph me in this, are you?'

'No.'

'Well then.'

'But it's not . . .'

'What? Supermodelly? Give me a break, Mimi. You'll get me out of this before I've even sat down at the place we're going. It's not as if there are going to be any paparazzi following us on the way, are there? I'm not letting the magazine down until you take bad pictures of me, right?'

Mimi shrugged. 'At least eat something before we go.'

'Stop mothering me, Mimi. I'm not hungry.'

'I'm not mothering you, I'm responsible for you. Where's your water?'

'God! Can't I look after myself for five minutes?'

'What're you complaining about? I'd love to be surrounded by people doing all my thinking for me and only having to turn up and look pretty for a job.'

'Would you just? Shall we swap places for the day?'

Mimi tried to lighten the weight of the atmosphere.

'Unfortunately I don't have long enough legs to do your job.'

'Right – let's go then. You can let the freak of nature inspire the rest of the world to do leg stretching exercises . . .'

'What's all this freak business?'

'And the freak will switch her brain off and . . . What did you call it? Oh yes, look pretty for the day.'

Mimi's forehead wrinkled with worry. Pandora usually stuffed herself with everything she could get hold of, wouldn't leave the house without a litre of Evian and never, ever, swanned down the street in a sarong and a T-shirt, neither of which looked as if they'd seen a price tag during the nineties. She wasn't even wearing any mascara to accentuate her record-winning eyelashes. Pandora saw Mimi's stricken expression and took pity on her.

'Oh ignore me. I'm just jet-lagged.'

'Don't you even want to bring a pack of cigarettes?'

'Mimi darling, I know you'll have thought of everything I might possibly need. And if you haven't provided it then our charming host will so I don't need to bring a single thing with me. After all,' said Pandora, ushering Mimi through the door and out into the bustling street and striding down the road, following the houseboy Faisal had detailed to show them the way to the Nizam House where they were to spend the day, 'I am only here to be transformed into whatever it is you decide is absolutely the last word in chic. No point in my even having an expression in advance, is there?'

'I wouldn't put it quite like that.'

In countries where the photographing of clothes is not an unusual occupation then the paraphernalia that goes with such an exercise is easy to come by. In Damascus this was not the case. When being photographed in London, Paris or New York, Pandora would have been collected by a large, sombre-coloured Mercedes, chauffeured by a man awed by the task he had of driving a princess of the media to a place where images of her would be made for worldwide consumption and worship. The old house in Damascus where Pandora was to be photographed on that first day was so close to the Mez'al House that a ride in a car would have been entirely superfluous; besides, the direct route involved steps and narrow streets and too many donkeys for the journey to be worth a Mercedes' while. So it was that she found herself walking through the old town to her first Syrian appointment with a camera. She passed a café where a fat man in an ill-fitting, greasy grey suit licked his lips at the sight of her; she climbed steps to round the Umayyad Mosque, whose minaret she'd admired so much the night before; she walked the length of a street lined with market stalls, where arrangements of finely turned chairs with rough wicker seats jostled for space with bins filled with spices, nuts and pickles, and trays piled high with quantities of paste diamonds and strings of pink plastic pearls. She caught only a glimpse of the ancient bazaar with its bullet-hole-spattered roof before their guide turned down a side street and stopped before another low door in a wall. Inside, Pandora was surprised to find a courtyard garden just like the one at the Mez'al House. It hadn't occurred to her that something so lovely could be duplicated.

In contrast with the lush abandonment of the Nizam House garden, the tools of Pandora's trade were laid out in disciplined ranks. Frankie was ready, brandishing a blusher brush, and an old swinging mirror on a stand had been brought into line so that Pandora could watch herself being transformed into the ideal woman. The portable rails had been carried along the streets, hung with the clothes Mimi had called in from the Italian designers specially for the Nizam House shoot, and George was lining up the shoes to go with them with military precision. However, unlike an ordinary shoot, the food laid out on other tables was not caviare and blinis and there was no iced champagne; there wasn't even Diet Coke or McDonald's quarter pounders with cheese to tempt the fashion team. Instead there was only water to drink, and the plates piled high with flat breads, salads, cold meats and cheese were unappetising to the jaded palates of the fashion crew. Besides, they'd all been warned that whatever they did they shouldn't eat the salad, and now everyone looked askance at what Faisal had provided, carefully wiping the necks of the bottles before sipping daintily at the water and fastidiously ignoring everything else.

'I must have a plug!' wailed Gavin from the hairdressing end of the make-up table. 'How'm I s'posed to do hair of any sort if there's no plug for my bits?'

Pandora pulled the pale pink ribbon holding back the mass of her shining black hair and shook it free.

'We'll just have to make do with it as it is, won't we?' she said, coolly.

'Don't panic, there's a plug here. I've been here steaming practically all night and as long as you don't take all day I suppose you can do hair in this area.' George, holier than thou and twice as magnanimous, stood back and pointed at the source of energy that he'd found. Gavin, pale with anxiety that he might actually find himself superfluous for the day, sighed loudly with relief and went to work.

'Come on, darling. Shall we make a start then?' he called to Pandora who was still standing by the Nizam House fountain, waiting to be told who to be that day. She submitted to having her hair rinsed in mineral water over the fountain basin which doubled now as a sink and smiled kindly at Gavin as he set to drying the black mess he'd made into the same long, straight style that she'd worn when she'd arrived.

Pandora breathed patience into her demeanour, forcing herself not to wring Gavin's neck for wasting everyone's time and smiling hard at him through her teeth.

'That was a useful exercise,' she said when he was finished, only a tiny glacial edge allowed to sharpen her voice. 'Mimi, what do you think? Could we use a ribbon?'

'Darling, you're brilliant. How could I have missed that as an idea?' Gavin said, grabbing the scrap of pale pink double-sided satin which Pandora passed him, and tying her hair back so that she looked exactly the same as she'd done when she left the Mez'al House over an hour before. Pandora clenched her fists and managed not to scream.

Next came her face. Frankie, laughing gaily at Gavin's ineffectual performance, began to clean Pandora's face prior to inventing another one. She cleansed it, spritzed it, patted and moisturised it, and then began to apply a secret formula of foundation and powder which left Pandora looking as if she were wearing an undecorated mask for a Venetian ball. At last, slowly, and with infinite care, Frankie began to create a new face for the supermodel, all the while waxing lyrical about her palette's bone structure. An hour later Pandora looked a painted version of herself. Frankie had reproduced her face perfectly, down to the tiny beauty spot on the right of her mouth, just under the place where her bottom lip curled down slightly and above the curve of her chin.

'There,' said Frankie, proud of herself and simpering victoriously at Gavin, completely unaware of the irony of the situation. Pandora looked at herself in the mirror. There she sat, a clone of the person underneath. She suddenly found that unless she pulled herself together she was going to cry. She had no idea what had caused this surge of emotion; being treated like a canvas had never bothered her before. She was being paid a fortune to be there. Why should she care if they insisted on painting a facsimile of herself onto the original?

She took a series of long, steady breaths, bit her bottom lip and concentrated, and no one took a blind bit of notice. She closed her eyes and tried to remember the sunrise she'd seen on Faisal's roof that morning, and slowly, while the scene around her grew more frantic, she managed to regain some sense of equilibrium. The beads of sweat on her upper lip disappeared into the ether.

To the others Pandora seemed to be immune to the competitive atmosphere around her. The calm at the eye of the storm, she sat drinking mint tea out of an emerald-green and gold painted glass, saving her energy, like the professional she was, for the performance she would be expected to give once the dressing up was completed. Courteney watched her for a moment and was awed at the model's ability to remain aloof, uninterested even in the quiet but heated argument between Mimi and George concerning the first outfit that Pandora was to wear.

'It goes with the pink one.' George was adamant.

'I don't care, sweetling. I like the orange better.'

'You'll get into trouble with Miuccia.'

'Don't be ridiculous. I can put a Prada suit with an Armani shirt if I like.'

''Course you can, but not when the entire outfit's Prada and is sold as an outfit all round the world and can only be bought as an outfit. You can't buy the Armani shirt instead of the Prada top so you can't have them shot together either.'

'George, let me explain something to you: this is editorial not advertising, OK? The whole point of magazines and the way editorial photographs things is that we can edit the season's look that the reader can buy in the stores. We're allowed to do anything we like, just as any of our readers can do anything they like with their wardrobes. Understand?'

'But the readers'll be annoyed when they go to buy and realise that they have to have a top they didn't see in the magazine instead of the one they did.'

'Give the poor things some credit, George. Firstly, the kind of people who buy Prada and Armani can perfectly well afford to buy a top and another shirt if they want to, and secondly, they understand that my editorial opinion is going to be a take on what the Italians have given us for the winter season, all right? I'm not simply going to reproduce what you see on the catwalk or we may as well just print pages and pages of runway shots and then we'd all be out of a job, wouldn't we? Now . . .' Mimi smiled carefully at George. 'Get Pandora into this little selection here, will you? Or would you like to go straight back to Manhattan and I'll get Nina's assistant sent out in your place?'

George sniffed furiously but acknowledged defeat and went to do what he was told. And Courteney and Joey, giggling delightedly at his misfortune, were forced to stifle their laughter as Mimi turned and glared at them.

'Sorry,' said Courteney.

'I should think so too.' Mimi went to check the film.

Later, when the sun had practically reached its zenith and the fine light of the early morning was long gone, it was, at last, time for Pandora to perform. Dressed in the offending orange Armani shirt, which was in fact pink shot with yellow making a delicate tangerine, and a sharp, fitted, navy gabardine, pleated Prada skirt suit, Pandora stared at the mêlée and realised that Nina was right; Mimi couldn't do it on her own and Pandora the freak was simply going to have to take charge if any photographs at all were going to be taken that day.

'Shall I sit here?' she asked, her voice quiet, but authoritative enough to seize Joey's attention.

'Flash!' said Joey, grabbing the photographer's arm. 'Look.' And Flash turned, a half-loaded camera in hand, and found Pandora doing what she did best. Perched on the edge of the central fountain, the delicate leaves of the orange tree sieving light onto her in a kaleidoscope of patterns, she'd crossed her legs, raised her chin, lit a cigarette, and was posing in a fashion reminiscent of Irving Penn portraits of Lisa Fonssagrives taken in the fifties.

So, at last, with nothing more than a sharp intake of breath, and an 'Oh babe!' Flash discarded the overweight bulging-pocketed safari waistcoat and finally began to work.

The shoot finished late, with Pandora posed on the window-sill of the old British Consul's office, the heart of the Nizam House. She wore a floating, empire-line, duck-egg blue Gucci dress and flat, white grosgrain mules, embroidered with hundreds of tiny blue stones. Flash took the picture through the marble-surrounded window so that she was framed like a Renaissance queen in marble stripes with the glory of the British Empire peeling off the walls behind her in a fantasy of green and gold leaf and time-spotted mirrors.

Faisal had dropped by and watched the professional flame burn behind her eyes, and saw also that the minute Mimi clapped her hands and announced that they were finished for the day the fire was instantly extinguished. Pandora slumped, rubbed her eyes, swallowed a litre and a half of mineral water in one go, and, kicking the mules off, marched back to Frankie's table where she began to take her make-up off herself.

'You look tired,' Faisal observed from his post leaning against the wall.

'Fuck off,' she answered. Faisal shrugged and began to back away. Pandora looked up, her face a mess of cream and mascara with only glimpses of the real skin underneath. 'Sorry. I'm never very gracious after a shoot.' She turned back to the mirror and carried on talking as she wiped off the mask she wore for the magazine readers to see. 'I'm even less gracious after a bad shoot. But you looked as if you were enjoying yourself.' She smiled up at him and took the cigarette he offered her and held it between slightly shaking fingers for him to light.

'It's mesmerising to watch.'

'So I'm told. I've been the person in front of the camera for so long I haven't got a clue what it must be like to be the other side. Personally I think I'd be bored rigid watching this lot circling me all day and turning me into a succession of people I'm not.'

'All the magazines claim you love your job.'

'Been mugging up on me, have you?'

'Are they wrong?'

'I don't love it or hate it – it's just what I do. I don't know anything else. I've been doing this since I was sixteen, before that if you count the days since I won the Pears Soap baby competition and did kiddies' adverts during school holidays. I like it most of the time, I suppose, but I'm afraid I'm always in a foul mood after a shoot's gone badly. I expect next time it'll go well and I'll be full of the joys of spring and glittery and shiny for hours afterwards and drive everybody mad. If you come to that, bring your dark glasses, I can be positively blinding. For the moment you'll have to allow me a little jet lag.'

'And what happens now?'

'What do you mean?'

'Do you all go to sleep and get up for the dawn again or what?'

'Oh no, tomorrow we drive up to that Crusader place, that castle. I think it's going to take all day, no pictures and I can be as jet-lagged as I like.'

93

'You look like you're perking up just at the thought of it.'

She pulled the Gucci dress she'd been modelling over her head, revealing only her perfect body, a little dusty from the long day's work but otherwise as naked as the day she was born. Faisal, confused, didn't know whether to blanch or blush so he passed her the sarong she'd worn that morning and she tied it neatly round her waist and dragged her now extremely grubby white T-shirt over her head.

'Right, let's go. As we're not shooting tomorrow you can show me Damascus by night if you like.'

'Aren't you afraid of me poking about behind your eyelashes to find out what makes you tick?'

'Promise me you won't and we'll get on fine.'

'Deal. I'll just check on Mimi and the others.'

'Oh they'll be all right. They'll spend all night steaming and folding and packing and labelling film.'

'Mimi too?'

'No, she'll oversee all that and then get on the phone to Nina to report back.'

'Don't you have anyone to ring?'

'Nope.'

Faisal and Pandora ducked through the street door of the Nizam House and headed into the maze of the ancient bazaar.

'Don't you have any family to check up on?'

'Just my Uncle Rory, and if anything happened to either of us we'd hear quickly enough through Nina. That's the thing about being a supermodel, even your family relationships are taken care of for you so that you can just concentrate on looking perfect.'

'Sounds horrible.'

'I've never had anything else so I don't know what ordinary sort of family dramas I'm missing.'

'No brothers and sisters?'

'Half-brother. He lives in Hampstead with his girlfriend and their baby. He paints and she's a lawyer. They represent sort of the last word in trustafarian living.'

'What?'

'You know what I mean . . . Wow!' Pandora stopped. They were standing at the gate to the Umayyad Mosque, and for a square mile around them the labyrinth of the bazaar bustled with its myriad businesses and teeming crowds. 'What's the time?'

'Nine o'clock.'

'Don't these people ever stop? It was this busy at six thirty this morning.'

'It's too much fun to want to leave and go to bed. Come on. I'll take you somewhere you can sit and watch. Or are you hungry?'

'Not hungry. Could do with a drink.'

'Tea or coffee?'

'Don't mind if there's a chance of slipping some whisky into either.'

'You're too young to be a blossoming alcoholic.'

'I've been slaving away all day. A shot of single malt would relax me and make me like you more.'

'Oh don't go all brittle on me again. Can't we try and be civil to each other just while you're here? Then, when you've gone back to the Big Apple, we need never speak to each other again.'

Pandora turned to Faisal and looked at him hard. They were practically the same height and she stared straight into his eyes while he fought the desire to look away. Eventually she held out her hand to him.

'Shake on it?'

'It's a deal.'

'Just while we're here?'

'Just while you're here.'

'And then I can be as horrible as I like when I get back to Manhattan?'

'I won't be there so I couldn't care less what you're like when you've left.'

'Right, where's that tea you promised me?'

He took her hand and led her towards a coffee shop he knew. There they'd get tea and perhaps a performance from a

95

storyteller, an old man who growled out his tales from a battered leather-bound book. But the short walk to the café was delayed by Pandora who stopped at every shop they passed and had questions about each one.

'And what's this one for?' she asked, stopping outside a door where a bead curtain hid the interior, but outside which an ancient black shrouded lady, who had only tiny sparkles for eyes, sat on a low stool, crocheting a white, cotton cap.

'Oh this isn't interesting. It's a fortune-teller.'

'Not really! And look, she's been waiting for us.' The expression in the old lady's eyes changed. She tucked her work into a pocket and sat, motionless, her hands folded in her lap, as patient as time.

'You're imagining things. She's not waiting for us. Besides, you don't need your fortune telling. You've already made it. What more do you want to know?'

'But I've always wanted to have my fortune told. What does she do? Does she hold my hand and look profoundly into my eyes, like you do only with a purpose other than to make me feel uncomfortable, or does she read cards or look in a crystal ball or what?'

'I haven't the faintest idea.'

The old lady interrupted before Faisal could drag Pandora away. She looked at the sheikh through her narrow, crinkled, parchment-surrounded firepoint eyes. Reaching for his arm she pulled herself upright and, taking hold of his hand, she pulled him into the gloomy interior of her shop. Pandora followed, her heart fluttering like the wings of a butterfly over a cabbage patch.

The darkness of the room where the old woman plied her trade seemed to be relieved only by a smoking oil lamp that hung low over a small deal table, around which were arranged four roughly finished wooden stools; but as Pandora's eyes became accustomed to the darkness she saw arranged on shelves covering every inch of wall a vast collection of shining brass and copper, everything from big, round, roughly beaten dishes to fine little coffee pots topped with tiny singing birds. And the glow from all this polished metal in the light of the lamp gave the room a comforting warmth, in spite of the fact that Pandora was convinced the old woman was a witch, a realisation which left her surprisingly unfazed.

The fortune-teller removed her rusty black veiling to reveal a face as creased as freshly screwed-up linen. Faisal kept out of the light, a shadow against a shining row of painted Saudi coffee pots. The old woman spoke to him.

'Tell the girl that I will look to the future for her. But know that in so doing I look into the future for you too. For your fortunes, good and bad, are bound together, and without each other you will not find what you are looking for.'

'She says I should translate for her,' said Faisal tersely.

'What else did she say?'

'Nothing.'

'Yes she did.' Pandora stuck her bottom lip out in stubborn determination to get the details from her interpreter.

'All right. I'll tell you. She says our fortunes are the same.'

'Ah, so she's going to tell your fortune too then.' Pandora's laugh tinkled; Faisal gave her a black look and turned back to the old woman.

'Go on then,' he said, nodding at the black-clad figure to begin.

'You must sit with us.' The old lady held out a hand for Faisal.

'Oh this is ridiculous! I don't want to know my fortune, it's all rubbish anyway.'

'For the sake of your friend here you must sit with us. You cannot translate from a corner.'

Faisal shrugged his shoulders and sighed elaborately. He perched on the edge of a stool. Pandora laughed.

'That's it, Faisal, be prepared to run off at any moment.'

'I can't believe I'm doing this,' he grumbled in English.

'Stop whingeing and listen. You might learn something.'

Pandora nodded at the old woman to start. The witch's teeth glowed like black pearls in the dull lamp light.

'Listen to what I have to say to you and repeat it all to the girl. Leave nothing out. You must both know this. Are you ready?' Faisal and Pandora nodded; Faisal fighting a secret curiosity, Pandora bright-eyed and breathless, glowing with excitement. The crone spoke; Faisal paused, frowned, shrugged and then translated.

'The moon marks time for you.
The sands lead you onwards.
Hearts hunt for treasure.
More successfully than minds . . .'

The fortune-teller looked up and the sparks in her eyes were gone; she was just an old woman again and her shop was nothing but a grubby hole in the wall housing an odd collection of dusty brass and a smoking oil lamp that should have been thrown out after the First World War. Pandora shivered. The old woman pointed a crooked nut-brown finger at Faisal.

'And you – watch out for that brother of yours. He's a bigger fool than he looks.'

'I wouldn't have thought that possible. What else?'

'Nothing.'

'Is that it?' Faisal asked, somehow disappointed.

'It is enough.' The old woman closed her eyes and wrapped her black cloak about her, covering her face and sinking onto her stool as if she were planting herself there. Faisal reached into his pockets for coins but the woman stopped him.

'Pay me and I'll never forgive you the insult.' He kept his hand in his pocket. 'Remember what I've said to you both and that will be payment enough.'

'Come on, let's get out of here.' Faisal took Pandora's arm and dragged her out of the shop.

'What did she say again?'

'I'll write it down for you when we get home.'

'But it doesn't make any sense.'

'I told you we didn't need our fortunes telling. They never do make any sense. And the person who tells them always makes them vague enough for you to take them any way you like and for them always to come true.'

'Still, I wouldn't forget what she said. There was wisdom in her eyes. She may not really be clairvoyant but age doesn't leave you entirely innocent, does it?'

'Thus speaks the great philosopher.'

'I may be uneducated but that doesn't mean I'm stupid.' Pandora shivered again. 'Gets cold at night in this country, doesn't it?'

'Come on, I'll take you home and get you something to eat.'

'And a whisky! Please.'

'I'm surprised she didn't warn you about the demon drink.'

'Oh shut up and hurry. Is it far?'

'No. Come on, we'll be there in a minute.'

Deep in the desert the dust storm grew; a purple stain on the horizon, it looked at first as if God had thumped the sky and dented it. In wordless complicity, Said and Faraj couched their camels, tying Sammy and Hassala's knees tightly together to prevent them running away from the wind. Wrapping their head cloths around their eyes and noses, they sat in the animal lea they'd created and hunched down to wait for the storm to pass. They were perhaps forty kilometres from the site marked on the Russian's map of the desert. They'd been travelling since dawn, crossing the undulating Badiyyat at a soft jog-trot, stopping for neither food nor drink. For the past hour or so their path had been lit by the gentle glow of the moon which had so fascinated Pandora the night before in Damascus. And it had been the disappearance of this moon that had alerted them to the danger of the coming storm.

'Should have made Faisal come himself,' grumbled Faraj into his dusty red and white checked keffiyeh.

'What?' shouted Said, squinting at his companion across the two feet filled with swirling dust between them. Faraj moved up and sat, cross-legged, shoulder to shoulder with him.

'I said Faisal should have come on this journey himself. He's the one who ought to be looking at this patch of desert. It's nothing to do with me.'

'So why didn't he come?'

'He's playing ostrich.'

'What are you talking about? If it's the sheikh's business, why are you here?'

'Misplaced loyalty. I volunteered to go out and put my life in danger so that he can swan round Aleppo with a bunch of American fashion editors.'

'Ah Faraj, are you really frightened of a little whorling sand? The storm'll be over in a minute. We won't lose anything, it's all fastened onto the camels and we've tied them down so they can't run away. It's not sandy enough here for us to be buried so we'll be perfectly all right. Where's your sense of adventure?'

'I left it in Damascus.'

'Rubbish. You've gone soft in your old age. You are a Bedu, this is your life. God only takes the moon away sometimes to remind us how good it is when it shines.'

And having pronounced his opinion, Said curled up in the shelter of the great bulk of his young bull camel Sammy and in minutes was asleep. And for a while Faraj sat up and watched him before realising that Said was doing the only sensible thing; sleep was necessary and in the shelter of the camels and lulled by the roar of the sand-thick wind it would, perhaps, be easy to come by.

The storm raged on. From his roof in Damascus, Faisal could see it bringing dust to the city and he feared for Faraj who must be in the thick of it. Perhaps he should have gone with his cousin. Perhaps he ought to be more concerned about this consortium who'd bought non-existent mineral rights to the Devil's Kitchen. So lost in contemplation was he that he failed to hear Ali's approach and jumped sky high when his brother spoke over his shoulder.

'Doesn't bode well for the fair, does it?'

'It'll be over in an hour or so,' Faisal snapped. 'Do you have to sneak up on people like that?'

'It might be the first of many storms.' Ali's voice was laden with doom.

'It might be the only one. Besides, who's afraid of a bit of wind and dust? It's not as if our kit isn't designed specially to deal with all this.'

'Our kit might be but I'm not.'

'What are you talking about? You're desert born and bred like me. You might not like a little sand in your eyes but you can cope with it. Which reminds me, when are you going east? Faraj's due to arrive the day after tomorrow. You'd better be at the fair before him or he'll bag the best site for his tents.'

'I was told he'd already left town.'

'He had an errand to run on the way.' Faisal looked out over the desert. Ali followed his gaze.

'Where?'

'None of your business.' Faisal could practically see the cogs beginning to turn slowly in Ali's brain.

Ali seemed to come to some conclusion and said, 'Anyway, I couldn't care less about the fair. I'm not going.'

'You are.'

'I'm not!'

'I'm not getting into an argument about this, Ali. You're going.'

'I don't have to take orders from you.'

'You do if you expect me to pay your salary, your allowance . . . your gambling debts.' Faisal pointed one of his famously expressive eyebrows at his brother and said, 'Besides, if you don't go, what are you going to do?'

'I have a life, Faisal.'

'Really? What, you and that Russian friend of yours . . .'

'His name's Ivan.'

'That is original.'

'I've got to talk to somebody while you keep the super-model you claim to be uninterested in away from me.'

'I'm not keeping her away from you.'

'Saying I could have first bite of the apple . . . I saw you two laughing when you so charmingly showed her round the bazaar this evening.'

'I was being polite. And you could've come and been intro-duced.'

'I wouldn't have dared to interrupt.'

'Well, how're you going to get to know her well enough to have a bite of the apple if you won't even meet her?'

'I don't want you to be in the way.'

'Afraid of unflattering comparisons?' Faisal couldn't help himself.

'Don't be ridiculous.'

'Well, you might have missed your chance, Ali. They're all off to Crac des Chevaliers tomorrow and you are off to the desert.'

'But what am I going to do there? Khaled and Walid can do it all in their sleep.'

'There has to be a representative of the family.'

'Faraj'll be there, won't he?'

'Eventually.'

'And you, you being so loyal to the family when you've just . . .' Ali changed the subject. 'Where did you say Faraj had gone?'

'I didn't. What have I just done?'

'Nothing.'

'What? You can't start a sentence like that and then not finish it. What've I done?' Faisal demanded. Ali grimaced, put one finger to his lips and raised a quizzical eyebrow before changing the subject again.

'All right – I'll go to your precious fair. Just give me a couple of days' grace. I could come and be helpful at Crac des Chevaliers.'

'Great help you'll be.'

'Brotherly love – there's so much between us it must move people when they see it. Have you ever noticed the way that when you're tired you forget to try and be nice to me?'

'What are you talking about? Just get to the fair sooner rather than later all right?'

'Your wish is my command.'

*

'Ivan! Ivan!' Ali burst into the Russian's communications room and held onto the door, bent double while he tried to catch his breath.

'What now?'

'I didn't tell you before because I didn't think it mattered, but now it does.'

'What are you talking about?'

'Faisal knows about the Devil's Kitchen.'

'Knows what?'

'That you know about it.'

'How?'

'He's had his spies in here and they saw the map with the markings on it.'

'What?' Ivan growled in a small man's imitation of the great Russian bear.

'It gets worse.'

'How can it get worse?'

'I think Faraj has gone out to look and see. He's left Damascus and isn't expected at the fair for a day or so. He left yesterday.'

'He could be anywhere.'

'Including the desert.'

'What'll Faisal do if he finds out?'

'Don't even think about it.' Ali slumped to the floor, still holding the handle. 'But you promised me no activity out there till after the fair so maybe it'll be all right.'

'Except they started shipping yesterday. I couldn't stop them. If Faraj is out there and avoids being caught he can watch the whole operation before reporting back to your beloved brother.'

Ivan was so angry that he slammed shut the lid of his laptop and barged out of the room before he found himself doing any serious damage to his valuable machinery. Bursting into the kitchen, he tried taking out his fury on an empty vodka bottle instead, sending it shattering against the fireside wall. His feelings not at all released, he poured himself a shot from a new bottle and slugged it back.

'Ugh!'

He spilled more vodka into his glass and drank it back. Ali crept into the room. He reached gingerly for the bottle but was surprised before he could help himself by Ivan's fat right claw, which took his left ear and twisted it until Ali's head had followed as far round as possible without his neck breaking. Ivan's anger was cold and precise. When Ali looked as if he was about to faint with the pain, Ivan let go and Ali fell to the floor, groaning and hugging his head in an attempt to ward off further blows. But Ivan's temper was always short-lived; once he'd hit out he found no satisfaction in following up the blow with further attempts at damage. He sat now, slouched on a rough deal chair, and waited for Ali to recover.

Ali dragged himself onto a seat, cupping his ear with a protective hand.

'So, damage limitation exercise: you stick to your brother like glue now and report back to me all the time – right? And I'll warn the desert to expect visitors.' Ivan growled this into his tumbler of vodka. Exhausted by his sudden bout of violence, his hooded eyes grew heavy; when he came to he found that Ali was gone.

Dragging himself to the computer room, Ivan opened a third bottle of vodka. He sat in the dark in front of the flickering screen, the prompt for e-mail flashing a repetitive reminder of what he ought to do. He slumped lower in his chair. He had a choice; he could either tell Pictikhov that the secret was out and risk death himself, or keep the secret and brazen it out if Faraj was caught peering over a cliff at the convoy of lorries rumbling south from the Caucasus. That way, Ivan might live to fight his corner. The vodka made the choice for him. His eyes closed and the bottle stood sentinel while he became a snoring heap.

Chapter 8

'THIS is the bus?' George stood aghast, staring wildly at the battered rust bucket in which the team were evidently expected to travel to Crac des Chevaliers; a supposedly three-hour ride was going to take all day in this charabanc. George's mood wasn't helped by the fact that he'd developed a fantastic dose of the runs during the night and was disabled in his battle for better transport by crossed legs and a mind half-occupied with prayers that the Immodium he'd taken really would work. He forced himself to concentrate. The driver saluted proudly and grinned from ear to ear.

'But isn't she a beauty?'

'No. She's fucking hideous. I wouldn't trust her to get us to the end of the road, let alone halfway to Turkey. No. You've got to get something built in the last year or two, not the last millennium.'

'But this is what you ordered, Mr George.' The driver waved a handful of faxes in George's face.

'I ordered a luxury air-conditioned loo- and TV-fitted steam-liner of a bus. Look, this hasn't got reclining seats, or a water dispenser with ice. I doubt it's even got four-wheel drive.'

'What?'

'Oh!' George rumpled his immaculate George Michael crew cut and stamped a Birkenstocked foot in frustration. 'I don't believe this. Mimi!' He turned back into the courtyard where Mimi was supervising the collection point for luggage and had almost disappeared behind the pile of black tin coffins containing the clothes.

'What now, George?'

'I think you'd better come and look at this.'

'Can't I leave you with one thing to take care of?' George looked stung. 'Oh don't do the hangdog Eeyore look with me, Georgie Porgie – it just won't wash,' she said as she stepped over the sill and into the narrow street outside the Mez'al House, where the bus was so tightly squeezed that even pedestrians hadn't a hope of passing it. 'Oh no.' She began to laugh.

'Well I'm glad you think it's funny. What are we going to do without a loo?'

'Oh darling, don't have such a sense of humour failure. I know you can hang on. Just keep taking the medicine. Where's Faisal? He'll sort this out.'

'No he won't. The bus driver says this is absolutely top of the range and the best we're going to get.'

'Well I don't believe him.'

George arched his eyebrows and folded his arms. 'We'll see if your lovely magician Faisal can do anything about this. Personally I don't see that he can solve anything that I can't.'

'There's no point in you letting the green-eyed monster get the better of you, sweetling, now is there?' Mimi grinned at her assistant and patted his arm. 'I think you'll find Faisal's being a local, a fluent Arabic speaker and a card-carrying member of the Syrian aristocracy might help, no? I mean, no offence, Georgelett, but you can't even speak French let alone persuasive Arabic, can you?' George scowled and vowed to resign when they got back to Manhattan. That'd teach Mimi. Besides, with the current state of his bowels he was already convinced that there'd soon be a touching deathbed scene, during which he could get his own back and make Mimi apologise. He looked back through the doorway to where Courteney lounged on a pile of photographic equipment laughing over some joke with Pandora.

'And as for that Courteney . . .' George's thoughts took an ugly turn as he marched through to the main part of the house to search for Faisal. No – he was forced into a change of plan; he ran, instead, towards the loo.

Faisal was not available; neither were Ali nor Ahmed to be

found. It soon became obvious that this old heap of a bus was going to be the only available transport to Crac des Chevaliers and Mimi's magnanimous mood turned murky as she realised that there was nothing she could do. She clenched her hands in her pockets and tried not to panic. What would Nina or Rory do in this situation?

Pandora watched the impending disaster balloon, resigned herself to wasting more of her precious energy keeping up the spirits of the rest of the team and took pity on Mimi. 'Shall we go?' she asked brightly.

'You haven't seen the bus.'

'Well, I can imagine from the stormy expression on your face that it isn't exactly what you had in mind. Still,' she hopped down from the pile of photographic kit on which she'd been sitting and started towards the door, 'may as well make the most of it, no? Face it, Mimi – if we're to spend the rest of the day broken down hadn't we better get a move on or we're never going to get as far as the main road let alone old lion-hearted Dick's castle? Come along children,' she cried as she ducked through the door and directly up the steps into the bus. If there'd been room between the doorway and the bus in which to laugh she would have roared. Mimi was right to look worried; this machine didn't look as if it was going to get them to the end of the street. Rather than encourage the rest of the team to refuse to board the vehicle, Pandora bounced up the rusty steps and was soon ensconced in the front seat, opening the window wide and arranging her belongings around her as if she were setting off on a Sunday school picnic. Shrugging their shoulders and silencing their complaints, the others followed, trooping onto the bus behind her leaving the weak and feeble George to direct the driver who was jamming the luggage into the hold.

'Did you see the crack in the back axle?' Gavin fought the desire to write all this down.

'And the holes in the floor of the truck. All our tools will be ruined by highway dust, let alone heat.' Frankie flicked a little Chinese fan in righteous indignation.

'And Pandora's so brave. Look at her, cool as a cucumber.'

'Don't know how she does it.'

'Well, she's a pro, isn't she?'

'Like us you see, prepared to put up with anything for a good picture.'

'And therein lies her art.'

'And ours, darling, and ours.' Frankie's face took on a thoughtful mien. 'You know, I'm reminded of the time we were shooting Tiffany diamonds in the Thai–Burma border hill country . . . I was riding a water buffalo . . . and the poppies . . . darling!'

Gavin and Frankie had settled in to enjoy the ride, telling one another the story of their journey as it happened, so as to be prepared to regale their colleagues with terrifying tales of derring do once they'd returned to the safety of old New York. They sat together towards the back of the bus, carefully embroidering each detail of the trip and making sure that the perfect ghastliness of it was absolutely clear to both of them.

Alone, Faisal pounded his way up and down Faraj's pool. His pump action crawl with its regular racing turns had nothing to do with a desire to keep fit. He'd spent most of the night watching the storm in the desert blow itself out, and when calm descended in the eastern sky he'd retired to the spartan comfort of his bedroom and tried to get some sleep. After three hours of lying on his back with his eyes shut while his mind whirled in imitation of the blown-out storm, he'd given up trying to rest and decided that he'd have to exhaust himself physically if he were to be able to shut his brain down. He couldn't believe what logic was telling him; and even if he did then it was too late for him to do anything about it, wasn't it? Hauling himself out of the deep end of the pool, he threw himself down on one of Faraj's planter's chairs.

Three hours later he woke up with cramp, his brain going into overdrive again. He gave up trying to rest and walked back to the Mez'al House, where he packed to go to Crac des Chevaliers. Faraj would report back sooner rather than later.

Until he heard from his cousin there was nothing he could do, except head into the desert himself.

'No,' he said out loud as he pushed his white Mercedes sports car into gear and headed for the main road north out of Damascus.

The bus was stranded somewhere south of Homs, irritatingly close to the turn-off to Crac des Chevaliers in mileage terms, but a potential lifetime as far as the ability of the bus to actually get there was concerned. Mimi was puffing with frustration. They'd been delayed before leaving Damascus by fighting off a selection of potential boarders, without whom their driver had insisted they'd never be able to complete their journey success-fully; two tour guides, a mechanic and three cousins of the driver who'd only come to gawp at Pandora had had to be firmly turned away. Now Mimi began to despair of their ever arriving at Crac des Chevaliers, let alone before dark.

For a while the journey had gone relatively smoothly. In spite of an obstacle course of seemingly unavoidable pot holes, a steady speed of about forty miles an hour had eventually been achieved. The air-conditioning was broken and the windows were all open so that everyone was soon covered with dust and choking from the crusty cake of pollution which permanently covers Damascus. These drawbacks simply gave the passengers plenty to discuss, look at, complain about and, in general, find entertaining. Pandora's shining stoic example was an inspiration and when, an hour out of Damascus, she started singing a bowdlerised version of 'Didn't we have a lovely time the day we went to Bangor' everyone forgot to be cool and joined in, Joey and Courteney even suggesting variations on the theme. Only George kept quiet; he was concentrating on surviving stomach cramps which threatened to kill him. And then the bus broke down.

Being stranded on the forecourt of a garage, which seemed to double up as a butcher's shop and a café, fazed everyone except Pandora. Realising, once more, that if she panicked then the rest of the team might give in to temptation and follow suit, she simply got out of the bus and took stock of the situation. Dressed in a sarong, an old Voyage cardigan, mis-washed purply grey, and a battered Panama of Rory's which she'd unrolled out of her luggage, she looked like a backpacker with unsuitably beautiful hair as she installed herself at a plastic table under a vine-covered trellis surrounded by fly-blown goat carcasses and accepted thickly sweetened mint tea.

Everyone else buzzed about the bus. The driver shouted at six useless garage mechanics who repeatedly appeared with small pannikins of water with which they doused the engine in a hopeful manner; Mimi and Courteney jumped up and down with fury; Gavin and Frankie stood, arms folded, at a small distance from the mêlée, 'I told you so' expressions on their faces, and making mental notes as usual; Flash lay snoring on the back seat of the bus, apparently immune to the disaster happening around him while Joey nervously wiped the photographic equipment which had been shoved so unceremoniously into the luggage compartment by the driver, and which was now covered in a thick, gluey mixture of oil and dust. George leant against the steaming sides of the exhausted machine and moaned quietly, prepared to forgive Faisal for making him feel inadequate in return for his turning up quickly in order to save the day.

They'd been there for nearly an hour when Faisal did arrive, a knight in a shining Mercedes, to save them from a fate worse than Syrian garage mechanics. In a swirl of dust he handbrake-turned to a halt in the wide arc of sandy waste ground that framed the garage. Courteney, very hot in up-to-the-minute but not very practical Chanel sample sale black silk knitted pants, waved at him, knocking over Pandora's mint tea in her excitement. Pandora looked up desultorily from the snooze she'd been enjoying behind her Gucci dark glasses and lit up the area with a smile.

'It's Faisal!' she said. 'How timely. Do you think he'll join me for some tea?'

'Pandora, this is neither the time nor the place to pretend Faisal's here to play your Rudolph Valentino. Leave the sheikh alone for a minute, will you? I need him now.' Mimi was only minutes away from suffering a major sense of humour failure.

'Be like that, why don't you?' Pandora huffed and leant back in her chair. Even with Faisal's help it was obvious they were going to be stuck in the garage for some time to come. Mimi obviously didn't realise how hard Pandora was working to keep everyone else from having a nervous breakdown so Pandora saw no reason to get in the way. She closed her eyes and tried to summon enough energy for keeping the peace once the bus set off again.

'What's going on?' Faisal unfolded himself from the navy leather interior of his shiny white car and ran a hand through his curls to shake the dust out.

'Thank God you're here,' began Mimi.

'It's been a nightmare,' joined in George, fighting back tears.

'The bus's broken down. That's what's going on,' Courteney explained kindly.

'I remember when I was doing great hair for a wedding dress shoot in Tadzhikistan . . .' began Gavin.

'Shut up!' chorused the others.

Faisal ignored the obvious disaster area which surrounded the fashion team and dragged the bus driver with him to the garage manager's office. Mimi watched, impressed as the sheikh simultaneously managed to ball out the driver, get hold of the bus company in Damascus and say something to the garage manager who organised the mechanics.

Five minutes later Faisal slapped the bus driver on the back, watched as the mechanics managed to get the bus started again, smiled at the assembled company and announced, 'There, that should get you to Crac des Chevaliers all right. The sort of bus you'd rather have will be delivered from Damascus tomorrow. Right – see you there then. Pandora,' he waved at her as she watched his masterful performance from under the grape-heavy vines, 'you're coming with me.'

She blinked at him and sniffed.

'No, I don't think so, darling. Come on everyone, let's go.' And dismissing Faisal with a toss of her hair, she climbed back to her place in the bus and stared, determined to ignore the sheikh, out of the window at a pair of kamikaze bantams playing chicken on the main road north.

'Be like that then.' Faisal, at a loss, jumped into his car without opening the door and sped off into the distance.

'Do you have to be so horrible to him?' Mimi asked.

'Mind your own onions, Mimi.'

Ali nursed his hangover with a glass of mint tea, successfully fighting the temptation to jump straight into a bottle of medicinal arak to calm the nagging headache caused by a surfeit of vodka as well as by the energetic head-twisting he'd suffered at Ivan's hands the night before. The tea finished, he threw a holdall into the boot of his three series navy blue BMW and installed himself behind the wheel. Passing the alley at the end of which Ivan's house was hidden, he spat neatly into the middle of the road. He'd teach that Russian to think that he could boss Ali around. Sitting suddenly straighter and putting his foot down as he reached the ring road to the motorway, his lip curled in loathing for his brother. Ivan didn't have the first idea why Ali was in this up to his neck; he thought it was about money. Ali laughed at the thought. Ivan obviously knew nothing about revenge.

Heading north, he pulled a baseball cap far down over his eyes, shading them from the relentless sawing of the sun. Focused firmly on the road ahead, he scapegoat drove the BMW, taking out on it the frustrations of his sad and lonely little life.

Guarding the roads from Turkey to the north, the Eastern Mediterranean to the west, the snow-capped hills of the Lebanon to the south and the final stage of the desert silk route to the east, nine hundred years old, impregnable, solid as the granite hill top on which it sat, Crac des Chevaliers was breathtaking. High above natural defences of sheer scree it appeared not much more approachable than it was a thousand years ago. The fashion team held onto their seats as the bus creaked and complained its way up the narrow road, winding in a series of hairpin bends through the old Crusader supply villages. They wondered if they were ever going to make it to the top. Pandora was looking down, admiring a twenty-foot-high granite needle, imagining Saladin's marauders using it as a people kebab stick in less peaceful times, when the engine began to give up the ghost entirely. A wall was being shored up, and a quantity of sticky mud mixed with a leaking hose had turned one bend into a skating rink. The bus crawled onto the slippery surface and stopped. There was a moment's hiatus, and then the rusty old thing began sliding gently backwards off the edge of the cliff. There was a crunch and any leverage there might have been in recovering it was lost as the ancient charabanc impaled itself on Pandora's pointed outcrop.

Silence; nobody dared breathe for fear that their precarious balance would be lost. Even George forgot about the acid party going on in his lower intestine and managed to focus on the fact that his death might come as a result of a mud slide rather than during a chic little scene where he died of dehydration and loyalty to fashion. Mimi began to shake; not only were her fashion team hanging off a small escarpment at a relatively sharp angle, but, much more seriously, a quarter of a million dollars' worth of clothes and accessories as well as the photographic kit and Gavin and Frankie's boxes of tricks were all about to be crushed by the rock on which the bus had been speared. Mimi had a vision of Nina howling at her like some kind of terrible queen of the furies for losing the Dior party dresses over the edge of a cliff. The driver sat, immobile, his knuckles white where they gripped the wheel.

It was Pandora who broke the spell. She leant forward and tapped the driver on the shoulder. 'Excuse me?' Her voice was as sugary as a pink penny mouse. He looked at her shakily and said nothing.

'Are you going to get out and look at the damage or shall I go and try and push this thing up the hill by myself?' He seemed incapable of speech. 'I guess I'd better get out then. Come on lads.' She called to the back of the bus. 'Time to prove your collective manhoods. It seems our friend here's lost his.' Pandora's move had given Mimi time to pull herself together. Hauling herself uphill from the back of the bus, she came forward to take charge.

'Don't be ridiculous, Pandora. These boys can't pull the bus out.'

'Too right they can't. But they might at least show willing and try. Or are you suggesting that you and I put them to shame and yank the old boat out of this jam ourselves?'

'This is not a good time to turn facetious on me, Pandora. Why don't you set an example by taking your bag and getting out of the bus and waiting on the other side of the road? Come on everyone, you've got to get out too.'

'Facetious! I'm only here to help, Mimi! I could have avoided this and been all supermodelly and got a lift in Faisal's handy little Merc. But no, I came with you lot because you obviously all needed help keeping your peckers up. So, if that's all the thanks I get for just trying to help when I really don't have to you can jump.' Pandora whispered this sweetly, giving the impression to everyone else that she was being kind to her editor, but her eyes flashed warning flares at Mimi as she headed for the door. She stopped suddenly; the bus rocked gently. 'Ooops, sorry honey, I don't think we're getting out this way.'

'Stop making life difficult, Pandora, and get out of the bus . . . Please?'

'Have you insured my long and beautiful legs against breakage?'

'What are you talking about?'

'A sheer drop of about twenty feet, pickle. Now what shall we do?'

The bus lurched drunkenly. 'Oh fuck!' Pandora forgot that she was busy being horrible to Mimi and made a dive towards the driver's door. 'Come on, whatever your name is,' she cried, 'we've got to get out of here.' And, prizing the driver's hands off the steering wheel, she pushed him out of the way and climbed over him, stepping neatly out onto a muddy verge, leaving the chauffeur open-mouthed with amazement.

On the road Pandora found Faisal, doubled up with laughter,

leaning helplessly on the bonnet of the white Mercedes.

'I don't know what you think's so funny.'

'Stop it, Pandora, this is not a time to get prickly with me,' he struggled to say.

'Fuck you, Faisal. Get us out of this one if you can.' She stood back and looked at the bus hanging at an impossible angle, only the stick of granite preventing it from hurtling down the hill to the valley far below. The passengers' faces were frozen with terror. With some effort Faisal managed to straighten his face and went to rescue the petrified team, leaving Pandora to give in to temptation and laugh away her tension from the other side of the mud-swamped road.

'And this is the dungeon . . . Listen.' The guide dropped a pebble into the huge black hole which he stood above with Pandora; it seemed an age before she heard it land.

'At last we meet.'

Pandora jumped and nearly fell over, hovering for a second on the dungeon's edge before finding her balance and grabbing the guard, who pulled her back to safety. She blinked and examined the man who'd caught her by surprise. He grinned at her and held out his hand.

'Ali,' he explained. 'I'm Faisal's brother. I'm sorry if I made you jump.'

'Jump! You nearly pushed me over the edge. Do you have any idea how far down this black hole goes?'

Solicitous, Ali took Pandora's arm. 'Then I suggest we get back to safety. I can't think what this man was doing bringing you here.'

Pandora disengaged herself from him. 'Actually I asked him to. We won't have time tomorrow and I'm curious.'

'But dungeons . . .' Ali stopped as if he had no need to continue explaining quite how unsuitable a place the dungeons were for someone like Pandora. 'Wouldn't you rather visit Richard the Lionheart's bedroom?'

'Seen it.' Pandora didn't like Ali's tone; was it patronising or slightly lecherous? She couldn't decide.

'So let me show you the rest of the castle.'

'Do you know it well?'

'Enough.'

Pandora picked her way towards the light across Richard the Lionheart's packed earth-floor kitchen. She wanted a better look at Faisal's brother. What she saw she didn't like – a strong, intelligent face, ruined by a spoilt pout. He had an uncontrolled quality which Pandora thought might prove positively dangerous should Ali ever find himself thwarted.

'Will you forgive me if I keep my guide? You see, he lives here and he knows the castle more than enough. You're right, this is a dangerous place and I'm determined to see every single back passage. I'd rather go with someone who knows the pot holes like the back of his hand.' Ali drew back. 'You don't mind too much, do you? Besides, I expect you're looking for Faisal and he's down at the hotel.'

Ali's eyes narrowed. 'He's put you off me, hasn't he?'

'What?'

'He's been telling you lies and warning you.'

'Who has?'

'That grasping brother of mine.'

'No. He's never even mentioned you.'

'The shit. He promised me. I'll get him for this.'

'But he hasn't said anything. He promised you what?'

'You must understand.' Ali leant towards Pandora where she sat on a window-sill, framed by its arch. 'He hates me you see.'

'I'm sure he—'

'No really. He's jealous. He loathes me. He tells lies about me all the time.'

'Well, I don't know what to—'

'So I'm just warning you. Don't believe him when he starts to tell tales about me. He's a little paranoid, that's all.'

'I see.'

'So now I'll show you round, yes?' Ali's face brightened as if the explanations he'd just given Pandora would make all the difference to her attitude towards him.

'I'm sorry, I really would rather . . .' Pandora thought hard.

She didn't want to offend Ali any more than she already had. It was her turn to be solicitous. Ali was evidently a little mad and being almost alone with him made her feel distinctly nervous. '. . . be by myself for a while.' She warmed to her task; taking Ali's arm she began to walk him towards the first arch on the long twisting curve which would take him down and out of the castle. 'I'm sure you understand. You must know what it's like to be under pressure. I need time to myself before I perform for the cameras tomorrow. And as for the guide . . .' she began to lie outright, 'I don't want to talk to him. He's just there to make sure I don't get lost.'

'I'm not convinced you'll be safe.'

'Of course I will be.'

'Just let me speak to him a moment.' Ali began to lecture Pandora's companion on the sanctity of her person. Pandora winked at the guide from behind Ali's back while he graciously accepted the large tip Ali gave him in an ostentatious moment, before standing with Pandora and watching while Ali sloped away.

'Phew,' said Pandora when Ali was out of sight. 'Close call. What a weirdo.'

'Weirdo?'

'Never mind. What's next?'

'How's George?' Faisal and Mimi were relaxing on the terrace of the eleventh-century convent which had been successfully transformed into a relatively luxurious hotel catering for visitors to the nearby castle.

'Moaning, but he'll survive. I've given him enough Diaralite to last him a lifetime, instructed him to keep taking it, and with any luck he'll be back on form tomorrow.'

'Can't he have the day off?'

'I'd love him to. But the thing about our Georgie is that he can't bear to miss anything. He has no intention of not being at the shoot in case his presence isn't missed and we inadvertently prove him dispensable.'

'You were nearly all proved dispensable this afternoon. Tell me again why you let the driver take that old heap round that particular hairpin bend.'

'Don't grin at me like that. How was I to know he was taking us the wrong way?'

'He must have thought you were going to jump out and take a few happy snaps of the castle and get back in the bus like most tourists do. Though he should have known better than to attempt that mud slide with so many passengers on board.'

'The poor man. I don't think I can remember seeing someone so upset.'

'Are you sure it wasn't just Pandora throwing herself over him with such gay abandon that took him by surprise?'

'Well, thank you for sorting the situation out for us so efficiently. Thank God we've got you to help us. Without you I expect we'd still be trying to get through immigration.'

'And tomorrow you shoot up there.' Faisal nodded at the great bastide, which stood, still almost intact, silhouetted against the late-afternoon sky.

'Hmm . . . an interesting mixture of the last word in American outfits for tourists. Pandora's going to steam. I've got two fur coats to put her in, not to mention the wool suits and cashmere roll-necks. Luckily she hardly ever breaks a sweat, when even the mercury's practically boiling.'

'Where is she?'

'Pandora? She's still up there. She seemed totally mesmerised by the place so I left her to explore it once I'd finished my plans for the shoot. I expect she'll have met up with your brother by now.'

'What?'

'He was here, looking for her. I told him where to find her.'

Faisal stood up suddenly, knocking his chair over and reaching hurriedly for his car keys and dark glasses.

'What's the matter?'

'I'll see you in a minute,' and Faisal was off. Mimi stared after him puzzled; he could be an extremely odd man.

Faisal found Pandora transfixed, listening to the Moslem call to prayer which was sung for her in the castle's tiny chapel-turned-mosque. Haloed by the failing sun, Faisal stood in the arched entrance and watched tears well in her eyes as the muezzin sang the old prayer through cupped hands, standing carefully angled towards Mecca. Faisal wondered for a moment why he'd been so concerned for her; after all, where should she be more secure but in the remains of a temple to the traditional English faith listening to the heartfelt entreaty to the same God by a supplicant from a brother religion?

There was no sign of Ali.

Embarrassed, feeling as if he'd intruded on some private mystery, Faisal turned away and sat on one of the stone circles that had surrounded the knights' round table and which still marked the central spot in the main courtyard of the castle. He lit a cigarette and watched the sun dip over the battlements, heading inexorably towards the Mediterranean. Behind him a half-moon rose and hung, pale and limpid, waiting for the sun to leave the stage. He allowed his gaze to linger over the elegant turns of the castle walls where shadow met light in finely contoured lines and the air was thick with ghosts.

His mind wandered . . . Pandora, beautiful, petulant, with a soul he kept glimpsing and losing as he might the answer to a problem in a dream. Pandora . . . he smiled to himself. If she were nothing else at least he could credit her with providing the ultimate displacement activity.

'Hi.' Emerging from the gloomy interior of the mosque, she sat on the stone next to him and helped herself to one of his cigarettes. 'Why didn't you stay?'

'I've heard that prayer before.'

'I bet you don't hear it that well sung very often.'

'Maybe.'

'What are you doing here?'

'You shouldn't be here on your own.'

'I'm not on my own. The guide's been looking after me and he's promised to get me a ride back to the hotel when I want to go.'

'I thought my brother might be with you.'

'So? Oh that's what the panicky face is all about. Did you rush up here to save me from him?'

'Of course not.'

'Yes you did.' Pandora was teasing. 'Is he as dangerous as he looks? He says you hate him and that you spread dirty lies about him at every opportunity.'

'He has a strange sense of humour.'

'Understatement. Anyway, no need to worry. I managed to get rid of him without any help from you.'

'Congratulations. I thought I should come and check on you all the same.'

'Oh, and what gives you the right to be my knight in shining armour?'

'I feel responsible for you.'

'You're so transparent. Ali said you don't want to share me.'

'Ali's a pathological liar.'

'He told me you'd say that.'

'And you believed him?'

'Why shouldn't I?'

Faisal blew a couple of nonchalant smoke rings and ground his cigarette butt under the heel of his battered brown suede Gucci loafer. 'Is that why you refused to come with me in the car today?'

'I only just met Ali. At the garage I decided you were behaving in a rather proprietorial manner for a man I've only made peace with for the duration of the trip.' Pandora lied. She didn't want Faisal to know that she hadn't been able to resist her own sense of responsibility to the fashion crew.

'Did you? It never occurred to you that I was just being polite to the princess of the party.'

'Princess! I work just as hard as everybody else.'

'Hmm . . . But you didn't earn your beauty, did you?'

'How dare you?'

'Sorry, that was uncalled for.'

'Too right it was, specially from a man who refuses to answer questions about missing tablecloths and sheep's eyes.'

'Touché.'

'I may not have earned my beauty but I didn't ask for it either. It's nothing to do with me, I'm a freak of nature, not a man-made work of art.' Pandora dragged herself back from the brink of fury. 'We really are good at rubbing each other up the wrong way, aren't we?'

'And for no good reason.'

'Maybe we're alike.'

'Don't be ridiculous.'

'Now you're getting all prickly. We are alike I think.'

Faisal raised a questioning eyebrow. 'Neither of us asked to be what we are. We're in powerful positions in spite of ourselves.'

Pandora looked at the sheikh through narrowed green eyes. 'And I don't think either of us is very happy with it but aren't quite sure what to do to remedy the situation.'

'Very perceptive. What makes you think I don't like the place I'm in?'

'If you did you wouldn't be following us around all the time, would you?'

'You're my guests.'

'So? You don't really have to shepherd us to this extent even if we are your guests, which we're not really. We're only staying with you at the camel fair. And you certainly needn't worry about me here.'

'It's instinctive with me, a tradition. I do come from a famously welcoming culture. It would be seriously against the grain if I didn't take personal charge of you while you're in Syria. Besides, you were my guests in Damascus. You only left my house this morning. And' – Faisal pointed his finger at Pandora – 'you'd still be stuck in a lay-by garage if I hadn't turned up today.'

'But I know you're not interested in the fashion stuff. I saw you in New York. It made you feel positively sick – or something did. Why the sudden interest now?'

'I've told you – you lot need looking after.'

'You're using us, aren't you? All this stuff about being our host is bullshit. You just don't want to do any work.' To Pandora

Faisal looked vulnerable in the dusk. 'You don't give much away do you? Professionally enigmatic.' Pandora smiled and waggled her eyebrows in a generally questioning manner.

'These facial acrobatics are supposed to get me to reveal my innermost secrets to you, are they?'

'I'm allowed to see if I can find out what makes you tick, aren't I?'

He stood up. 'Shall we?'

'Shall we what?'

'Go?'

'OK, I give up. I won't force you to talk.'

'Let's go then.'

'No. I told you, my guide said he'd get me a lift back when I was ready to go. What is it with you al Mez'al boys? You seem determined not to give me any time alone.'

'All right. What is there left for you to do?'

'What?'

'Here, before you go back to the hotel. What else do you want to have a look at?'

'Faisal! Leave me alone. I want to explore this place on my own.'

'You can't.'

'Why not?'

'I told you. It's dangerous.'

Pandora snapped. 'Faisal, I hardly think the spiritual muezzin's going to jump on me from behind the arras. And I've sent your lecherous brother off with his tail tucked firmly between his legs. I don't smell danger.'

'You're obsessed with sex! I'm not talking rape and pillage. I'm talking broken legs.' Faisal looked askance at the kitten-heeled Manolo's Pandora'd borrowed from George. 'You could do yourself some serious damage on those.'

'I've been all right so far.' She didn't mention the near miss at the dungeon.

'So let's go back to the hotel and avoid tempting fate any further. You are spending all day here tomorrow after all.'

Pandora sighed elaborately and shrugged. 'All right, I give

in. But only because after all this meaningless chat it's too dark to see much anyway.' She set off towards the first of the long gothic arched descents to the outside of the castle. 'God, you're worse than Nina and Mimi put together. I've never been so mothered.' Pandora kicked off her unsuitable sandals and cantered barefoot down the steps crying, 'For God and King Richard!' her voice echoing round the arching twists of the stone-paved route to the great main door. 'I wish I had a white charger to gallop about on while we're here. I'm sure all the princesses had them.'

'Yes, Pandora.' Faisal followed her, patient as a nursemaid, his eyes glued to her as she pranced about. Even without heels, her legs, long and fragile as a young doe's, didn't look too safe on the uneven surface of the road she'd chosen.

'I told you about the fortune-teller warning me against him. Pandora believed her.'

'Since when did you become so superstitious, Faisal?'

'I just don't need any more complications in my life than I already have.'

'I'd hardly describe your brother as a new complication.'

'He's turned up here to make trouble with Pandora.'

'I thought you weren't interested in her.'

The door opened and Ali slipped into Faisal's room unnoticed.

'Ahmed, I'm not,' he overheard, 'but that doesn't mean I don't mind being accused of spreading malicious truths about him. No news from Faraj I suppose?'

'Not a whisper.'

'I shouldn't have let him go off like that.'

'I told you you'd get bored with those Americans.'

'I'm not bored. I'm irritated by the suspense while we wait to hear from Faraj. My brain tells me there'll be nothing worth reporting but since you and he have made such a mountain out of this molehill I can't wait to be vindicated.'

'You've made your bed, Faisal, but you don't have to lie in it. You could always—'

'—Go and find him? No. That'd be admitting that he might be right.'

'Stubborn as ever.'

'I'm right, Ahmed, you'll see. I'll see you at the camel fair.'

'I'll look forward to it.'

'Sound a bit more enthusiastic, can't you? I know you secretly love the excuse the fair gives you to dress up.'

'Rubbish!'

'I'll speak to you later.' Faisal grinned down the phone. 'Forgive me, Ahmed, but you are the easiest man to tease.' He put down the receiver before lighting a cigarette and staring ruminatively out of the window.

'Faisal?' Ali hovered near the open door. Faisal turned round slowly, his dislike for Ali hidden behind a glacial expression. Ali shivered.

'I heard you'd followed us up here. What d'you want?' he asked, grinding out his cigarette.

'Brother . . .'

'I thought you were supposed to be in the desert.'

'Not yet. I did warn you I might come up here to help for a day or two. Is this a bad time?'

Faisal leant against the edge of the desk from which he'd been telephoning and crossed his legs. He examined Ali through narrowed eyes. 'Is this a bad time? . . . You have such a nice way of putting things, along with a talent for understatement that leaves me constantly amazed. Watch my lips. I'm on holiday, not just from work but from you too. If you refuse to get to the camel fair till the last possible moment then why don't you go and play at the knee of that Russian friend of yours?' Ali shrugged. 'Bored with you, is he?' Faisal gave a teasing little laugh.

'Do you have to be so sarcastic?'

'I'm sorry. You have just as much right as I do to be here. So long as the fair goes without a hitch.'

'You know perfectly well I won't be allowed to do a thing at the fair.'

'Representing the family . . .'

'That's rich coming from a man who seems to have taken up

supermodel-chasing as a career. Where's your sense of respon-sibility, Faisal? Has Pandora snatched it?' Faisal's eyebrow overhang lowered further. Ali held himself tight. He wasn't sure if he'd gone too far. He couldn't bear the silence. 'Hey, I'm sorry. That was unnecessary.' He stood up and held out his hands in supplication.

Faisal sighed. 'Why do we bother, Ali? Go away. Why talk? We'll only fight.'

'Maybe that'd clear the air between us,' Ali shrugged. 'We could get everything out and then, if we haven't actually killed each other, we might finally get on. And I know you've got things to tell me.' Ali winked conspiratorially.

'Like what?'

'You will when you're ready. We could have a slanging match and see if it brought it all out.'

'No. It'd be a waste of both our time.'

'Confrontation was never your strong point was it, Faisal?'

'I just don't see the point of fighting, specially when I'm going to win.'

'Oh, it's a competition is it? Of course, I'm too dumb to argue effectively hm?'

'I didn't say that.'

'No, you wouldn't deign to say what you really thought.' Ali bit his lip. 'So, when does Faraj get to the fair?'

'I don't care, Ali. In case you've forgotten, let me remind you that I put you in charge of the fair so I suggest you get out there and get on with it, all right?'

'One night here and then to the fair.'

'Why not now?'

'Let me have one chance with Pandora. Besides, I haven't had a proper night's sleep in ages and I'm exhausted.' Disingenuous to the last, he carried on. 'Frankly, I think it would be just plain dangerous if I set off now. I had a terrible journey up here . . .'

'Well, I wish you luck.'

'Don't need it. She found me perfectly charming up at the castle.'

'Not literally I hope.'

'What do you care? I thought you weren't interested.'

'Allow me brotherly curiosity.'

'You wait – just give me one proper chance . . .'

'Nina!'

'Mimi – I can hardly hear you.'

'I know. I'd send you a fax if the machine here wasn't broken so I'll just have to shout. Is that better?' Mimi said, talking into the mouthpiece of the old Bakelite telephone at the hotel as if she were using a walkie-talkie.

'No.'

'What?'

'How's the shoot going?'

'We haven't used any boots yet. Why do you want me to?'

'Haunted? Can you move?'

'No, the bus crashed down the mountain and Faisal had to ferry us and the luggage one by one to the hotel. It was a narrow escape from total disaster.'

'Plaster! Who's broken what?'

'Mimi!' Pandora stood in the doorway, still swinging her borrowed Manolo's, exhilarated from her evening at Richard the Lionheart's castle.

'What, Pandora? Go away. I'm trying to talk to Nina.'

'Ever heard the expression "These people are talking at cross purposes"?' Mimi began to laugh.

'Porpoises! I thought you were miles from the sea.' Nina's voice echoed from across the Atlantic.

'Nina, I'll try and call you from Aleppo.'

'What?'

'Bye, Nina.'

Mimi put the phone down and rubbed her eyes. It had been too long a day. She felt as if she'd been run over by the now defunct bus. Pandora smiled at her, uncharacteristically gentle, and pulled Mimi out of the too-low chair from which she'd been calling New York. She made her editor skip with her down the stairs to dinner.

'Please God may the food be edible,' was Mimi's heartfelt prayer. Pandora laughed.

'You'll be lucky. And just so you know, I'm going to be eating the salad tonight.'

'Oh no, Pandora, don't.'

'But I'm fed up with bread and over-cooked bits of unspecified meat. And the salad looks so good. Go on, Mimi, let me try the tabbouleh and if that doesn't kill me in a matter of minutes then let me move on to the tomatoes with that delicious hard goat's cheese. I'm starving!'

'I can't have you ill, Pandora. At least I've had Courteney to help when George's been incapacitated but we don't have a second model.'

'I've got the constitution of an ox. I promise I'll be all right.'

'Just be careful.'

They arrived in the dining room. The rest of the fashion team sat like an expectant family round the table waiting for their star and their manager to join them. Even George, pale, shaking, but feeling marginally better, was waiting there to eat. Only Faisal didn't sit with them. He could be seen out on the terrace. Framed by fruit-laden vines, silhouetted against the half-moon-lit castle, Faisal smoked a cigar and nobody dared interrupt his solitude by inviting him to join them for dinner.

Pandora ruthlessly ignored the view and sat down to attack the tabbouleh.

'May I?' Her munching was interrupted by Ali. Leering at her, and dragging a chair, he was evidently intent on squeezing in to sit beside her. Forgetting her hunger, she dropped her fork.

'By all means.' She gave him the full eyelash smile. 'I've already finished. You can have my place if you like.' She escaped to the solitary Faisal, hungry but skin no longer crawling, as it did when Ali was near.

Faraj's binoculars glinted dully where he lay flat on the top of a sharp escarpment, which lined one side of the spot marked on Ivan's desert map. Below, to the uninitiated eye, lay nothing but sand, a basalt pavement, a place known as the Devil's Kitchen. Once, three millennia ago, this had been the site of a small town on the silk route from the Far East. Watered by the Euphrates, Hittite merchants had grown rich on passing trade, until disaster struck in the shape of an earthquake, which swallowed the town whole and threw up the escarpment that Faraj now used as his vantage point. Now the place appeared barren as a burnt moon, a huge crater filled with nothing but black basalt slabs paving the place between escarpments where once people had lived and trade had flourished. The only remaining evidence of the Hittite town lay underground. Between the great slabs of basalt pavement there were holes, entrances to a warren of catacombs, in places several stories deep, the underworld of the long dead, ancient city. Faraj strained his eyes to see more through the dark: nothing, not even smoke from a fire. Turning onto his back he looked up at the sky.

'What the hell's going on here?' he asked. Said, holding the camels which they hadn't couched in order to prevent drawing attention to themselves by the roaring Sammy and Hassala would make in protest, didn't attempt to answer. Faraj turned onto his stomach once more and crawled towards his companion. 'Come on, let's put a couple of miles between us and this place and bed down for the night. We'll come back at sunrise and get a better look.'

He didn't bother to mount his camel but followed Said's lead to a spot where smoke from their fire couldn't be seen by any lookouts. They set their camels free to browse and, while Said built a small fire and began to cook flat bread and bring cardamom-flavoured Bedouin coffee to the boil, Faraj leant back against his camel saddle and watched the stars dance round the moon.

Chapter 9

4.30 AM flashed in sickly fluorescent green on the screen of Mimi's travel clock as the alarm beeped insistently in her ear. She groaned and turned over, feeling blindly to turn off the noise. She forced her eyes open and sat up, steeling herself to begin the day; allowing herself no time for dozing, Mimi went straight into her morning routine. Pushing her unruly black curls out of her eyes, she washed her face, cleaned her teeth, dressed and, sitting at the little table under her bedroom window which served now as a desk, she made a list of what the day held in store. Once the list was finished she could face the future; without it she would have been lost.

Dressed in old denim capri pants, a sleeveless, white poplin, Equipement shirt and immaculate white Superga tennis pumps, her hair tied back in a white cotton Peter Jones man's handkerchief, Mimi trotted down the corridor off which were the rooms where her team were sleeping, knocking loudly on each door as she went. There was no muffled 'I'm up' from Pandora's room so she tried the door. It was open; there was no sign of Pandora. Mimi shrugged and ran downstairs to where hair and make-up tables had been set up under the vine-covered terrace. Here she found her supermodel already hard at work doing Gavin and Frankie's jobs for them.

'What are you doing up? I usually have to inject you with adrenalin to make you open your eyes at this time of the morning.'

'Hmm . . . ?'

'Well?'

'Couldn't sleep. Get me some more tea will you?' Pandora smiled from under the huge rollers round which she'd wound her hair, and through a thick layer of Jo Malone cream which smelt simultaneously of wood smoke and roses. Mimi obediently went to the buffet, where cheese and salads along with sugar-crusted doughnuts and hard-boiled eggs were laid out framing two huge Thermos flasks in which were steaming weak coffee and fresh sage tea. The tea smelt of the hills around them and Mimi smiled involuntarily, looking out at the view, and for the first time taking in the size of the sky, the age of the hills. She gave Pandora her cup.

'All right, I see why you're up.'

'Good. Pass me the cotton wool please.' Mimi passed it and Pandora began to clean the cream off her face. 'What would you say to my not wearing any make-up at all today?'

'I'd say your nose would shine, you'd probably burn in the sun and what makes you so uninterested in making the most of your magnificent eyelashes all of a sudden?'

'What about my hair?'

'Darling, you know we need it up today. It's in the Polaroids.'

'Oh well, if it's in the Polaroids then I suppose there's no point in asking questions.'

'I hope you're not going to be all crabby again today.'

'Crabby! I'm just asking if you want my opinion, that's all.'

'Of course I want your opinion.'

'Wouldn't you ever like to take pictures of me? Just me? After all, I'm supposed to be the be-all and end-all of womanhood, aren't I? I'm supposed to represent what everyone wants to be?'

'Yes . . .' Mimi wondered a little nervously where this line of conversation was going.

'So take pictures of me then, not of Frankie's not inconsiderable talents with a blusher brush and Gavin's overrated abilities with hairspray and pins.'

'But you are you.'

'Under four inches of make-up and a couple of cans of Elnett.'

'Hardly any make-up the day before yesterday actually

130

and no hairspray at all if I remember rightly.'

'So why don't we dispense with them altogether?'

'Because, sweetling, we have to use next season's colours so that everyone knows what to buy and we have to practise next season's hair styles so that everyone knows how to look.'

Pandora sighed. 'Sometimes I wish you didn't have to practise on me. Would it offend the cosmetics companies so much if my face was just there, clean and open and showing me?'

'Come on, Pandora, you know as well as I do that the real you is hidden so far down inside you that I'm not convinced even you know what you're like.'

'Don't be horrible.'

'I'm not. I'm being honest. I've always thought you were such a chameleon that you could literally get up in the morning and decide from a wardrobe of characters which one you were going to wear each day.'

Pandora frowned and drank her tea. 'I don't do that.'

'Admit it, darling, you can be different, as only you know how. I count you as a really good friend but even I never know quite what to expect when I'm going to see you.'

Pandora laughed nervously. 'You're being ridiculous. Nobody's like that.'

'Most people don't have the imagination. Don't be offended, we love being taken by surprise by you.'

Pandora narrowed her eyes at Mimi. 'I should be cross with you but the view's too good. So I'll forgive you for accusing me of being shallow.'

'I didn't accuse you of being anything of the sort. I think you're lovely, and you are, without a shadow of a doubt, the most beautiful girl in the world. You've spent a lifetime telling everyone that that's all you want to be. Why suddenly start asking questions now?'

'Maybe you're right.' Pandora squared her shoulders and watched the sun gain on the sky. 'I'm just being stupid.'

'No, not stupid. You shouldn't be so touchy. Don't take life so seriously. You're a supermodel – enjoy yourself like you're supposed to.'

Pandora couldn't begin to frame the words to describe her reaction to Mimi's comments. Fortunately there was no time to sit and think about what her secret longings might be; there was hair and make-up to do and a whole day of photographs to take. Pandora gritted her teeth and let Mimi think they were sitting in companionable silence, while the rest of the team came down and behaved as tourists do when faced with unusual breakfast; they picked up each different type of food and looked at it nervously before finally making a choice most closely resembling what they might have eaten back in their own homes. Only Pandora ate cheese and humous for breakfast, wrapped in flaps of warm flat bread. Only she and Mimi drank the sage tea. Everyone else drank coffee and tried to treat the bread like toast, spreading it with unsalted freshly churned butter, which they didn't trust because it didn't come in individually wrapped packets, and with jam, which they trusted because it did.

'What do you think?' Faraj passed the binoculars to Said, who stared thoughtfully through them for a minute.

'There are six men running about on the desert floor. They'll die out there if they don't cover their heads.'

'What else do you see?'

'Nothing. No transport, no smoke . . . oh yes . . . there it is.' A tiny trail of grey made a tentative appearance perhaps half a mile away, seemed to check the air for safety, and then became a stronger plume smudging the pale, dawn air. 'Well that's all right then.'

'What?'

'At least we know they're not devils.'

'How's that?' Faraj laughed.

'Devils don't need to cook.' The smell of cooking meat reached Faraj and Said atop their sharp cliff. Faraj's stomach rumbled loudly. 'You've gone soft from city living.'

'I'm hungry.'

'I gave you bread.'

'I'm hungry for more than bread at breakfast.'

'Like I said, you've gone soft.'

Faraj snatched back the binoculars and changed the subject. 'The problem is there's no way of telling how many men there are, what kind of kit they've got or what they're really doing without getting inside. And I can't see an American flag.'

'Should there be one?'

'I hope so. We'll just have to get in there and have a look.'

'I'm not going in there.' Fear twisted Said's face into a comic grimace.

'Why not? You played in those catacombs all through your childhood. What's the matter with them now?'

'There are ghosts and genies and spirits and all sorts of things inside. They'll take away your manhood. You won't have children if you go in there.'

'Where did you hear this mumbo jumbo?'

'Your mother told me. No man should go there once he's reached adulthood.'

'Said, I thought you were a modern man.'

'No point in taking any chances.'

'You're ridiculous. Are you seriously suggesting I have to go down there and get in and out on my own?'

'You see, you're frightened of the jinn too.'

'I'm not frightened of any evil spirits, Said. I'm frightened of men slinging their Kalashnikovs about with gay abandon. I'd like a little back-up.'

'Oh.'

The surprised tone alerted Faraj. He whipped his head round and found himself staring into the dangerous end of an AK47. Another gently stroked the back of Said's neck. At the trigger ends of the guns were a pair of Action Men clones, dressed from head to foot in ex-USSR army surplus desert fatigues. They jerked their rifles in a 'stand up, very slowly' sort of way. Faraj saw no reason to disobey these two gun-firing machines with faces so impassive that he wondered briefly if they were in fact robots being worked by remote control. In any case, they didn't look like the kind of people who would react favourably to discussion of any kind.

'Somehow I don't think we're going to find any stars and

stripes down there,' said Faraj. The butt of the rifle jammed against his upper lip. He tasted blood in his mouth and grimaced. He stood up, very slowly, leaving the binoculars behind.

By 6.00 am Pandora was ready for the first photograph. Dressed like the most expensive type of American tourist, in classic navy pin-striped Ralph Lauren, she aimed one of Flash's cameras, empty of film, at Richard the Lionheart's shield, which was carved above the arched entrance to the council chamber at the heart of the castle.

'Babe, lose the elbow!' Flash was directing operations with a kind of gung-ho Indiana Jones sort of attitude, aided in his performance by his ubiquitous bulging safari waistcoat, which was never going to inspire Pandora to shine for the camera. Mimi winced while he coaxed his supermodel to heights of absurdity, all the while leering at her and calling her babe. Nothing could have been calculated to annoy Pandora more. Mimi was beginning to wonder why he was so respected as a photographer. So far Pandora had done all the work.

'What about my elbow?'

'It's in the way, babe. Can't you just hold the camera with your left hand and let the other one go?'

'What are you talking about? Let it go where? I'll look ridiculous!' Pandora turned a furious face at Flash and pointed his spare camera at him in a threatening manner. 'You, Flash Harry, haven't the faintest idea what you're doing.' Her hands came down to her hips and she bent forward to make her point. 'I've been in this game since before I could talk, Flash, and you're behaving like this is a catalogue!' Flash smiled quietly to himself as he pressed the remote control and took pictures of an angry supermodel making magic shapes with the sharp contours of the classic suit.

'All right, gorgeous, gotcha. Did you know how fabulous you are when you're angry?' He turned away from her, passing his camera to Joey, who started changing lenses and reloading film. 'Right then, shall we try something else?' he asked. 'Courteney, let's get out some of those velvet dresses and turn our heroine into Richard the Lionheart's sweetheart *à la* end of the millennium.' Mimi took Pandora by the arm and led her to the knight's library which had been turned into a wardrobe for the day. Flash was left behind to supervise Joey while he labelled and tucked away the film; a wide grin covered his face.

'I'll kill him!'

'Don't be cross, sweetling, he's just getting his own back for your Lisa Fonssagrives impersonation in Damascus. And you know how he hankers after you. I'm sure he thinks that the nastier he is the better his chances of getting into your pants. Just let him take the pictures and it'll all be over before you can say "a thousand and one nights".'

'You're disgusting. I know he'd like to get up close and personal with me but you're not seriously suggesting that he thinks he stands a chance. Who does he think he is? He's twice my age and that David Attenborough outfit he seems to have adopted for this trip makes him look like a pink slug in sandy khaki. And as for his lean, mean look! Is he so impressed with it that he hasn't noticed that he's getting decidedly pear-shaped around the hip area? He can't really think he's attractive, can he?'

'Perhaps we should just pity him and admire him for trying? And you know all the trouble we're having on this shoot so far is my fault. I'm too tired to be much of a stylist so he should be taking over. Allow him to be cross because you did all the creative work at the Nizam House. He'll feel better now he's been horrible to you for a minute.'

'Minute! Hour or two more like. Ugh, there's nothing more disgusting than a straight boy lecherous male chauvinist pig.'

'Neatly put, "babe".' Pandora playfully hit Mimi, swiping off her editor's bandanna and setting free Mimi's riot of black curls. 'Thanks!' Mimi began the process of taming her mane.

'Well I hope the happy snaps he's just got a roll of are perfectly hideous. That'll teach him to make fun of me. Why couldn't he have just asked me to act angry?'

'I think you'll find those unhappy snaps will be perfect. Let him do his job, Pandora. Don't be mean to him.'

'I'll think about it. But you tell him if he calls me babe one more time I won't be responsible for my actions.'

'He calls everybody babe, sweetling.'

'It's sexist, derogatory and patronising.'

'And it's not just aimed at you.'

'Just tell him not to do it, even if we both know he'll ignore you. At least you'll have made an effort.'

'I promise.'

Pandora let Courteney pull the suit jacket she'd been wearing off her and perched on the edge of an arrow slit while George removed a pair of red patent leather J P Tod's and then the suit trousers. She felt her hair, styled by herself into a smooth chignon wrapped high on the crown of her head. 'Where's that Gavin Cheveux gone? I know I did my own hair this morning but he might at least come and make sure it's still up where I put it. I can't do everything around here,' she complained. Gavin appeared, blushing at being caught lounging by the buffet table which was laid outside in the shade of the library wall. He'd been eating the Hershey Bars he'd brought with him from New York, washing them down with gallons of weak, Thermos-warm coffee while watching the proceedings with Frankie. Frankie bustled in as well and started repowdering Pandora's nose before she too could be accused of loitering without intent.

And George, with due reverence, brought a fish-tailed, bias-cut, burnished bronze coloured velvet evening dress for Pandora to wear. With a professionalism born of dressing for photographs countless times a day for the past eleven years, Pandora stood naked but for a skin-coloured G-string and waited while George lowered the dress into a pool on the large white linen sheet, which was being used to protect both Pandora's precious feet and the equally valuable clothes from the broken stone floor. Then she stepped into the dress and stood stock still while George hooked the hundred or so open velvet-covered buttons which followed the curve of Pandora's spine from the nape of her neck, round the bias cut, over her left hip, and down to the place where the fish-tail hem of the dress scooped up to just above the hollow behind her right knee.

'Wow,' said Gavin. For once he had no situation halfway up the Himalayas with which to compare this moment.

'Phew,' added Frankie, equally dumbstruck.

'Good,' said Mimi, triumphant; this picture would be magnificent.

'Blimey!' Courteney and George said at the same time.

'Hair up or down?' asked Pandora, unimpressed by the awe with which the people surrounding her were staring. 'Joey!' she called. 'This lot are dumbstruck. Come and help, will you?' Joey appeared in the doorway and stopped, trying to stop his jaw grazing the unprotected ground at his feet.

'Oh for God's sake.' Pandora, exasperated, started pulling out the pins holding up the chignon she'd built so carefully while watching the sun rise that morning. 'Hair down it is. And if any of you are ever freed from the spell which has turned you all to stone, can someone get me some coffee? I'm off to have my picture taken at the head of old Lionhearted Dick's dining-room table.' Holding the hem of her dress high off the ground with one hand, she went herself to the hanging rail, under which shoes for each outfit were arranged in careful George-like order. George was the first to escape from his petrified state.

'Stop!' he cried. 'Don't touch them. You don't know which are the right ones.'

'Well, pickle, with all of you incapacitated by my overwhelming beauty, I had to choose some shoes for myself. I think I'll wear these ones.' She held up a pair of perspex-heeled Manolo slingbacks.

'But you're supposed to wear these ones.' He went for a pair of flat Chanel pumps; they were dark bronze leather with black watered-silk toes.

'You've got to be joking. They are the most disgusting pair of shoes I have ever seen in my life. Mimi!' Pandora pleaded with her granite editor who finally came back to life. 'Look, George says I have to wear these and not these. Please, Mimi. You know I have exquisite taste.'

Mimi bared her teeth at George. 'Will you stop being so dogmatic with everyone, George. Let Pandora wear those sandals if she likes. If she wants to not wear shoes at all that would also be an option.' Mimi marched back out of the library. 'The point I'm trying to make is that it's already six thirty and if we don't get a move on we won't take any pictures at all because the light will be gone. That would be a shame wouldn't it? We'd all get fired. Now take that sullen look off your face, George – you never know, the wind might change and you'll be stuck with it.'

So Flash spent the rest of the morning taking pictures of Pandora dancing round the circle of stone seats which would once have framed the knights' round table. She swung her perspex-heeled Manolo's as if they were a handbag and she waltzed for the camera, turning her fish-tailed dress into her dancing partner; and she did all this because it was her job to do so and she wouldn't know how to do it badly even if she tried.

Faraj and Said sat opposite each other on the floor in an underground chamber. Their little prison was dark. The entrance was barred with the back of an Action Man lookalike. Faraj scratched his chin, his moustache, his head. Said rolled a fat and generous cigarette. He saw no reason to save his tobacco as he was convinced that it would be sooner rather than later that they were to die in this hole.

Not far away, through the rabbit warren of passages, a satellite phone was being used to call Ivan.

'We've got two men.'

'Bedouin?'

'Certainly.'

Ivan picked at a mosquito bite which was festering in his ear, and it began to bleed onto the grimy collar of his black nylon shirt. 'Who are they?'

'How should I know? We speak no Arabic and they speak no Russian . . .'

'Did you try them in English?'

'No joy.'

'What? You didn't try them or they didn't understand?'

'Don't see why it means so much to you.'

'It means, you twit, the difference between just letting them go because they're innocent passers-by, or blowing their heads off because they're Faisal's spies.' Ivan hoped the desperation in his voice wasn't carrying to the catacombs. The mantra 'please don't let it be Faraj' kept repeating itself in his head.

'Oh, we tried English.'

'And?'

'They didn't understand. They're country boys, Ivan. Why are you panicking like this? The problem is we brought them in and kept them, and then a couple of the boys got a bit over-excited and did a bit of target practice on their camels.'

'I don't believe this.'

'So we don't know what to do with them.'

'Can they drive?'

'We haven't got enough jeeps to just give them one even if they do. There are more coming with Pictikhov when he arrives.'

'Well just let them go then.'

'They'll die!'

'I didn't think you'd be squeamish. If they were so obviously country boys why did you take them in?'

'Couple of the guards were a bit too keen. Besides, they were staring down at the camp with binoculars.'

'So they're not that technophobic.'

'Very, very old binoculars – in a leather case. They looked like an old war relic.'

'What exactly were they looking at?'

'This place.'

'How can you be so sure?'

'You haven't been here yet – there's nothing else to look at! Overground it's an oven with nothing but burning black stone for miles and miles, and underground it's a series of dusty caves that never warm up. I'm shivering here!'

Ivan was bored now; convinced that the Bedouin at the catacombs were not Faisal's spies, he stopped concentrating while his colleague in the desert carried on listing his litany of complaints. He was jerked back to consciousness only when he heard, 'Of course we'll have to tell Pictikhov.'

'Why?'

'Don't sound so astonished. He'll guess that there've been people here because of the camel carcasses.'

'Burn them.'

'Well if they're nothing to do with anything then I don't see why we shouldn't tell him.'

'Just bring the picture of our boss into your mind's eye for a second, will you? Do you see there a man who'd be forgiving about not only over-enthusiastically arresting a couple of passing peasants but then blowing their transport away and taking them prisoner, so that sooner or later they'll be free and therefore able to spread the word among their friends and family that there's an arms depot being built up in a patch of desert not far from home?'

'I hadn't thought of it quite like that.'

'No, evidently not. Now, listen to me. Put them in a jeep, drive them fifty miles away from the catacombs, chuck them out with no food or water and they'll never bother you or anyone else again. And burn their camels. And whatever you do, don't tell Pictikhov!'

'Right.'

'Just do it before Pictikhov finds out or we'll all be strung up with razor wire with no questions asked.' Ivan slammed the phone down, exhaling cigarette smoke, praying that he'd got away with his lies. At least he'd escaped the conversation without giving away the fact that, according to Ali, Faisal knew the exact location of the Russians' camp, thanks to a neatly marked map he'd so kindly left for them to find pinned to the back of his office door. He wouldn't have got away so scot-free if Pictikhov had arrived, but his plane wasn't due to leave T'bilisi until two days later. Tearing the incriminating map from its Scotch tape pinnings, he lumbered out of the room and headed for the kitchen to burn it and pour his first vodka of the day.

*

Out of spite for Ivan, who was enjoying himself in the relative luxury of Damascus, the Action Man in charge of the catacombs decided to tell Pictikhov all. Then he sat in his office all day, waiting for instructions, leaving Faraj and Said to rot, unfed and without water, under guard.

The shoot carried on all day. The team worked their way round the castle, each room demanding a different outfit, a different narrative. There were pictures of Pandora in DKNY jeans and a black cashmere polo-neck framed in the window of Richard the Lionheart's bedroom, looking out over the snow-capped hills of the Lebanon; Anna Sui orange and pink shot taffeta and a mole-coloured, fake-fur-trimmed, short-sleeved, round-necked sweater for the kitchens; a Marc Jacobs Louis Vuitton duck-egg blue dress and coat, and camel-coloured, patent leather, severely chic Mary Janes for the princesses' boudoir. Even Ali, who arrived after lunch thinking he'd get another chance with Pandora, was completely shattered by the end of the day and he'd done nothing but watch and get in the way. And Pandora? Pandora submitted to necessity and was so concentrated on the job in hand that neither Flash nor Ali could get past the glassy perfection of her performance.

Hell-fire flames framed the sinking sun and the silhouette of the village, to the dramatic accompaniment of a recorded muezzin calling the faithful to prayer through a scratchy tape machine and very loud speakers. A pale two-thirds moon loitered as if with intent above purple bruise mountains towering over the gravelly desert floor. At last Pandora's day was over.

'How did it go?' Faisal asked her, absent-mindedly, actually wondering whether Faraj was on his way back from his spy mission yet.

'Fabulous!' Pandora threw herself along the length of a wicker sofa on the verandah of the hotel, kicking off the Louis Vuitton Mary Janes which she was still wearing from the shoot and shaking her river of hair out until it pooled on the floor behind her. 'Though I say it myself, I was magnificent.' She stretched and closed her eyes. 'You should have come and watched. Your brother was quite open-mouthed with amazement. Where's he gone? I thought he'd be worshipping at my altar after the kind of performance I gave today.'

'Ough, my feet!' Mimi slumped into another, smaller chair; even her exuberant hair seemed to be suffering from exhaustion and, unlike Pandora's, it hung in tired ringlets over her half-shut eyes. She ignored Pandora's over-excitement and turned to Faisal, attempting and failing to re-tie her now grubby white handkerchief round her head.

'I don't suppose you've seen Joey on your travels? He seems to have vanished.'

'No.' The sheikh stood with his back to the girls, watching the sun disappearing in a blaze of glory.

'What's up with you then, grumpy?' Pandora reached for the gin and tonic she'd made herself at the untended bar and drank half of it in one go. 'Delicious,' she pronounced, not waiting for Faisal to answer. 'A little taste of Uncle Rory. I wonder how he's getting on in Vegas.'

'Even more magnificently than you are here I should imagine.'

'Mimi, you're too, too sweet.' Pandora started to hum a tuneless medley of Cole Porter songs.

'This is absurd!' A flustered Flash appeared, sweat rings making the already grubby multi-pocketed waistcoat even less attractive to Pandora, who wrinkled her nose and made a little moue of distaste at the photographer-cum-adventurer who'd so rudely interrupted her.

'Shh Flash, I'm entertaining the troops. They need some very serious cheering up. They feel overwhelmed by their responsibilities and don't have time to acknowledge quite how fabulous I was today.'

'Babe, with respect, would you mind putting your admittedly very beautiful self aside for a moment while I worry about the fact that my already useless assistant seems to have made himself even more unpopular by doing a badly timed runner?'

Pandora sat up suddenly, interested. 'No!'

'Yes. Not a note, not a clue, not a thing to tell me where he's gone.'

'How very selfish of him. Where's he supposed to be?'

'Guarding the kit of course. How can I relax if he won't do his job properly?'

'Well, if you gave him a break once in a while then he might prove a bit more obedient.'

'Pandora does have a point, Flash. He's not really disappeared, has he? Has he taken his luggage?' Mimi asked the sensible questions.

'How would I know? I don't have the key to his room.' Flash looked at Mimi as if she must be immensely stupid.

'Well then, shall we go and look?' Mimi dragged herself out of the comfort of her little wicker chair and took the photographer's arm.

'What's this "we" business, Mimi?' Flash installed himself in Mimi's erstwhile chair. 'You go and find him. You're in charge. I'm having a drink like the one Pandora's guzzling.' Mimi couldn't be bothered to argue; she puffed a little and went off in search of the wayward Joey.

'She'd better find him quickly. Aren't we supposed to be going to Aleppo tonight?' asked Flash, slouched so far down in Mimi's chair that Pandora wondered if he were about to slide right off it and onto the floor. He sat, legs wide apart, as if the advertisement of his evidently plentiful wares would make her fall for him; he made her feel slightly sick.

'We can't go anywhere now,' she said, just to annoy him. 'Do you have any idea how dangerous these roads might be in the dark? I've heard all sorts of horror stories about these mad Baghdadi truck-drivers lurching down the wrong side of the road at impossible speeds with no brakes and no headlights.'

'You're so helpful, Pandora.'

'My pleasure, Flash. Anything I can do, don't hesitate to ask.'

From the darkened edge of the verandah where the world fell away towards the hills between the hotel and the sea, Faisal's voice surprised them.

143

'She's right. You can't drive to Aleppo now it's dark. You'll have to go in the morning.'

'My, Mr Faisal,' said Pandora in a breathy imitation of Scarlett O'Hara, 'I'd quite forgotten you were out there. You did make me jump. Would you get me another drink please? Just to calm my nerves.' Faisal clapped his hands sharply and he barked an order to the boy who came at his command. 'And you can be so masterful too when you put your mind to it.' Pandora batted her inch-long eyelashes and grinned a wicked grin. He ignored her.

'I hope that stupid Joey hasn't got himself into any serious trouble.' Faisal's hands were buried deep in his pockets. He began to pace.

'Don't see why you're so concerned. Oh, I forgot, you feel responsible for us.' Pandora dispensed with the *Gone with the Wind* impression and sat up, resting her chin in her hands and staring out into the darkness. 'Can't you do one of your knight on a white charger acts and magic him up from somewhere?'

'I'd have to know where he'd got to first.'

'Snap again at the drinks boy and see if he knows.'

Faisal didn't answer and turned back to stare hard into the darkening night. Flash stood up to go. 'You two are about as good company as a mismatched pair of out-of-sorts monkeys tonight,' he pronounced.

'Now there's an interesting comparison. I tried performing for you, pickle, but you said you didn't like it. This is the real me. Too much like hard work, am I?'

Flash threw Pandora a twisted, angry look. 'I don't believe this. I'm actually going to have to go and look for the little waster myself.'

'Bye! Hope it takes you forever to find him.' Pandora glanced over her shoulder to make sure he'd gone. 'Don't come back at all if you can help it, you overweight, lecherous old slob. Call yourself a photographer! I've met more talented baboons.'

'Are you always this vitriolic with people you don't like?' Faisal asked from the shadows, where he'd stopped pacing and leant now against a vine-dressed pillar.

'Of course I'm not. I'm bored that's all.'

'I thought you were all over-excited because of your marvellous performance today.'

'I was . . . I am.' She shook her head and looked at the sheikh. 'The adrenalin's gone. Now I just feel thoroughly flat. You know what . . . ? It's your fault; whenever you're around I stop believing what I've always been told.'

'What's that?'

'That I'm the be-all and end-all, of course. You make me feel as if I'm just a spoilt little girl who spends all day prancing around in front of a mirror and smiling at herself. Enough to dampen anyone's enthusiasm, you must admit.'

'I'm sorry. I don't mean to. I'm sure you're brilliant at being the most beautiful girl in the world and you evidently work hard at it too.'

'Patronising bastard!' She looked at the remains of her drink and slugged it down. 'Besides, you're right. I've got no right to swan around feeling pleased with myself. I'm totally uneducated. I've never done anything else to earn my daily bread but stand and look pretty in front of a camera. I wouldn't even know where to look for my brain, let alone how to test drive it.'

'Takes a good mind to make good pictures, doesn't it?' Faisal tried to be helpful. He wasn't sure he was up to another bout of introspection from Pandora; it only made him start to stare at his own navel, an occupation he'd never found particularly edifying.

'You flatter me. It takes years of practice and lovely legs, that's all. And one day I'll have to start spending half my income to keep up my appearance so that I can command ever higher prices for the image of my face.'

'Sounds tough.'

'You wouldn't do it.'

'I don't think my looks are the kind they'd have much use for on the cover of a glossy magazine. Besides, I'd look a bit peculiar in a flouncy mini-dress – the hair on my legs wouldn't do the clothes any justice.' He dropped into Flash's recently vacated chair and crossed his long, angular legs. Pandora didn't laugh.

145

Faisal watched her, her forehead wrinkled in uncomfortable thought, and she watched him, the dark overhang of his brows hiding the true expression in his fiery black eyes. The silence was suffocating. Faisal stood up.

'Come for a walk?' he asked.

'Good idea.'

In the still-inhabited Crusader village, Ali and Joey were enjoying a moan in a back street café where the click clack of twenty games of backgammon was joined by their own. They had a narghile each, stacked high with rough local tobacco, and their glasses of sage tea were kept replenished by a waiter, awed by their air of big-city glamour. On the edge of the café's light a shepherd with black teeth and sad eyes played whisky tunes on a little tin flute. Ali and Joey ignored his fine, mournful song; they were much too thrilled with each other to acknowledge anything or anyone else.

'I mean it's hell, you know. I could be in the same position for the rest of my life if I'm not careful. That Flash Harry, he's got an ego the size of fucking Manhattan and I just get ignored. It's like I'm a bit of machinery that's expected to switch on in the morning and perform endless miracles all day and then just disappear and be ready next time I'm needed. I mean, the man doesn't even speak to me. He just holds his hand out and expects me to know what he's after. Luckily I'm no mean photographer myself and I can usually tell what he wants so at least he doesn't try and hit me any more . . .'

'I know exactly how you feel.' Ali, morose, his moustache drooping in sympathy, looked dolefully into his glass of tea. 'At least you can move on. I haven't any choice. For the rest of my life I will be the great Faisal bin Ali al Mez'al's little brother. The one that's cute and charming.' He allowed himself a small, deprecating smile at this point. 'But ultimately I'm useless because I don't hold the purse strings. That control freak, who had the great good fortune to be born two years before me, won't let me touch a single thing. Imagine being forced to be overwhelmed with gratitude just because I'm allowed to go and be in charge of a stupid camel fair! I mean, I ask you, what's that got to do with the price of bread? You know what he's really up to, of course. He's been trying to keep me away from Pandora. Not because he's interested himself, like any normal red-blooded male, no, he's just bloody-minded and selfish and never learnt to share.'

'You don't like your brother much then?' Joey was beginning to realise that this wasn't going to be so much a mutual moaning session, but one where he played audience while Ali showed off his grudges.

'I tell you, this isn't some simple case of sibling rivalry. Oh no . . .' Ali, a little wild now, knocked over his narghile in his excitement, scattering smashed glass and tobacco and burning coals across the road. The awed waiter appeared instantly to replace it. Ali didn't even acknowledge him. 'He took everything from me. And you know what?'

'What?' Joey leant far back in his chair as if to protect himself from being infected with this rambling fury.

'I'll get my revenge, you'll see.'

'Right.'

'And it will be sweet . . .' For a moment Ali's eyes glazed over as he gazed into the future, glowing at the thought of his brother's sticky end. He brought himself back to the present with a shake of his head. 'Right, let's play,' he said, shaking his dice as if they were maracas and laughing with pleasure; he looked just inches away from turning quite mad.

Neither Ali nor Joey noticed Faisal until he came between them and the light from the old hurricane lamps which crowded a nearby table. Ali jumped.

'Faisal! Do you have to sneak up on people like that?'

'I thought you were exhausted and getting an early night.'

'It's only ten o'clock. I was just suggesting we pack up and make tracks, wasn't I Joey?' Joey, a little slow and embarrassed to be caught playing truant from the fashion shoot by the only supermodel in the vicinity, didn't answer.

'Cat got your tongue, Joey?' Pandora's voice was as friendly as a barbed-wire fence; Joey made no attempt to cross it. He stood up.

'Come on, Ali. Let's go.' He started ambling up the street with all the enthusiasm of a schoolboy caught playing truant.

'You might remember to drop in on Mimi and let her know you're OK. I doubt she'll forgive you but at least she'll be relieved not to have to send back to Manhattan at great expense for a replacement photographer's assistant.'

'Glad to hear she was so worried about my welfare and not how much my leaving was going to cost her,' said Joey, sulkily walking backwards up the hill, his hands deep in his pockets, his words defiant, while all the time he was secretly relieved to have this chance to get away from Ali's raving.

'You're in the wrong industry, Joey, if you seriously expect people to care about you, and not about what you can do for them. I'd have thought you'd know that by now.' Pandora heard the bitterness in her own voice. She turned and walked away so that she didn't have to see by the expression on his face whether he'd heard it too. She stopped where a small river was bridged by a Crusader arch and leant on the balustrade, ignoring Ali and Joey as they trundled slowly back to the hotel.

Faisal came and stood beside her and watched the trickle of water dawdle under the bridge.

'Lonely too.' Pandora turned and looked at Faisal. 'Like you.'

'Time to go back, don't you think?'

'Or is it time to go forward?' Pandora laughed and linked arms with Faisal. 'You do make me come out with some funny things sometimes.'

'Oh the way your mind works is my fault, is it?'

'Absolutely, it's all that staring deep into my eyes and ignoring my legs that does it.'

'Pandora, are we flirting with each other?'

'No, darling, this is escapist banter. Flirting with me is a much more energetic exercise.'

'Is it?'

'I might show you some time.'

'I'll look forward to it.'

'Ha!'

*

148

Deep inside the catacombs under the desert floor of the Badiyyat ash-Sham, Faraj and Said argued over escape routes mapped out in the dust. The Action Man who guarded them had long since given up listening to the unfamiliar sounds of the foreign language they spoke; he couldn't understand a word. Besides, what threat could a pair of desert idiots in dresses and tablecloths pose to armed Russian security? Faraj leant back against the wall and listened to Said's persuasion.

'Listen. I'm more desperate to escape than you are.' Said was determined that they would take the way he'd chosen. 'I'd like to be able to have children, thank you. Follow me and I'll get you out. If I'm wrong then you can have all my possessions, including my wife.'

'If you're wrong then I shouldn't think that either of us is going to have much use for possessions, let alone wives.'

'We've got to get out of here!'

'OK, let's go. Your route.'

'At last!'

'There's one final problem. What about big boy there?' Faraj nodded at the back of their impassive guard.

'That's easy.' Said reached under his cloak and, silent on bare feet, took the unsuspecting soldier by surprise. The two of them were out, escaped, celebrating moonlit freedom before the guard had regained consciousness from the blow to his head from the turquoise-studded handle of Said's trusty dagger. He came to later to find his eyelids stuck together by the congealing blood from a nasty head wound and Said's head cloth wound round him as both gag and blinding hood. Faraj's red and white checked keffiyeh bound his feet, and the black silk rope which usually kept it in place tied his hands to his feet, behind his back. The guard was well and truly stuck, unable even to raise an alarm. On the desert surface, Faraj and Said skirted round the basalt pavement searching for the bigger entrances to the caves which they knew perfectly well were there somewhere.

'Here!' Said ducked back into a long dark passage and stopped, breathing heavily, waiting for Faraj to catch up with him and for his eyes to become accustomed to the gloom. 'I can smell diesel,' he said to his panting companion.

'Come on then. Let's follow your nose.'

At last a reply from Pictikhov whizzed to the catacombs via satellite from T'bilisi.

> Message received and understood. Keep prisoners to attend my pleasure. Under no circumstances must they be allowed to escape. I don't believe they're innocent Bedu – it must be a plot. I don't trust Ivan's story. Keep tabs on him but don't rattle Ali's cage by calling him in yet. Sheikh and his brother get to desert in two or three days. Suggest welcome committee prepares. Are my quarters ready?
> Pictikhov.

Chapter 10

'**O**w!'

'Shh!'

'I've gashed my leg.'

'I don't know what you think I'm going to do about it.' Faraj ploughed on through the crumbling grey velvet underground. 'If you'd been right about the diesel we'd have been out of here by now.'

'It must have been ghost diesel.'

'Stop banging on about ghosts, will you? There are no ghosts, no genies, no evil spirits.'

'So why haven't we been able to find anything? We haven't even heard a word from the people who locked us up.'

'They're all asleep, dimwit . . . wait!' A sliver of light, a hint of colour; Faraj rounded a corner, finding nothing but a tiny hole allowing a spotlight of early-morning sun to show yet another dead end.

'Shit!' He couldn't bear the fact that they'd actually escaped before voluntarily diving back for a second spell incarcerated deep underground. Neither was he much pleased with his or Said's memories; they really had spent large chunks of their childhoods scooting round these passages when their families had been camped on the top of the escarpment only half a mile away. He couldn't understand why the place looked so different now. And he was ready to clout Said, who blamed everything on evil genies who had nothing better to do than make life tough for these men, desperate to escape.

Said sat down and put his head in his hands. 'They must be searching for us by now. If the sun's up so are they.'

'Don't panic. We don't know how many they are. They

might not have found their battered companion yet.'

'Yeah – right.'

'Come on, Said. We can't just sit here and hope for a miracle to save us. We've got to keep looking.'

'I can't.'

'Try.'

Said forced himself to his feet. 'Which way?' Faraj closed his eyes, turned round and round until he had no idea which direction he faced, stopped and pointed. 'Very scientific.' Said wasn't impressed.

'That's rich coming from a man who believes in ghosts.' Faraj set off in the new direction. Said followed a little way behind. The passage they had taken shrank, smaller, narrower, disintegrating around them, threatening to collapse altogether; Faraj kept going.

'You can't go this way – it's another dead end.'

'Trust me. I've got a feeling about this.' Faraj got down on his hands and knees and crawled into the space in front of them.

'I'm claustrophobic,' wailed Said. 'We're going to die.' He squeezed his shoulders between the crumbling basalt walls and tried not to cry. They couldn't turn round and go back. There wasn't room.

'Tough!' said Faraj, struggling on in front. And it seemed an age before his unscientific approach to escape was vindicated. Suddenly the passage opened. Faraj stood up; Said followed. 'Look!' They were in a cavern and Faraj, triumphant, pointed at four jeeps, lined up facing a wide, clear exit. There was nothing to stop them now . . . except for a guard. Faraj saw him first. Then they heard him. The shots from his semi-automatic handgun flew wide, hitting only the petrol tank of a jeep before Faraj had whipped off his old camel-hair cloak, thrown it over the man like a net and grappled him bodily to the ground. He sat on the guard's back and caught the rope Said tossed from one of the jeeps. Faraj tied up the guard and left him, face down, disarmed and terrified.

In a matter of minutes, the two Bedu were out in the early-morning light, faces hidden by stolen ex-USSR army caps, and heading west to the site of the camel fair. Said drove. They had sixty kilometres to go, it was dawn, they had a full tank of petrol, and neither of them was wearing sunglasses. Glancing at the bodies of his bullet-burst camels smouldering with flies, Said winced. Faraj passed him a cigarette. Said took it, slammed down the accelerator and roared away from the horrible sight.

'Pandora, if you do the "We're all going on a summer holiday" thing again I'll wring your neck.'

'You are much too stressed, Mimi.' Pandora, climbing into the new and improved coach which Faisal had magicked for them from Damascus, ticked off her editor. 'Look at this lovely conveyance. You should be joining in the singing with me for at last we have a suitable thing in which to sing. And if you give me another filthy look like that one, then I'll just have to check with God to see if we can't get the wind changed and your usually very pretty face'll be stuck like that for life.' Mimi relaxed a smidgin. 'That's better. I suggest that while we're on our way up to jolly old Aleppo you get out your pecker and give it a bit of a polish. We can't have a sorry stylist now, can we?'

'No, Pandora.'

'Good. Now you'll be glad to know that I have no intention of singing and that, having been haunted by Captain Bluebeard and his henchmen all night after a late evening walk with Faisal the freak, I'm suffering from an uncharacteristic bout of post-panic attack exhaustion.'

'Panic attack!'

'Yes, pickle, night sweats, hyperventilation, the works. As you can see, I'm keeping myself ruthlessly calm, largely because I recognise that you are in no fit state to handle any more crises. So, as I'm in need of a great, big slice of beauty sleep, I'd be grateful if you'd ask the others to keep the noise down while I get a bit of shut-eye on the way.' Pandora pulled a navy satin Virgin Atlantic eye-mask out of her bag, helped herself to the back row of seats and lay down. Within seconds a little snore escaped her. Mimi looked at her friend in amazement; if only she could fall asleep like that wherever and whenever she felt like it.

'Shall we all get on too?' Gavin and Frankie stood at the top of the steps.

'Yes, of course.' Mimi began to count the rest of the team onto the bus.

'It's just that I thought you might have been giving our Pandora a little pep talk in private before we go. If you want my opinion, she's getting a bit big for her boots, that one, and could do with being taken down a peg or two.' Gavin spoke carefully into Mimi's ear, his arms folded, his chins doubled in conspiratorial bitchiness.

'Just because she did her own hair yesterday!'

'Well, if she's going to complain of exhaustion then she'd better stop doing everyone else's jobs for them, hadn't she? Hmm?' Gavin pursed his face into cat's bottom disapproval.

'Sit down, Gavin, and leave the poor girl alone.'

'Only saying—'

'Well don't.'

'Really!' Gavin turned to Frankie who looked just as horrified as he, and like the pair of old trouble-makers that they were they crowded into their seats and settled down to enjoy a long and fruitless moan.

Mimi ignored them and marched to the front of the bus, where she sat behind the driver and stared nervously out of the window, chewing her nails and worrying.

Bits of the shoot were going well and thanks to Pandora's unflagging professionalism the photographs so far would be good. But Mimi worried that her supermodel wouldn't be able to keep up the pace. Was this talk of panic attacks just keeping up with the Joneses or was the indomitable Pandora really cracking? Mimi chewed her nails harder, drawing blood around her right thumb and swearing quietly to herself as she searched deep in her capacious Gucci holdall for a Kleenex; she felt as if the last creative impulse she was ever likely to have had been left behind in her office in New York. She was failing to keep up her own morale, let alone everyone else's. And Joey's disappearance the night before had proved to her what she'd suspected all along: not only was Flash Harry a shit man to work for but she herself lacked the authority to make up for his endless inadequacies. And now they were running twelve hours late because she hadn't realised that they couldn't drive through the dark so, instead of being rested, Pandora was going to have to perform again after a long and potentially painful journey to the Church of St Simeon Stylite.

The stolen Russian jeep ate up the kilometres between the catacombs and the camel fair. The erstwhile prisoners didn't care what interesting activities might have been going on beneath the basalt pavement from which they'd so recently escaped. They were simply relieved to have got away. Said drove. Faraj chewed his bottom lip and thought out loud.

'Russians not Americans. No sign of surveying for minerals. High security.' He turned to Said. 'We should have had a better look. Turn back.'

'No way.'

'Why not?'

'They'll kill us, that's why.'

'We could just ask to be shown around.'

'I'm sure they'd be delighted – like they weren't yesterday.'

'We still don't know anything much.'

'It's simple. We just tell the sheikh they're there and he'll go and get rid of them. What right do they have to be there?'

'You're so right, Said. As far as I'm concerned they've got no right at all.'

Behind them the Action Men had no time to torment themselves with the disappearance of their prisoners; they were occupied with the second delivery, the installation of the merchandise deep in an Aladdin's cave three stories below the desert surface, the endless activity preparing for Pictikhov's arrival.

Ivan squinted as he looked at the screen of his computer in Damascus, in case the e-mail from T'bilisi was frightening enough for him to need to close his eyes against it. The message from Pictikhov gave nothing away. It read:

If the sheikh's in Aleppo then you should go too. Meet him. Go and have a look at him and report back. I need to be prepared. No more second-hand reports from the jealous brother. It's time I knew more about the man I'm really interested in. Sykes told me practically nothing. I want more from you. Any screw-ups and I'll hold you personally responsible. Report to me as soon as you've met him.

Ivan breathed a sigh of relief and went to pack for Aleppo and the desert.

It was five hours before the bus drew up outside the Church of St Simeon Stylite. Mimi wished she'd splashed out on a helicopter; these long road journeys were not only getting her down but were obviously taking it out of Pandora. George had spent the second half of the journey from Crac des Chevaliers to this Byzantine village a little to the north-west of Aleppo hanging the clothes Mimi'd decreed Pandora would wear that day from the luggage racks. Now he rushed out with the steamer to find a plug and water so that by the time the hair and make-up were finished the clothes would be ready to wear. For Gavin and Frankie, tables and chairs were taken from the hold of the bus and set up on the grass in front of the church facing the remains of the pillar, chained to the top of which the first ascetic saint spent thirty-five years embodying the early Christian ideal. Two hours later Pandora would be transformed into a different ideal, born of fifteen hundred years' social and scientific evolution since the glory days of St Simeon.

Mimi bustled about, concentrating on her star.

'Courteney, where's the food I ordered? Pandora needs a drink.'

'Yes ma'am.'

'George, can we get an umbrella up to give Pandora a bit

156

more shade? These trees are dappling but not overly efficient.'

'Aye aye Cap'n.'

'Gavin, careful darling, Pandora's very tired. I'm sure she'd appreciate your treating her hair with some gentle concern.'

'We're all tired, Mimi,' he answered, tugging at the mess made of Pandora's hair by the snagging carpet seats of the bus. Mimi glared at him. He shrugged and gave in, stroking the tangles away and giving Pandora a discreet head massage at the same time.

'Frankie, can I have a word?'

'Of course, Mimi.' Frankie, mixing a palette of powder, foundation and moisturiser onto the back of one of her hands, went into whispered conference with Mimi under a spreading cedar which must have been as old as the church itself. 'What's the matter with our little supermodel? She didn't say a word the whole way here and she wasn't sleeping.'

'How do you know?'

'Because I can tell when someone's sleeping and when they're not, that's why.'

'Oh . . . Well, can you just give her a little powder and nothing too heavy today? We'll take wide shots to get the whole church in and no close-ups. She's got black bags the size of cabin trunks under her eyes. I think we'll just get her hair hooked up gently and she can wear those long Ann Demeulemeester coat suits and we'll take her from behind.'

'Ooh Mimi, you do have a wicked sense of humour. After all . . .' Frankie's laugh tinkled round the ancient church walls like breaking glass, 'her bum's hardly going to show signs of exhaustion, is it?'

Mimi forced a smile. 'Just be nice to her, Frankie, please. And there's really no need to be bitchy.'

'Only teasing honey, only teasing.'

Mimi lost her temper and turned on the make-up artist. 'Well don't.' She marched off, wishing that she was better able to control herself, that Pandora would come out of her strange trance-like state, that she was back in Manhattan, that she had a simple job, like being a rocket scientist. 'George?

George! Where is that boy?' The umbrella he'd placed to shade Pandora's alabaster skin wobbled fearfully and Mimi shored it up with a couple of acanthus leaf carved stones which lay scattered about all over the ground. George appeared, the petulant pout that he'd worn since leaving Crac still ruining his otherwise attractive face. 'Oh stop sulking, George. I can't bear it when people make an atmosphere. Can you get those Demeulemeester suits first please? The very plain grey and the pale lilac wool. She can have the white Yohji shirts underneath and for shoes . . . Why don't you choose for once? In the kind of mood she is in I don't think she's going to fight with you today.'

Much cheered, George skipped off to make his mark on the styling of this shoot. Mimi turned back to Pandora. Frankie and Gavin were finished working on her. Her hair was piled in a simple twist so that her head could be seen, Brancusi perfect on the fine sweep of her neck. Even with bags under her eyes she was exquisite. She wore her old, pink, miswashed grey Voyage cardigan, a floor-length loosely tied, faded red sarong, white Superga pumps, like Mimi's only not quite so immaculate, no jewellery and only a fine dusting of make-up. Mimi wished she could photograph her as she was then. But these pictures were for the Christmas issue and she could hardly credit the pages with endless 'model's own' comments and miss out the designer beauties she'd gone to such trouble to bring with her.

'Are you all right?' she asked Pandora, perching her own rounder behind on the edge of the make-up table.

Pandora looked up at Mimi and blinked. 'What?'

'What's the matter?'

'Nothing.'

'You still seem a bit . . . out of it. Did you not sleep on the bus?'

'I'm fine. You'd better photograph me in those sharp-edged Demeulemeester suits so I can just make shapes in them and you can get Flash to forget to focus on my face.'

'You've read my mind, darling.'

Pandora almost rubbed her tired eyes, remembered the make-up, and didn't.

'You're not coming down with anything, are you? After all, you have ruthlessly been eating the salad,' Mimi asked, already mentally searching her bags for the Immodium.

'There's nothing to look so concerned about. My stomach's fine.'

'You're not though.'

'I just feel a bit . . . disjointed, or floaty, or sort of slightly out of focus. I don't know. Don't worry, when I'm all dressed up and ready to go I'll perform to your heart's content.' Pandora leant forward and patted Mimi's knee. 'Panic not, pickle. I won't let you down.'

Mimi smiled a little faintly. 'I'm not worried about the shoot. I'm worried about you.'

'Well don't, fatso.' Pandora switched the light on behind her eyes that turned her into the valuable commodity for which the fashion industry treasured her. 'You see! All I have to do is concentrate.'

'I'll never understand how you make that transformation. One minute you're just a bog standard person and the next you look like you're your own likeness only made out of light.'

'Very poetic, darling. That's why you stay so cleverly behind the camera and I take up all the space in front of it . . . Apart from the fact that you're just a tiny bit overweight, about a foot too short and have much too much character to be transformed into a different editor's dream every day. Eeek!'

'You cow!' Mimi leapt up and chased Pandora round the grass, until they both fell down laughing, by the main door to the great old church. Pandora rolled onto her stomach, cupped her chin in her hands and looked up at the diminutive remains of St Simeon's pillar.

'Did that man really stand on top of this pillar for thirty-five years?'

'My, you have been doing your research.'

'Nothing like a little Gertrude Bell to educate the uninitiated Middle Eastern keeno. Well, did he?'

'I don't know. But if that's what the book says it must be true.' Mimi stood up and walked round the base of the pillar. 'He must have been clinically insane.'

'How do you think he went to the loo?'

'Over the edge I suppose.'

'Hmm . . . that must have been fun for the pilgrims. Or perhaps he had some acolyte whose special job it was to receive a bucket of saintly waste from him every morning. Still . . .' Pandora got up and wandered over to look out of the empty arches of the church windows onto the patchwork of limestone-scattered fields on the plain below. 'He had a fantastic view.'

'Come on. I thought we'd got you out of that pensive mood. Don't slip back in. Let's get you dressed and photographed. The light's magnificent and I know we can make some magic pictures here.'

Pandora turned back to Mimi from her overview of St Simeon's landscape and for a split second Mimi didn't recognise her friend at all; in that splintered moment her soul flashed behind the supermodel's eyes, wide and deep and green and lovely. Mimi, surprised by the apparition, blinked, and looked again. And, ashamed to find herself relieved, now she saw only the Pandora she knew – a supermodel, an extraordinarily beautiful English girl who lived in Manhattan, with a life so high that only a tiny slice of humanity could even imagine it.

Pandora smiled. 'You look as if you've seen a ghost, Mimi. Come on, let's get on.'

Mimi shook herself and turned back to the business in hand. Pandora walked towards the place where George had five perfect and almost identical Demeulemeester suits and five equally immaculate and practically identical Yohji Yamamoto shirts waiting with one pair of pale lilac, red-satin-lined, silk grosgrain slippers all the way from Jimmy Choo.

'George! Courteney! Come on children, let's get dressing.' The two assistants hurried forward and started stripping Pandora of her own simple clothes before applying the others. Even Flash and Joey stopped arguing over which cameras and film to use with the heaven-sent late-afternoon light, so that by the time Pandora was ready to hang off St Simeon Stylite's pillar and catch the flaming evening in her magical emerald green eyes Flash was there to capture the moment and the shoot, somehow, went without a hitch.

Faisal parked the dusty Mercedes in the garage garden of the Baron Hotel in Aleppo. The unctuous attentions of the receptionist did nothing to improve his mood as he marched up the steps to the hall of the hotel which echoed emptily with ghostly grandeur. He took off his dark glasses and allowed himself to be shown upstairs. He hated the place; he hated the peeling flowery wallpaper, the prints of pointers on vague Scottish hills, the ugly rose-covered counterpanes, and most of all he hated the bathrooms, symphonies of dripping taps on echoing stained porcelain. Why Mimi insisted they stay there was beyond him. Waiting for the fashion bus to arrive, he went down to the bar where he ordered a stiff whisky from a barman known as Charlie. Installing himself in an old brown leather-covered armchair he called Ahmed on his mobile.

'Any news?'

'Not a whisper.'

'Where's he got to?'

'I don't see what's stopping you going and searching for him yourself. Surely your precious cousin is more valuable to you than a supermodel. Or perhaps not?'

'Don't be ridiculous . . .'

'I'm not. I'm simply trying to explain your behaviour to myself.'

'I wish you wouldn't. I do have my own conscience you know. You don't have to stand in for it.'

'So listen to it.'

'I am. And it's telling me to sit tight and wait for news.'

'Then stop fussing about Faraj and calling me about him all the time. For a man who doesn't care . . . Are you drinking?'

'What is this? Do you have special powers so you can see me down the airwaves to Aleppo?'

'I know your voice and it's got whisky on it.'

'OK, let's make a deal shall we? Give me one more night to relax. Tomorrow, if we still haven't heard from Faraj, then I'll go and find him. Meanwhile . . .'

'Meanwhile what?' Faisal heard the kind patience in his old secretary's voice and felt suddenly like a small boy who's being forgiven for something for which he's not sure he deserves to be excused. 'All right, Faisal, I'll cut you a bit of slack. And I know you are worried about Faraj. You're not completely heartless. I just hope this determination to put off until tomorrow what you could easily get on with today doesn't become too much of a habit.'

'I promise.'

'I'll call you if there's any news. And don't drink too much. You know it'll only make you sick.'

'I know. Thanks for the concern. Bye.' Faisal called the Queen Zenobia Hotel in Palmyra. They had received no word from Faraj. They asked if they should expect him and said that yes, Ali had stopped there and left his BMW with them. He'd gone on to the camel fair in a land cruiser and had left no message for Faisal.

Faisal put the phone down on the table with his whisky. His head drummed with an ache which had a Faraj-Pandora-Birthright rhythm to it, irregular, confusing. He picked up the whisky glass, swallowed the contents, waved for the bottle.

'Faisal, Faisal, look, here's our Lawrence.' Faisal blinked. Pandora stood looking at a painting of TE – the reason the fash pack were staying there – in the hotel lounge. 'Isn't he gorgeous?' Faisal couldn't think of anything to say. This didn't seem to bother Pandora. 'Mind if I join you?' She batted her impossibly long lashes at Charlie and sank into the comfort of a brown leather chair. 'Can I have a pint of gin and tonic and don't stint on the ice and lemon?' she asked Charlie who, smitten, provided a dish of nuts to chew on, as well as (for lack of a pint glass) a pair of gin and tonics at her elbow.

'You're incorrigible.' Faisal grinned at her, the insistent beating in his head retreating behind this whisky-washed vision of

Pandora in a grubby sarong, grubbier gym shoes and her grotty Voyage cardigan, misbuttoned.

'Thanks.' Pandora swallowed the contents of the first glass in one go and reached for the other. 'What's the matter?'

'What do you mean?'

'You look worried about something. Why don't you send some underling round with us to make sure we're all right? Why do you have to be here yourself? You can't be interested in the fashion shoots 'cos you don't come. What do you do all day? Don't you have business to attend to?'

'Nope. My father cashed in the Mez'al family chips. No business to run, no nothing . . .' The shutters came down over Faisal's eyes. He poured more whisky. 'Don't let me bore you with my troubles. It's my pleasure to make sure the shoot goes well for Nina.' He instantly regretted the ice that had slipped into his voice. Pandora seemed to fold into herself, away from him. Down went the contents of the second gin and tonic and Pandora waved for more. Charlie, smitten, obliged.

Flash stood before the fly-spotted mirror in the mildewy corner of his bathroom. He slicked down his pale lemon-coloured hair and looked carefully at both his profiles. He thought himself lean, tigerish, and devilishly attractive; not an ageing roué with a flat fat bottom, whose chances of seducing Pandora that night were about fifty million to one. He took off his over-stuffed safari waistcoat and reached for a battered Armani cream linen jacket, which he slung over one shoulder trying unsuccessfully to look cool.

Five minutes later he sauntered into the bar humming 'Luck be a Lady' and snapped his fingers, prancing lightly on old Adidas Green Flash. He spread his significant arse on a pair of bar stools, waved magnanimously at Pandora and Faisal and ordered.

'Whatever they're having, barman, and mine's a beer.' It wasn't until that moment that Flash turned to check if Pandora was as bowled over by his performance as he was. She gave him a steely glare. Flash winked at her; he loved a challenge.

Faisal took all this in and finished his current glass of whisky. Since offending Pandora, the rhythmic reminder of his responsibilities was back with a vengeance, a little pulse beating visible time with it in his right temple. He didn't care about Flash; Faisal was tired, he was after oblivion. Flash, innocent of the atmosphere around him, rubbed his hands in anticipation. Pandora finished the gin and tonic he'd ordered for her and forced herself to be nice to him. All too aware of the tensions thickening the air, she couldn't have cared less: Faisal could go jump as far as she was concerned. Faisal fingered the beating pulse and talked in the hope that no one would notice how terrible he felt.

'So, where do we eat tonight? Has your George organised something or do we go out and take pot luck in the city?' Faisal asked Pandora, instinctively rather than pointedly excluding Flash. The photographer wasn't to be so easily left out; he hadn't gone to such efforts with his appearance to be usurped by this young swank. His intended victim tossed her hair out of her eyes.

'Mimi, at last, there you are!'

'Sorry I've been so long. Frankie and Gavin seem to be suffering from a touch of the runs – I've been filling them up with Immodium and lecturing them on their eating habits.'

Pandora grinned wickedly. 'I hope that means they'll be laid low tomorrow.'

'Don't be horrible.'

'Oh I can't bear their chitter chatter all day long. This might give them a real story to tell instead of all that exaggeration they've been giving us up till now. Can I borrow one of your hankies to keep my hair under control?' Mimi smiled, not unduly concerned about Gavin and Frankie who were notorious hypochondriacs. She reached into her bag for a baby-blue cotton square, which she proceeded to fold and tie about Pandora's head while perched elegantly on the arm of her chair. 'We were just discussing dinner. Where to, Mimi?'

'Why don't we let Faisal advise us? Apparently the place George thought he'd booked and paid for doesn't actually exist, and they don't do dinner at the hotel unless you order it weeks in advance.'

'Sissi House it is then,' said Faisal, smiling broadly through his headache, his expression only a little forced and lightly glazed by the whisky. He unfolded himself from the unsprung depths of his chair. 'Shall we walk?'

'Oh I think so.' Mimi took his arm, leaving Flash to escort Pandora while George, Courteney and Joey brought up the rear. 'That was atmospheric, darling,' said Mimi as they made their way towards the old town of Aleppo. 'Do you want to tell me what's going on?'

'Not really,' was all the answer Faisal was prepared to give. So they walked along in silence, Mimi uncomfortable and embarrassed, Faisal counting the beats as they pulsed like flashing lights on the right-hand side of his head.

The camp for the camel fair was up and running by the time Faraj and Said roared into it and handbrake-turned to a halt at the edge of the swelling sea of tents. They were drunk with relief at their escape from the Russians and could hardly wait to get the formalities of their arrival over before they could tell the tale of their adventure.

They hurriedly washed in water from a tanker-fed stand pipe and dressed in clean white shirts and immaculately starched red and white checked head cloths. Faraj's father, Abdullah, was already installed at the fair with his household and had turned his black goat-hair tents into a home from home. The sandy desert floor had been cleared of rocks and covered with fine old rugs and huge, kelim-covered cushions and highly decorated camel saddles. The two heroes leant on a pair of these during a celebration feast of camel calf served on a great mountain of rice. And only then, when the food was finished, and while the bitter Bedu coffee was passed round again and again, did they finally tell their story.

Ali missed nothing in the telling of this tale. He stood apart, leaning against a tent pole and smoking. He took in every word. When he'd had enough of the Russian camp's arrangements, the cruel imprisonment in the surely haunted cave, the battle with the terrible guard, the daring escape in the stolen jeep, the fate of the fly-blown camels, he turned and slipped away. Ducking under tent ropes and clinging to the darkness behind the temporary village, he returned to his own tent and scrabbled about in his saddle bags for his mobile phone. Faraj clocked the disappearance of his younger cousin and, passing the reins of the story to Said, he followed, silent on bare feet; it was time for a confrontation.

He caught Ali rattling his phone as if shaking it would raise a signal.

'Why don't you beat it against the tent pole? I'm sure that'll make it work better.' Faraj's voice was acid. 'Calling your Russian friend, are you? Why don't you let me talk to him? I can fill him in on what his colleagues are up to first hand. Tell me . . .' Faraj settled down on the floor, using a saddle as a back rest, 'did you know all this or were you as in the dark as you'll have to be if your brother is ever to forgive you for getting involved with these rogues?'

'I don't know what you're talking about.' Ali gave up with the phone and let it drop.

'Really? Haven't heard anything about a bunch of Russians moving in to a set of catacombs that hardly anybody knows about?'

'Why should I? Those catacombs belong to us.'

'Not any more they don't.'

'What?'

'Oh come on, Ali – you know perfectly well your brother's sold the mineral rights of that particular patch of desert.'

'I had no idea!' Ali's voice was breathy with feigned surprise.

'I don't believe you for a second.'

'Honestly. Mineral rights? I thought there was no oil there.'

'Join the club. So, come on, Ali, for once you're the one holding all the cards. What are these Ruskies doing here?'

'Why should I know? Faraj, you're talking rubbish. I'm not even sure whether I should believe your tales of adventure. You and Said might have made all this up.'

'Might we just? And why would we want to do that?'

'I haven't the faintest idea. If you're so curious why didn't you have a better look?'

'Oh you obviously missed the bit about us being taken prisoner and having to escape. Ali, I know you're lying. Your Russian friend had the exact spot marked on a map on his office door – so either he's involved with the people who've bought the mineral rights or you told him about it. Either way the whole thing stinks.'

'Think what you like. I'm just relieved my beloved brother saw sense and sold that useless patch of land. I hope he got a fortune for it.' Ali's face cleared as if he'd suddenly had an idea. 'Oh that's why he's got nothing better to do than hang around with Pandora. He can afford to now. Of course it never occurred to him to tell me what he was doing with the family business.' Ali didn't have to pretend spoilt fury now. 'If he did include me then things might be a lot easier for him.'

'You'd help him spend his new found wealth would you? What on? Horses? Backgammon? Paying off your gambling debts? You're a bad actor, Ali. We'll get to the bottom of this somehow.'

'What's this "we" business? If I'm not very much mistaken my brother couldn't care less about people in the catacombs – if he did he'd be here now wouldn't he and not wining and dining Americans.'

Faraj had no intention of admitting that Ali might have a point. With an old-fashioned swish of the spun-gold edging of his camel-hair cloak, he was off into the night leaving Ali sweating and wondering if Faraj was bluffing; how much did he and Faisal really know?

The basement of the Sissi House had been turned into a nightclub decorated with a delight of naked ladies sporting about the walls in drunken, concrete bas-relief. The clientele sat on low, kelim-covered banquettes drinking anything as long as it was arak and playing backgammon in the gloom. Upstairs the sixteenth-century merchant's house was a perfectly restored dream of sandalwood screening and elegant service. Even the fountain in the courtyard of the old house played quietly enough not to disturb the fine layers of fuchsia-pink rose petals which had been scattered over the surface of the water. Eating in the courtyard, the fashion crew and Faisal were attended by a swarm of waiters who wanted to get a good look at the porcelain beauty of the supermodel as well as have some glamour rub off on them from the great name of Sheikh Faisal bin Ali al Mez'al. Pandora glowed; she hadn't been treated like this since she left New York, and the aura of discreet worship with which she found herself surrounded was as familiar as a comforter is to a child. She relaxed into it and forgot the snapping session she'd had with Faisal. She felt dizzy, pleasantly haunted, half alive, but not half dead; she felt something other, a sort of fey weightlessness.

It wasn't until after dinner that things started to go wrong.

The assistants had been sent back to the Baron to guard the kit, and Faisal and Flash persuaded Mimi and Pandora that the basement was worth a visit; against their better judgement, the girls agreed. The two men had been drinking steadily for the past three hours and there was an unhealthy atmosphere of competition which had come with them from the Baron.

They were on their way to a corner table already furnished with arak and glasses and smoked salted almonds when the owner of the house took it upon himself to introduce the only other client in the basement, a man Pandora remembered hissing at her from a pavement café in Damascus.

'You!' Faisal took a step towards Ivan who stood, hand outstretched in greeting, obsequious in his greasy grey suit. After the event Pandora couldn't decide if she thought Faisal had been intent on greeting or gashing the Russian; before he had time to do either, a brass table-top sang out in protest as Faisal tripped over it and hit his head hard on a protruding nipple from the concrete frieze on the wall. Pandora and Mimi waited for Flash or Ivan to dive forward and help, and when neither of them did Pandora sniffed with disapproval and went to pull Faisal up herself. She hauled him onto some cushions before turning to face

168

the Russian and examining him with the full force of her curiosity.

'Do you always have that sort of effect on people?' Pandora installed herself on a banquette and patted an ottoman beside her coyly. 'Who did you say you were?' Ivan gave his inquisitor a lop-sided, drunken smirk and arranged himself on the little red velvet-covered seat. She wrinkled her nose in distaste, but curiosity about this unattractive little worm, who had something to do with Faisal, was stronger than her aversion to his smell. She smiled at him and let him see the length of her eyelashes.

'I am a business associate of his honour the sheikh. I had heard that he was unable to support alcohol.' He wiggled his eyebrows conspiratorially at Pandora. 'It seems my informant was correct.'

'And that would be?'

'Oh somebody in Damascus.' Ivan waved his hand dismissively. 'And you are the famous mannequin. I can see why our little sheikh can not keep away from you.'

Pandora giggled sweetly and laid her hand on Ivan's arm. 'You're too kind . . . So . . .' She sipped her arak in a ladylike fashion and let her sarong fall open a little as she crossed her legs; Ivan nearly fell over at the sight of them. She made sure she didn't laugh. 'What is it you and the sheikh do together?'

Ivan laughed, cocked his head to one side and tapped the side of his bulbous, squashed strawberry of a nose. 'Classified information I'm afraid.'

'How exciting. I won't pry.' She simpered prettily and gave Ivan an appraising look. He blushed. 'You're a Russian, aren't you?'

'Not difficult to tell.'

'A compatriot of mine then.'

'I thought you were American.'

'English, actually, well, half English. And half Russian,' she said like a magician pulling a rabbit out of a hat. Ivan was suitably amazed.

'A true Russian beauty. You are living proof of the saying that Russians make the most exquisite women.'

'Not one I've heard before myself. Oh do tell me about yourself, what you do, where you come from.'

Ivan's face was momentarily tragic. 'I've lived my life in exile.'

'Oh?'

'I grew up in Georgia reviled by the local peasants for being Russian. And now I'm even further from home – I never would have imagined that I'd end up in Syria, off to do business in the oven of the desert.'

'Can't you go home if you hate it so much?'

'Business is business and we all have to make a living and mine, unfortunately, is here.'

'I wish you'd tell me more about it.'

'Let me say only this . . . I provide people with the ingredients for keeping the peace.'

'Like the UN?'

'Perhaps a little different in approach but with the same end in mind.'

Pandora's eyes widened. 'You're not . . .' She grasped Ivan's knee.

'What?' Ivan looked about him nervously.

'But I've always wanted to meet the real thing.'

'What kind of . . . ?'

'And you're just right for the job.'

'What job?' Flash and Mimi didn't have the first idea what Pandora and Ivan were talking about.

'Ivan's an arms dealer!'

'Shh!' Ivan flapped his arms as if to disperse the announcement Pandora'd just made.

'No!' Mimi and Flash were childishly impressed.

'Of course . . . don't deny it. You are, aren't you?'

Ivan blushed with pleasure from the attention Pandora was giving him and forgot that until now he'd been successfully concealing his vocation in life. He shrugged dismissively. 'It's not so much to be excited about.'

'But that means Faisal's an arms dealer too.' Pandora pressed on. 'Did you hear that, Mimi? Faisal's an arms dealer!'

'Not exactly . . .' Ivan was desperate for the conversation to change direction.

'How do you mean?' Pandora wasn't giving up this easily.

Ivan grabbed the arak and filled their glasses. 'A toast!' he cried, standing up and brandishing his glass, spilling arak in Pandora's lap. 'To Russia, my homeland, my love.' He swayed slightly and reached out to the offending nipple for support. Pandora recognised defeat; Ivan was too drunk to tell her anything much, he might have been lying all along.

'To Russia, with love.' Pandora stood too for the toast and slammed her arak back over her right shoulder and onto Faisal's face. He spluttered and turned over. Pandora thought she might have heard him snore. Ivan reached for the bottle and filled their glasses again. Mimi's face was stunned.

'But we're shooting in the morning!'

Pandora ignored her editor and raised her glass. 'To steppes and mountains, snow and ice, vodka, dumplings and . . .' She stopped and searched for an end to her rhyme. 'The gambling vice!' she announced triumphantly. Ivan downed his arak and she poured hers over Faisal's face again. The sheikh began to come round from his stupor. And Ivan was swaying on his feet. They needed perhaps one more toast before he would be first under the table. She filled their glasses for the last time.

'Nasdrov'ya!' she cried and she watched Ivan swallow the contents of his glass in one go before the sound of it shattering against the wall finally brought Faisal round and the concerned patron down to the gloom of the club to prevent these foreigners fighting.

Faisal sat up, rubbing his face blearily. 'What happened?'

'You had a little rest, pickle, and now we're going home. Come along, Flash, you can take the other side. No, Ivan, we don't need your help. I think we've had enough of you for one night.'

Ivan sat down heavily and felt the arak hit the back of his head; he hoped he wouldn't be sick in front of all these people. He needn't have worried. Pandora took charge, linking arms with the swaying Faisal and pulling him up the stairs, out of the

Sissi House, down the narrow passage which led back to the main road and turning right for the short walk back to the hotel. She needed air if she was to take in, let alone decide if she believed, what she'd heard.

Ivan stared about him, bereft of his audience and wondering quite what had happened.

'Where did they all go?' he asked a cavorting concrete lady, his voice blurred, his balding pate sweating pure alcohol.

Pandora leant out of her bedroom window at the Baron looking at her moon. High above the old town of Aleppo it shone a pale, smoky white; the orange glow of the street lights were drab and grubby in comparison. There was a knock on the door. It was Mimi.

'Hello.' Pandora smiled at her.

'What a night! Did you get Faisal to bed all right?'

'No thanks to anybody else.'

'You didn't look as if you wanted anybody else there.'

'Did you notice how Flash didn't once offer to help?'

'He's jealous.'

'Don't be ridiculous.'

'He thought he was getting somewhere before dinner when you and Faisal were being all icy with each other. What was that all about?'

'He gets all touchy when I ask him questions about himself. Now we know why.'

'Arms dealing?'

'Must be. That's why he was so cross in the Sissi House. He didn't want that horrible Ivan there to spoil the image he has of the clean-living type.'

'No, he was just drunk.'

'And that's another thing. What happened to him tonight? Even Rory doesn't drink like that, you know, as if he won't stop until he passes out and the sooner that is the better.' Pandora untied the blue bandanna from her hair and sat at the wobbly dressing table looking at herself in the mirror. Mimi came and stood behind her and began to brush out Pandora's river of long, black hair.

'Well, we're certainly getting more than we'd bargained for on this trip.'

'And we'd bargained for a fair amount.' Pandora smiled at Mimi's reflection. 'It's interesting though, don't you think?'

'I just want to get it over with and the Christmas issue finished and go home quickly to safe old Manhattan.'

'Where's your sense of adventure?'

'From the girl who practically had to be tricked into coming here.'

'I'm allowed to change my mind.'

'You were brilliant tonight.'

'Why thank you, kind miss.'

'I can't tell you how glad I am that I don't have some other model on this trip with me. So far, every time there's been a crisis, you've taken over and managed everything. Any other girl might have demanded that I let her go home by now. I feel very small and incapable next to you.'

Pandora turned to face her friend. 'You may be small, my darling, but you are anything but incapable. We're good for each other, you and I. We keep each other going.'

'Maybe.'

'Don't put yourself down. Just because I'm the one everyone makes a noise about doesn't mean you don't get a look in. I may be good at crisis management but I'm easily bored when there isn't a crisis to manage.' Pandora looked wistfully out of the window. The moon was too high to be seen from her seat so she got up and went to find it. Before she could stop herself a sigh of perfect misery escaped her.

'What has got into you, Pandora? Something's very odd about you on this trip. If I didn't know any better I might go so far as to accuse you of being depressed.'

'Don't be ridiculous.' Pandora tried to bluff her way out of Mimi's sudden prying. 'I'm just feeling a bit funny. Funny peculiar. And I'll tell you what, at first it was dead unnerving. But now I'm starting to like it. I feel as if I'm starting out on something and I've got no idea what it is or where I'm going and for once I don't mind. It's strangely liberating.' Pandora lied with the ease of many years of practice.

'Such wisdom for this time of night.' Mimi smiled with relief.

'Go to bed then, Mimi. I'm not the only one who needs their beauty sleep around here.'

'If you're sure you're all right. I'm not convinced I like all this talk of freedom and not knowing where you're going.'

'Why not?'

'Well, you might leave the rest of us behind. We love you, Pandora, we need you.'

'Yeah, I know. Go to bed, Mimi, and don't worry about me. You wait, we'll get back to Manhattan in no time. And then it's the shows and the winter season and all that photographing bikinis in snowscapes – business as usual.'

Mimi kissed Pandora good night. Pandora hugged her friend back.

'Night, pickle.'

'I'll wake you in the morning.'

'You bloody well better. I'm so shattered I might need a volcano to get me out of bed tomorrow. God! When we get home I'm going to sleep for a fortnight.'

'Except for when you're prancing down a catwalk.'

'I can't bear it! If we go on like this I'm not going to get booked for any of the shows – except perhaps Marc Jacobs might use the bags under my eyes for inspiration for a new line of luggage at Louis Vuitton.'

'You never know your luck.'

Faisal lay in bed where Pandora had heaved him. He was wide awake and stone cold sober. He stared at the reflection from the street lights on the rose-wallpapered ceiling. He felt sick, not because he'd had so much to drink but because of what he'd heard in the nightclub – arms dealing.

The little pulse was back, beating hard at the side of his head. He wondered how he could have been so stupid, how he could have been so blind, how he could have made that decision to sell the desert without asking anybody's opinion but a banker who didn't care. The blood ran cold in his veins; not only had he sold his birthright but it looked like he'd invited in the means to destroy it into the bargain. Faraj had been right; Ali must have known about it all along. The gall of it; to be taken in by his own little brother!

He crossed his legs at the ankles, crossed his arms behind his head and began to make a series of mental lists. So much for his jolly holiday with Pandora. Ali had forced his hand and Faisal knew why: revenge.

Chapter 11

FAISAL woke up early. The whisky, wine and arak he'd drunk the night before made uncomfortable bed fellows in the depths of his bowels, and somewhere above his right eye he could feel a drill making holes in his skull for the fun of it. He treated his condition with a long, cold shower before an early breakfast of bread and olives and muddy Turkish coffee, which came in a cup half full of gritty black silt. He sat alone in the empty cavern of the dining room and called Ahmed on his mobile. A sleepy voice answered in Damascus.

'No word from Faraj?' asked Ahmed, stifling a yawn.

'He'll call soon enough.' Faisal's voice was terse. 'Tell him when he does that apparently the new owners of the catacombs are a bunch of arms dealers.'

'They can't be!'

'Oh yes they can. And as far as I'm concerned I sold that desert for its mineral properties, not for the catacombs to be used as a storeroom for land-mines.'

'What do you mean?'

'Well, it's obvious, isn't it? I've got to take it back.'

Ahmed's sigh of relief was audible all the way from Damascus. 'What will you do?'

'Find that Russian slime ball first and deal with him. Where's Ali?'

'At the fair by now.'

'As soon as we know that Faraj's all right you'd better go and prevent that brother of mine from getting into serious trouble. I'm finding it tough believing he's been stupid enough to get involved with arms dealers. He must believe their story about mineral rights. He'll deny all knowledge of the situation and feign surprise. Frankly I don't care what he does so long as he doesn't get into any more hot water. As long as you keep a close eye on him he won't be able to do much at all.'

'Right.'

'I'll speak to you later.' Faisal switched his phone off, stood up, finished his coffee, grimaced, and headed to the reception desk, bumping into a bleary-eyed Pandora on the way.

'Morning.'

'You're very chipper for a man who had to be carried home last night.'

'Can't stop. See you later.'

Pandora shrugged and went to pick her own way through some breakfast before the onslaught of the day.

Aleppo is a dapper city where old men, dressed with sartorial elegance in silk ties and crisp white shirts, black suits and immaculately laundered white crocheted caps, lounge like latter-day Lotharios in the doorways of the ancient khans; and on this particular day they had a fine sight to feast their eyes on. Among the carpets and jewellery, coffee-pots and fine stretches of silk that crowded the bazaar, Pandora waited while Flash and Joey struggled with a selection of small lights which Joey had magicked out of one of Flash's endless bags.

Pandora was dressed in an *haute luxe* version of winter shopping gear: blood-red Chanel silk grosgrain pants, a sleeveless lilac cashmere turtle-neck, a matching lilac Stephen Jones beret sparkling with sequins on her otherwise undressed hair, and black patent J P Tod's on her feet. She sat on a pile of carpets outside the shop they'd borrowed for lack of a studio van, while the proprietor brewed sticky sweet tea on a leaky camping stove and pressed her to accept red Marlboros from him before presenting her with a selection of filigree silver and amber necklaces, which he seemed convinced would be just the thing to go with her outfit. Pandora smiled vaguely at him and ignored his necklaces. Frankie dived forward with powder and pencil to mend the place where the tea had smudged her upper lip. Pandora brushed the make-up artist away; not only did she have a stinker of a hangover, but the strangely liberating feelings she'd been so enjoying the previous evening had turned to vertigo this morning. She felt isolated, odd-one-outish, like the ugly duckling who has yet to find his fellow swans. She drew deeply on the cigarettes she'd accepted from the shopkeeper and felt thoroughly sick.

'Polaroid ready.' At last Flash had finished playing with the lights and wanted to get a move on. Pandora put down her glass of tea, ground out the cigarette under the bobbly heel of her J P Tod's and stood up.

'Ugh, head rush.' She grabbed the wall beside her and held on, waiting for someone to catch her so that she could give in to the desire to faint. No one noticed her distress; fortunately there was a pile of carpets for her six-foot frame to fall on.

'Pandora!' Mimi grabbed a list off George and began frantically fanning the star of her show. Pandora didn't move. 'I shouldn't have made her wear the cashmere in this heat. No wonder she's fainted. And I know she hardly touched her breakfast. Courteney, get some cold water. George, get . . . oh I don't know . . . don't just stand there gawping! Do something.' Pandora lay on the comfortable pile of carpets coming to and listening to the nervous bustling going on around her.

'Courteney, don't poor water all over her hair, we'll only have to do it again,' Gavin snapped.

'And watch the make-up. It took me two hours to make her look pale and interesting instead of like a lightly boiled fish.' Frankie flashed. Pandora lay very still wondering how long she could keep up her fainting fit. She felt Mimi tucking a sheet over her, covering the fragile lilac of the cashmere turtle-neck. Somebody removed the beret she'd been wearing, she could hear the rustle of tissue paper being wrapped around it to protect the beading. She tried to breathe through waves of nausea, failing to fight off the conviction that the cold sweat she felt prickling everywhere was, in fact, despair. She found that she could take no more than little panting sips of air. From under her tightly shut eyelids great pearly tears forced themselves onto her cheeks, cutting through the mascara and the make-up and running slowly but with increasing force towards the little pink shells of her ears.

'Pandora, wake up darling.' Mimi stroked wayward strands of hair off Pandora's forehead. Pandora sobbed. 'What's the matter? What can I get to make you better?'

Pandora shook her head. 'Nothing,' she groaned.

'You're not worried about the pictures, are you? You look fantastic. Not a soul would know that you didn't get to bed till late and had drunk enough to lay most people low for a week. You look marvellous.'

Pandora rubbed her eyes, ruining what was left of Frankie's hard morning's work, and sat up slowly. 'I'm just tired.' She looked up at Mimi, searching for something in her editor's face that would excuse her from explaining herself, that would somehow understand; she didn't find what she was looking for. Leaning back against the ancient brick of the khan wall Pandora allowed the threatening tidal wave of helplessness to overwhelm her. The only image she had of herself was broken. For the first time in her life she saw Pandora Williams as she really was: a scrapbook filled with nothing but pretty Polaroids of a supermodel, a stranger transformed into a lifetime of other people's idea of perfection. What was she without the pretty clothes and the make-up, the hairdos and the photographer's compliments? Pandora gave up trying to hold on and felt herself tip slowly over the edge of the void and begin the vertiginous descent into the big black hole inside herself; she pushed Mimi out of the way and was violently sick into the gutter.

'Oh my God. I knew we should have brought another girl with us. If Pandora's got gippy tummy too then the shoot'll be a disaster and we'll just have to go home and studio shoot it all on somebody else. The story won't work, we haven't got enough to use already—'

'Frankie, shut up. Stop being such a panic merchant. George? Do you think you could find some water and wash away this mess?' Mimi turned back to Pandora and tried to stay calm as she squatted on her haunches before her, holding her friend's hands and praying that this attack would pass so that they could get pictures taken that day. 'Come on, sweetling. I know what great reserves of strength you've got inside you. Let's see if we can't draw on some of them and try and get some work done, eh? You'll feel better when the day's over. You're just tired. Let's get this shoot finished and then you can relax. No more pictures till tomorrow night after this lot.'

'What on earth is going on?' A voice of Lady Bracknell proportions thundered from no distance away. Mimi looked up and thought she must be going mad. This couldn't be Rory Williams descending on them, could it? It had to be; who else would march about the bazaar in the unlikely get-up of cream linen suit, a fez and an Edwardian red silk parasol festooned with tassels and with a profusion of hand-painted orchids decorating the lining?

'Rory?' she breathed, uncertain, yet increasingly hopeful.

'What have you done with my baby?' he cried, discarding parasol and fez with one swift movement and pulling from his breast pocket a huge fuchsia silk handkerchief scented with Eau de Hadrien, with which he proceeded to wipe away Pandora's tears. She looked up and began to cry again.

'Rory!' She blinked. 'And now I'm seeing things. I must be going mad.'

'Panic over, precious. I knew I should have come on this shoot. I've just had the most ghastly time in Vegas and eventually I just threw my expense account in Nina's face and jumped on the first plane here. She doesn't know where I am. But that's not unusual. She seldom does. And I know Mimi's a magical editor but she's really not experienced enough to cope with this many egos in one bus so I thought I'd come and impress everyone, not mentioning any Flash Harrys in particular, with my gravitas, and then things would be bound to go smooth as silk velvet, bias cut over a perfect bum.'

'Rory, I love you.' Pandora buried her head in his narrow, but still accommodating, shoulder.

'Come on, precious. I know you're upset but there's no need to get mascara on my suit now, is there?' She looked up and he wiped her eyes again. 'There's my girl. You're my brave girl. What has that nasty Mimi done to you? Has she made you wear something you don't like? Has she been horrible to you? I'll kill her if she has, you know. Or are you just suffering from a tiny bout of exhaustion?' Pandora nodded. 'Well let's get some sugar down you, shall we, and see if the rush doesn't give you enough pick-up to get us all through the day. And don't you worry about a thing, darling. I'm here now and I won't let even the smallest fly hurt you.'

Faraj stood under the shower in the Hotel Zenobia at Palmyra and let the dust from the storm and the sand from the desert and the sweat from his incarceration pour off him. He shook himself, grinning like a dog being cooled by a stream. He'd left the camp of the camel fair at dawn that morning and had made Palmyra in time to shower before he had to call Faisal. Tucking a small towel around his hips, he lay back on the bed, settled the phone onto his washboard stomach and dialled Faisal's mobile number.

'Hey Faisal, it's me.'

'Where the fuck have you been?'

'Nice to hear your dulcet tones too, cousin.'

'I've been worried sick.'

'Not enough to come and find me, eh?'

'Stop it. What happened?'

'We were taken prisoner.'

'What? Who by?'

'Ah . . . interested at last are we?'

'Get on with it.'

'All right, all right. I found Said, it took us forever to get there on his trusty steeds, we had a cosy night with the camels and the next morning while we were taking a leisurely look at the Russians' camp we were rudely surprised by a pair of Action Man lookalikes armed with lethal-looking semi-automatic rifles. They proceeded to shut us in a tomb underground for no good reason before we effected a miraculous escape, leaving only a little blood but not one single body.'

'I don't believe you.'

'Oh you should. And I haven't told you the best bit yet. We had a riot beating up a series of guards in order to escape in a stolen jeep and képis at dawn yesterday.'

'What happened to the camels?'

'They got used for target practice. An untimely end. Said's devastated. I had to put my life in his hands and let him drive me back to the camp in a sad effort to cheer him up.'

'And what did you find in the catacombs?'

'Not much – between breaking out of our little prison and stealing the jeep there wasn't much time for sight-seeing.'

'Did they look like they were surveying for oil?'

'As if I know what that looks like.'

'Use your imagination.'

'Well, I don't know what they're doing there but I'd put money on it being a mineral-interest-free operation.'

'Thank you.'

'But if they're not digging for oil then what are they doing?'

'Arms dealing.'

'Woah . . . That's quite a jump from mineral surveys. Where did you get that from?'

'Are you sure you didn't see anything?'

'Faisal – be grateful we're alive! By the time Said'd used his initiative and KO'd the man guarding us, all we concentrated on was finding a way out of there. I mean, after we'd found a jeep and tied up another of the heavily armed bad guys. You want details, you can go and do your own dirty work out there. We didn't really want to get ourselves killed when we didn't have much more than a couple of blunt daggers to help us.'

'That Russian friend of Ali's has turned up here, you know?'

'What's he doing in Aleppo?'

'No idea. We were introduced at the Sissi House last night.'

'And?'

'Pandora charmed him into telling all and sundry that he's an arms dealer.'

'But that means I was right about the mafia!'

'Maybe.'

'You're so gracious in defeat.'

'Anything else to report from the sandy east?'

'Spent the night at the camel fair last night. Khaled and Walid have done an admirable job.'

'What about Ali? Has he actually turned up yet?'

'Oh yes. And he's shaking with fear about something.'

'What do you mean?'

'I'd describe him as a gibbering wreck with desperate murderous impulses. His eyes are full of loathing for you. He's practically psychotic.'

'*Plus ça change.*'

'I think you should take finding out his connection with these Russians a bit more seriously.'

'I am.'

'You see, revenge looks sweet to any man possessed by the green-eyed monster. Having said that, he was a bit shocked about us being taken prisoner in this camp bristling with big guns. I think he has a vague idea what's going on but I'll bet he's desperately trying to get hold of that Russian friend of his to find out more. I caught him abusing his mobile phone with a tent pole when he couldn't make it work from that far east.'

'What are you going to do next?'

'Now I've spoken to you and had a long shower I'm going to eat an enormous breakfast and then go back to the fair. I'll keep Ali within arm's reach while I get Said two new camels. I'll put them on your bill.'

'Thanks.'

'When do you get there?'

'Palmyra tomorrow. Shoot there tomorrow evening. Camel fair day after.'

'No earlier?'

'Why panic the bad guys? Besides, I need to make a plan if we're to get my birthright back.'

'Raiding!'

'Hold your horses. I don't know what we're going to do yet.'

'Still, I'll get out my armour to protect me from stilettos in the night and sharpen my dagger just in case.'

'Where do you get your energy?'

'I'm easily bored . . . Faisal, do I detect a hangover?'

'I can't hide anything from you and Ahmed, no matter how far away I am from you.'

'Why did you do it?'

'Desperation.'

'Headache?'

'And how.'

'What did you do?'

'What do you mean?'

'You always make a total fool of yourself when you're plastered. Don't tell me you managed to drink yourself into oblivion without any mishap this time?'

'I knocked myself out at the Sissi House when I lunged at Ivan.'

'Oh great. Well done. That'll really impress him with your ability to keep cool under pressure.'

'Actually it might not have been such a terrible thing.'

'How do you make that?'

'He wouldn't have showed off like he did to Pandora if I'd been a bit more focused. And if he thinks me a weakling then perhaps he'll keep his guard down. He's a useless twit really. What were the Russians in the desert like? More efficient than this Ivan character?'

Faraj gave up thinking of breakfast and concentrated. 'Put it this way. I have no idea if they worked out who we are or if they care. What I do know is that they incarcerated us for no good reason – and the man who looks after the cars was armed like a mercenary; not the usual kit for a chauffeur.'

'Hmm . . .'

'Listen, they may be kitted out with big guns but they're not efficient enough to stop us stealing a jeep and getting away, are they?'

'I'm just wondering whether I should summon some of the troops.'

'Faisal, the whole tribe's going to be at the fair. You can always mount a midnight raid and disarm these Russians in one easy move from there.'

'Right.' Faisal ran his hands through his badly behaved hair and, letting Faraj go to his longed-for breakfast, he started making two lists; they were headed 'pros' and 'cons'. The 'pros' column held nothing but the word 'cash' in it, the 'cons' list was long and detailed, starting with 'mafia' and ending with 'arms dealing', with variations on those themes filling a page of his notebook in between.

'More sugar.'

'More sugar?'

'I said more, didn't I? Are you profoundly deaf or just stupid?' Rory stared at George until he put more sugar into the glass of tea being prepared for Pandora.

'Still more.' George nearly fainted at the thought of a super-model being forced to take in so many calories in so few mouthfuls.

'Keep going, keenie. If you want her to be up to being pho-tographed at all today then I suggest you pour as much sugar down her throat as you can find.'

'But . . .' George looked up at Mimi for support. Mimi gave him a rueful little smile.

'Do as the man says, Georgie. Disobedience is not something I'd recommend where Rory's concerned.'

'Thank you, Mimi. I love being reminded quite how power-ful I am. Now . . .' he re-examined Pandora who, still shaken but a little less stirred, sat on the same pile of carpets, a pale flush replacing the blanched calm of her pre-panic face and a tiny smile attempting to take over the corners of her mouth. 'Are you feeling a little more secure in yourself, darling?'

'What do you mean, Rory?'

'That's my girl. Just forget that little episode ever happened. Let's see you pull yourself together and get on with the job in hand, shall we? There'll be time enough for self doubt when we get you back to Manhattan. Today we must practise earning a living.' Rory stood up, flourishing the handkerchief that Pandora had soaked with a long hour of tears. 'Come along everyone, we're ready to perform so I hope none of you are going to hold us up now we're in the mood.'

Frankie dived forward, the tools of her trade at hand; Rory took them from her and did Pandora's face himself. Gavin didn't even try to get near her hair; he passed Rory the hairbrush and the lilac beret and stepped smartly out of the way. Satisfied with his handiwork, Rory reached down and pulled his niece to her feet. 'Go for it, gorgeous. We'll worry about your insides later. Let's make the most of your face while it lasts.' Pandora forced herself to laugh.

'That's my darling. Stop worrying about the things that go on in that silly little head of yours.' Holding her hand, he helped her pick her way down the narrow causeway between stalls selling mountains of clashing coloured spices or heaps of fat, pale biscuits studded with gleaming glimpses of sugary black dates, or great copper barrels from which olive oil dripped into coagulating pools, which gathered in the dips left between time-worn flags. Flash walked backwards in front of them taking pictures paparazzi fashion while Joey cleared their way of over-laden donkeys and excited schoolboys playing truant and the crowds of people going about their business – crowds who couldn't be less interested in the circus performance of a fashion shoot come to town. Rory carried on talking to Pandora in whispers, which gave the pictures an air of moments stolen from the lives of their protagonists. And Pandora, taut with white-knuckle calm, tossed her hair and smiled and looked at jewellery and bargained for a brass Bedouin coffee-pot painted with a pattern of red carnations and silver jasmine blossoms

Mimi, so worried that even her eyes were pinched with the effort of hiding her concern, watched Rory whisper to Pandora as one might when calming a fractious filly and thanked God that he'd come to her rescue. Now he was there she could relax and let him take over, not only the morale of the shoot, but, more importantly, the state of mind of the star of the show. Mimi wondered what would have happened if Rory hadn't arrived in such a timely fashion; the thought made her feel slightly sick and she took her mind off the situation by being unusually strict with George and Courteney, who buzzed around Pandora like bees round a honey-pot, feeding her with calm by being, for once in their careers, truly efficient.

It wasn't until they were ready to photograph in the court-yard of the Aleppine Umayyad Mosque that things threatened to go downhill again. The pictures of Pandora in her cashmere turtle-neck, flushed with the exertion of keeping herself under control and holding hard the hand of her uncle would be cute and useful, and both Mimi and Flash were pleased. However, the mosque was a different matter. Pandora had changed into a Cristo outfit: white silk organza shirt, so fine that the outline of her dark raspberry-pink nipples showed clearly through the fabric; black silk matador pants, high-waisted; spray-on tight, salmon-pink silk stockings with scarlet clocking round the ankles and black patent leather men's dancing shoes with double velvet bows which hung loosely in the dusty floor of the dry, sun-dappled khan. The shopkeeper who'd hired out his shop to be Pandora's styling studio for the day looked at her when she appeared dressed, shaking her half-plaited, black-velvet-rib-boned pony-tail, and he clapped his hands in admiration, calling the rest of his staff to come and admire this vision. 'Where is this picture to be?' he asked.

'In the courtyard of the mosque. We know we can't go inside with her dressed like this, but the courtyard should be all right.' Mimi smiled, proud of her beautiful friend. 'And the mosaics and the marble's kind of Spanish feeling which'll be lovely with the matador pants you see?'

'I don't think so.' The shopkeeper was apologetic.

'Why not?'

'With her . . .' he demonstrated Pandora's breasts, too embarrassed to say the words, 'out like that?' He shook his head. 'I don't think so, lady.'

'They're not out. They're covered.' Mimi flushed, bile rising; she couldn't bear it if the shoot started to go wrong again.

'Not enough. No, to use the mosque you must really cover.

Even only in the courtyard. Dressed like this, your lady will cause a lot of trouble.'

'What can we do?' Mimi wailed. Pandora, switched off from her performance, was in no mood to help. She sat on her pile of carpets and watched disinterestedly as a group of tiny ladies with high red hats and tattooed faces bargained ferociously over bolts of fabric across the way. She wished Rory would stop telling her how marvellous she looked and would just get her some gin.

'I know,' the shopkeeper smiled, 'I have just the place.'

'Where?'

'The lunatic asylum!' he announced with pride.

'Loony bin! We can't photograph there. This isn't a "copy cat princess looks after the poor unfortunate foreigners" trip. Pandora's half mad herself at the moment. Going to the lunatic asylum would probably send her over the edge.' Mimi didn't quite manage to keep the panic out of her voice.

'It's not still a loony bin.' Pandora spoke up from behind her air of lethargy.

'What?' Rory and Mimi turned to her, pointed eyebrows implying that Pandora should be quiet and let them deal with this new crisis.

'Don't panic, Mimi. I'm sure the man means the old loony bin. It's thirteenth century or something. I've seen pictures of it. It's lovely. Come on.' Pandora stood up and took the shopkeeper's arm. 'You can lend me one of those wonderful Turkish waistcoats to cover up my nakedness as we walk through the streets, and if you're very, very nice to that assistant over there' – she pointed at George – 'he'll write down all your details and credit your lovely little shop and all its magic carpets in the magazine when we publish and then all the readers will come with loads of lovely hard cash to spend with you because I've implied by being with you that you are the last word in chic.' The shopkeeper blushed with pleasure at being made so much of, and Mimi and Rory stared at one another in amazement. Where did Pandora get all this information?

'Don't look at each other like that.' Pandora was suddenly

furious. 'The whole point of my existence may be to provide the ultimate displacement activity in the glamour department, but that doesn't mean I'm not allowed to read a book every now and again while some underpaid fool gets to do my nails for me.' In a deeply unattractive but extremely expressive manner, she hawked into the gutter and marched off with the shopkeeper, Mimi, Rory and the others scurrying after them, their tails tucked firmly between their legs.

Of course, the heat of the day was the time when Ali felt his isolation most keenly. Friendless and ignored, he lounged in solitary splendour in the grand expanse of his tent on a pile of cushions, smoking a narghile and wishing he'd brought more arak with him. He massaged his neck, his temples, his eyes. He shook his mobile phone again in case it might suddenly burst into life. He changed the battery. It still didn't work. He changed into a clean, cool, white shirt, washed his face, poured water over his pounding head. And, as if by magic, when he turned away from the brass basin of water and picked up the phone again, planning on smashing it on a rock, it finally began to ring. He almost dropped it he was so surprised and then found that he had to angle himself uncomfortably round a tent pole in order to keep the signal.

'Your brother is a drunk, you know that?' Ivan's voice was faint from Aleppo.

'Only once a year and then his hangover's so terrible he doesn't drink again until he's really desperate. It's nothing to do with his religion. I think he's just allergic.' Ali groaned; talking made his headache worse.

'I don't care when or how he drinks. I'm just glad he does. Makes him more human, don't you think? Till now I thought him a really cold fish. And last night there he was in a nightclub slavering all over this model woman and falling down drunk like any normal man should occasionally. We're going to get on fine.'

'Ivan, I wouldn't get too over-excited. Faisal tends to hold the witnessing of one of his annual fall-outs against the witnesses 'if you see what I mean. I doubt he's suddenly going to think of you as a jolly drinking companion, slap you on the back and promise you anything you like while he attempts to drink you under the table.'

'Why not? He was friendly enough yesterday. And the girl . . . I tell you, Ali. She wasn't interested in him at all. No, ha ha ha . . .' Ivan's lecherous laughter turned into a great phlegm-filled cough. Ali heard him hawk and waited while his co-conspirator caught his breath.

'I'm amazed.'

'Don't sound so astonished. She is, after all, a compatriot of mine. We have a lot in common.'

'You don't say.'

'Did you see Faraj?'

'He's seen your camp. Well done for leaving that map on your wall. Now he knows that the buyers of the catacombs are Russians and he also thinks that men rushing about in army surplus old USSR uniforms are bound to be mafia.'

'Did you tell him anything?'

'Played perfect ignorance.'

'Did he see anything . . . you know . . . ?'

'Incriminating? I don't think so. He wouldn't have asked me so many questions and might have been more accusing if he'd found out more. He told the whole story to the camp here like it was some adventure out of the Arabian Nights. All he needed was a genie in a lamp to finish off the effect of his tale. He didn't mention any of the special arrangements though, so they can't have got hold of any of the plan, and anything they overheard they wouldn't have understood because it would've been in Russian.' Ali stared at the pale cream sheep's wool stripes in the black wall of his tent, narrowing his eyes slightly so that the stripes blurred and the ache at the back of his head relaxed its hold a little. 'What did you say to Faisal when you met him? How did you explain away your chance encounter in this club?'

'Didn't need to. He passed out. Oh, and just so you know, I let the model girl guess that I was an arms dealer.'

'You did what?'

'I let the—'

'I heard you the first time. Why?'

'Double bluff. She didn't believe me. She thought I was joking. We spent the evening toasting each other in arak and ignoring your brother, who snored throughout.'

'And you think Faisal didn't hear, do you?'

'I told you, he was snoring!'

'And it hadn't occurred to you that she might pass on this juicy bit of information to her host for the evening once the poor love came round from his over-indulgence?'

'You fuss so. Who cares what she tells him? He won't believe it either.'

'Just so long as you're sure they weren't bluffing too. Faisal might have been wide awake behind the noise he was making, and taking everything you said seriously.'

'You weren't there, Ali.'

'All the same – I should watch my back if I were you. When are you coming out here?'

'Tomorrow. I'll come in convoy with that supermodel. She'll appreciate my keeping an eye on her.'

'She couldn't care less, Ivan. I should get out here now if I were you. That way if there's any covering up that needs to be done before my beloved brother arrives we'll have time. Have you spoken to your friends at the catacombs?'

'Are you telling me what to do, Ali? Because I should shut up if you are. Just remember your position in this operation all right? Don't worry your pretty little head about how I should plan – just keep your mouth shut till I get there tomorrow and that'll be enough contribution from you. Understand me?'

'Fine – ignore my advice if you like. But don't say I didn't warn you when my brother sneaks up behind you and hangs you from the walls of Aleppo by your armpit hair until you tell him all the gory details about your employers.'

'Do you have to be so imaginative? Just think of the money and smile.'

And Ali did smile; he smiled at the thought of revenge.

*

It was the end of a long day for Pandora. She'd used up the last of her reserves of energy to perform supermodel feats of chic in the calm courts of the old lunatic asylum. Posing under falling showers of dusty old roses, she'd charmed the mesmerised shopkeeper who, dressed in an unlikely outfit of Rory's fez and his own grubby grey and blue striped jallabiyya, had happily been photographed with her. She'd been patient with Flash, who wasn't happy with the film he had, and Joey, who broke the Polaroid camera, dropping it on the marble floor of the rose-festooned lunatics' courtyard. She'd smiled encouragingly at the concerned faces of Mimi and Rory. She'd born the inade-quacies of George and Courteney who may have been as keen as puppies but were, in Pandora's opinion, about as useful. And now, exhausted and shocked by her publicly performed panic attack of the morning, she sat in the cool of the borrowed shop, being plied with fresh tea and cigarettes and ignoring everyone as they packed up the day's equipment. Rory kept trying to talk to her, pecking at her with conversation like a worried hen. She didn't acknowledge his fussing and sipped her tea. She'd done what she'd been paid to for the day. Now all she wanted was to crawl into a soft, comfortable hole and in sleep find oblivion and an escape from all the questions which her life seemed to have become.

Faisal rounded the corner to find Pandora the calm in the eye of the clearing-up storm. He sat down beside her on the pile of carpets and said, 'Busy day?'

'That's one way to describe it.'

'Everyone's got that pinched nervous look you lot get when things aren't going well. What happened? Did Flash finally jump on you?'

Pandora laughed, a thin, sad little sound like the mewling of a sick cat. 'No. I just had a fainting fit and now they don't know what to do with me.'

'Give you a glass of water and the day off I should think.'

'No chance. They gave me a glass of water, my Uncle Rory made a miraculous appearance, poured sugar down my throat, and we went on working. I'm exhausted.' She dropped her head in her hands so that her hair fell in a screen over her face. The last thing she wanted was for Faisal to see her cry. He'd only start giving voice to the difficult questions that were already buzzing round her head like a cloud of angry hornets from which she couldn't escape. She felt a kindly arm go round her shoulders. 'If you're nice to me I'll cry,' she said, too late, the tears already coursing down her cheeks.

'Wouldn't dream of it.' Faisal grinned at her. 'Seems like that fortune-teller was wrong after all.'

'What do you mean?' Pandora blew her nose on a huge starched white handkerchief which Faisal produced out of his jeans pocket.

'She didn't say anything about working too hard or taking a holiday.'

'No.' Pandora was relieved that Faisal was going to blame her tears on overwork, not panic. She tried a smile and her face didn't crack.

'Working tomorrow?' he asked.

'Yes. Palmyra. We go in the morning and shoot in the afternoon and then on to your camel fair the next day. I can't believe they're doing this to me. I feel this shit and they're sending me to a place where there'll be no ice, let alone hot running water. And how hot does it get during the day?'

'I think I'd better not tell you.' He stopped. Pandora looked as if she was about to internally combust. It obviously wasn't a good time to go into details about 110-degree heat and no shade and the fact that the drinking water was always hot enough to bathe in.

'You see? And I've got to look cool and lovely while I wear winter clothes for them. Everyone else can sweat to their heart's delight. But not me. Everyone else can look tired. But not me. Everyone else can walk around in a sarong and a T-shirt and a big hat to save them from the sun. But not me. No, I must be cool in cashmere while I sit on a camel with some poor grinning fool holding on to the head rope and look like the most unlikely tourist in the history of travel. I mean, doesn't it strike you as a little ridiculous that a magazine whose readers would no more

193

go to a place without five stars emblazoned above the door than they would shit in the street are being given ideas of which designer's clothes they should wear for camel riding?'

'The thought had crossed my mind . . . Tell you what, I'll drive you to Palmyra and then at least you'll have a lovely journey instead of being thrown about in the back of that bus.'

'And it'll keep me away from Rory, who I love dearly but who can be a tad over-protective at times, and Mimi, who's gone into cahoots with him to keep me glittery and shiny enough to finish the shoot before I collapse with nervous exhaustion on the plane back to New York.'

'Great. I'll be outside the front of the hotel at four thirty.'

'A.M.?'

'Not worth going if you miss the sunrise.'

'Fine. Anything to keep away from my fashion cronies.' Pandora pushed her hair back and tied her tiny double satin pale pink ribbon round it. Faisal accepted tea from the shopkeeper, who took this as a sign that the sheikh might like to buy something. Having been extremely reticent with the hard-sell side of his nature all day, he began a sort of dance of the seven sales, using Persian carpets instead of silk mousseline as props. Faisal couldn't help laughing. Even Pandora's spirits were a little cheered at the sight of the diminutive man playing hide and seek behind his carpets to an improvised song of dollars, cash or traveller's cheques.

'Faisal, why did you allow us to come?'

'It's good publicity for the fair. And I've got a few demons of my own that I've been trying to avoid and you guys were providing the perfect distraction while I ran from them.'

'Ivan the arms dealer?'

'How did you guess?'

'I thought you knew all about him. I thought you tried to throw yourself at him last night so that he wouldn't tell us all about the politically incorrect side of your business.'

'Me! An arms dealer!'

'Why shouldn't you be? You appear to have more money than sense and you won't talk about where it comes from and 'you get all tetchy when anybody asks you what you do for a living.'

'I can't believe this. What kind of a person do you think I am?'

'I've no idea – you shroud yourself in mystery all the time.'

'But—'

'That's why we're all being so nice to you now. We're frightened you'll turn your stock of Kalashnikovs on us if we're not!'

Faisal was horrified. 'I can't believe you really thought I'd be an arms dealer – or have anything to do with arms dealing for that matter . . . I'm getting out of here before you accuse me of white slavery or being a drugs baron or any other stereotypes you can think up for money-grabbing Arabs.' Faisal stormed off before Pandora could stop him, pushing Rory – who, having seen him, had bustled forward like a Victorian chaperone eager to make his acquaintance and vet him for suitability for his niece – roughly into the wall.

'Well!' huffed Rory, pink with indignation on Pandora's behalf, and dusting down his cream linen jacket. 'I can see why you find him so objectionable, although there's no denying he's an attractive man is there?'

'Rory!'

'A little joke, to cheer you up. Come on.' He offered her his arm and she pulled herself up and hung on to it. 'Let's go and admire old T.E.'s likeness in the lounge room of our hotel. Do you think they'll have a bed for me? I must say, I dropped my little bags off there this morning and they were most unhelpful and thoroughly musty. I slightly wondered if the staff were in fact mouldy ghost survivors of the twenties when I suppose it might have been a relatively grand place.' He sighed and turned a corner, his long strides causing Pandora to trip awkwardly in her gym shoes as she tried to match his step and nearly lose her badly tied sarong in the process. She may have been six foot, but Rory, the same height, had a stronger vein of energy at that moment, one with which Pandora simply couldn't keep up.

Rory ignored her difficulties. He knew her well enough to realise that if he stopped to question her about her weakened

195

state now he'd never get her back to the hotel. So, with talk of hot baths and pints of gin, he dragged her back the few blocks from the walls of the old town to the Baron and pulled her upstairs to bathe her. Behind him, as if he were fashion's Pied Piper, the rest of the team struggled, bowed down with luggage, even Mimi carrying a pile of linen shrouded suits and six pairs of shoes in chamois-leather drawstring bags, struggling to keep up herself.

Back at the Baron Mimi found a doom-laden pile of messages from Nina. She squared her shoulders and went upstairs to do battle with the phone system and then, if she ever managed to get through to New York, explain to her editor-in-chief how Rory'd found them.

'What's he doing there, Mimi?' Nina's voice was brittle from the other side of the Atlantic. For once the phone had connected first time and the line was crystal clear.

'I don't know, Nina. He just appeared this morning, bright as a button and twice as shiny. I didn't give him our itinerary and I've no idea how he found us in that maze in the bazaar.'

'Send him back.'

'I can't, Nina.'

'Why not?'

'I hardly have the authority to send the style director of the magazine packing, do I? I'm just a lowly editor with about as much clout as a dishcloth.'

'You'd be surprised how much they can hurt when flicked efficiently.'

'Nina, you know what I mean.'

'You know he'll ruin the shoot. He'll chase the boys, distract Pandora, double the cost of the whole thing and, worst of all, he'll keep having a better idea all the time. Before you know it the shoot will no longer be yours and the most important styling of your career so far will be credited to the famous Mr Williams and you, my dear, will be swept away with the forgotten Polaroids before the perfect print of his achievement.'

'Thanks.' Mimi's ears burnt at this onslaught.

'So I suggest you send him home, darling. Or shall I sack him? That'll bring him back Stateside quickly enough. He's always enjoyed fighting his own corner.'

'To tell you the truth, Nina . . .'

'What?'

'Well, to be perfectly honest . . .'

'Yes?' Mimi could hear Nina tapping her immaculate Chanel red fingernails on the chic grey lacquer of her Franck de Vos desk.

'OK – I'll admit it . . . I'm really relieved he's here.' And before Nina could interrupt, Mimi launched into the tale of woe which represented the shoot so far. 'The pictures'll be fine, Nina, but Pandora's behaving very oddly and I don't think I can manage her and the rest of them. Flash Harry's turned into some kind of wannabe lady killer in safari pants around Pandora, and George, Gavin and Frankie have all nearly died of the squits, and then Joey ran off with Faisal's brother and we all thought he'd been abducted. The food's disgusting and tomorrow we go to the desert and everyone's moods are going to be much, much worse because the amenities here might be a little basic compared to what we're used to in New York but can you imagine what they're going to be like there? And it's so hot!'

'Take a breath, Mimi!' Nina shouted down the line. 'All right, I get your point.' Mimi blinked back tears and hoped that Nina couldn't hear how close her voice had come to breaking. There seemed to be a grapefruit-sized lump lodged in her throat and Mimi wasn't sure how much longer she was going to be able to keep up this conversation without giving away quite how desperate the situation had become.

'You're obviously over-tired, darling, and if I must let you have Rory to keep a lid on things then . . .' Mimi gave way to tears of relief. 'Oh for goodness' sake pull yourself together, Mimi. You're a senior stylist, not a junior assistant. It's not the collections, it's a jolly shoot before the shows start. If you can't cope with this what are you going to be like in Europe?'

'At least there's hot running water and croissants at any time of the day or night in Europe. Here if you don't have a bath at certain times of the day there's no water at all and the electricity keeps failing and the food—'

'I don't want to know.'

'I don't care. I'm going to tell you. It's awful.'

'I bet it's not as bad as that time I was going down the Zambezi with Gavin, or was it Frankie?'

'Oh don't start that, Nina. Gavin and Frankie have done nothing all trip but try and make out that they've had worse experiences before and I just don't believe them.'

'Make the most of it, darling. Think of the book you can write when you retire, burnt out by your efforts, at the tender age of thirty. I can just see you downshifting to some Brazilian hideaway to grow beans or corn or something and live on organically grown vegetables and wind-generated light . . .' Nina humphed in disgust at the idea. 'Now, I suggest you calm down, have a bath quickly before Rory uses all the hot water for his own ablutions, and go and have a stiff drink in the bar. Then go to the best restaurant in town, take the whole team out for a slap-up meal, make sure nobody gets drunk, get to bed before ten and everything will seem much more manageable in the morning. Yes?'

'I'll try.'

'How's our friendly sheikh in all this?'

'He's been very helpful till now, but Pandora accused him of being an arms dealer tonight and he stormed off in a bate so I shouldn't think we'll benefit from his help any more.'

'Arms dealer! How preposterous. Where does that girl get her ideas from? All right, you can keep Rory. It sounds like you could use him.'

'Thanks, Nina. I will.'

Pictikhov's arrival at the catacombs inspired a flurry of activity in an atmosphere already tense enough to slice with the barrel of one of the shiny new Kalashnikovs he brought with him in hundreds of skull-and-crossbones-stamped boxes. By tacit agreement the men holding this underground fort didn't mention Faraj or Said, or the fact that they'd managed to beat two armed men into submission without any fire power of their own before escaping. They knew it would only be a matter of time before Pictikhov demanded to see them and they knew better than to bring the sky down on their heads before it was absolutely necessary. In the meantime boxes of Pictikhov's precious merchandise – everything from rocket launchers to a selection of branded land-mines – were installed in what was rapidly becoming an arms dealer's Aladdin's cave.

Chapter 12

ITS engine turning over, purring like a finely bred cat, the gleaming white Mercedes waited, roof down, outside the dining-room terrace of the Baron Hotel. The dawn was still only a hopeful smudge on the horizon between the modern apartment blocks which ringed Aleppo. Pandora shivered and wrapped her pink pashmina tightly round her shoulders.

'How can a place that gets so hot during the day be so endlessly freezing at night?' she asked Faisal, a shadowy form in the grey half-light, leaning on the bonnet of the car and drinking Turkish coffee as she came towards him.

'Land of contrasts, Syria. Never a dull moment.' His teeth gleamed, pearly in the gloom. He passed her the coffee he'd had prepared in case she actually turned up. She took a deep breath; she didn't often find herself forced to apologise and was unsure where to start.

'Thanks for waiting. I thought you might have burnt off in a fit of pique after our tiff yesterday.'

'You're not the only one who's tired and emotional. I'm sorry I got tetchy with you too. You hit a raw spot, that's all.'

'Ditto. I'm so relieved you're not still cross with me. I mean, you would have perfect reason to be. I had no right to accuse you of whatever you thought I was accusing you of yesterday when I know all you were doing was being friendly. Let's make a deal.' She held out her right hand. 'As we're both feeling a bit fragile then I suggest we keep off delicate subjects and just try and have a nice time without bruising each other on the way?'

'Deal.' They shook. 'When does the magazine charabanc leave?'

'Not for another hour or so. And now Rory's on board I'm

afraid that, however hard they try to get him up, he'll probably delay them even more. Never been any good at either travelling or early mornings, my Uncle Rory. Put the two together and you're asking to be days late before you've even started.'

'Great, we'll have the road to ourselves then. Have you got a hat?'

'Better – a scarf.' Pandora produced a faded and much washed old sarong from Simrane in Paris.

'You are efficient.'

'I'm not as green as I'm cabbage looking.'

'And brighter than I'd have given you credit for at this time of the morning.'

'Careful of those tender spots, Faisal.'

The sheikh gave Pandora a wry smile and put down his cup on the little tray the waiter had left with fresh rolls and butter on the edge of the verandah, picked up the rolls and balanced them on the dashboard of the car. He opened the passenger door.

'Shall we?'

'Why thank you, kind sir.' Pandora simpered and exercised her eyelashes. Faisal grinned at her and batted his better ones back.

'Let's go.'

And so Faisal drove Pandora to her first real encounter with the desert. He turned off the Aleppo Damascus highway where the sown ground peters out against the vastness of the uncultivated not far outside Homs. He headed directly east on a road as old as the silk route of which it is part towards a smudge of far-off mountains which, in the pale dawn light, were outlined as if with brushstrokes of violet ink. Pandora lay back and let Faisal do all the work. Her hair tied fast under the old sarong, her pashmina wrapped tightly around her shoulders to protect against the early morning chill, she stared through the windscreen as the clean lined purity of the desert enveloped her.

And she saw that, contrary to her expectations, the desert was neither barren, nor particularly sandy. The sunburnt grey of the spiny desert scrub was transformed at this time of the day by dew into a gentle green, giving depth and shadow to the endless pale yellow of the earth. Sheep and goats tended by small boys sitting sideways on donkeys meandered along the edges of the road. The animals tore at thorny herbs and the occasional patch of rough grass; and where there were goats there were tents, black goat-hair camps squeaking with the laughter of small children accompanied by the clatter of pots while women tended breakfast fires. The little shepherds laughed and waved at the flash car speeding past them. Faisal waved back and, picking up his cue, so did she.

Pandora ate one of the rolls left for them by the hotel; it was filled with cumin seeds which gave it a sweetly aniseed taste. Faisal saw her relax a little; the hard hunch of tired, angry shoulders slacked an inch or so; she uncrossed her ankles which had been so tightly twisted round each other that he'd wondered for a while if she was double-jointed. Eventually he saw her close her eyes and put her head back to inhale this air, redolent with the smells of goat-trampled herbs, woodsmoke and Bedouin breakfasts. And as the sun licked the summit of the lowest eastern hill, so did a smile touch the corners of Pandora's mouth. It was the smile he'd first witnessed on the roof of his house in Damascus; the whole glory of a new day was mirrored in the pallor of her face. Faisal drove on; at least one of them was happy.

Pandora knew he was looking at her and she didn't mind. She didn't mind about anything much with the dry sweet desert wind in her nose mixing with the aftertaste of cumin seeds and bitter Turkish coffee. She thought of all the things that had combined, connived even, to make her sick in the bazaar in Aleppo the day before. Keeping her eyes shut she took each one of them and shredded them mentally: exhaustion – pouf, she let it go in the wind; sudden terror of an inability to perform – off it went like a handful of dust tossed into the breeze; the howling void inside her – perhaps it was time to fill it with something new, with whatever she chose. She peeled away all of these things, the protective layers of her life, and eventually, squinting mentally in case what she saw was the monster that she feared she'd become, she found what she was looking for. Under the self-doubt and the fear, and the knowledge that she simply could not carry on pretending to be the people endless editors, photographers, features writers and even biographers invented for her to play, she came to a new blank page lying waiting in her heart.

And opening her eyes to the rising sun, she began to laugh. She laughed until she cried. She sat up and leant across to Faisal, kissing him for being with her.

'What?' Faisal couldn't believe the change that had come over her.

'Ha!' she cried. 'I'm not sure I should tell you – it's a powerful tonic but are you ready for it?'

'What?'

'No . . . I'm not telling you.'

He screeched to a halt. 'What?'

'You'll think I'm clinically insane. There isn't a way of telling you what's just occurred to me without it sounding like wanky, new-age, soul-searching stuff.'

'Try me.'

'You've got to be joking. If I told you now you'd get out of the car and throw up and recommend I go and write a little book of empowering thoughts for over-protected, over-bred, poor little rich girls just like me.' Faisal looked at her, puzzled. 'And there's no need to stare at me as if I'm completely mad.' She laughed again. 'I can't believe I could have been so stupid!'

Faisal started the car again and roared towards Palmyra at about twice the speed he'd been travelling before, raising a tunnel of dust behind them that could be seen for miles.

'Can't wait to hear all about it,' he shouted above the roar of the whipping wind.

'What?'

'Never mind.'

'What?'

'I said . . .'

*

Faisal and Pandora weren't the only people on the road to the desert that morning. Ivan followed an hour behind them, battling with a hire car that claimed to be a five-speed Daewoo but which, upon closer inspection, proved to be a Daewoo exterior housing a Lada engine with only four unhappily grinding gear changes available. Ivan hated this car; in T'bilisi he drove a five series BMW, with original Czech plates, straight from the motorway service station from which it had been stolen. In Syria, not only was he driving a horrible car, but there was the added worry of a strangely shaped orange light which flashed ominously at him from the dashboard whenever he turned sharply left or went up hill for longer than a mile or so. To take his mind off possible mechanical problems, he sang a gruff rendition of 'Thank you for the Music' in Russglaise as he drove along, tapping his fingers in time on the steering wheel. Abba's greatest hits should get him as far as Palmyra, he'd move on to the screeching remembrances of Fleetwood Mac on the next leg of his journey to the camel fair. He slurped occasionally from a bottle of water, an act that left him with the unfamiliar feelings of virtue and health and abstemiousness all at once. He pushed back his fake Wayfarers, opened a window, hung the pasty pink flesh of his left arm out to burn. He lit a red Marlboro. In spite of his dissatisfaction with his transport, he felt that life really could have been considerably worse.

It was well past nine when the rest of the fashion gang hit the road for Palmyra. Mimi, clenching her smile in place, had to encourage Rory into the bus gently, as if he were a recalcitrant thoroughbred objecting to being boxed in. She was beginning to regret persuading Nina to let her keep him with her. The rest of the team sat and stared while she tried to make Rory do as he was told; George deeply disapproving, Courteney giggling not far from outright hysteria, Flash disgusted, Joey distracted by the worry that he might have left something behind, and Gavin and Frankie making endless mental notes.

'Ooh look at her!' cried Gavin, laughing at Rory while displaying self-righteous good behaviour. 'Who does she think she is! I may have behaved like that in my time, but Frankie, you and I both know that when you get to a certain age in this business it just doesn't pay to play up like that.'

'Oh I know,' answered the indefatigable Frankie. 'I don't suppose you ever heard about the time I was doing dinner services and Pratesi sheets for the design section at the top of the Matterhorn . . .' And so they went on.

Faisal's camel fair was almost ready to welcome the fashion gang. For days people had been arriving, populating the ghost town laid out by the sheikh's henchmen. There were tents and camels, land cruisers and water trucks, generators, satellite dishes, goats and piles of aubergines, dates, pomegranates, chick peas, tomatoes and cucumbers along with great bundles of mint and jars of cooking fat for feasting to last a week. Khaled and Walid had spent the time since the meeting at Faisal's house in Damascus arranging the fair on the flat plain where it traditionally took place. Between a fold in the hills and a tiny oasis – where great old palm trees did battle with the heat and shaded a fifty-yard long, clear, if slightly brackish, spring, which provided water and shade for both camels and people alike – the fair had been taking place, sixty kilometres south-east of Palmyra, since time immemorial.

Khaled and Walid's job was to arrange plots for tents, plots for camels, plots for racing, plots for rubbish. This year there was one unusual task: Walid organised a task force of curious Bedouin boys keen to earn some extra pocket money into a gang to dig a cesspit for the lavatories which were to be installed for the fashion groupies. So while Pandora and Faisal sailed across the crumbling sand and basalt plain to Palmyra in a modern version of the ancient ship of the desert, Khaled and Walid supervised the construction of the modern version of the old-fashioned 'dig a hole in the sand and just go' sort of arrangement. Pink plastic loos, on a specially built platform, and cubicled off in brown and white striped deck-chair ticking, were built downwind of the camp. Each cubicle had its own tiny table and a pale blue plastic bin for used paper. The doors had latches and there were strings of white bulbs, not only along the front of them so that there would be no doubt which were in use during the night, but from the corner of the fashion tents to the edge of these unlikely conveniences. Khaled and Walid stood back with their team of workers and couldn't decide whether to smile with pride or just laugh at the ridiculousness of pink plastic lavatories perched hundreds of miles from anywhere in the middle of the desert.

'I like the platform best,' Khaled said, beginning to chuckle.

'No, the tables for the paper,' Walid joined in. And soon the group of loo builders were creased with laughter, they had never seen anything quite so absurd.

'Now, who's going to see if they work?' Tears poured down the workers' faces at the idea; no one volunteered.

Sulking in his tent, Ali heard the laughter. He was smoking, sucking hard on the cigarettes and squashing the ends flat with his teeth. His mood was not improved when Faraj popped his head round the edge of his tent and grinned at him.

'Glad to see me back?' Faraj's voice boomed through the quiet gloom of Ali's quarters.

'Not particularly.' Ali was in no mood to be gracious. Still, Faisal would arrive the next day, the fair would be more bearable if he made peace with his cousin. He forced a friendly teeth baring. 'Sit down. Let me call for coffee.'

Faraj was proficient in the teeth baring department too so he smiled over the coffee and lit a proffered Marlboro. Leaning back against an ornate camel saddle, he stared at the dappled shadows coming through the loose weave of the tent. 'Everything ready?'

'I suppose so,' Ali agreed.

'You've done a good job.'

'I haven't done anything except sit here feeling totally useless. It's Walid and Khaled who've done everything. I did offer to help but Khaled managed to brush me off with his usual obsequiousness. He wouldn't let me touch his precious fair with a barge pole. I really have no idea why my brother made me come out here at all. When he used to be in charge of the fair I always wondered what he did when he got here early and I still haven't got the slightest idea. I mean look . . . with the best will in the world there isn't anything to do. It's just plain boring. There aren't even that many people here yet. There's no one to talk to, there's no gambling to speak of.'

Faraj grinned, remembering the years when he and Faisal used to get to the fair a good two weeks in advance to start acclimatising their camels for the races. 'You don't race, Ali. I wouldn't expect you to understand.'

'You really can be deeply patronising at times.' Ali leered at Faraj through the gloom and poured more of the bitter Bedouin coffee. 'Perhaps I have different priorities from you. You must respect that.'

'Must I? I didn't realise that there could be more important priorities, as a member of a sheikh's family with a long and honourable history of upholding the ways of their tribe, than participating in tribal traditions and helping to continue a sense of community – working for the common good.'

'Even more patronising, Faraj.'

'Thanks, it was intended to be.'

'But you see, you're wrong.'

'How's that?'

'My priority is the success of the tribe. The only problem is that I disagree rather fundamentally with my great good brother, who, by the way, has been seen falling down drunk in Aleppo. A fact which does nothing to add lustre to his evidently easily tarnished reputation.' Ali was getting into his stride. He held up a hand to prevent Faraj from interrupting. 'If you would just let me develop my point . . .' He sat up and crossed his legs, jabbing his finger at his cousin. 'Here we have, no distance away, a team of crack scientists who've already spent considerable funds setting themselves up here in order to help us make enormous sums of money which can only benefit the tribe as a whole.'

'And you particularly. I must say, they didn't look much like wannabe Nobel Prize winners to me, more like oafish, dangerously armed bouncers up to no good.'

'Of course they have to protect their interests. Everyone has security. And they will benefit the tribe. I'm not in this for myself, Faraj, but for all of us.'

'Not in it for yourself? Pull the other one, Ali.'

'All I ask is that my gambling debts are paid off. A small price to pay as a consultancy fee considering the amount of work I've already put into this project. And imagine what it'll do for you. I can't understand why you're being so dense, Faraj, you'll be rich beyond your wildest dreams.'

'I'm not badly off now, thank you very much.'

'But what we have is never enough, is it? Imagine how you could improve your art collection, hey? Imagine the furniture you could buy!'

'Ali, stop it.'

'What?'

'They're not surveying for oil.'

'Yes they are.'

'They're not. You know perfectly well why they're here. You've known all along.'

Ali's face was a picture of childlike innocence. 'What on earth are you talking about?'

'Arms dealing, Ali.'

'Oh don't be ridiculous.'

'Ivan was boasting about it in Aleppo.'

'He was bluffing. Can't any of you take a joke? And who did you hear this from? My drunken brother? How do you know he heard right? Ivan told me he was out cold all night having bashed his head on a concrete tit.'

'Why would Pandora lie?'

'What's Pandora got to do with this?'

'Precisely – there's no reason for her to make things up. Ali, you and I both know that if there was a serious quantity of oil under this desert it would have been exploited years ago. These Russians don't want oil, they want a warehouse for their rocket launchers. And stop pretending you don't know about it either. They are Russian mafia, Ali, and you've known that all along.'

'They are bona fide businessmen and I see no reason not to

trust them until I'm given proof positive that I shouldn't.'

'In which case you're a bloody fool.' Faraj stood up. 'Thanks for the coffee, cousin. See you around.'

The Queen Zenobia Hotel in Palmyra sits audaciously in the middle of the city burnt in the third century by the Emperor Aurelian, lived in by Diocletian, and ruled before the arrival of either of these Romans by the glamorous, self-aggrandising, ambitious queen herself. Outside the hotel, rows of tall pillars line the streets of the city while the remains of churches, temples, baths and a theatre, houses, shops and courtrooms spread out from the main roads in perfectly recognisable patterns. Sheep graze under the benevolent eye of old shepherds in the shade of a temple courtyard. Small boys set up shops in the ruins of shops built two thousand years ago, using original fireplaces to make their tea while touting to tourists the kind of tat that is sold to travellers the world over.

The same souvenirs can be bought from the cool marble interior of the Zenobia Hotel; little carved bone camels, stuffed plastic camels with tinsel reins, sandstone camels, every variation on the theme you can think of. You can not, however, buy American standard luxury, let alone the kind of luxury to which this team of fashion shooters had long since become accustomed.

Their bus cranked into town along the road that snakes through the middle of the ruins, sandwiched between two Baghdadi trucks after a journey fraught with pot holes and kamikaze goats playing chicken on the road. Courteney throwing up down Joey's back had done nothing to improve either the smell of the bus or the feel of anyone's temper. Even the bus driver was a little ragged round the edges by the time he put the handbrake on in the forecourt of the Zenobia; the Baghdadi truck drivers had decided to play cat and mouse with him all the way from Homs, terrifying the passengers to the extent that even Gavin and Frankie had stopped twittering for an hour or so. To make matters worse, on arrival at the hotel they found that a convention of German tourists had taken all the best rooms and that George's reservation faxes had been misunderstood; everyone was expected to share, three or four to a room. With some horror Rory found that there wasn't room for him at all. The receptionist smiled sweetly and suggested they put another bed in the only available single room and that he should share with Flash. Rory stamped his foot on the slippery marble floor and had to grab hold of the reception desk to stop himself falling over. 'Now listen here . . .' he began. The receptionist smiled again with the benign expression of a china doll and with about as much understanding.

Leaving Rory and George to sort out the mess, Mimi went in search of Pandora. She'd seen Faisal's Mercedes parked outside, but there was no sign of him nor her precious model. Shoving her dark glasses onto her face as if she had some kind of vendetta against the sun, Mimi marched towards the ruins hoping that Pandora and Faisal would stand out from the crowd of Germans, who wove about the ruins in obedient crocodile formation dressed in matching white short-sleeved shirts with green logos on the pockets and green baseball caps with white logos on the front. They were heading towards the great Temple of Baal. Mimi took the opposite direction. On a hill not far away was a castle; she decided that if she could get up there she'd find not only an overview of the situation but perhaps some peace of mind as well as a clue as to Pandora's whereabouts.

She zigzagged gently uphill for perhaps half an hour, finding herself soon at the height of Diocletian's camp where there was a platform. She sat cross-legged on this ledge and watched the business going on in the little Bedouin household beneath her. They were packing to go somewhere. A three-wheeler truck, lavishly decorated with what looked like coat-hangers twisted into heart shapes and painted with a pattern of camels and palm trees, was piled high with pots, pans, a tent, a box of chickens, and two children, balanced on the top; they were holding on for dear life and grinning expectantly, waiting for the off. Mimi wondered vaguely where they were going. It never occurred to her that it might have been to Faisal's camel fair.

She jumped when Said appeared beside her. He smiled through the generous bush of his moustache and said, 'Can I sit?' A little taken aback, she made to get up and leave. 'No. Don't leave on my account. You're a friend of Faraj and the sheikh.' Said's English was slow, careful and correct. 'If you're looking for Faisal and the girl they're under the paintings in the Temple of Baal laughing at the Germans and examining the soldiers.' Mimi looked puzzled. 'The paintings are of soldiers. The Germans are around them and the sheikh translates for your friend. You're here to take photographs?'

'Yes.' Mimi sat down again; she liked this man with his expressive moustache, out of which sprouted the worst rolled cigarette she'd ever seen. It smouldered dangerously close to the badly clipped hair on his upper lip. Said seemed unconcerned about any imminent conflagration and she saw no reason to worry him. He held out his hand to her.

'I am Said,' he said. She shook the proffered hand.

'Mimi.'

'Mimi.' He said her name, testing it for himself.

'Do you live here?' Mimi asked.

'Yes. I used to rent out my camels for tourists to ride on.' Said stared out wistfully over the ruins.

'Used to?'

'Now I rent out my jeep for driving through the desert.' He picked tobacco off his bottom lip, looked at it and flicked it away. 'I'm one of the drivers taking you to the camel fair.'

'Oh . . . but we've got a bus.'

'It's off road most of the way. The bus will get stuck in the sand.'

'I didn't realise.' Mimi scratched her head, distracted.

'Don't panic. The great Sheikh Faisal bin Ali al Mez'al has arranged it all.'

'Has he just?' Mimi failed to keep the sarcasm from her voice.

'I take it you aren't happy with the arrangements.'

'I would have liked to have been informed.'

'But you're guests of the sheikh. He will always make the best arrangements for you. There is no need for you to concern yourself with these things.' Said smiled, crinkling leathery skin around his eyes.

'But I have to concern myself. I'm responsible for this circus. I have to get back to Manhattan with material for twenty pages of the Christmas special featuring Pandora dressed in a selection of the least suitable clothes for the area, the idea being that the contrast between the clothes and the place will bring out the best in both. So far the photographer's been useless and done nothing but lech over Pandora, my assistants may as well not be here, the amount of help they've been, and now the delightful Rory Williams has turned up I should probably just hand over the reins to him so that he can do everything and then take all the glory. I may as well not have bothered coming at all.' Mimi could hear the screeching crescendo of nerves in her voice and found that she could do nothing about it. Said grinned at her.

'I think you're very tired, Miss Mimi. Why don't you come and have some Bedouin tea? It'll calm you.' Mimi gulped; she liked this man and his bushy moustache and sparkling mischievous eyes but wasn't sure she was up to nipping to his tent for a glass of tea and who knew what else. Said laughed at her expression. 'I like your face, Miss Mimi. It prints your mind clearly on it.' He stood and offered her his hand to pull her up. 'Look, tea is over there, just by the hotel. There is nothing improper in my proposal.' Mimi blushed, smiled through her confusion, took his arm and headed down the ancient street with him, letting him guide her round seventeen-hundred-year-old pot holes, over Queen Zenobia's personal baths, down a side street to a temple, and finally to a hollow made by fallen pillars just outside the hotel, where Said lit a small fire and began the ritual of Bedouin tea-making in earnest.

Relaxing against the cool pillar, Mimi stared up at the sky; perfect azure, scudding clouds, a wheeling hawk. She thought she'd never seen anything so perfect. In the distance she could hear the tinkle of Pandora's laughter and relaxed. If Pandora was happy then she could allow herself five minutes off before beginning to panic about buses and bedrooms and sleeping arrangements.

'I've sorted it all.' Rory's shadow loomed. Mimi found him looking down on her in a self-satisfied sort of way. Shaded by his scarlet parasol, he was dressed otherwise as a sort of Gaultier sailor-boy dream: striped Breton T-shirt, wide, French blue, flap-buttoning, rough linen pants, a little red and white spotted kerchief tied neatly round his neck. The marine theme was finished off with navy and white old-fashioned plimsolls. Mimi smiled up at him weakly.

'I'm so glad, Rory. I knew you would.'

'Turns out the German tourists had used up twice their quota of rooms. I've selected a little peach of a suite at the end of the corridor for you and me and Pandora. Your beloved assistants don't seem to mind sharing so I put them together. Frankie and Gavin never stopped talking for long enough to realise that I'd put them together. Besides, they're frightened of me in spite of what that old queen Gavin says, so they'll do what they're told. It was a bit mean of me to put them in a double bed but I just couldn't help myself when the opportunity presented itself.' His face gleamed gleefully. 'And as for that ghastly photographer, with the character of an over-cooked prize marrow but the unfortunate ability to take good pictures, I put him on a mattress in a box room with his horrid little assistant. Kill or cure, that's what I say.' Smug with achievement, Rory spread a clean red silk handkerchief on a piece of stone, sat on it and crossed his legs. He extracted a cigarette from a battered packet of Silk Cut and, after tugging at it for a second to straighten it out, lit it and inhaled deeply. Mimi looked at him fondly and all the resentment she'd felt towards him earlier in the day disappeared in a blur of goodwill. Said passed her a tiny glass of tea and then gave one to Rory.

'You are a joy, my man,' said Rory, glittering at Said. Mimi introduced them, forcing herself not to wince too openly when Rory held out his hand as if he expected it to be kissed. Rory sipped his tea and examined Said critically. Said didn't seem to mind. He rolled another paper-bag cigarette and sat and smoked it happily while Rory's eyes roamed over him, staring hard. 'I don't suppose you've ever had your photograph taken for an American magazine?' Rory asked. Mimi groaned; she didn't want Said in the pictures; he was hardly pretty enough. 'Don't whinge, Mimi. He'll look heavenly with Pandora. She's only about six inches taller than him, we can do those killing sort of little and large type pictures.'

'And get a post bag full of complaints about racial stereotyping.'

'What?' asked Said. 'You must take my picture. I take very good pictures.' He produced from the capacious depths of his grubby sand-coloured jallabiyya a pile of photos and letters from grateful tourists who'd been entertained by him during their trips to Palmyra. It was true; he photographed beautifully. The crinkle-framed glittering eyes shone out of the pictures as they do when people are totally unselfconscious and couldn't care less what they look like and are simply enjoying themselves.

'Told you so.' Rory raised an eyebrow at Mimi who shrugged.

'Listen. We photograph here this evening then we go tomorrow. If you insist on using Said in some of the pictures then I won't fight you. But let's make a deal, he mustn't be in all of them, all right?'

'Perfect, darling. That way you'll have a control which will show you how much more successful my little experiment will be than yours. That's as long as the half-wit photographer and his assistant manage to get the film back to New York all right. I saw their baggage, you know, bundles of unlabelled film, half of it from the dark ages and not been in a refrigerator since, if you know what I mean,' he said darkly. 'Tell me, Said. Do you have a camel we can borrow?'

Said's face fell. 'I had two beautiful camels. They were the kindest, gentlest, fastest camels. My Hassala, she was pale like the dawn with big soft eyes . . . But Faraj will get me new ones and for now I have a jeep instead.'

'What happened to your camels?'

'They disappeared in the desert. It was a tragedy. But I always wanted a car and I got one in exchange for my camels so it's not too bad.'

'Do you know where we can get a camel?'

'For the photograph?'

'Yes.'

'But you should use the jeep.'

'We want a camel!'

'Why do you want a camel? A camel is old-fashioned. The camel is finished. Jeeps are the way to travel in the desert now.'

'Rory, I should think we'll get plenty of camel opportunities at the fair.'

'You may have a point, Mimi. But this gentleman won't be at the fair with us, will he?'

Pandora's laughter was getting louder. Mimi looked up and could see her dancing along the road with Faisal. The passing locals stopped and stared at the strange mixture of the sheikh and the show girl, one dancing, one dawdling along; both dodging the occasional Baghdadi truck which thundered through the ruins in great clouds of burning diesel on the only passable road.

'Polaroid.' Joey passed the spare Polaroid camera. 'Hold it, Pandora.' Pandora held it. The sun, for so long the danger of the daytime sky, was burning out in a blaze of glory behind the silhouettes of the old city's pillars. Pandora posed on the plinth where Mimi had met Said earlier in the day, a statuesque beauty in floor-length black Chanel mousseline-de-soie, the white silk of the signature camellias at her breast catching fiery reflections from the sun. Her skin too glowed with reflected glory, as did the shining black of her hair which glinted now with points of flame. She held herself upright, posed with her arms reaching for the sky as Mimi and Rory and Flash examined the Polaroid. It was perfect.

'Camera.' Joey passed the loaded camera and Flash began to shoot. And for the first time in her life Pandora didn't feel she had to perform: she simply stood and felt the earth living under her feet and watched the sun curve over the lip of the same hill she'd seen it rise behind at dawn that morning. This was what made these the photographs that defined Flash Harry's career; not the dress, not the pose, nor the hair, nor the make-up, not even the perfect ideal of girlhood represented in the exterior of Pandora. The rare quality of the photographs lay in Pandora's realisation that this was the first day of her life during which she'd seen the sun rise and the sun set and had watched it all day in its arch over the world and the experience left her breathless, thrilled to be alive.

Afterwards everyone ate dinner seated on white plastic garden chairs at acanthus-leaf-carved Corinthian capitol tables on the terrace in front of the hotel. The atmosphere was muted. Perhaps it was the effect of the sparkling breadth of the velvety sky, perhaps it was the quiet that creeps up on this desert town and takes possession under cover of darkness and which interrupted even Gavin and Frankie from their ceaseless chatter. Only Faisal seemed unaffected by the night. He leant back in his chair, flicking his father's lapis lighter and puffing on a postprandial cigar.

'It's good to be home,' he said.

'I thought Damascus was home to you.' Mimi wondered why she was whispering.

Faisal waved at the night sky and laughed. 'How could home be anywhere but here?'

'Do you have a house here?' Mimi was confused and so relied on the rules of English dinner-party conversation to get her through this difficult patch. She didn't like this dreamy atmosphere, it made her feel unsafe. She didn't even like the size of the sky much; she was used to perspective given by buildings and street lamps.

'No. I only have a house in Damascus. Here I live in three-sided tents. You know why I think they're three-sided?'

'No.'

'So you can always see the sky. When I was still at school I'd come home for the holidays from England and my father would send me out here. It was supposed to toughen me up I think and to teach me the ways of the desert and obvious things like that. All I really remember is racing camels with Faraj and spending long nights staring up at the stars. If you lie still and stare for long enough at one star eventually all the others start shooting in at the one you're staring at and the sky looks like a kaleidoscope. Have you ever done that?'

'In Brazil sometimes. But the sky there's different. Maybe because the horizon's not so smooth – there's always something in the way of it that cuts the edge up a bit and makes it less . . . I don't know . . . you don't feel that it surrounds you so much.'

'I know what you mean,' interrupted Pandora. 'In other places the sky feels like the roof of the world. Here you know that it goes all the way round and we're just floating in a bubble.' Her voice was breathy with excitement.

'Aren't we getting poetic in our old age?' Sharply cynical, Rory lit a Silk Cut.

'Makes me dead nervous.' George sipped at a warm, flat beer and made a little, forced smile. Pandora grinned.

'I love it,' she said, standing up, grabbing her cigarettes and the gin and tonic she'd been toying with all evening.

'Don't go for a walk now, Pandora. You'll break your leg in the dark.'

'Panic will get you nowhere, Mimi. Come on, Faisal. If you're so at home here you can come and warn me where the pot holes are.'

'My pleasure.'

They left a profoundly unsettled group. The oil that greased the lives of these New Yorkers in order that the wheels of the magazine should grind smoothly was missing. So far that evening no one had showered because there had been no running water at all, let alone hot running water, as a result of which everyone felt decidedly sticky and kept their noses far from each other's armpits. The hotel, the smartest in Palmyra, served nothing but warm, flat drinks, and the wine had been described by Rory, who'd spat a mouthful out under a nearby acacia tree, as *exécrable*. Frankie was practically hallucinating about a glass of iced champagne. The food was more of the same: humous, tabbouleh, flat bread, olives, oil, cheese, and meat kebabs. Courteney would have been prepared to pay a month's rent for a McDonald's at this stage of the trip. And the soles of George's black patent leather Birkenstocks had shrunk when he'd left them in the sun on the shelf at the back of the bus that day leaving him tearfully forced to sport a shameful pair of last season's Nikes.

'I don't know how she does it.' George watched the disappearing Pandora with awe.

'What do you mean, young man?' Rory puffed himself up and prepared to hold forth. 'It's terrible what she's doing. She's letting the side down unforgivably. Have you noticed the way she's not even powdering her nose? And where she got that unsightly collection of ancient sarongs from I have no idea. And they're all the same. And she seems to have only one pair of shoes with her and they've frankly had it. If I trusted the machinery I'd get them to give those tennis shoes a whiz in the washer but I doubt that they'd come out any cleaner than they are, and I'm not sure Pandora could care less.'

'I rather admire her for being so blasé.' Courteney dared to speak. 'I mean, look at us all, desperate for little luxuries from civilisation and still getting up in a new outfit every day and nearly dying from exhaustion from the added pressure we're putting ourselves under and she's cool as a cucumber.'

'It's a bad sign, Courteney. And admire her though you may, I don't see you following her example so I know you're talking crap. I know you need the armour of your oh-so-up-to-the-minute fake Chanel capri pants.'

'They're not fake!'

'No darling, of course not.' Rory lit another Silk Cut. 'Now don't be upset. Work hard and long and one day you'll be able to afford the real thing. I don't mind if assistants wear fakes, they've got to wear something and you can hardly walk around in last summer's combat pants even if they were made by Isaac

Mizrahi. I know it's impossible to work with Nina and Mimi and me and not be ahead of the trends, darling. You wouldn't have got the job otherwise. And if your salary only pays for fakes then that's all right too. As long as you try, precious, as long as you try.'

'Thanks.'

'Nothing like a few home truths. I must say I think my baby Pandora is being very badly influenced by her not so chic sheikh. And there I was thinking that a multi-national upbringing like the one he had would mean he fitted in neatly with her life. Not a bit of it. Did you see what he was wearing this evening?'

'Shh . . .' Mimi was desperate for the hotel staff not to hear Rory go into a great tirade against traditional Bedouin dress.

'Oh put yourself down, Mimi.' Rory wasn't having any of her PC approach. 'Has it never occurred to you that being so hyper aware of other people's sensitivities is simply patronising in the extreme? And presuming that these other people could-n't possibly defend their position, or might not like a little discussion on the relative merits of burnous versus prettily cut Yohji jackets, is worse than speaking one's mind and letting dif-ferences be differences, no?'

'Rory, you know what I mean.' Mimi gave in, too shattered to fight.

'I'm not sure I do, darling. I'm not sure I do.'

'Well I think Rory's right,' Gavin interrupted. 'We may have had our differences over the years but I must say I agree. It's very worrying the way she's behaving. And, with respect Rory, it's not just that she's been wearing the same outfit since she got here. She doesn't care what clothes Mimi puts her in, she does-n't care what I do to her hair, she couldn't care less what Frankie does to her face. If I didn't know better, I'd think she couldn't wait to escape from the camera all together. The expression on her face when she took off that magnum opus of a Chanel party dress this evening! I thought she was going to trample it under her bare feet for a minute. I was all ready to rush in and rescue the thing before she did it any permanent damage.'

'He's right.' It was Frankie's turn to speak. 'Is it safe to have her round the clothes if she's going to be like this?' George stiffened and closed his eyes in horror at the thought of such sabotage. 'I mean, she's paid to be a coat-hanger, not to suffer from hysteria; she's supposed to do what Mimi tells her, you know, not throw up in the street and make us all nervous and then rush off in the morning with a perfect stranger.'

'You are all being ridiculous.' Flash's voice came from the gloom under the acacia tree where Rory'd so recently spat.

'I beg your pardon?' Rory was indignant.

'Stupid girl's stubborn that's all. She doesn't know which side her bread's buttered on. But hey, as long as she comes up with the goods tomorrow then I don't see that there's much point in trying to stop her exploring a ghost town in the dark with that sheikh, who, and I agree with you here Rory, I wouldn't trust with a fucking lens cap. If any of you'd looked this evening you'd have seen that the pictures I took of her were better than ever before. Brilliant in fact.' Flash seemed almost awed.

'Thank you for your insight, Flash.' Mimi stood up and smoothed her creased Nicole Farhi trousers, 'And on that note, I suggest you all go and get some sleep. I'm afraid it's going to be a bumpy ride across the desert before we get to take more pictures and I don't think there's much point in any of us waiting up for Pandora, do you?' Rory shook his head, resigned, depressed and burning inside with a slow fire of self-righteous anger.

Pictikhov was in his Aladdin's cave counting out his land-mines. He had four men with him, having left one guarding the garage and one his communications room.

'If I'd brought more men with me you know, I'd have happily strung you up with some of this razor wire, one by one. How could you have let those Arabs get away?' No one dared answer. No one took responsibility. Pictikhov stormed about the cavern three stories under the desert floor. Icy cold and pitch black in the corners where the strings of naked bulbs didn't shine, the cavern rang with his fury. 'For God's sake, they're Arabs, desert nomads, about as threatening as a fly and with half the intelligence.' He grabbed one of his men by the neck and began to squeeze. The man didn't fight back, not even when his eyes began to bulge and his face went purple with dammed blood. Pictikhov dropped the man and marched back, following the string of lights, to his office at the centre of the warren of underground caves. He sat down, slung his feet onto his desk and lit a cheroot. His men were ranged before him. He waved all but one away.

'How soon can we get them all here?' he asked.

'According to the brother the sheikh arrives at the fair tomorrow night.'

'So then bring them to me.'

'How?'

'Fetch them.'

'They'll be surrounded by people all the time.'

'I don't care. Lure them. I want them all here, the ones that escaped, the sheikh and his brother, the girl maybe, and specially that lying Ivan Ivanovitch so that I can deal with them personally. Do you understand' The catacombs rang with the echoes of Pictikhov's fury. 'I will not have my ownership of this place questioned. It is mine and it will stay that way, whatever I have to do to protect it.'

'Sir!'

'They're really cross with you.' Blissfully ignorant of the fate Pictikhov had planned for him, Faisal held Pandora's hand as she climbed down the steps over Zenobia's bath and crossed the road with him to the theatre, where Said and some friends were gossiping while stewing tea in a burnt kettle which bubbled over a tiny fire.

'I know. They hate it that I'm having a good time and they're not. They can't imagine what there is to enjoy here. And even if there isn't anything for them to enjoy they're much too cool to just forget about it and get on with the trip in case maybe, inadvertently, they might find they were having a good time in spite of themselves. I can't be horrible to them. It's easier to humour them and try not to irritate them too much by shoving my love of this place into their faces and making them feel even more inadequate.'

'You do have the most bizarre way of being over-confident one minute and convinced you're right about everything and then letting everyone else get away with murder in case you're proven wrong and throwing up in the street next.'

'It's called hedging your bets.'

'It's called not trusting your judgement. You can see what's out there, what's over the sill of the door to your silken prison, but you daren't jump free.'

'Maybe I need something to jump for.'

'Frightened of the void, eh?'

'Aren't you?'

'But it isn't a void. Look, the earth's solid.' Faisal stamped on the step where he sat.

'That's not earth, that's marble.'

'You're picking nits.'

'So? How can you lecture me about not jumping into the void when you're just using this trip as a massive excuse to avoid all the devils which are crowding at your door and hammering to get in?' Faisal raised his hands in surrender. 'Don't be like that. You're the one who insisted on breaking the agreement we made about not mentioning touchy subjects.' Pandora was indignant.

'No I didn't. Those so-called friends of yours did that while we had dinner. From what you say hadn't you better have a nervous breakdown about your hair or something tomorrow to make them all feel better?'

'No point. We're spending the day in open-topped jeeps going to your camel fair and then there's no washing water there. They'll be too busy freaking out themselves to notice anything I might get up to.'

'You know them too well.'

Pandora held out her glass for more tea. Said leered at her as he poured. She leered back and he blushed.

'No, I won't jeopardise my trip to your camel fair by doing

222

the slightest thing to give them an excuse to go home. And the photographs will be magnificent. And we'll all be rich, famous, and live happily ever after.'

'In fairy tale Manhattan!'

'Why not?'

'Not much of a fairy tale.'

'Lots of fairy tales happen in New York.'

'You mean you really are going to just peer over the threshold and then lock yourself into your jewelled prison again?'

'No. I might make an educated choice to stay there though.'

'I'm not convinced.'

'What do you want, Faisal? Do you want me to give it all up and stay here with you?'

'Now you really have missed the point. I don't want you to do anything for me. I want you to do something for you.'

Pandora stared into the shadows from the fire which danced against the carved backdrop of Zenobia's stage and drank her tea. Faisal passed her a cigarette and wondered if he'd gone too far. She shivered. Faisal took her glass and passed it to Said.

'Come on,' he said. 'It's really late. And we do have a seriously early start. I'll take you back. You'd better get some sleep.'

Pandora looked up at Faisal, her eyes glistening. 'If I do jump, will you hold my hand and jump with me?'

'You've got to do it on your own, Pandora.'

'Help!'

Faisal took her hand and led her back across the ruins. Their path was lit by the benevolent moon. Pandora looked up and stared at it.

'It looks as if it's going to burst a bit, doesn't it?'

'It is. Tomorrow.'

'How do you know about the moon?'

''Cos that's when the fair starts.' He laughed. 'I can't wait.'

Chapter 13

DAGGER points of light broke through the underskirts of Ali's tent to pierce Ivan's veined and blotchy eyelids. He screamed and woke Ali, who sat up, reached for something to use as a weapon and found only his own ceremonial dagger which was as blunt as a cake-slice and not nearly so useful.

'What?' Ali was on his feet, crouching low, circling for danger. Ivan groaned. 'What?' Ali insisted in a stage whisper.

'I don't know why you're whispering loud enough to wake the dead.' Ivan covered his eyes with his sweaty suit jacket and lay flat on his back, the great mound of his stomach making him look like a cartoon snake who'd swallowed a horse, only lumpier. Ali slumped onto the floor, holding his dagger like a fan and waving it around ineffectually as if it might actually cool him.

'Don't ever do that again,' he said.

'What did I do? I didn't do anything. I don't know what made you decide that this should be the day to take up prancing around like some kind of dwarfish ballerina with a knife in your hand. It's nothing to do with me.'

'You screamed.'

'Screamed! You don't know what a scream sounds like.'

'You did. You screamed like you'd been stabbed in the back.'

'If I'd been stabbed in the back I'd more likely have gurgled as the blood from my punctured arteries flooded my lungs and drowned me.'

'Do you have to be so specific?'

'Do you have to speak at all? Shut up and bugger off or . . .' Ivan heaved himself onto his side. 'Why didn't you bring in proper mattresses, and more of them, to make me more comfortable?'

With an expression like that of a beast who'd been kept awake by a pea, he sat up only to be deafened by the sounds of the camp waking up around him. Nearby a camel roared as it was forced to its feet. Ivan cradled his head in his hands, smoothing back the oily strands of his coiffure.

'Coffee,' he said, and then jumped visibly as the satellite phone beside him burst into life. Incongruous among the larger satellites at the fair which the Bedouin campers used to fuel their television sets, Ivan's Inmarsat equipment was altogether too small, too shiny; there was no sign of coat-hanger engineering to take away from its evident efficiency, and the volume was turned up high. 'Leave me alone,' he groaned but answered it anyway. It was Pictikhov with instructions of which Ivan took haphazard note.

Pandora, Faisal, Rory and Said rode in the stolen Russian jeep at the front of the fashion cavalcade making its way across the sand. The sun was already high in front of them and Palmyra far behind; the shady groves of date palms and the relative comfort of the Queen Zenobia Hotel now memories to dream of in the burning days ahead. Pandora was loving the drive; she'd smothered herself in a thick layer of Clarins factor 35 and now she turned her face to the sun and worshipped it, spreading her arms wide to catch the wind as they passed. She felt as if she were flying.

Rory, on the other hand, was not having such a good time. His travelling companions were either practising selective deafness when they ignored his complaints or they really couldn't hear him above the roar of the jeep as it sped over the sand leaving wide arcs behind it in the burnt yellow of the desert floor. Rory's discomforts were as follows: sitting on a bench facing the collection of water and petrol cans which littered the floor of the back of the truck made him feel sick; there was no shade, and in spite of having remembered, like Pandora, to cover his face with total sun block, he was convinced he was burning; the water in the bottle he'd been given to drink – and informed that he should have finished by the time they arrived at the camel fair or he'd probably suffer from sunstroke – was tepid; and to add insult to injury, Pandora seemed to have gone completely mad and was exposing quantities of precious, fragile, over-insured skin to the sun in a manner that suggested she hadn't a care in the world. Didn't she remember that her skin must be pearly white for the shoot scheduled for that evening when she would be photographed with camels and draped in Faisal's recently acquired emeralds? Emeralds and burnt Pandora might be Christmasy as far as colour schemes went, but were hardly the thing for a supermodel to sport. Rory felt a little faint and dabbed at his neck with a lilac silk handkerchief which he'd doused in advance with Eau de Hadrien to remind him of Nina whenever he felt panicky.

Pandora took pity on her uncle and took his hanky from him. She soaked it from his luke warm water bottle and then tied it round his neck where the wind caught the water and cooled the feverish style director of the biggest fashion magazine in the world. Today, dressed in lightly tied at the waist linen pyjama pants, a black silk, short-sleeved, v-neck T-shirt and black patent leather Birkenstocks just like the ones George mourned in another jeep half a mile behind, Rory was perhaps a tiny bit more suitably dressed for the occasion than he had been. Forced to abandon his parasol for fear that the wind might damage its delicate tassels and the sun might burn off the painted flowers on the lining, instead he wore an old panama which Pandora had stolen from him and which he'd now, gratefully, reclaimed.

'How far?' he shouted into the wind.

'What?'

'How far?' Pandora shrugged with impressive nonchalance. Rory turned to Faisal who grinned up at him from the front seat, filled with the excitement of a man within sniffing distance of home. 'How far?' he repeated. Faisal pulled Rory down towards him.

'See those hills?' He pointed to a blurry purple mass directly under the sun in the far away distance.

'Not that far! I'm going to be sick.'

'You wait, it'll be worth the journey. I promise you, Rory, you are going to have the time of your life.'

'Oh I hope not.'

Said had been practising handbrake-turns in order that his arrival at the camel fair should suitably impress the waiting crowds. Having practically blinded a group of curious fair-goers when he came to a spectacular halt, he was already unloading when two more jeeps arrived in quick succession filled with the rest of the team shakily hugging their kit. Joey wondered whether there'd be a single unsmashed lens left for Flash's cameras. Gavin and Frankie were particularly nervous – they were going to a place where there really was no running water, no fridge, no power shower, no phone and, in spite of their many reminiscences about travails past in pursuit of their art, they were still whirled into a flat spin whenever they were forced to leave behind the comfort of their fashionable, urban lives.

Mimi, hoping her legs wouldn't give way beneath her, hung on to the side of the jeep she'd arrived in; she realised now why she'd been thrown about so much during her journey: not only were the jeep's shocks evidently shot but there was no air in the tyres to absorb the shot shocks' shocks. She smiled a little shakily and squared her shoulders to face the fray. At least she didn't look as bad as Rory who was breathing through his damp lilac hanky as if he longed for it to be doused in ether rather than Eau de Hadrien, the sharp lemony scent of which worked more like smelling salts and was therefore less useful at a time when oblivion would have been infinitely preferable to the rigours of real life.

Everyone was tense with anticipation at the idea of seeing their tents; even Pandora was convinced they'd be beyond basic and as uncomfortable as anything any of them had ever experienced.

Sweating with the effort of accommodating the expanse of his stomach, Ivan sat cross-legged on the floor of Ali's tent, his tongue sticking out as he concentrated on his e-mail. Outside he could hear the commotion caused by George directing the unpacking and Flash shouting in his macho fusspot way about the minutiae of installing his photographic equipment in his tent.

Ivan's e-mail to the catacombs read:

Message received and understood. Prepare to welcome all guests within next 24 hours. There may be added bonuses for which I shall expect extra compensation.

Pictikhov, reading this on his underground screen, roared with laughter.

'I'll give him a bonus he'll never forget,' he said, lighting a cheroot and leaning back in his campaign chair. He had spent the morning counting his treasure while his office was set up to his satisfaction and now there was nothing left to do but wait. Pictikhov was a patient man, as long as he knew that he would eventually get every single thing that he wanted.

Rory surprised everyone by pronouncing that he was delighted with the tents which had been assigned to the fashion team. His relief stemmed from the fact that everyone's fears had been unfounded: no one was expected to sleep on the floor and the tents had been furnished with smart, old-fashioned camping cots, tables and chairs, mirrors, wash-stands and strings of white fairy lights which were hooked up to a generator far enough away that the sound didn't ruin the atmosphere at all. The tent floors were even furnished with antique rugs in rich Persian colours which Rory felt did everything to accentuate his and Pandora's natural colouring; they made them both look pale and interesting. He smiled for the first time since Aleppo, took Pandora and marched her proprietorially into his tent, where he promptly collapsed onto the larger of the two camp beds and let his eyes well with tears, angling himself carefully so that he was staring straight at the fairy lights in order that his misery would shine at Pandora clearly through the gloom.

'Pickle!' she said, perching on the edge of his bed and taking one of his hands in hers. 'What on earth's the matter?'

'Pass me the whisky, precious.' He reached for a ruby red tea glass which sat with others on a tray by the bed. 'It'll take the edge off this water.' Pandora passed duty-free Balvenie and looked at her uncle quizzically. He'd stopped crying in order to concentrate on the whisky for a minute. But as soon as his drink was ready, more tears welled and fell elegantly down his pale, fashionably chizzled cheeks.

'At last you notice that something's wrong,' he said, wiping his eyes before trumpeting into his by now extremely grubby silk handkerchief. Pandora fetched him a fresh one and he sighed his grateful thanks. Little vertical lines creased the space between Pandora's eyebrows.

'I've been so terribly worried.' Rory pulled himself together enough to speak.

'About what?'

'About you my darling. I can't bear it when you're unhappy.'

'I'm not unhappy.'

'Yes you are.'

'I'm not!' Pandora was indignant.

'Then tell me what that panicky, sicky, teary moment in public in Aleppo was about. I don't call that the behaviour of a happy person.' The lines between Pandora's eyebrows deepened and Rory sat up, forgetting his own tears for a moment, to smooth the lines away. 'Careful of your face, darling,' he reminded her. 'After all, you're twenty-seven, and you should remember that sooner or later the creases will come to stay and there's no need to encourage them in advance.'

'I don't mind the odd line or two.'

'Why waste money on air brushing them out all the time when you don't have to have them in the first place?'

'Can't I have just one crease in a picture? Can't I have one single laughter line, one sign that I might have some character after all?'

'So that's what all this is. Don't be silly, darling. We know you've got more character than all the other girls put together. I'm just hurt that you felt you could go off and talk to Faisal about everything and shut me out. I'm your Uncle Rory, darling, I'm the father and the mother you never had. You always tell me everything. Why go off with some stranger like that? I can't bear it when you're unhappy, and it's even worse if you go round telling everyone else why and keep me out of the loop.'

'But I'm fine. I really don't know what you're talking about. Faisal and I have some interesting chats that's all. I'm not miserable, I'm just a bit confused. And I don't see why I should force myself to be all glittery and shiny every day even when I don't feel like it just because you can't bear it if I'm not. Why should my state of mind have anything to do with what you can or can't bear? It drives me mad when you talk like that.'

'You're depressed.'

'I'm not. I'm just having a bit of a think that's all.'

'But why think when you don't need to? Look at the creases it causes!'

'Oh for God's sake you're being ridiculous. I'm twenty-seven years old. Isn't it time I learnt to think for myself? I can't be a supermodel for the rest of my life, can I? I can't rely on other people to do all my thinking for me for ever. Besides, it's suddenly occurred to me that I don't always like the decisions other people make on my behalf, and even though I've spent my life believing that you and Nina and the rest of you fashion gurus know better than me what is and isn't good for me, I think maybe it's time I learnt to make those decisions for myself. Admit it, darling, you and Nina might get run down by a bus tomorrow and then where would I be?'

'More likely to be run down by a tearaway camel out here in this God forsaken place.'

'But that's just it, Rory. That's my point. I think this desert is the most gorgeous place on earth. I mean, look at the sky, it goes all the way round the world and doesn't just stop at the New Jersey Turnpike like it does in Manhattan. I love it here. I love it because I don't matter. Nobody could care less what I do for a living or how much looking after I need on a daily basis in order to do it. I've never felt so free in my life.'

'You'll regret it back in New York when you see the old womanly lines. Believe me, precious, I've spent a lifetime trying to get rid of the marks your mother's death left on my own not unattractive face. Why do you want lines when, as you say, there's nothing happening to give them to you?'

'But—'

'No buts, my precious little darling. I think all that sun you got in the car this morning's boiled your brain a little.' Rory stroked Pandora's hair away from her face, revealing the fine fragility of her head and smiled. 'You are the only constant beauty in my life. Please let me do the worrying so that you, please, for my sake, can simply be your own, exquisite self. It's my job to see that no harm ever comes to you and it's yours to shine like a perfect diamond in the darkness all around us. Admit you have the better role in all this.'

'But not much of a choice.'

'Choice, schmoice! Does a pearl long to be an ordinary oyster for a day? I think not.'

'But—'

'I can't believe you're still butting. Now, go and rest and keep that porcelain skin out, out, out of the sun. We'll take your picture at sunset and I must go and find you a camel to pose on. Do you think there's time to get it shampooed before the shoot so the smell doesn't make you crease your nose up as well as your worried little forehead?'

Pandora gave up the fight, laughed and slapped him playfully. 'You wonder why I never come to you with my troubles! How can I when all you care about is how to shampoo a camel?'

'An important consideration, my love, don't you agree?'

Pandora kissed her uncle and smiled at him. 'Of course it's important, and I suggest you get a move on or there won't be time for Gavin to finish blow-drying the poor beast before he has to start on my hair for the shoot.'

'Oh my Lord you're right!' And Rory was up and off into the glaring, late-morning sun before Pandora had time to give in to hysterical giggles at the thought that he might seriously think that not only was there enough water and shampoo available for the purpose of coiffing a camel but that the beast would put up with it if they tried.

She retied her sarong and took Rory's abandoned panama. She stepped out, looking for trouble to occupy her until it would be time to be lovely for the camera again.

She heard Mimi and Rory setting off in search of a camel and took the diametrically opposite direction from the sound of their voices. Cutting behind the fashion team's loos and smiling at the sight of George's carefully waxed ankles showing between his out-of-date Nikes and the cuffs of immaculately pressed, iron-grey, silk Gucci pants, she slipped away from the heart of the little tent village. She tucked her sarong into her knickers and climbed a steep rise, at the top of which were a circle of flat rocks and the remains of many small fires. She perched on one of the rocks; warmed by the sun, it was like sitting on a large, flat radiator, and, resting her chin in her hands, she settled down to watch the fair below her.

'Tell me more.' Faisal, Faraj and Ahmed were inspecting the camels lined up for sale. Faisal loved the sound of the beasts roaring as they were bartered over, as if they too wanted to have a say in the discussion of their value.

'You're very relaxed,' Ahmed accused Faisal.

'With you two representing my conscience I hardly need worry, do I? You'll remind me when I have to.'

'When are you going to go and confront these Russians?' Faraj rubbed his hands in anticipation.

'All in good time. Let's wait and see if my beloved little brother makes any silly moves first, shall we? I'd like to give him the opportunity to incriminate himself properly.'

'The Russian's here in his tents. Isn't that enough?'

'Ahmed, Ali's allowed a guest. I've got about twenty.'

'He's got a satellite phone.'

'Not exactly a criminal offence. What do you think of this young man?' Faisal began a close inspection of a young bull camel with sturdy hind quarters and shortish legs which would make him a talented porter one day.

'He's no racer.'

'Oh don't sound so sulky, Ahmed. We promised to keep an eye out for camels for Said. Didn't you say Sammy was a bit like this one, Faraj?' The camel's owner bobbed forward, eyes gleaming at the thought of negotiating the sale of this camel with his sheikh.

Pandora jumped a mile when a little boy came up behind her, leading his own camel, tapped her on the shoulder and asked in Arabic if he might sit down. She nodded and watched, impressed as he couched the beast, who roared in protest, furiously grazing her leathery knees on the rough, rock-strewn ground, before availing himself of her for shade as well as a comfortable back rest. The boy grinned at Pandora, displaying two rows of perfectly shiny white teeth in a smooth, nut-brown face. His eyelashes were almost as impressive as those sported by his camel, who bared her own rather fearsome, greige teeth in turn, and growled at the supermodel. Pandora thought she was beautiful. A pale gold colour with a curly coat like fluffy astrakhan, she had double rows of eyelashes looped round huge, watery brown eyes, and her flaring nostrils were dressed in cashmere down. She may have been beautiful, but she was also evidently easily bored; having given Pandora a close inspection with eyebrows raised more expressively than either Rory's or Faisal's, she snorted once more before laying her head on the ground and sinking into heaven as her owner scratched between her ears with a stick.

The little boy pointed at himself and said his name was Attallah, and he and Pandora began the kind of strangely informative conversation that people who have no common language but are deeply curious about one another can do, using only a mixture of signing and laughter in order to communicate.

And while she and Attallah talked, thoughts of the photographs which would be taken that evening were ruthlessly banished from Pandora's mind. If she did allow herself to think about prancing about for Flash the whole idea made her feel slightly sick; so she didn't. Instead she watched the business of the camel fair, the people who couldn't care less who she was, what she represented, or who paid her millions for pretending to use their shampoo . . . Here she was happy, looking out instead of in.

Below her she could see the sheikh as he made his rounds of the camp, his progress hampered by a constantly babbling gang of small boys, who seemed to inspire in him a sort of fond distraction; they evidently loved him, running after him, tripping him up, pulling him about and dancing with him, their voices a sing-song of jokes and laughter. Pandora had expected that traditional Bedouin desert dress might look slightly out of place on the urbane, cosmopolitan Faisal; on the contrary, any touch of spoilt Eurotrash playboy that might have played over his features and lurked in his stance in jeans and Ralph Lauren shirts was banished now by his long white robes and keffiyeh.

Some time later Pandora was brought back to reality by her companion, who jabbed her in the ribs and pointed at the tents where the fashion ant army was beginning to mass. She pushed herself to her feet, slipped and scrabbled down the slope and took the shady route under guy ropes and behind tents back to where she knew the wardrobe would be set up and ready for her. It was the sound of English being spoken that stopped her in her tracks. She didn't recognise fashion-team voices; it was Ivan and Ali speaking.

''Course I'm ready. I've been ready for weeks.'

Peering through a hole in the loose weave of Ali's tent, Pandora could see Ivan examining the fine and shining lines of a pint-sized but powerful automatic pistol he was polishing. His reflection shone in it, sweaty, excited, relieved that this project was nearly over.

'What time are they expecting us?'

'First thing tomorrow.'

'And Faisal suspects nothing?'

'Who's the only person who could have given all our secrets away, Ali?'

'How could you imply I might lose faith at this late stage?

What a suggestion from the man who told the whole world what he did for a living in a certain drunken moment in Aleppo!'

'I told you, they thought I was bluffing.'

'Yeah – right.'

'And are you sure he'll take the bait?'

'Take the bait! The emeralds must be his most precious possession if he was prepared to sell his birthright for them.'

'I hope you're right.'

'Trust me, I'm his brother.'

'And tonight?'

'Piece of cake – so long as you don't get drunk and let me down.'

'Don't you—'

'Joking, Ivan, a little bluff of my own.'

'Very clever . . . I don't think.' Ivan and Ali punched each other gleefully in their excitement.

It occurred to neither of them that Pandora, returning from her afternoon with Attallah, might have overheard their conversation through the back of the tent and would have paused to listen. Too busy congratulating one another on their batch of unhatched eggs, they didn't hear her stumble over a guy rope in her haste to report back to Faisal.

'Shit!' She stopped stock still. Ivan and Ali carried on their joyful jigging. Pandora edged away.

She found Faisal at the fashion tents. She hadn't realised how quickly time had passed and they were about to send out a search party for her.

'Where the hell have you been?' Rory's voice was sharp with worry.

'Only up there.' Pandora pointed to the crest of the hill where she could see Attallah and his camel still watching the afternoon pass by. 'You would have seen me if you'd looked. Faisal . . .'

'I thought I told you to get some rest.' Rory was really angry.

'I have been resting, out of the way of your mother-hen fusspotting. Faisal . . .' Faisal was gone. 'Where is he?'

'Who cares? Time for work if you're so rested.'

'But I just overheard Ali—'

'Yes, and that Russian fellow too I expect.' Rory's hands were on his hips, his lips pursed, his right eyebrow raised to heaven. 'Honestly, Pandora, Faisal knows all about that.' Rory looked pointedly at his watch. There was no time for Pandora to go rushing after the sheikh if they were to catch the light. 'Come on. Let's get you ready. He'll be back in a minute with the emeralds.'

'Rory, I should tell him now, it might be important.'

'Look, you sit tight and let everyone make a start on you and I'll go and get him all right?'

Pandora's patience ran out. 'Don't patronise me you horrible old queen. You're just jealous that you can't be me.'

'Pandora!' Mimi was horrified. Rory stormed out, chin high, tall enough that no one could see that he was blinking back tears.

This touching little scene was watched by the rest of the team, nervously giggling behind their hands; they couldn't wait to tell *le tout* New York about Pandora losing her rag and accusing Rory, the great and good style director of the biggest fashion magazine in the world, of being a fussy old woman who wouldn't let Pandora do what she wanted because he was jealous! Pandora turned on her gawping audience.

'And I don't know what you lot think you're staring at but I suggest you get a move on and turn me into today's ideal princess before I lose patience with you too and ruin everything by riding off into the sunset on one of those lovely big camels.' She sat down hard in a tall director's chair placed in front of the hair and make-up table and ripped off her T-shirt so that when her face had been done she wouldn't smudge it; she sat, naked from the waist up, an angry Amazon, barely tamed.

The atmosphere during the preparations for that evening's shoot was predictably horrible. While Pandora sulkily submitted to Frankie's attentions, Mimi paced up and down the portable clothes rails, half her mind ticking off the things she wanted

Pandora to wear for the photographs while the other half thought seriously about whether it was time she considered a career change. George followed her, pad at the ready, bare-footed rather than embarrassingly old Nike shod, the blood running cold in his arms as it does when assistants fear that their superiors are about to lose their temper with them. Massively over-compensating for any mistakes he may have made, he started every sentence with 'sorry' which served only to push Mimi closer to the edge of the hysteria that she'd been fighting ever since she stepped off the plane from New York.

Only when she realised that she'd ticked off the same pair of Manolo Blahnik, perspex-heeled, pale-grass-green, satin sling-backs for the third time without moving on did she come to the conclusion that she was going to have to do something to clear the air. She turned and looked at the team that surrounded her: Frankie and Gavin, silent for once, hardly daring to touch Pandora in case she bit their hands off; Courteney and Joey quietly getting ready for Flash, in fear of having their heads bitten off; George, shaking with nerves, standing too close to Mimi's back; Flash pacing up and down outside the tent, great circles of sweat on the back of his sweat-stained Indiana Jones outfit; Rory, off, elsewhere, not helping. Mimi pull the shoot together. She gritted her teeth and began to speak.

'Can I have your attention everyone?' She heard her voice quaver and tried to breathe some authority into what she had to say. 'Now I know you're all really tired and I think you're doing a poptastic job in very difficult conditions.' Her eye-brows arched in amazement at her own ability to understate. She pushed the sweaty curls out of her eyes and then clenched her hands around her block to stop herself fidgeting. 'But this is the second last day, people. We shoot tonight and tomorrow morning and that's it. After that we get back in those jeeps . . .' Frankie groaned at the thought and Mimi, slowly getting into her stride, sent the make-up artist daggers. 'We get back in those jeeps, Frankie! And then we go straight back to Damascus, where we arrive late tomorrow night and then we fly home on a real-life, bona fide aeroplane with cold water, blankets, air-conditioning and air hostesses who are paid lots of money to get us anything we ask for, within reason.' Nobody laughed at Mimi's bad joke. 'We'll even have beds to sleep in because I promise to upgrade all of you to first class when we check in, no matter what the cost. I'll be the first to admit that this whole trip has been a complete nightmare and I think you've been marvellously brave. After all, what with terrible runny tummies in Damascus' – she smiled kindly at George, whose hip bones would be sticking out at an unsightly angle for some time to come since his unfortunate encounter with a street vendor's pickle, which had looked delicious, tasted even better, and practically killed him off as an unexpected bonus; 'Lost assistants in Crac des Chevaliers' – little glare at Joey; 'Plagues of insects in Aleppo' – sympathetic smile for Courteney whose bed had been infested with tiny red bugs who'd tried their best to piranha her to the bone. She'd been forced to fight them off bravely with a cigarette lighter and a torch. 'And disappearing models in Palmyra' – kind but stern look for Pandora, who knew perfectly well what Mimi was trying to do and did nothing but stick her tongue out in return rather than bite it and not say a word. Mimi's little remonstrating look turned into a more serious glare.

'I'm sorry.' Pandora seemed to have stopped sulking and was perhaps making an effort to look contrite.

'I should think so too. And don't give me that look or you'll make me laugh.' Pandora was forgiven. Mimi pulled herself up to her full height of five foot two and a half inches and smiled generously. 'I guess that what I'm trying to say is that if you'll all just pull together for twenty-four more hours then we can go back home and leave all this behind us and pretend it never happened.'

'But I've had a lovely time.'

'Oh Pandora, I love you for the way you only ever think of yourself.' Rory was back, posing at the entrance to the tent, shining with excitement, his fury with his niece apparently forgotten for the moment. 'Now then, look what I've got.

This should cheer you all up a bit.' And reaching into his pocket he produced a handful of green fire. Faisal's emeralds, which Pandora was to wear as she posed with a camel in Dior couture. Pandora gasped. She reached for them, the act instinctive rather than premeditated. Rory held them high out of her reach. 'No, no precious. You can hold them in your greedy little paws only on one condition.'

'And what's that?' Pandora's green eyes danced, reflecting the emerald lights hanging from Rory's pale white hands.

'You behave yourself!' He'd forgotten nothing.

'Beast!' Pandora leapt up, pulling away from Gavin, who held her hair in a complex knot in one hand, seconds away from pinning it into place.

'Pandora!' he groaned.

'Oh don't be such a whinge-bag.' Pandora skipped about the tent, naked but for the slip of the sarong she'd doubled about her waist, and grabbing for the emeralds.

'What did I say about behaving yourself?' Rory asked, leaping onto a chair and laughing. Mimi began to laugh too. All of a sudden Pandora stopped and stamped her foot in frustration.

'Don't laugh at me!' she cried, her mood flipping from elation to frustration.

'Put your nether lip away, Pandora, and we'll let you wear these beauties.' Rory came down from his chair and kissed her. 'But first we'd better get you dressed.'

'What about my hair?' wailed Gavin.

'It's not yours, it's mine!' Pandora answered. 'What do you think, Rory? Can't I just wear it down?' Rory rope-twisted Pandora's black mane high above her head.

'I think we need it up, up and away,' he said, 'otherwise we won't see the earrings.'

Pandora took the weight of her hair-rope into her own hands. She looked up at Gavin, who hovered, his face full of nervous anticipation, and gave him a daring grin. 'I know . . . Let's cut it all off,' she said.

'What?' There was a sharp intake of breath and general chorus of shock from around the tent.

'Cut it off!'

'We can't cut your hair. You've spent all your life growing it. You're the only person anyone knows who can sit on their hair. What are you talking about?' Mimi was horrified.

'If I'm such a stunner to look at then I can afford to lose my hair, can't I?'

'But . . .' Mimi was practically speechless. 'Everyone loves your hair. Little girls around the world are desperately growing their own in an attempt to look like you. What will you do to them after all their hard work?'

'It's not my problem if they've not got minds of their own and insist on copying someone else. Come on, Rory, agree, it'll make the shoot more amazing.' Rory simply flung his hands in the air in horror. Pandora had evidently lost her mind. 'It'll sell more copies. Everyone'll want to see what I look like with short hair.'

'They'll have seen it already in the weeklies and the dailies – all those pictures of you prancing about at the shows. Today's photographs won't hit the streets until mid-November.'

'OK then, how about I give you exclusivity and cancel all my bookings at the shows? You could even photograph me having my hair cut, crunch by crunch if you like.' She wriggled her sarong up over her breasts. 'Look, now I'm perfectly decent. Go on, Mimi. Say yes – it'll be a riot.'

'Nina'll kill me.'

'What's Nina got to do with it? It's my hair! Please, Mimi – I want to know what I look like without this veil.' She let the hair drop over her face and then tossed it back, whipping Gavin in the process. 'Surely there's more to me than my hair? Please, let there be more to me than my hair.' She turned back to Mimi and Rory, united in their determination that the hair should stay firmly attached to Pandora's head. 'I can't believe you won't let me try. None of you believe I'm worth anything without my hair. That's all you care about, not me.' She picked up a handful and looked at it, calmly reflective. She looked about for Gavin's scissors, then picked them up and stared at them for a moment. She made a few tentative snips in the air to make sure they worked. Everyone held their breath. She wasn't really going to do it, was she?

And now the scissors, razor sharp and lethal, crunched in slow motion. It took a whole minute before the great rope was separated from Pandora's head and she held it up and examined it curiously as if she'd never seen it before. She gave it to Rory who looked as if he'd been given an invaluable relic. Pandora examined herself in the mirror, her face strangely blank.

Gavin gingerly took the scissors from her. He couldn't help himself; he had to take charge of the operation. If Pandora wanted short hair at least he could make sure she had chic short.

She didn't notice Faisal come into the tent. Nobody noticed him. He leant against a corner tent pole and watched as the tension mounted with the pile of hair around Pandora's feet. Gavin gave Pandora a chin tickling bob.

'Shorter,' she demanded. Gavin cut it shorter – still girlish, feathery layers. Pandora looked at it speculatively and shook her head.

'Shorter,' she said again. So Gavin cut her hair really short. He gave her a skull-hugging crop; tiny hair, tiny fringe, immaculate on Pandora's perfectly shaped head. Only when there was no more than two inches' length at any point on her skull was Pandora finally satisfied. She sat up straight and felt her head with both hands. She looked uncertainly at her reflection in the mirror. And she smiled.

The room was silent, the assistants waiting to be told how to react, the photographer and the stylists undecided. Nobody moved until Faisal stepped forward from his gloomy corner and stood behind Pandora. He'd never touched the magnificent head of hair which until so recently had adorned the Brancusi perfect head. Now, without thinking what he was doing, he reached out to stroke the new head, shorn of all its former glory.

'Is it pretty?' she asked him.

'Never mind what it looks like – how does it feel?' Pandora blinked back tears of relief; she was light-headed with joy. And then Faisal bent and whispered in her ear, 'I think everyone's been turned to stone. If I were you I'd summon all that performance energy and put it to some use. They're not going to move a muscle till you do.'

'Oh not again.' Pandora grinned at Faisal. 'Will you stay?'

'Nope. I'm off hunting.'

'What?'

'Try the hawks out.'

'And you're leaving me here to pose with a camel?'

'Looking at the dresses they've got for you I don't think they had hunting in mind when they chose them.'

'Nor camel riding neither.'

Silhouetted against the sun, Faisal wheeled at the entrance to the tent and saluted her. Behind him Faraj waited with camels, hawks and dogs. Pandora thought she'd never seen anything so beautiful; did they really have only one more day of this? She waited, brushing off the attentions of Frankie and Gavin and George and Mimi who wanted to get on with the job in hand. Faisal mounted his camel and jog-trotted away from her; he rounded a corner in a fold in the framing hills before she finally turned back to her stylist.

'Right,' she said. 'Time to grin and bear it. What do I wear first?'

'Don't you have a preference?' Mimi asked, hoping to coax into Pandora some enthusiasm for the shoot.

'Couldn't care less.'

'How about this lovely soft green Dior?'

'Fine . . . Shit!'

'What?'

'I never told Faisal what I heard.'

'Never mind. It's too late now. You'll have to tell him later.'

'Bugger!'

Pandora stripped again, and began to get herself into a floor-length, pale-grass-green, satin-backed crêpe creation, so cut that it slunk about her finely lined figure in one long stroke. She helped herself to the emeralds which Rory was holding loosely in his hand. 'Anyone feel like doing up the clasp on this little

242

number for me?' she asked, holding the ring of stones around her neck. 'George?' She had to physically shake him out of his mesmerised state. 'And Courteney, get a move on, will you? There's sand in my slingbacks; if you want me to wear them you'd better give them a shake too.'

Pandora turned and faced the assembled throng, a clover-coloured silk-mousseline stole finishing an ensemble fit for a fairy queen.

'Ready, Flash babe? Or am I going to have to kick you into action?' He wasn't fast enough for her. 'Come on! I want to be done before Faisal gets back.'

'So, are you going to tell me what's going on?'

'What do you mean?' Pandora folded her arms tight over her chest and stuck her chin out. She and Mimi were in the wardrobe tent. The shoot was over and they were catching their breath before going to look in on the gambling in Ali's tent. Mimi sipped at a luke-warm bottle of water. She stared at her shorn-headed friend.

'We can start with the panic attack in the bazaar in Aleppo if you like, or move swiftly along to the hair-cutting incident. Whatever. I don't really care. But I'm going to need some explanations or were you planning on saving it all for Nina?'

'You're really angry.'

'Don't look so surprised. Stop playing with us, Pandora.'

'I'm not playing with you.'

'Yes you are, you're teasing us with all this panic one minute, take charge the next stuff.'

'Rory's put you up to this, hasn't he?'

'It's nothing to do with Rory.'

'What is it then?'

'Well, what are you going to tell Nina? You've lost interest in modelling, you suddenly think we're all a total bunch of time-wasters, you couldn't care less whether a sleeve is cap or long or whether the beading took a thousand man hours and every piece is a semi-precious stone or that the inspiration is pure Vionet or—'

243

'OK, you've made your point. I'm not bored of modelling.'

'You're bored of me, all of us . . . What?' Mimi was close to tears. Pandora wasn't to be so easily moved.

'No I'm not. I'm just . . . different. I'm sort of lost here.'

'You can say that again.'

'But I'm found too.'

'Ah, the born-again, new-age model – a likely concept. I can't believe this is more fun than that shoot in St Barts after the ready to wear that time. Don't you remember?'

'But all those shoots just blur into one long over-protected champagne party after a while. This is different.'

'Be careful. This is my livelihood you're slamming.'

'Mine too. I'm just not sure what I think about it all any more. Admit it, Mimi, I've been prancing about on a catwalk or in front of a camera ever since I can remember. I've never done anything else. I can't remember the last time I went somewhere where the people I was with couldn't care less who I am or what I do or who I know or whose my dress is.'

'What's so different here?'

'Faisal, and Faraj and the others. They notice I'm not your average shape but they don't really care about it. They don't treat me like a weirdo because I'm tall with camel eyelashes. That's the lovely thing about Faisal. When I'm with him I don't feel like I'm the odd one out any more. I don't feel like a freak.' Pandora sat down on her director's chair and uncrossed her arms. She took Mimi's hands in hers. 'Mimi, that panic attack in Aleppo, that was . . .' She shook her head, lost for words.

'What? What was it?'

Pandora scratched her shorn head in an effort to find words to explain how she felt. 'Maybe I woke up to the fact that I'm . . . I'm a coat-hanger . . . that's it. All I am is a coat-hanger. And I don't like it any more.' Pandora gave Mimi a wry smile. 'Don't worry, I am perfectly aware that my hands are a bit tied because, let's face it, I'm really good at being a coat-hanger and I haven't got the first idea how to do anything else.'

'But this is ridiculous. Before we left New York you were storming about furiously with a bee in your bonnet about nobody liking you for your eyelashes any more and getting all steamed up about nineteenth-century French novelists.'

'Premonition of disaster. And in the end the disaster was a good thing – I've got some perspective at last.'

'Oh great. It's that simple, is it? You leave modelling and go off and get into a little light Zola?'

'Who?'

'Never mind.'

'Don't patronise me, Mimi.'

'I'm not patronising you. He's a nineteenth-century French novelist.'

'Oh fuck French novelists. This is more . . .' Pandora waved her arms about, including the sky and the desert and the great space of it all. 'I like the size of this. I like the smell of it. I like the way I'm irrelevant and so I can just be me without offending anyone.'

'But I thought you were saying you didn't know who you were any more?'

'OK, then it lets me not know and doesn't care.'

'I'm so confused. I want to help you but I don't know what you want. What about the hair thing? Have you any idea how long it's going to take you to grow it back?'

'Who says I want to? I can't tell you how light-headed I feel without it. Who needs drugs when you can get a haircut instead? Safer, cleverer, and so fabulous. I feel like I'm flying all the time and I haven't come down yet.'

'And I'm not sure I want to be there when you do. What are you going to do when you get back to New York?'

'Who says I'm going to New York?'

'Oh Pandora . . . no.'

Late that night the heart of the camel fair beat firelit red against moonlit cool, everywhere alive with activity; dancing, drinking, gambling. Ali's tent had been transformed into a sort of desert nightclub and all the fashion team were there, drinking away the tension of the afternoon, keen to forget that they would have to go through it all again the next day. All around them low voices competed with the clackety-clack of dice and backgammon pieces. Ivan manned a makeshift bar which served nothing but arak and vodka. Khaled and Walid guarded the entrance to the tent; should there be any trouble inside or out it was their responsibility to quash it. They sat quietly, their ceremonial daggers sheathed in their belts, drinking coffee brewed on a little fire. They rose and bowed low when Faraj and Faisal at last arrived with Said, who wanted to celebrate the fact that Faisal had bought him two new camels that afternoon. Now he had a jeep and two beasts, basic equipment for a tour company; he saw himself soon becoming rich.

Pandora, curled up against a camel saddle, watched Ivan and the tent opening. She hardly touched the vodka Ivan had given her, and when Faisal entered the tent she waved at him, carefully nonchalant, in case the Russian or Ali saw her being too keen. She didn't want to give herself away. They might, after all, have heard her, or suspect her, or . . .

'Hey.' Faisal sat down beside her.

She held out her warm, half-drunk glass of vodka. 'Can I tempt you?'

He shook his head. 'I think after my last performance under the influence . . .'

Pandora laughed. 'You may have a point.'

Faisal looked around him and spied little Attallah playing an energetic and voluble game of backgammon with Joey. 'It would blow out of the window any illusions that boy may have of my being a responsible adult.'

'No windows . . .'

'Still. Nice to see Ali's got the gaming going. He's good at it. If only he'd realise it, when he does the organising he doesn't play, doesn't lose any money and makes a packet fleecing his customers. He should open a casino.'

'You sound almost fond of him.'

'Don't tell anyone.'

'He's a fool.'

'You know that, I know that, even that oily little Ivan knows that. Ali, naturally, remains sublimely ignorant of the fact.' Faisal stood up and held out his hand to Pandora. 'Come outside?'

'Yes, I wanted to tell you something.'

Tar-dipped flares lit the path that Faisal and Pandora took towards the ridge where Pandora had sat that afternoon. She followed him, picking her way behind him up the steep rise to the flat stones at the top, where they sat, with their backs to the fair, facing a night sky so velvety Pandora had to stop herself from reaching out to see if she could touch it. Instead she lay back on the still-warm stones, pillowed her head on her arms and crossed her ankles.

'It's magnificent,' she said. Far above them, the moon, full to bursting, lit the surrounding desert with a pale, pearly glow. The stars, outshone, hung back, twinkling like so many moon groupies. Faisal watched Pandora drink in the glory of the sky. She caught him looking at her.

'Penny for them?' he asked.

'I was doing that "star light, star bright" thing I used to do with Rory when I was little.'

'And what did you wish for?'

'Ah . . . that would be telling. Anyway, I can't tell you or the wish won't come true. And what were you staring at?'

'I was just wondering what happened to that girl I met at the Four Seasons.'

'Which one?'

'You. I've never met anyone who could change so much so fast and only throw up once in the gutter out of shock.'

'Am I supposed to take that as a compliment? You should count yourself lucky that I'm in much too good a mood to get all tetchy with you for that kind of comment. The moon might take umbrage and disappear.'

'Don't be offended.'

Pandora turned to lie on her side, leaning on an elbow, resting her newly shorn head in her hand. 'I'm not. I'm sorry all that lot down there are having such a horrible time. I wish they'd come and look at this and then perhaps they wouldn't mind so much that there's no air-conditioning.'

'And who needs air-conditioning on a beautiful night like this?'

'And none of them seems to have worked out that during the day you're just going to get hot so there's no point in trying to do anything about it – you'll only get hotter. Let it go and you stop over-heating and . . . I've never been so frustrated with people before.'

'No, you've never chopped off a lifetime's growth of hair before with no explanation. It's bound to be confusing for everyone concerned.'

'You do think you know me well.'

'I used to. I'll have to get to know the new shorn-headed version.'

'Is it awful?'

'Do you care?'

Pandora laughed. 'No.'

'I believe you.'

'Do you?'

'Why shouldn't I? That calculating look's disappeared from your eyes and the spoilt curl you used to have in the corner of your top lip has gone and the lines on your forehead that old Uncle Rory's so concerned about have disappeared entirely and your shoulders, which used to be superglued somewhere round your ears, have dropped about a foot.'

'My, we are observant.' Pandora sat up. Faisal breathed her in deeply; she smelt of lemons and flowers, of his garden in Damascus. Pandora could smell him too, a mixture of soap and fresh perspiration, lanolin and goat hair, a combination that would usually make her crinkle her nose in distaste, but on this occasion suddenly made her feel quite faint with desire. She shook her head and dragged herself back to reality. He'd run off as fast as his legs could carry him on meeting her dressed up to the nines in New York, he certainly wasn't going to find her attractive now when she couldn't remember when she'd last had a shower, and her hair, short or otherwise, was certainly in need of a wash. She felt filthy, grainy, dusty all over; not a sexy combination.

'So, seems we've sorted me out,' she said. 'What about you?'

'I'm not thinking about anything until after you lot go.'

'We go tomorrow, Faisal. You haven't got much time left.'

'Twenty-four hours. Until then I can just be plain old Sheikh Faisal bin Ali al Mez'al and enjoy the fun of the fair.' Turning back towards the grouped tents below them, he looked down. Pandora knew what he felt for what he saw – for the people, the camp, the hobbled camels, all fitting so neatly into this flat space between the folding hills and the oasis in the vastness of the Eastern Syrian desert.

'You're never going to put all this at risk, are you?' she said.

He shook his head. 'Nope. I'll protect it with my life if I have to.'

'Which reminds me—'

Faisal put a finger against Pandora's lips. 'Shh . . .'

He took her hand and kissed it, an action as impulsive as it was surprising, to both of them. She kissed the hand that held hers. Their eyes met and held, and the blue-black velvet of the night came close around them, wrapping them in a cocoon, protecting them from the sounds of the fair, the drums of the dancing, the clackety-clack of the backgammon, the sight of two figures stealing out from the back of Ali's tent, mounting two dark camels and beginning a wide circle of the camp, avoiding Faisal and Pandora's perch before striking out eastward, towards the Euphrates.

Chapter 14

'FAISAL! Faisal!' Faraj puffed up the slope to the little eyrie, breaking the moon-cast spell. 'Stop drooling over each other and concentrate, will you? Didn't you see them go? Where are they?' He scanned the horizon. Pandora looked up and for a moment saw nothing but a scattering of shooting stars.

'Wow!'

'Faisal! I can understand our pretty girl here being overwhelmed by her first meteor shower but you should know better.' At Faraj's insistence Faisal began to come back to earth. Pandora got there first.

'Where did who go? What are you talking about?' she asked.

'Ali and Ivan have done a runner with the jewellery.'

'You're not serious!' Pandora looked about her wildly as if a follow spot would suddenly light up the fugitives if she searched hard enough.

'You bet your life I'm serious. They waited till all the people in Ali's tent were comatose and then they picked Rory's pockets and legged it with half a million dollars' worth of emeralds. I hope you've got them insured, Faisal.' Faraj scanned the horizon once more. 'I can't believe they're off to Damascus – they've gone on camels and it's too far – and Palmyra's too obvious, we'd find them in a second. There's only one route anyway that doesn't take them through the salt lake and even Ali's not stupid enough to try that. I reckon they're off to the catacombs . . . That way.' Faraj pointed into the distance, in the direction of the slowly sinking moon.

Faisal, coming back from some far-away place where Pandora's face and the moonlight had become one interchangeable and utterly sublime thing, had to push his hair off his face and rub his eyes before he asked Faraj to repeat himself.

'Concentrate, Faisal, can't you?'

'Ivan's done a runner with Ali and the emeralds,' Pandora explained gently. 'Faraj thinks they've gone that way.'

'Well we'd better get after them.' Finally awake, Faisal was on his feet and heading down the steepest slide of the slope, slipping through the rocky scree with no thought for Pandora, Faraj, or his feet, which were cut up through his sandals as he battled to the bottom. Once there he turned to the other two making a hurried, but less precipitous descent. 'Come on!'

Pandora grabbed Faisal's hand. 'But that's what I was trying to tell you before you started getting all hypnotic. I heard Ivan and Ali talking today.'

'Very edifying for you.'

'Don't be horrible. I meant to tell you before the shoot but I got distracted . . .' She touched her hair. 'And then I wanted to tell you in Ali's tent but you dragged me out here instead.'

'Tell me what, Pandora?' Faisal pulled her along as they hurried through the tents, dodging tied-up goats and loose late-night children.

Pandora, breathless but gripped with excitement, said, 'Something about being ready and bait and bluffing and . . . Someone's expecting them.'

'A little more specific?'

'That's all it was.' They'd reached the camels. Said was there, saddling up four beasts with the help of Attallah whose camel was already prepared, dripping water skins from her saddle bags like unlikely extra breasts. Faisal raised an eyebrow at Attallah who instantly fell to his knees, begging to be allowed to go along. Faisal shrugged and made the boy's year.

'You can come, but only because your camel's in milk. And you do what you're told, OK? Your mother will have me strung up if anything happens to you.' Attallah's grin split his face in two, his smile so big his huge brown eyes all but disappeared. Faisal went from camel to camel, checking equipment. 'Come on, Pandora, think. What exactly did he say?'

Suddenly as desperate as Attallah to ride out after the

emeralds with Faisal, Pandora crossed her arms, defiant. 'I'm not telling you unless I can come too.'

'You're unsuitably dressed.'

'You're letting a five year old join in.'

'He's twelve. And he knows the desert.'

'Well I speak Russian and I bet you don't have anyone else handy who does. Give me five minutes to get suitable and then I'll tell you exactly what he said when we're under way.'

And before Faisal had a chance to reply, she was off to the fashion tents. From Rory's bag she stole his cream linen, drawstring pants and the panama; she put on a loose, cotton, long-sleeved shirt which she whipped from Mimi's luggage, tiptoeing in and out of her editor's tent trying not to wake the gently snoring figure tucked neatly in her camp bed; from her own backpack she grabbed a handful of sarongs, the ancient boiled grey Voyage cardigan, her pashmina and some sun cream; she was already wearing her battered white tennis pumps; they would have to do. She tied her belongings into a sarong-bound bundle and was back with Faisal in an instant. He'd been briefing Ahmed. Pandora spied them pointing at her from a distance; Ahmed was shaking his head vehemently and hugging his disapproval to his chest.

'Have you ever ridden a camel?' he asked Pandora, confident that this one factor might be enough to save her from joining in the raid.

'Ahmed's right,' added Faisal. 'If you're going to hold us up then I can't afford to take you along.'

'Hah!' Pandora was triumphant. 'Fortunately for you I'm a Cossack by blood. I can ride anything.' And as if she'd been doing it all her life, Pandora mounted her already moving camel like a pro, using her left foot on its neck for a leg up. 'Come on, we haven't got all night.'

Wheeling her camel round as if it were a stallion, Pandora was off towards the east before the others were even mounted. Faisal shrugged, Ahmed scowled, Faisal grinned wickedly and pushed his camel after Pandora before Ahmed could get a word in edgeways. The sky above the horizon was striped with colours; the warning lights of the encroaching dawn edged the hilly foreground in fantastic fluorescence. Pandora breathed the clean, cold air, felt her pink pashmina billow about her as her camel picked up speed, and laughed out loud, quickly, before she was moved to tears by the beauty of the place. The sand beneath her camel's feet was tarnished silver in the pre-dawn light, the desert hills surrounding the circle of Bedouin tents folded away gently, like so many huge, crumpled, linen sheets. Pandora had never felt safer nor more at home anywhere. This chase may be serious, dangerous even, but for now her only thoughts were for the freedom of the desert, the size of it, the way it let her race around upon it; her relationship with it was mutually unconditional and she loved it.

Dawn at the camel fair was just as magnificent . . . for those who saw it; those who didn't were mostly littered about the floor of the tent where Ali and Ivan had so lately run their gambling-cum-drinking den. Of the fashion team only Mimi was tucked up like a good girl in her own quarters. Long before her alarm call she woke, cosy in her camp bed which Faisal had thoughtfully had made up with linen sheets and blankets. The gentle dawn light inspired her to be up and dressed, appreciating the cool air and drinking coffee and nibbling on flat bread and cheese. She checked her watch; the others weren't due to be called for another half an hour. Deciding against taking the opportunity of a little peace and quiet to call Nina and tell her about the hairdressing disaster, Mimi climbed the rise where Pandora and Faisal had been spellbound in the night; she sat on their flat rock and watched the camel fair come to life.

Far on the other side of the tents the camels were pulling themselves to their feet assisted by hordes of chattering children, who watered them, fed them and set about preparing for another day of selling, bartering and racing. In the camp a hundred crackling fires cooked flat bread and coffee. The good smells mixed with the scent of the spiny herbs she'd trodden on as she climbed the little slope and the aroma curled round Mimi who breathed it in gratefully. She stretched her neck, pulling the tension away from her head.

Too soon she came back to reality. It was time to get them all up; they'd need to get all the photography over before ten o'clock if they were to make the most of the early-morning light, let alone make it back to Damascus before dark that evening. She forced herself to her feet, promised herself she'd never forget the sight or smells of the desert dawn, wished she'd borrowed Flash Harry's Sure Shot to preserve what she'd seen for posterity, stretched her arms high to the sky, yawned cat-wide and shook herself before scrambling back down towards the fashion tents at the bottom of the hill. For a split second she was almost sad that this was their last day in the desert and that twenty-four hours later they'd be on their way back to Manhattan, home, Nina, and the safe, familiar hysteria of the office of the biggest fashion magazine in the world.

Ducking into wardrobe first she found Joey, George and Courteney, hungover silent, but conscientious nonetheless, sorting out camel-riding clothes for Pandora to wear; Ralph Lauren wannabe eccentric English hunting clothes, so far removed from what people might actually wear when out in the mud in la Gloucestershire profonde that there was really no comparison. Mimi knew this didn't matter; she was photographing for Americans who would no more want to wear real thick thermals or antique pinks bloodied by history than they would shop at Marks and Spencer for their underwear or wear Woolworths poppit pearls, having sold the real ones to pay for a new roof for the crumbling family pile.

'Morning,' said Mimi. Her assistants looked up and nodded. Courteney rubbed her eyes and poured bitter coffee from the jug that had been left for them. 'Any sign of the rest of our jolly team?' Mimi, forcibly bright, grabbed herself more coffee, grimaced at its bitterness, and leant against the trestle table covered in all sorts of accessories, everything from riding crops to top hats with elegant little veils which had looked so lovely on Pandora when her hair had pushed them forward into a perfect rakish angle, the force of her chignon fighting for supremacy with the high satin crown of the hat. Mimi tried not to think what it would look like on her new little boy crop.

'Nope. No sign of anyone,' said George, disapproving to the last and endlessly holier than thou. 'They all got pissed over at Ali's and they're still sleeping it off on the floor.'

'Oh great.' Mimi felt her calm, dawn-inspired mood beginning to slip away. 'I hope they're not in any worse state than you two are or we won't get anything done.'

'You went to bed early.' George, undaunted, stood hands on hips, eyebrows raised in conspiratorial gossip mode. 'You should have seen them all. That Russian man poured alcohol of very dubious origin down everyone's throat as fast as he could and then fleeced them all for their dollars playing backgammon. Even Rory played and if I'm not very much mistaken I'm afraid he lost his oyster Rolex.'

'Shit!'

'Do you want me to go and get them all?' George asked, zeal for the task ahead glittering in his eyes. 'I'll wake them up all right.'

'No. No, George. Thank you. I think you might be a bit too enthusiastic for them. I'll go. You two ready otherwise?'

'More or less. Can I go back to bed till we start?' Courteney rubbed her eyes.

'No, darling, you'd better guard your precious charges now they're out.' Mimi was referring to the clothes. 'But I won't tell Nina if you sit down and put your feet up for a minute or two.'

'Mimi, you're the best boss in the world.' Courteney sank into Pandora's director's chair, her eyes already shut, and swung her feet onto the accessories table. Mimi marched over the empty space between the tents to Ali's headquarters, her face set like that of a housemistress about to break up an illicit schoolgirl party.

Inside she tripped over Rory first. His howl of pain from being kicked in the solar plexus so early in the morning was cut short as his over-indulgence in rough arak hit his head. He looked for the time on his finely curved left wrist and memories

255

of the evening began to flood back. He pointed woeful eyes at Mimi.

'I lost my watch,' he said.

'More fool you, Eeyore,' she replied, looking around the tent, counting up the fashion figures.

'What happened to the fear and respect with which you used to treat me?' Rory moaned.

'At the moment you are in no fit state to be either feared or respected, sweetling. Oh no . . .' In a far corner Mimi saw Frankie and Gavin, lying side by side, sleeping peacefully, like an old married couple effigied in a church. In the middle of the tent Flash Harry lay sprawled, a beached whale of a man, the expanse of his livery stomach bursting out from his safari shirt and gleaming pink in the early-morning light.

'Where's Pandora?' Mimi asked nobody in particular. Rory sat up, holding his head gingerly, as if it might break if it were moved too quickly.

'Pandora?'

'Yes, darling, your niece, the star of this show, the girl with no hair? Remember?'

'She was here,' he said. 'No she wasn't. I saw her sneak off into the night with that rogue of a sheikh. I expect you'll find her warm and cosy in his arms. It was only a matter of time for those two, don't you think?' Rory stood up, using the swaying sides of the tent for not very reliable support. 'What do you think the chances of a Bloody Mary are around here at this time of the morning?'

'Rory!'

'Don't look so shocked, my dear. I may no longer be a coke head but that doesn't mean I've given up the demon drink too.'

'I can see that.' Mimi did an about turn. 'Right, well, for lack of a Bloody Mary, can you get this lot up and moving and I'll go and see if I can't rustle up Pandora?'

'Oh you can be so masterful sometimes.'

'Only when the people who are supposed to master me are in no fit state to do it themselves.'

'Ouch! We are sharp this morning.'

'Well, I just thought that after my uplifting little pep talk last evening everyone would have got a sensible early night, would be raring to go this morning and then we could be back in Damascus in time maybe to catch an earlier flight. I'm not sure why I bothered now. I've obviously got all the authority of a wet blanket.'

'We are keen to get home, aren't we?'

'I never thought I'd see the day when I'd actually miss the office.'

'Happens to us all sooner or later, darling; it's called growing up.'

'I don't care what it's called. I want to go home!'

'Now you're the one doing the Eeyore impression. Pecker up, pickle.'

'Only if you set me an example. I'll leave you with this lot and go and find the P word. Shame we haven't got any cold showers to put everyone under.'

'Or even a handy hose to spray them with.' Mimi kissed Rory. 'Get on with you . . .' Rory waved her out of the tent before turning to deal with his collection of bodies.

Mimi checked Pandora's tent first; the little truckle bed had certainly not been slept in. Then she looked around for the tent that seemed most likely to belong to Faisal. Next to Ali's tent was one she knew belonged to Faisal's cousin, Faraj. She couldn't knock on the door so she just ducked inside smiling nervously and hoping that Faraj would be there so she could speak English to him. She found only his ancient father entertaining Ahmed to breakfast.

'Excuse me,' she said.

'Welcome,' answered the old man. 'Sit down. Will you have some tea?'

'No. Thank you. I was simply wondering which tent belonged to the sheikh?'

'The one next door to this one. You will recognise it in its lack of decoration. He has, as you may have noticed, rather ascetic tastes.'

'Thank you,' said Mimi, turning to go.

'But you won't find him there.' Ahmed smiled helpfully.

'Oh? Is he out with the camels?'

Abdullah laughed. 'Sort of. He's gone on a good old-fashioned raid. If only I were younger and my hips were up to a day or two's riding I'd have gone with him. But alas, no amount of oiling will get me on a camel again.' He lifted opaque orbs to Mimi. 'And my eyes aren't what they used to be. I've gone soft in my old age.' Mimi didn't have time to listen to Abdullah reminiscing all morning about his past life as a raider.

'Where? What's he gone to rescue?' she interrupted.

'Do you not know?'

'No.'

'I think you'd better sit down and I will get you some tea.' Ahmed patted the rug beside him and Abdullah clapped his hands for service.

Her camel, a fine pale female, bred for racing like the camels of the others, covered the miles at a smooth jog-trot and Pandora sat proud, cross-legged, like her Bedouin companions, her balance perfect, her back straight, her head held high, her eyes narrowed against the glaring, rising sun. She didn't feel the heat, nor the stress, or wonder how the adventure would turn out. She gave herself over to pure enjoyment of the moment. And Faisal watched her ride, eager, controlled, happy and he saw in her himself. Her natural courage screwed into place his own determination to save the desert from the results of his own thoughtless greed. He took a deep breath, sat up high in his saddle, whipped his camel into a gallop and threw his head back in pure excitement as he and Pandora raced across the sands.

'What?'

'Where?'

'With who?'

'Why?'

'I don't know. All I do know is that Faisal's brother and that Russian man who was running the bar last night have gone off somewhere and that Pandora and Faisal and Faraj have gone after them. We're presuming that the emeralds that were stolen from Rory last night are with Ali and the Russian.' Mimi forbore to mention that the emeralds had been stolen while Rory was too drunk to notice; he might have lost the right to be treated with fear and respect in private but he was still her superior and she would never do anything to harm his reputation in public, especially with Gavin there to spread every single word when they got back to Manhattan. 'I don't know which direction they've gone in, how far they'll have got or when they'll be back.' Mimi sat on the floor of the wardrobe tent, her head in her hands, trying to explain to the rest of the fashion team what had happened to their star performer; she prayed that someone would come forward with a brilliant idea.

'I take it we won't be going home this evening then?' Gavin and Frankie sat together, holding hands, faces filled with the tragedy of having to spend another night in the desert.

'How can you be so selfish?' Rory snapped at them through his hangover. 'My niece, my Pandora, the light of my life has disappeared into the wide blue yonder and all you two can worry about is missing your flights! I'm horrified!'

'Oh hark at her! Who let the emeralds go in the first place?' Gavin's highly coloured cheeks wobbled in indignation.

'Please, you two, don't fight. We've got an emergency on our hands. Blaming each other isn't going to do any good. We've got to work out what to do now, not fuss over whose fault all this might be.' In Mimi's voice was a desperate, last ditch appeal for everyone to keep calm; it worked, for a second.

'The only thing I know for certain is that you're going to have to call Nina and tell her. She might get the National Guard out looking for them or something.' Rory's face was vaguely hopeful.

'More like get onto the insurance people.' George was sensible to the last.

'Oh God.' Rory began to howl; so much for calm.

'Right.' Flash Harry, beating down his hangover with a third litre of weak American coffee which he'd made from a secret supply concealed in one of his bags, began to pace up and down one end of the tent. 'It is evidently time that I took charge.'

'What?' Mimi looked up in amazement.

'You may not realise this,' he said with all the self-importance of a prize pig, 'but I am, actually, not only an expert tracker, but a gifted and experienced negotiator in the realm of getting hostages released.'

'If you don't mind my asking . . .' Rory was so shocked by this pronouncement that he stopped wailing and started snapping at Flash's self-importance like a jack russell who'd cornered a prize pig. 'Where exactly does this suddenly useful experience come from? Should we call now for references? Who, precisely, do you imagine to have kidnapped Pandora? Tracking!?!? Have you entirely lost your mind?'

'There's no need to be belligerent.' Flash was offended.

'Such a long word from one so pear-shaped.' Rory didn't back down an inch.

'Well, if you don't want any help I won't give you any. But I'm too much of a man to stand back and ignore cries for help from a maiden in distress. For Pandora's sake I will go in search of her. And I hope you all get sun stroke while I'm away.'

'How are you planning on going on this mission?'

'I'll requisition one of those jeeps.'

'Oh, yes, and a driver too I suppose?'

'I'll take an Arab boy with me to help dig me out of sand dunes should the need arise, yes. But I will do the driving.'

'Because you happen to have a handy qualification in wadi bashing, is that it?'

'How difficult can it be?'

'Hah!' Rory threw his fist in the air in a victory salute. 'You haven't the first idea what you're talking about, have you? You couldn't track an elephant in a small, muddy field. You've no more idea what's happened to Pandora than any of us. And she's not been kidnapped; she's gone with Faisal because she wants to. And you can try and persuade her she'd rather be with you till you're blue in the face but I can tell you now you'll be wasting your breath. You're just grasping at the opportunity to play hero 'cos you fancy the pants off her and you're under the sad delusion that misplaced heroics would be just the thing to consolidate your so-far unsuccessful seduction of her. This isn't a John Buchan adventure, Peaches,' he carried on. 'This is real life. And I should shut up about little Arab boys if I were you, you patronising creep, or you might find yourself with a knife in your back before you've had a chance to set out on your rescue mission.' Rory's eyes narrowed and he paused for breath.

'Well . . .'

'Right.' It was Rory's turn to stand up and start pacing at the opposite end of the tent. 'Here's what we're really going to do.'

'Got her!' George interrupted, waving the handset of the satellite phone about frantically.

'Who?' Mimi was confused.

'Nina of course . . . Here she is.' George passed the phone to Mimi, whose blood ran cold and who managed to stop herself from being sick only by hugging her stomach tight with her free arm.

'Down.' Faisal slipped down his camel's neck and handed the head rope to Attallah, who subsequently took charge of Faraj, Said and Pandora's animals as they slid down their necks too before crawling, commando-style, towards the edge of a sharp ridge. Pandora knew that this would be a bad time to ask what was going on, so she kept her head down, peered gingerly over the edge and waited to be told what to look at. Faisal pointed. Far over the plain she saw a dot. She squinted and looked harder; the dot grew into a man . . .

'It's Ivan,' she said, forgetting in her excitement that she ought not to speak.

'Shhh.'

'Why?' she whispered. 'There's only him.' She knew she should keep her voice down but didn't like being told what to do. Besides, he seemed to be miles away.

'He might be a plant,' whispered Faisal.

'What do you mean?'

'You know, a plant!'

261

'Oh a plant! Sorry, I couldn't see his leaves from here. I'll keep my mouth shut.' Nerves turned a stupid joke into something killingly funny. Faisal tried not to laugh and failed.

'Odd sort of plant.' He spluttered, knocking his head on a piece of stone, which he then watched, horrified, as it rolled down the side of the hill beginning a small avalanche. They might as well have stood up and waved. Ivan, far in the distance, looked up at them, his face gleaming in the mid-morning sun. He began to run towards them, wobbling on his fat little legs. Flash wasn't the only person looking like a prize pig that morning.

'Now look where your juvenile sense of humour's got us.' Faraj was furious; Faisal and Pandora were gigglingly contrite.

They waited as the rolling Russian slowly stumbled towards them. Eventually he stood below, panting fit to burst, his whole head purple with exertion. Pandora peered over the edge. He saw her.

'Pandora! My love, my countrywoman, the answer to all my dreams, help me.' She turned to Faisal, eyebrows raised like question marks.

'Leave this to me,' he said, inching a pistol from his belt, a sharp, silver beauty of a machine, at the sight of which Pandora felt marginally more secure. She grinned at him.

'Go soldier,' she said. Faisal raised himself a little above the top of the cliff, letting Ivan see the gun. Ivan stopped short, raising his hands like a stick-up victim in an unlikely eastern Western.

'I come in peace,' he said.

'That's a crap line.' It was Faraj's turn to give into nervous laughter.

'Shh . . . We've got to frighten him.' Faisal leant over the edge so he could see Ivan clearly. 'How did you get here?' he shouted to Ivan who was frightened enough already, shaking in his unsuitable crêpe-soled loafers, which were threatening to melt in the rising desert heat.

'I was abandoned.'

'Who by?'

'Who've you got up there with you?' shouted Ivan. 'Can I come up and join you? I'm unarmed. Do you have any water? I thought I was going to die out here.' So saying he began to climb up the little hill, stumbling to keep his balance, his hands held high.

He reached the top and collapsed, writhing.

'Give me water,' he moaned.

'Keep your hands where I can see them and stop being so melodramatic.' Ivan's hands came up again, Faisal's pistol was trained on the fat man's heart. 'Get him some water, Faraj.'

'You are a good man, a credit to your creed.'

'Oh shut up.' Faisal's patience was wearing thin. 'Where are the others?'

'What others?'

'My brother for one.'

'They took him.'

'Who took him? Where to?'

'My so-called colleagues. They took him to their camp.'

'Faraj, you were right. How far's the camp from here?'

'Another thirty k's. We're about halfway.'

'Right let's go. Thanks for the information, Ivan. You can stay here. I saw some hungry vultures earlier. I expect they'll be grateful for the gift of you.'

'You can't leave him here to die!' Pandora was horrified.

'Why not? He would have died anyway. If we'd passed by a hundred yards to the north we wouldn't have seen him.' Pandora's face pleaded with Faisal.

'Search him.' Faisal directed Faraj who, with distaste written all over his fastidious face, began to go through the Russian's pockets and check him for weapons, jewellery . . .

'You can't really mean to leave him here.' Pandora stood with her hands on her hips determined that on no account should Ivan be left behind. 'That would be murder!'

'Of course I'm leaving him. Why should we take another drain on our water? If we miss the landmarks we might be days finding the caves. We can't afford to have another hanger-on to slow us down.'

'Liar. You told me you've been to this place millions of times and Faraj was there only last week, and even if you hadn't been before, with you and Faraj to get us there we'd be no more likely to miss the caves than we are the sunset. You can't leave him behind. I won't have it.' Habit made her stamp her foot. Faisal raised a single eyebrow and folded his arms in stubborn refusal to give in. Pandora mirrored his actions and snorted too. 'Sorry,' she said. 'But I mean it. Either he comes with us or I stay with him to die.'

'Now look who's being melodramatic.' Faraj wasn't impressed.

'You'd go that far to avoid having your picture taken again?' Faisal's voice was full of sarcasm.

'He's clean.' Faraj stood up and kicked the prostrate Ivan for no reason other than that he thought he deserved it and to remind him who was boss; he hadn't noticed the tiny transmitter bleeping his position to Pictikhov from behind a shirt button.

'You sure?'

'I can't find anything. You look as if you don't trust me.'

'All right, I believe you. Attallah.' The boy appeared, pulling the camels; he was wide-eyed with excitement at being allowed to join in this real-life raid. Ivan cowered at their roaring discontent.

'Where will he ride?' asked Pandora.

'With Said.' Faisal's face was hard. Ivan was helped up onto Said's camel. It wouldn't be a comfortable ride for either of them, but Ivan deserved a little discomfort for causing all this trouble in the first place and Said was a stoical sort. Faisal mounted his own camel and turned to Ivan. 'Try anything and I'll kill you. Do you understand?'

'Yes.'

'Said, you're in charge.'

'Thanks a bunch.' Said bared his teeth at Ivan, who shivered in spite of the heat and then, disingenuous to the last, asked, 'How are we going to find the place where my colleagues are camped?'

'We know the way.'

'You do?' Ivan feigned surprise.

'Shut up Ivan and thank your lucky stars I'm not leaving you behind.'

'I do . . . I do.'

'Nina, I'm going to pass you Ahmed who's Faisal's secretary. He'll tell you what he knows and then I'll call you back when we've made a plan.'

'You bloody well won't call me back.' Far away in New York, Nina's voice crackled with impatience as she paced her cool grey office, ignoring her assistant who was trying to press upon her a small glass of brandy which she repeatedly pushed away. 'Keep the line open. I want to hear what's going on over there. Hurry up and pass me this Ahmed person then. Come on, quick!'

Mimi gave the handset to Ahmed, smiling apologies for Nina's understandably black mood.

'Hello?' Ahmed was suitably deferential.

'What the fuck's going on?' Nina screamed unchicly from the other side of the Atlantic.

Ahmed's face remained impassive. He even managed a smile. 'Please don't worry. Your Pandora couldn't be in safer hands.'

'You and I obviously have different ideas about the meaning of the word "safe".' Nina's voice was acid.

'She has gone with the sheikh and his cousin. I can personally vouch for them. You know Faisal, you know he will not put her in any danger. And with his cousin . . . there are no two better gunmen, trackers, or more proficient desert travellers than these two men.'

'Gunmen! My, I am relieved!'

'Madam.' Ahmed had had enough of Nina's hysteria. 'This is no time to panic. I suggest that you leave the arrangements for the recovery to me. I may not be a desert Bedouin but I'll be happy to accompany your friends in a jeep and follow the sheikh as far as they go. I simply hope that our actions are not too precipitous and that we don't' – he stopped and thought for a moment – 'blow their cover, I think is the term you Americans might use.'

'I'm not an American.'

'No? I am surprised. If you were as English as you sound then I would have expected a little more sang-froid from you, madam.'

Nina took a deep breath. She took a gulp of the brandy; perhaps Ahmed had a point.

Pictikhov lit a celebratory cheroot and then thought to offer Ali one; Ali refused. The heart of the catacombs had been transformed into campaign headquarters; Ali sat now in an office furnished with every comfort that might be required by this Russian mafia boss on the move, including a computer which currently featured a map of the desert being crossed by a little flashing red light; Pictikhov pointed at it with a cane which he affected as a sort of military accessory.

'Look at your brother. Is he always this easy to manipulate? So far he's followed the lure, taken the bait and now all we have to do is wait for him to walk into the trap. You look a little pale, Ali. Perhaps I could get you something to calm your nerves?'

Abdullah and Ahmed huddled in Abdullah's tent.

'We can't let them go.' Ahmed was frantic.

'Why not?'

'Have you seen them?'

'No.' Abdullah pointed at the opaque orbs of his eyes.

'Of course. I apologise.'

'I don't mind. Why can't they go? Explain to me.'

'They are completely unsuited to desert travel. I'm surprised they've survived their journey here. They'd die if they went to the Devil's Kitchen.'

'The girl went.'

'The girl's different. And even she shouldn't have been allowed to go. She's turned Faisal's head and he'll do anything for her.'

'Really?'

'Abdullah, this is not the time to speculate about the love life of our sheikh. We've got to stop those lunatics getting into jeeps and driving off into the wilderness and dying of sunstroke miles from anywhere.'

'Calm down, Ahmed. I'd never have taken you for such a panicker. I thought you were more of a stoic. We'll just use delaying tactics.'

'What?'

'Take all morning to find suitable jeeps, take all afternoon to fill them with petrol, refuse to drive in the dark, find they've been unpacked during the night tomorrow. Faisal and the others will be back before they've had a chance to leave.'

'You're a genius.'

'My pleasure.'

'We might have one problem.'

'What's that?'

'They're all fighting over who should be boss of this. I suggest I take charge of the tall dark one who shrieks all the time. You can have the one in the peculiar waistcoat who swaggers a lot.'

'Which one of us has the short straw here?'

'I think you'll find they're as dreadful as each other.'

'What about the nice girl?'

'Mimi? She'll flit between the two. She'll be all right. She's actually no fool. It might be worth taking her into our confidence.'

'Now?'

'No, let's see how we go. We might need her later.'

'Stop here.' Said and Faraj recognised the place where they'd camped before and slipped off their camels, dropping silently to the ground. Only Ivan, camel sore and moaning gently, made any sound. Even the animals, perhaps sensing the solemnity of the occasion, were couched without complaint, and laid their weary heads flat upon the ground, asleep almost before they'd had their saddles removed. Faisal, Faraj, Said and Pandora walked the last mile or so, binoculars at the ready, to get a look at the Russians' camp before the remains of the sunlight left them in moonlit darkness. Attallah, armed with a pistol and a dagger, proud as punch and twice as jumpy, guarded the camels and the trussed-up Ivan and kept an eye out for patrolling Russians, ready with a hawk's cry should the others need warning.

'Still can't see anything.' This from Faraj, peering through binoculars at the bare nakedness of the basalt blocks which paved the great expanse of desert far below them.

'What do we do now?'

'Shhhh!' Faraj and Faisal turned on Pandora for speaking at all.

'Well, if you two are going to get all "women should be seen and not heard" on me I'll go and check on Attallah,' she said, standing up, forgetting she might be seen, and finding herself being yanked roughly back to the ground by Faisal and Faraj, furious that she should put them at risk in this way.

'There's nobody down there. They've all gone to ground. What are you hiding from? Look there's nothing there!'

'Just keep down and shut up, all right?' Faraj was losing patience; he thought of Pandora as a dilettante adventurer.

'Stop arguing you two. Pandora, why don't you go back? You're right, there's nothing much to see here but I'd like to have a look anyway.' Faisal tried to be diplomatic.

'I can't go on my own. It's miles . . . I'll get lost.'

'Then please . . .' said Faisal with a friendly flash of teeth, 'be quiet.'

'Fine. But I was only trying to help.'

'I know.'

'So, what do we do now?' whispered Faraj, who took the binoculars back from Faisal and looked at the empty space before them.

'We'll raid them in the morning.'

'Raid!' Pandora squeaked before clamping her own hand over her mouth in order to prevent herself making any more noise.

'Yeah . . . We'll take them by surprise.' Faisal turned to

Faraj and laughed. 'Don't look so panicky. You were the one who wanted to go raiding! I know you got lost the other day, but you'll remember your way this time. And with the three of us we'll be all right.'

'I'm not going back in there.' Said was determined.

'Then why did you come with us?' Now Faisal was stumped. 'Come on, Said, for me, for the family . . . I know you can do it. I need you. You and Faraj are the only two who know the way.'

'What about Ivan?' Faraj interrupted.

'I'll deal with him.'

'How?'

'You wait and see. Right.' Faisal began to edge his way back before standing up. 'I expect they patrol this place so now we've had a good look at nothing much let's get out of here. I want to eat, sleep and raid in the morning.'

'Are you just raiding for the emeralds?' Pandora piped up, daring to speak at last as they made their way, Indian file, back towards Attallah, Ivan and the camels.

'What do you mean?'

'You're not raiding for Ali too?'

'I'll see how I feel when I see him. I might just slit his throat for disloyalty.' Faisal unwound his keffiyeh and scratched his head. 'So much for avoiding decision-making till after you lot go.'

'You have no idea what's really at stake here, Pandora.'

'Shut up, Faraj, you'll only frighten her.'

'Don't worry about me. I'm fine. You know we were supposed to have gone today.'

'Oh no . . .'

'What?'

'They'll be beside themselves about you.'

'No they won't. They'll know I'm in safe hands. They'll have gone back to Damascus as planned, and they'll be having a nice hotel dinner somewhere and revving up for their plane home tomorrow. Mimi will have called Nina, who'll be cool as a cucumber, and they'll expect me when I turn up. They didn't

269

like my short hair anyway so it doesn't matter if they didn't take my picture today.'

'I wish I had your confidence.'

'Trust me.'

'Not much I can do now anyway.'

'Precisely. I should concentrate on the job in hand if I were you and forget I'm even here.'

'You wouldn't honestly want me to do that, would you?'

'You two!' Faraj stopped and pointed a bossy finger at Pandora and Faisal. 'I did not come all the way out here to play gooseberry while you flirt with each other. Can you just save it till we're out of here? Come on, Faisal, if we're raiding in the morning you do not need female distraction.' Faraj humphed and marched back to the camp, his back a picture of rigid fury and perhaps a tinge of envy; Pandora and Faisal, chastened, followed him in silence.

'Look, Ali. You can see them just there. And we are here.' Pictikhov proudly pointed at the screen of his Notebook. 'They haven't moved for over an hour now. Perhaps they're eating a picnic. I presume they'll attack in the morning.'

'Do you?'

'You seem very unsure of yourself, Ali. I think we should make sure they do, let's give them an added incentive.' Pictikhov waved over a couple of Action Men and began to give them orders in Russian. They nodded, clicked their heels and about turned, Kalashnikovs primed.

'What did you tell them to do?'

'Never you mind. A surprise. Now, dinner. More than a picnic for us. I hope you won't mind eating with me.'

Ali nodded shakily; he wouldn't dare refuse Pictikhov anything. The man was extraordinary, a mixture of old fashioned courtesy that meant nothing when Ali looked in his eyes, and cold steely determination. Ali found him terrifying. So together they sat down to steaming bortsch and a thick stew in which dumplings and whole stewed potatoes jostled for space with chunks of goat and massive quartered carrots. Pictikhov ate until Ali thought he must surely burst; oddly enough, his own appetite seemed to have disappeared entirely and he found he could do nothing but pick at his dinner and try not to be sick.

Attallah had built an efficient little camp; the camels circled the people, who circled a tiny, crackling fire. He cooked flat bread on a battered iron plate over the glowing embers of the fire and gave Pandora a handful of dry, sandy dates to eat with it, all of which she devoured with alacrity. After dinner they sat and watched while Attallah built up the fire and made coffee, bitter-tasting nectar to Pandora. Even the drinking water, warm, and slightly brackish from the skins where it had broiled quietly all day, tasted sweet to her that night.

Ivan had been banished and was tied to a hind leg of Faisal's camel. He'd been fed one or two dates and a mouthful of water. Pandora knew he was too faint from heat and starvation to make much of a fuss. So now she sat, cross-legged, like Scheherezade herself, and told stories to entertain the others. Faraj and Said were open-mouthed with amazement as she talked about fashion shoots, fashion shows, fashion parties, the life in which she'd played a protagonist's role, ever since she could remember. Sitting under the stars, the full moon behind her, the warmth of the fire sparkling, the friendly faces of her companions shining in front of her, Pandora couldn't remember a time she'd been happier. Faraj was smiling at her again and Faisal laughed at her stories and seemed, for the moment, to have entirely forgotten that his brother was incarcerated a few miles away with the enemy, that he was currently down half a million dollars' worth of emeralds which weren't insured to be outside his house, and that the desert he'd sold to a bunch of Georgian investors was about to be used as an arms market unless he and his motley crew of raiders could do anything about it in the morning.

'And then when I asked if anyone had seen my pants . . .' Pandora told her favourite story about the boil-washed M&S underwear and the La Perla contract.

*

271

Mimi could hear Rory's helpless bleating from where she sat with Ahmed, while he explained the situation to her.

'I'm sorry but there's no way we're allowing any of you to go to the Devil's Kitchen.'

'But why?'

'None of you have the first idea how to exist in the desert.'

'It's only sixty kilometres away — we're not asking you to take us across the Empty Quarter.'

'I wouldn't take any of you further than that hill. I don't understand why the sheikh's allowed you this far.'

'It's a free world. We could have come on our own if we'd not been invited by the sheikh.'

'With respect, the desert is not free, it comes at a high price.'

'And with respect to you, if you don't help us go and fetch Pandora out of the trouble she's got herself into then we will simply requisition some jeeps and go. And then, if it's as dangerous as you say, you'll be responsible for our deaths. Would you leave a friend alone in the desert?'

'She's not alone. She couldn't be with better people. I promise you she's safe. If all of you go haring off after her then I won't guarantee anything.'

'But—'

'The man with the waistcoat . . .'

'Flash?'

'Yes, he's dangerous, he's too busy showing off to take notice of how the ground is or where the sun is.'

'But he's not in charge, Rory is.'

'I rest my case.'

'But . . . I . . .'

'And none of you is comfortable here, you are all a little frightened here, and this camp has everything you need — water, tents, food, electricity, lavatories . . .'

'I know, but we'd manage.'

'You wouldn't. It would take only one of you to panic and the whole mission would be a disaster.'

'But I thought you'd come with us.'

'We must stay here. Abdullah's practically blind, I may look like a Bedu but I'm really as urban as you are. I come because I must, not because I want to. And the only people I'd really trust to go with you are Khaled and Walid but they must look after the camp. We have a thousand people here. I won't be responsible for the administration of the place on my own. Not even for twenty-four hours.' Mimi's face fell. 'You must let your Pandora be safe with my sheikh. They will return, I promise you.'

'How are we going to explain this to the others?'

'We thought we wouldn't. They don't really want to go. It's taken very little sabotage to make sure you didn't set off today. We can carry that on tomorrow. And the others will be back the day after. Please, be reassured.' Mimi shrugged.

'It looks as though I haven't got much choice.'

'Go and get something to eat. We will pretend to attempt to leave again in the morning.'

Mimi left the tent and Ahmed shakily lit a rare cigarette. He hoped she hadn't seen that he was no more convinced that Pandora would come back alive than she was.

Mimi wandered off, up the little hill where she'd breakfasted that morning, deep into the velvet embrace of the night. She sat facing away from the camp, waiting for her double-time beating heart to calm itself, and, resting her chin in her hands, began to examine the stars.

It was late. Attallah's little fire had died down. Faisal threw Pandora a thick camel hair cloak.

'We should get some sleep,' he said.

'I need to go and find some white heather first.' Pandora stood up and looked about her for a suitable rock behind which she could pee in privacy.

'What?'

'You know, I need a moment to myself.' She was suddenly coy. Faisal's amused expression made her feel fidgety and girlish.

'Go on then. But don't lose sight of us.'

'But . . .'

273

'It's all right. We promise not to look.' She saw Faisal's teeth gleam in the moonlight.

'Don't you laugh at me. I'm going behind that rock all right? If I'm not back in ten minutes then you can send out a search party.'

'Ten minutes? How long does it take?'

'These things can't be rushed.' And Pandora was off to the other side of her rock, fighting the acute embarrassment of having been caught short: it wasn't that she hadn't peed all day, it was just that now, under the stars, in the quiet of the night, with the tension high and the air thick enough to cut with the blade of Faisal's dagger, she wanted to be above such pedestrian needs as the desire to go to the loo. Crouching down, she stared at the sweeping breadth of the sky; she knew she'd never tire of it. She heard footsteps.

'I told you not to send a search party for ten minutes!'

Cold steel stroked the back of her neck. She hurriedly pulled up Rory's drawstring pants and turned round. 'Faisal!' She opened her mouth to scream. A hand blocked the noise a split second before it started. Russian Action Man lookalikes turned her around, away from Faisal and their cosy little camp.

'March,' said Action Man one in Russian, and, understanding not only the word but the spirit in which it was said to her, march she did.

'My name is Pictikhov. Please sit down.' Pandora blinked like a rabbit caught in the headlights in the sudden glare of this underground office. She perched, gingerly, on the edge of a Napoleonic campaign chair, a work of art in tooled leather and rosewood stamped with bees. The man in front of her leant against the matching lines of his desk, crossed his arms and narrowed his eyes at her through the smoke from his cheroot. 'You must be Miss Williams. You know your reputation for beauty does you no justice. You are . . . truly exquisite.' He cocked his head to one side and examined her, as if she were a precious *objet* which he'd recently acquired. 'What happened to your hair?' Pandora didn't answer; she simply glared at him. 'No

274

matter. It is a pleasure to welcome you here. I am fortunate to be surrounded by so many of our sheikh's valuables. Now . . . it's late.' He stepped forward and offered her his arm. 'And from what I hear you didn't sleep at all last night. Allow me to show you to your quarters. I'm afraid they're hardly the Ritz, but I'm sure you'll be more comfortable than you would have been sleeping on the ground in that ramshackle little camp that the sheikh has built. Did no one ever warn him of the dangers involved in building one's house on sand? What a shame.' Pictikhov led the way down a series of passages, lit by naked bulbs, to a hole in the ground. He indicated that Pandora should make use of a ladder which led deeper into the earth. Pandora stopped.

'You want me to go down there?'

'Please.' The Action Man guards crowded forward a little. Pictikhov barred any attempt to escape. Pandora descended and watched from below as the ladder was removed.

'Great,' she said in a voice not much stronger than a whimper.

There was gnashing and grinding of teeth all around Mimi that night: Nina swore revenge down the phone from New York if Pandora was permanently lost; Flash had yet to tire of swashbuckling about and effing and blinding and calling fire and brimstone down on Faisal; and Rory wept, convinced that he was never going to see his beloved niece again. Fortunately George seemed to be prepared to take on the role of comforting Rory, leaving Mimi free to listen to Flash as he raved throughout the night.

Chapter 15

ANOTHER dawn, the same desert; armed with little more than pistols, daggers and an impressive determination of spirit, Said, Faraj and Faisal sat looking down at the Russians' camp. It was cold in the grey first light. Faisal shivered. The desert dew, a tiny hint of moisture in the air, hung in a frail mist between them and the basalt pavement below. Faraj sniffed and wiped his nose on his sleeve. He picked a sprig of spiny silver thyme and crushed it between his fingers while he waited for Faisal to decide what to do.

Faisal's eyebrows lowered like storm clouds.

'They'll have Pandora well hidden.' He chewed his lower lip. 'I can't believe how stupid we were.' His companions waited. 'We've been well and truly had.' Faraj didn't dare argue. 'Emeralds, Ali, Pandora . . . my desert . . .'

'The situation might not be so bad.'

'Thanks for the platitude, Said.' Said shrugged.

'Security's going to be tight. They'll be ready for us.' Faraj was gloomy.

'Why don't we all state a few more obvious truths?' Faisal snapped. 'Let's just hope they take us for the fools they must have thought you were instead of the wily Bedu that we really are. Right,' Faisal stood up, unfolding his tall, angular frame. He squared his shoulders. 'Let's go.' He began to make his way down the escarpment towards the hidden entrances to the cat-acombs beneath the desert floor. 'There is only one certainty in all this: they're bound to be expecting us.'

'I thought you said we were going to sneak in and out without being noticed,' Said whispered through his exuberant moustache. 'Why don't we use the passage?'

'Why didn't you use it last time?'

'We were taken by surprise. And then we escaped in the jeeps. Besides, I'm not sure I'd have been able to find it, the place is so changed.'

'Well we can't use it this time because we need them to know we're coming. Just to make the situation a little more fantastic, we've the added bonus of a maiden in distress to rescue. We're going to have to play decoy ducks as well as knights in shining armour. The secret passage entrance is out of the question,' said Faisal through determined, gritted teeth.

'Why don't you send Said through the secret way?'

'No, he'd only pop up in the middle of the boss's office and be totally useless to us. If I remember rightly the trap door comes out into that big chamber in the middle, the one that all the passages end up leading to. They're bound to be using it for something. Besides, the trap door might be covered with furniture or something. It might be useless. We'd better go in together.'

'Fine.' Said headed out over the pavement. 'We may as well go in through the garage exit just to remind ourselves where the jeeps are in case we need to make a quick getaway.'

There was no cover. The three men walked straight over the desert floor, tense, scanning the flat ground around them for danger. They arrived at the garage entrance unchallenged. None of them believed for a moment that they hadn't been seen.

They ducked into the underground garage. The stolen jeep had been replaced. There was no sign of a guard. Faisal whispered to his companions.

'Faraj, you come with me. We'd better go and find the camp commander first. We can keep them busy for a while, I expect they're only interested in me. Said, you go off and see what you can find. Try not to get caught. If you do, play dumb. I expect we'll bump into each other later, but get as much of an idea of how to get in and out of this place as you can before they put you back in that hole they hid you in before, all right?'

Said, loyal to his sheikh and determined not to let him down in spite of his fear of ghosts, slipped away down a passage, his eyes scanning the walls for distinguishing marks and, where there weren't any, making them in Arabic with the freshly sharpened point of his old ceremonial dagger.

Faisal and Faraj crept down passages listening for Pandora, keeping an eye out for Ali, absorbing as much information as they could before their inevitable capture. They too marked the soft porous stone walls as they went, eyeing them constantly for signs they recognised from their childhood game-playing. The passages were almost dark; only the light from an occasional bulb slung at a crossroads showed Faraj and Faisal the way.

'Shh . . .' The two men stopped short; Faisal's head snapped round – voices. They couldn't understand a word, but edged forward nonetheless, listening hard, feeling their way through the gloom towards a strip of naked bulbs which hung across an opening. They peered round the corner; their eyes were met by the dangerous ends of AK47s.

Faraj smiled at the men who pointed their rifles so energetically at their chests. 'Looks like they're pleased to see us. Be nice to them. I nearly lost a tooth last time.' He raised his hands slowly. Faisal did the same. The men nodded for them to turn around. Marched briskly down the well-lit walkway, AK47s muzzling between their respective shoulder-blades, they were soon installed in the office where Pandora had been welcomed earlier. Pictikhov greeted them with a tigerly smile; his incisors gleamed. Immaculate in starched and creaking desert-storm type army fatigues, he looked like somebody Flash Harry might emulate in his dreams. He carried a revolver on each hip, a small stick tucked under an arm, and wore the shiniest black army boots that Faisal had ever seen.

He nodded to Faraj, who grimaced in reply and gave Pictikhov a finger-crunching handshake. The Russian didn't wince. He turned and shook Faisal's hand, a gentler experience. 'You must be the famous Sheikh Faisal bin Ali al Mez'al. I'm fascinated to meet you at last.'

'You should have telephoned. I'd have asked you to Damascus for a chat.'

'I was more interested to meet you here. I felt it would be easier to come to an understanding on my ground than on yours. There are too many distractions in your great city. We would have spent all our time enjoying ourselves and never managed to do any business.'

'So instead you lure me here with my brother, my emeralds, my—' Faisal stopped himself.

'Your Pandora?' sneered Pictikhov.

'In the middle of the night. You might have simply invited me.'

'Perhaps I felt you were unlikely to accept my invitation. I apologise for my rather unorthodox manner of . . . shall we say . . . tempting you here. But now you are with us I hope that our business will be concluded swiftly so that you can return to your little fair.'

'You have got Pandora?'

'My good fortune.'

'And my brother, he is here with you?'

'Ah yes, the delightful Ali. Now there's one member of your family with whom I've always seen eye to eye. I hope that after today you'll understand what I'm intending to do here as well as he does. After all, he may be charming and he may be useful but why do business with the monkey when the organ grinder's standing here before me?' Pictikhov smiled his tiger smile. 'Can I get you some tea? Coffee? I have one or two things to attend to before we come to signing any agreements. Please, make yourselves at home. I will be back with you soon.' And Pictikhov turned on his heel and was gone, leaving the Action Men guarding both entrances, facing the interior of the room.

Faisal and Faraj were left with coffee, water and warm croissants made from tinned croissant kits. Time passed. Faisal began to pace. The guards didn't take their eyes off him for a moment. He turned to one of them.

'Can we have some more coffee?' he asked in Arabic. The guard looked at him blankly. He tried the other. 'How about a proper drink? Or a brace of children to grill for our lunch?' The guard simply shrugged.

'They could be pretending,' Faraj said.

'Nope. They didn't understand you last time, did they?'

'They didn't try very hard. Besides, if you think we can use our Arabic as a secret code then you're mistaken; Ali'll understand and Pandora won't.'

'At least we can tell Said what's going on.'

'So long as he can hear us.'

'It won't be such a bad thing if Ali knows we're here. And Pandora might not get what we're saying but hopefully she'll recognise our voices and know we haven't abandoned her. And we can say anything we like to each other. You know where we are, don't you?'

'No, apart from being in Pictikhov's den.'

'You are so slow! This is where the secret passage comes out.'

'No it doesn't, that's a squa—'

'This is a square chamber. It looks different with Pictikhov's furniture in it, that's all. It's the right room; look, behind the desk, there's the carving on the wall.'

'My camel!' Faraj was delighted.

'Your very own childish artwork, Faraj.'

'But where's the trap door?'

'It must be under the desk. We'll have to be ready to get shoving when the time comes.'

'Great. Any other cunning plans?'

'Well, if we had an indiarubber ball and a trained mouse . . .'

'Don't even think about it.'

Ali turned over, muttering in his sleep. He dreamed that Ivan was taking him to the casino in Monte Carlo. Ivan was laughing, slapping him on the back, pushing him forward, telling stories of great gambles which paid off; but every time Ali turned round to look there was nothing but money. Behind him the ground fell away into a cloud of currency – American dollars, South African rand, French francs. The past was gone, drowned in cash. The casino loomed like a palace on a hill, and when he arrived Ali realised that it wasn't the casino; it was his family's house in Damascus. He peered through the low door in the wall. In the courtyard he could see Faisal surrounded by all his extended family, and to one side Flash Harry was ready with his camera. Ali was being forced over the threshold but he knew that the moment he stepped into the cool marble interior then it too would begin to dissolve as everything he'd walked on so far had dissolved behind him. And the photographer would record the moment in which Ali destroyed his family's heritage with a monstrous camera whose lens seemed to grow, coming nearer and nearer. The flash went off. Ali woke up, shouting, dripping, in a pool of sweat.

He caught his breath. He sat up. He blinked. There was Pictikhov, smoking a cheroot, sitting in a campaign chair with his legs crossed.

'Bad dream?' he asked. Ali blinked again. 'Your brother's on his way,' Pictikhov lied and knocked the ash off his cheroot onto the packed earth floor. 'So . . . Now you can decide how much of this cake you keep for yourself and how much of it you offer to him.' The mafia boss pared his fingernails thoughtfully with a blade from the Swiss Army knife which hung on a chain from his belt. 'We've got the girl, we've got the emeralds . . . but they don't really matter. The question is are you going to take this on for yourself or are you really just a mouse who'll let your brother win again?' Ali didn't answer. He stared stupidly at Pictikhov while the dream still played at the front of his mind. 'Of course, you do realise the implications of the deal I'm offering you.'

Ali shivered.

'Fratricide.' Pictikhov savoured the word.

'Don't say that.'

'I didn't think you'd be so squeamish.' Ali sat on the edge of the truckle bed, beads of perspiration decorating his upper lip and circling his hair line. His hands shook as he wiped the sweat away. Pictikhov's patience was running out.

'You understand, Ali, that I couldn't care less which one of you takes this on. Or if neither . . . although you must see that if you don't agree to my terms then empty-handed is a massive understatement when it comes to describing the state in which you won't even be able to crawl away from here.'

Ali twisted a sodden handkerchief between his hands.

Pictikhov stood up slowly. He dropped the butt of his cheroot onto the earth floor and ground it out under his mirror polished army boots. He reached into his pockets and withdrew the emeralds. The pile of fiery green stones landed on the bed beside Ali, who picked them up gingerly and held them in his hands. The light reflected from them onto his lily-livered face.

Ali looked up and saw the total absence of compassion in Pictikhov's face. And at last he understood the true implications of being involved with these particular Russians. He examined Pictikhov for signs of remorse, excitement, an emotion of any kind born of the determination to kill a man; he saw nothing. And Ali knew that he'd run out of options. He peeled his lips back into a semblance of a smile.

'I'm all yours.'

'I thought so.' Pictikhov snapped his cane against his thigh with a satisfied thwack, then he rounded the corner and was gone. Ali dropped his head into his hands. The emeralds spilt out of his palms, he was shaking uncontrollably; he scrabbled around to catch them before, like so many pieces of silver, they fell in a glittering stream onto the floor. How was he going to warn Faisal?

Said was completely lost. His exploration of the crumbling passages of the catacombs had taken him what seemed like miles underground. The only useful information he had was that the huge cave at the deepest level below the desert floor had been turned into an arsenal, a storeroom heaving with boxes stamped with skull and crossbones. Dust camouflaged, he hadn't been seen by the guards. He'd worked his way back up towards the surface, marking the walls and turnings as he went. At last he saw a light. He turned a corner and stopped, taking a step back before he could be seen. Ali sat in front of him, his head in his hands, the emeralds dangling from them like a stream of solid tears. Said removed his keffiyeh, stretched it, twisted it until it made a passable rope, and lunged at Ali, who, taken completely by surprise, found himself seconds later gagged, his hands bound behind his back, watching as Said stuffed the emeralds in his own pockets. Said then dragged the uncomplaining Ali back down the passages through which he'd travelled. Keeping an eye out for the marks he'd made on the walls, he soon had his prisoner hidden in a distant cave. Here he slammed Ali against the wall and kneed him in the groin. His prisoner fell to the floor, winded. Said hurriedly tied Ali's ankles to his wrists before he could catch his breath. Then he waited, lounging in the entrance. Ali tried to shout; he found he could hardly breathe. Eventually he looked up at Said, who smiled at him.

'You can nod your head or shake it for your answers.' Ali groaned. 'If I think you're lying I'll have some fun with this.' His dagger gleamed in the gloom. 'You do understand?' Ali nodded fiercely.

Rory and Flash sat upright and united in the front seats of the three-wheeler van Mimi had last seen waiting to leave from the little house in Palmyra.

'What are you doing?' Mimi was horrified.

'Nobody seems to take this situation seriously so we've taken things into our own hands.'

'That thing won't cross the desert!' Mimi couldn't believe they were about to set off into the wide blue yonder in this over-decorated tin pot on wheels.

'It got here from somewhere so it must.'

'But there's a track from Palmyra to here.'

'How do you know this came from Palmyra?'

'Rory, please, be sensible.'

'But—'

'Please . . .'

Mimi gave in at last and burst into loud and out-of-control tears. She knew perfectly well that neither Rory nor Flash could resist a woman in distress.

'Oh darling, I'm sorry.'

'Babe.' They were out of the van in a second.

Said crept along another passage. If Ali really had changed his mind and finally seen the error of his ways, then, according to the instructions he'd given Said, Pandora's dungeon must be nearby. Said's ears hurt from concentrated listening. He tripped in the gloom and fell.

'Ough!' He lay still, forcing himself not to make any more noise. He opened his eyes and began to feel around. He'd certainly sprained an ankle in his fall, if he hadn't broken it. He groaned quietly.

'Hey!' Pandora kicked him in the face when he came across her in the dark.

'Thank God!' he whispered in Arabic. 'Pandora, it's me, Said.'

'Help at last! I thought you were going to leave me here to rot for ever.'

'Shh . . . We've got to get out of here.'

'Where's the ladder?'

'What ladder?'

'You've fallen into a hole. We're both stuck in it if you didn't bring us something we can climb out with. Oh shit!'

'Ali didn't say anything about a ladder!'

'Ali's on our side. At last!'

'Not necessarily. He didn't tell me about the ladder. I've just walked straight into his trap.'

Pictikhov swept back into his cavernous office, wreathed in smiles and oily graciousness.

'So, down to business. Your brother may have facilitated this meeting but he can't sign the papers, can he?' He laughed and sat down behind the desk. One man brought coffee, another a pile of documents which Pictikhov began to lay out.

'I thought all our business was done. I've sold you these caves for the mineral rights. End of story. In fact, I can't think what we're doing here. Why don't you just give me Pandora, my brother and the emeralds and we'll leave you to your surveys?' Faisal stood up as if about to leave.

'If only things were that simple. No, the deal is not quite done.'

'It isn't . . . ?' Faisal sank slowly back into his chair.

'Well, thanks to the indiscretion of my associate, you know perfectly well that we haven't the slightest intention of surveying for mineral deposits.'

'You amaze me.'

'We want the catacombs for storage.'

'Spell it out Pictikhov. What kind of storage?'

'Shall we say there is a huge market for equipment which governments find it is no longer either politically expedient to supply or politically correct to demand. As a result, entrepreneurs around the world are grasping the opportunity provided by this new hole in the market.'

'Arms dealing.'

'If you must put it so bluntly.'

'And what, precisely, do you think I might like to have to do with this?'

'Well, if you'd read the small print in the contract which you signed in Manhattan the other day you'd have noticed that there were certain conditions involved in receiving the balance of the twenty million dollars.'

'My banker assured me that there was no catch to the deal.'

'My dear Faisal, just because your man Sykes wears a suit and a watch chain, that doesn't mean he's not going to be interested in a little underhand dealing himself. Besides, even if he wasn't directly involved, he's hardly likely to encourage you to turn down twenty million dollars when he's probably going to get custody of it, is he?'

'The bastard.'

'I'm afraid you've been outmanoevred.'

'Not necessarily. If you're trying to appeal to the "hard done by I'll teach them to ignore a Bedouin" side of my nature then I'm afraid you're not going to get anywhere. As far as I'm concerned I've sold you the catacombs and you still owe me sixteen million dollars for them if you're to fulfil your side of the bargain. If you don't pay up, I simply take them back.'

'And so long as you understand that the total twenty million doesn't simply buy the caves here but also your silence, your protection, your facilitating of visitors to my discreetly hidden market place, then I think we'll be able to do business.'

'And you expect me to sign more papers to that effect?'

'Of course.'

'It doesn't seem to have occurred to you that since this kind of market place is strictly illegal, not just in Syria, but according to all sorts of treaties worldwide, any documents I sign now won't even be worth the paper they're printed on?'

'Not under international law perhaps. But I think it's important that you understand how seriously I take my business, how determined I am to avoid risk, how much of yourself you lay on the line when you break these agreements.' Pictikhov's eyes were arctic cold. He stroked his cane thoughtfully. Two of his men hovered, all the more menacing for the total lack of expression in their killer faces.

'I don't have any choice, do I?'

Pictikhov shrugged and smirked. 'You shouldn't feel cornered, Faisal. Feel free. You are going to be richer than in your wildest dreams.'

'What a comforting thought.'

'And where's the harm in filling this hole in the market? If I don't somebody else will and neither of us will benefit.'

'Well in that case . . . Where do I sign?'

'What?' Faraj blanched in horror.

'Find me a pen. I'll sign. Don't look so surprised, Faraj. He's convinced me. I don't want to die, which I will obviously do if I refuse. And I love the idea of the money.'

'Good thing I cut my hair off.' Pandora was talking herself calm, pacing up and down the confined space of her prison, her hands deep in Rory's linen pockets, frowning, thinking, determined to get out of the caves alive.

'Why?' Said sat on the floor, his moustache drooping in the

gloom, his ankle throbbing. He'd felt so confident when he'd left Ali tied up, but now he was imprisoned himself he felt lost, panicky and as if he'd let Faisal down.

''Cos I'd be even bloody hotter with that extra eiderdown to deal with. Your problem, of course, is that you've an overactive imagination.' Pandora wasn't going to let Said lose heart.

'What?'

'Instead of thinking of practical ways of getting us out of here, you're simply conjuring up a series of ever worse scenarios in which you and I both die a horrible death and—'

'You don't know about the ghosts in this place.'

'You've never heard of friendly ghosts I suppose? Listen, I've been in this kind of situation before. And I escaped. And if there's one thing I remember from that experience, which, you should know, was infinitely worse than this one, it was that there's no point in panicking under any circumstances. Either you escape, or you're rescued, or you die. There aren't that many options to get excited about.' Said sighed mournfully. So much for all the markings he'd made for his escape route; he could see no way of getting out of this hole. And how were the others going to find them even if that was an option? 'In this case, of course, there's the added bonus of my Russian ancestry.' Pandora frowned, she wasn't sure exactly how her Russian blood might help, but Said didn't seem to want more details. He simply allowed Pandora's rambling to wash over him. He stared up at the hole above them, through which he could see nothing but the dimly lit roof of the upper passage. 'You see,' she obviously wasn't going to stop, 'last night I was as gibbering a wreck as you are now.'

'A gibbering what?'

'Wreck, Said. I'd forgotten that there's no point in panicking because at some point something will happen to resolve the situation one way or another. Time will always win.'

'Will it?'

'You don't sound convinced.'

Said answered her with a sarcastic swing of his eyebrows, invisible in the gloom.

*

287

Ali pulled his hands free, his wrists burning from the effort. He untied the keffiyeh Said had used to gag him and rubbed his face to encourage circulation in his numbed cheeks. He tiptoed forward and peered round the corner into the dim corridor. Seeing no one he crept on, wondering as he did so why he was moving so carefully; after all, he had a perfect right to be there, he was still a guest of Pictikhov. He kept close to the wall and carried on heading towards a brightly lit spot in the distance. Only once did he look behind him to see if he was being chased by hordes of money. Reaching his own room unchallenged, he slipped his dagger into his belt. He wished he had a gun. Then he headed back into the maze of corridors. He'd made his decision: it was time to act on it.

The ladder slipped into Pandora and Said's hole in the ground. A face peered into the gloom.

'Ali!' Pandora didn't care that he was supposedly the enemy. She would have been thrilled if it had been Pictikhov or the devil himself who'd come to save them. She scrambled up; Said followed closely behind.

'Quick. This way.' Ali led them away from the lights to a little cave where they'd be able to talk undetected.

'What are you doing?' Pandora's voice was a hoarse whisper.

'I'm saving your life,' Ali answered.

Said snorted. 'How did you escape from where I tied you up?'

'I wriggled a lot.'

'Now don't be cross, Said. You may have tied Ali up but luckily for us he managed to get away so he could save us,' said Pandora.

'Cross! He's brought us here to kill us, I can promise you that.' Said drew his dagger, grabbed Ali round his neck and squeezed.

'Don't! Ali, what's going on? Tell us quick before Said slits your throat.'

'Pictikhov's forcing us to sign the papers which will make us business partners with him.'

'What kind of business?'

'Arms dealing, drugs, anything you like. If all goes according to Pictikhov's plan this place will become a world centre for the anti-personnel mine everyone's going to have to officially get rid of.'

'But Faisal won't allow it!'

'Unless we do something to help him he hasn't got an enormous amount of choice.'

'But I thought you wanted all of this. I thought you were on the Russian's side.'

'Let's just say I changed my mind.' Ali's voice was grim. Said's grip on Ali's neck slackened slightly. 'I need the money, Pandora, but I'm not that stupid.'

'I would've thought the money he'd be offering you would be enough to pay for any amount of stupidity.'

'He doesn't just want our desert. He wants us to be involved. But I've spent enough of my life being a fall guy already. I need the money but not in return for half the international arms dealing community cutting off my extremities one by one whenever they don't get what they want from me.'

'Right.' Said let go of Ali entirely now. 'Let's go.'

'Wait, where are the emeralds?' Habit made Pandora worry about the pretty things first. She kicked herself. 'Who cares?'

'I've got them.' Said was itching now to get them all out of the catacombs. 'Which way, Ali?' As far as he was concerned he'd achieved what he'd come for: saving Pandora, the emeralds and Ali as a bonus.

'Don't we need a plan?'

They started at the garage.

'Ough!' The single guard was down before he had the safety catch off his rifle. A minute later he was stripped of his weapons and his USSR army surplus outfit and tied up in Said's cloak. While Pandora and Ali made two jeeps ready for a speedy departure with jerry cans of petrol and huge plastic bottles of water, Said dressed in the guard's outfit. When the jeeps were ready, Pandora flashed Ali her expensive American dentistry, relieved him of the keys to both the jeeps and tossed them over to Said; in spite of what she'd said to Said, she didn't trust Ali further than she could throw him.

Leaving the jeeps ready and waiting and facing the wide exit of the cave, the unlikely trio made their way back towards the centre of the catacombs, looking for Faisal, Faraj, and Pictikhov. Pandora led the way and Said played guard with Ali jammed between them in case he thought he'd lead them to a trap. Said pulled the peak of the stolen hammer and sickle embroidered cap far down over his brows and pointed the stolen Kalashnikov at the backs of Pandora and Ali as they were marched along, almost at a jog-trot in order to keep up with Pandora, who was bursting with the adrenalin, too excited now to feel nervous about what might be going to happen next.

Faisal signed the final document with a flourish. Pictikhov grinned and called out, 'Fetch the vodka!'

Faisal's eyes narrowed. 'Now we must pray,' he said in English so that Pictikhov would understand. He knelt down. Faraj looked at him confused. 'Come on, Faraj, it's time,' Faisal insisted. Faraj shrugged and joined his cousin on his knees.

Faisal began to cry out in Arabic. 'Said, Ali, if you can hear us, we're in the big man's office waiting for you. There isn't much time. He's breaking out the vodka. If we're lucky then we can get them all trolleyed before shooting the lot of them. Where are you, Said? Can you hear me?'

Thud! Pictikhov's bodyguard, mesmerised at the sight of these wild-eyed Bedu praying in his boss's office, didn't hear the catlike Ali's approach. He hit the floor thanks to a side swipe from a spanner Ali'd stolen from the garage. Pictikhov spun round.

'Wha . . . ?' He didn't have time to call for help before Ali, Faraj and Said all fell on him at once. Gagged and bound, he found himself staring into the barrel of his own revolver, which Pandora levelled at him from her perch on the edge of his desk. Pictikhov stopped struggling; his starched army kit seemed to wilt on him as he sat terrified, on his Napoleonic relic of a chair.

'Vodka, hmm . . . lovely. Just the thing at this time of the morning,' said Pandora in Russian. Pictikhov stared at her in amazement. The silence was broken by the arrival of a man carrying a tray on which condensation was just beginning to form on the outside of the iced glasses. He faltered when he saw the company gathered in the office, dropped the tray, and before anyone could do anything to stop him, he ran. They heard him scamper down the passage, calling for help as he went.

'Now what do we do?' Pandora asked, not taking her eyes off Pictikhov for a moment.

'First we burn these.' Faisal took the recently signed documents and, lighting each one with his father's lapis lighter, dropped them, flaming, into a steel wastepaper basket. 'Good thing this office is so well equipped,' he said as the last document floated, fine as burnt Amaretti paper, down to join the others.

'But the Action Man's going to be back in a minute with all the other guards!'

'They are three down including Pictikhov so there can only be four left to go, and there are five of us,' Ali said to his brother, tossing the fallen guard's AK47 to Faraj.

'Have this, you're a better shot than I.'

Faisal nodded. 'So, we're even equipped to surprise them all, aren't we?'

This was much too relaxed for Pandora's liking. 'With one rifle?' She didn't give up.

'No, I think we should get out of here before we find we're cornered.' Faisal went behind Pictikhov's desk. He physically picked up the Russian, immaculately shiny boots and all, kicked the chair the man sat on aside and, holding Pictikhov firm, turned to Pandora.

'Scrape the floor there.'

'Here?'

'There.'

Pandora scraped. The outline of a trap door emerged.

'Wow!'

'Open it.'

She pulled at the handle carved deep in one side. The door

wouldn't budge. She pulled harder. The door was still stuck. Faraj came forward to help. They could hear the thudding feet of the other guards coming to help now. There was no time to waste. Faraj took charge of Pictikhov, Faisal and Pandora bent to pull at the door together.

'Heave!' The door burst open. 'Get in quick.'

Pandora was first down a series of dark stone steps. Said and Ali followed, then Faraj, then Pictikhov at the butt end of his own revolver. Finally came Faisal, revolver in one hand, torch in the other. He tossed the light to Pandora. The trap door slammed behind them.

'Which way?' asked Pandora in a loud stage whisper.

'Just carry on. You'll come to a fork eventually. Take the left hand one. It should slope uphill.'

'Will the torch last?'

'No idea.'

'Great. Will the guards follow?'

'I hope so.'

Pandora picked up the pace, already imagining the rattle of rifle fire cutting them all down from behind. Ahead of her was the fork Faisal had told her about.

'Is this it?' She shone her torch down each black hole in turn. The void before her didn't inspire the slightest hint of vertigo.

'Go left. Take it slowly. Be careful, it's steep.'

Pandora didn't alter her pace at all. The others panted along behind her. Far away they could hear the Action Men shooting helplessly at the trap door, a solid rock barrier. Why don't they simply open the door? The passage began to climb sharply. There were roughly hewn steps carved out of the solid basalt ground. Pandora felt like a Lara Croft manqué as she gripped the torch between her teeth so that she could haul herself up with both hands. Ten minutes of hard climbing and she burst into the sunlight.

'We're here!' After the cool of the catacombs, the heat was suffocating. Blinded and panting, Pandora turned round to get her bearings. The escarpment dropped away on one side to the basal pavement below. And behind her she found Attallah, grinning, offering her Rory's panama and a tin cup full of water.

'Thank you,' she said.

Leaving Faraj and Said covering the entrance to the secret passage, the others took Pictikhov and tied him up with Ivan; back to back, like two sides of the same bad penny, the Russians were left to roast under the relentless weight of the midday sun. Pictikhov made less and less effort to struggle free, hampered by the disillusioned Ivan, who not only was too tired and hungry to make much of an effort to escape but knew perfectly well that Faisal would let them go only if and when he wanted to; until then there was nothing they could do but wait.

'Now what?'

'Back to the catacombs.'

Pandora gave her tin cup back to Attallah, stood up, and brushed herself down. 'Come on then,' she said.

'Not you.'

'That's not fair.' Pandora fought a sudden wave of panic. Now they'd surfaced from the dreamlike netherworld of the underground caves the adrenalin had drained away; she felt vulnerable, her Lara Croft bravado melted in the sun.

Faisal grinned at her. He threw her Pictikhov's pistol. She caught it. 'You'll be all right,' he said to her. 'Attallah'll guard your back. Can I trust you to keep an eye on these Russians for me? We'll be back before you know it. There's not much for us to do.'

'But they're incapacitated. Why can't I come too?'

'Partly because you're too precious to put into any more danger, but mostly because what we're going to do now is between us and the desert. It's ours to do. I hope you understand.'

'But what about Ali?'

Faisal took a deep breath. 'It's his desert too so I think he'd better come with me.'

And he was gone, he and Ali hurrying towards the edge of the escarpment where the others waited. Shaded by a sarong,

Pandora sat next to Attallah, her gun trained on Pictikhov and Ivan. Attallah pretended not to notice her slightly shaking hands; he gave her a handful of dates to eat and made coffee for her. His little hum in time to the rhythm of the pestle and mortar grinding up the coffee beans was calming and Pandora soon found that the sugar in the dates gave her confidence enough to last the rest of this assault course.

Seeing her relax with coffee and dates under the shade of a sarong, the Russian captives growled. And knowing that she was safe, she laughed at them.

'All right, Ali, this is your big moment.'

'What do you want me to do?'

'Are you sober?'

''Course I am.'

'Have you eaten?'

'Not much, but I won't faint on you.'

'Water?'

'I'll live.' Ali was exasperated.

'Fine. You come with us then.'

'What?' Faraj was aghast.

'He's a traitor.' Said's face was a picture of uncomprehension.

'Don't look at me like that,' protested Ali. 'I made a mistake. Believe me, I'm not going to let you down again.'

'Faisal . . .' Faraj couldn't believe what was happening.

'He's my brother. I'm afraid we're all going to have to take a risk and trust him.'

'Forgive me if I remain sceptical.'

'Come on, Faraj, you must see that I'd rather trust him where I can see him than just hope he'll sit like a good boy with his two trussed-up ex-colleagues and Pandora over there.'

'So you don't trust me!'

'I'm challenging you to earn my good faith, Ali. Is your arrogance such that you expect more than that after what you've done?'

Ali held out his hand to his brother. Faisal hesitated, his mouth set firm. They shook.

'Just give me the chance to show you what I'm made of.' Ali was surprised to find himself choked with emotion. He cleared his throat. 'Right,' he said. 'So what's the plan?'

'A little explosive engineering. Follow me, boys.' Faisal ducked into the entrance to the secret passage. 'Let's see what we're really made of, shall we?'

At the end of the passage they found the trap door still closed. They could hear nothing above them. Ali and Faisal put their shoulders to the stone; it opened marginally. They stopped, listened, could hear nothing. They put their combined weight behind the door and a minute later they'd shoved it back and were out, in Pictikhov's office. Hardly stopping to check that there was no one about, they headed down one of the passages, knowing what they had to do. Soon enough they found the communications room. Faraj levelled his stolen Kalashnikov at the screens. Ali shook his head and unplugged everything; the machines were incapacitated. Ali was about to make a smugly sarcastic remark when voices warned them into running to hide behind an opening in the crumbling wall beyond the drop to Pandora's erstwhile prison. Stock still and silent, they waited in shadows while guards sprinted past them; none of them dared breathe.

Only when they were certain that they hadn't been discovered did they carry on their search, Said leading, following his own markings which he'd left on the walls. Stopping at a scribble he'd made hours before, he thought for a second, scratched his head, and turned right. The passage sloped downwards.

'I remember this.' Faraj suddenly recognised where they were.

'Good. You'll remember how to get out to the garage then afterwards.'

'I said I remembered this, not that I'd suddenly had a vision of how all the passages fit together.'

'I know the way,' said Ali.

Faraj humphed, still annoyed at being bettered by his cousin in the communications room.

'Shut up you two.' Faisal took the lead. Far below they could see lights and, as they drew closer to the great cavern, three stories underground, there was the noise of frantic activity.

At the end they stopped, blinking in the sudden glare from powerful spotlights. A spray of bullets hit the wall behind them. They threw themselves down behind a barrage of boxes. Faisal lay flat in the dark space between a wall of land-mines and the ancient earth. He felt the dull ache from where his ear had been nicked begin to smooth its way around his skull. He blanked out the pain and looked up to check on the others. Said was gone, crawling catlike behind the boxes. Faraj had moved off too, finding a space between mines where he could examine the activities of the guards. He couldn't see where Ali had got to. Faraj looked back at Faisal holding up four fingers. Faisal nodded. Taking a deep breath, he raised his hands above his head and prepared to stand up. He was too late. Ali had already done what he'd been planning. He stood now, hands high, four guards facing him, training their Kalashnikovs at him. They were wary, knowing that, in spite of his apparent submission, they were surrounded. The guards jerked their rifles to bring him forward. Ali smiled at them and took a step back. On Ali's first step Said, who'd circled the whole of the great cave, appeared at the top of a pile of boxes marked 'Anti-Personnel Mines' in English. He held a camouflage net. On Ali's other side, Faraj lined up the guards in the sights of his stolen Kalashnikov.

Faisal, redundant, could do nothing but watch the proceedings as if they were freeze-framed in crystal-clear slow motion. Said dropped the net. Before it landed on the guards they opened fire on Ali. Ali threw himself sideways behind the only pile of boxes in the cave which weren't stamped with skull and crossbones. Faisal prayed that they didn't contain explosives. Faraj opened fire in return, winging the men as the net landed on them and they collapsed.

With the guards incapacitated, Faisal stood up, shaking the flour from the exploded storage bins out of his hair. And there was Ali, greyish and shaking from the shock of his unmeditated act of courage, but otherwise unscathed. There was no time for Faisal to do more than clap his brother on his back; Said and Faraj were dragging the wounded bundle of Action Men towards the exit. Faisal threw away the guns they'd dropped and, dashing about the great cavern and laughing like children, he and Ali poured petrol from the already bullet-sprayed barrels over all the boxes. When the arsenal was soaked they took a last can each and followed the others, pouring petrol as they went.

They headed back up the steep slope and hurried along the route signposted by Said to the garage. There the two other Russians, seeing their colleagues netted and bleeding, turned into gibbering wrecks and didn't protest when Said bound them in the back of one of the jeeps. Ali took the keys to this jeep and the other Russians were jammed into the back of it. He roared out of the cavern with his terrified passengers and paused, waiting, his engine idling. The others leapt into the second jeep, and, still pouring petrol behind him, Faisal held on for dear life as Faraj threw it into gear and roared out of the cave. Outside he stopped, the last of the petrol dripped onto the bare desert ground, the fumes joining the heat haze to rainbow the midday mirage of basalt-coloured water. Faisal drew out his father's lapis lighter. He lit it, kissed it, paused. He threw the lighter to Ali, and as Faraj revved the jeep ready for their flight Ali threw the flame, in a high, piercing blue arc, towards the last of the petrol. It caught. The jeeps made for the wadi and the steep road to the camp above the escarpment. And as they arrived at the top the earth began to shake.

Ivan and Pictikhov were jammed unceremoniously in the back of Ali's jeep. Pandora and Attallah leapt into the back of Faraj's and, as the convoy headed back down the hill, towards the wadi, away from the old, cracked earth of the escarpment – which, under the pressure of the underground explosion rumbling behind them, was beginning to disintegrate, crumbling slowly, then gathering speed, and finally collapsing in an avalanche of sand and basalt – a mile-high cloud of dust and debris was thrown up behind them, obliterating the sun, the sky, the ground between them and the horizon. Ali looked back and he roared with pure glee; he saw in the explosion that the past was disintegrating, not into money, nor into revenge, but into a cloud of broken desert and a bevy of saved lives. He put his foot down and raced with Faraj, covering the sixty kilometres back to the camel fair in record time.

Pandora thought the sunset that evening more magnificent than any she'd seen before. After a day in which she felt that her whole being had been tried and tested, she sat now on the warm rocks on the little hill above the camel fair encampment. The sun made its inexorable decline in a blaze of glory and, low on the eastern horizon, the moon waited its turn, a perfect circle shining silver in the still blue sky. Pandora sat and breathed the cooling desert air, oblivious to the frantic activity in the camp below her.

Her fellow fashionable travellers were all of a twitter, congratulating themselves on her survival, bravely showering under buckets of bottled water, preparing in their heads the tales they would tell on their return to New York. Pandora could see Mimi gesticulating wildly as she related her adventures over the satellite phone to Nina in Manhattan.

The Bedouin had other concerns; once the sun had set and the light of the moon had turned the desert to silver then at last their camels would race. Pandora could see Faisal making his way along the camel lines. He looked up and saw her, and he left his ubiquitous band of little boy admirers behind and climbed up to sit with her, taking off his head cloth and shaking out his hair as he arrived.

'Hey,' he said and folded his long fine legs, sitting down next to her.

'Hey,' she answered. 'Busy day.'

'You could say that.'

'You've burnt your boats as far as making a quick buck's concerned.'

'I know. I'll have to buckle down now.' He gave her an uncertain, lopsided grin. 'So much for life as one of the idle rich.'

'But at least anything you make from now on will be yours

and not the leftover efforts of your illustrious forebears.'

'And that's supposed to be inspiring, is it?'

Pandora laughed and shrugged.

'What about you?' Faisal asked her.

'What do you mean what about me?' Self-conscious, Pandora smoothed her flat, cropped hair.

'You know. What are you going to do now?'

'I don't know. I suppose I'll go back to Manhattan with the others. I'm not sure I want to stand in front of a camera any more though.' She laughed. 'That's a huge lie. I'm positive I never want to stand in front of a camera again.'

'So why go back to Manhattan?'

'Because that's where I live.'

'Not where you have to live . . .'

'Maybe I think there's a limit to the number of momentous decisions you can make in one day, and deciding to give up an extremely lucrative career is one thing, but moving somewhere different at the same time is something else.'

'You could . . .'

'What?'

'Well . . .'

'Yes?'

A horn sounded below them. There was a sudden flurry of activity. Faisal stood up. 'Let's talk about it later,' he said, holding out a hand for her. 'Now I've got to start the racing. I hope you've got some money to put a bet on.' They slipped and scrabbled their way down the hill and hurried through the tents to the starting line where thirty or so men sat astride their finely bred beasts ready for the off.

High on danger and the testosterone-charged atmosphere, the fashion people were having the time of their lives. Relief that none of them had been seriously hurt and that Pandora's adventure had been successful had turned them all slightly manic. Even Frankie and Gavin, their desire to be back in Manhattan forgotten, had been transformed into mad gamblers; they'd organised a sweepstake for the fashion team which Frankie was administering with an efficiency that Mimi wished she would remember when she was being paid to keep the shine off Pandora's nose.

Courteney and Joey were like children set free at a fun fair.

'Look!' Courteney cried. 'Look, look at everything.'

George, flushed with excitement, skipped about too; he'd bought a Bedouin outfit of long white shirt and keffiyeh and dressed in it now, with a dagger plunged into his belt at a rakish angle; he thought himself absolutely gorgeous. Rory, in an unlikely mixture of linen drawstring pyjama bottoms and a sort of grey silk shalwar-kameez top which he'd magicked out of his capacious luggage, thought George a fairly delicious proposition too. Mimi kept an eye on both of them; she couldn't decide which would be worse, Rory running off with a selection of Bedouin or with her own assistant who she couldn't bear to lose.

Pandora couldn't care less what her uncle was up to. She had eyes only for the racers. The camels were resplendent, slung about with twisted silk ropes and spun-gold bordered saddle cloths. Their riders were immaculate in white shirts, polished, bullet-heavy, dagger-hooked, leather bandoliers and perfectly folded, red and white checked head cloths, tucked up into turban shapes to keep them out of the way. Faraj and Said jostled for pole position with the other riders, the whites of their eyes and their incisors gleaming.

'They look positively murderous,' said Pandora, waving at Faraj.

'Do you want to start the first race?' Faisal asked her.

'I can't, can I? Doesn't it have to be the sheikh?'

'No reason why it can't be a guest for once.' Ali appeared at her side. He passed her an ancient rifle, a relic of the first world war. She grabbed it, took a deep breath, pointed it high in the sky and pulled the trigger.

They were off!

The feast which followed the racing was as impressive as Faraj's murderous teeth had been. Whole goats and sheep and young camels had been roasting for hours over deep, charcoal-filled pits; now they were roughly pulled apart and laid on great piles of rice on battered brass dishes six feet in diameter. People gathered round each dish in laughing circles while dancing boys in red sashes sashayed between the feasting groups to the accompaniment of hand drums and the leaping sound of a tinny little flute. Even Ali seemed to be enjoying himself, drawing maps of the day's adventures in the sand and explaining the part he'd played in saving the desert in endless detail to Flash.

Pandora sat with Faisal under the awning of his tent.

'Sheep's eyes?' he offered her. They roared with laughter, happiness singing out of them, gilding the air; they were phosphorescent with glee.

Later, when the children lay sleeping in their parent's laps, and the camels were couched, and the last celebratory gunshot had long since cracked the air, Faisal took Pandora's hand and led her out into the night. Skirting a faltering band of red-sashed dancers, who skipped about with only Rory and George for an audience, they ducked under guy ropes and round the back of the fair and climbed to the top of their favourite hill. Crouching on his haunches, Faisal watched the business going on below.

'You love this, don't you?' Pandora stood behind him, her pashmina pulled tight about her shoulders for warmth.

'It's home . . .'

'It won't disappear, you know.'

'Sometimes I'm convinced it will.'

Pandora knelt down beside him, putting an arm round his shoulders. 'You don't single-handedly inspire this fair every year. I bet nobody knows how long ago it started, and it'll go on forever, long after you're dead.'

'Maybe . . .'

'Faisal, don't you think it's time to cut down on the things you worry about?'

'Like what?'

'Like that lot for instance.' Pandora waved at the camp below. 'Those people down there, that huge extended family of yours. I think you think they're each and every one of them your personal responsibility. All you've been doing is worrying about too many things and so spreading yourself too thin to actually achieve anything. Try really delegating to Ali instead of pretending to. He's proved he can rise to an occasion now.'

'Maybe . . .'

'You've been so busy worrying about the mess your father left you that I think you've missed the point entirely.'

'And that is?' Faisal raised a questioning eyebrow at Pandora's earnest homily.

'Being born a sheikh doesn't make you some kind of *wunderkind*. You've been so overwhelmed by the size of your problems that you've only seen things in terms of extremes – you know, take the Russian's money or go under entirely. So now you're going to have to make something of yourself by yourself, on your own merits, by your own—'

'All right, I get it!'

'So long as you try.'

'If you say so.'

'And you know these people will be behind you whatever you do.'

'Well . . .'

'Even Ali now. You are their sheikh.'

'That's nothing to do with me. I was just born their sheikh, it's an inherited position. It doesn't really mean anything.'

'Bullshit. You are the sheikhest chic sheikh I've ever heard of.'

'Oh yes? And your sheikhly experience is wide and varied, is it?'

'Let me be nice to you, will you?' Faisal blushed in the darkness and bit his self-lashing tongue. 'Listen, you are a sheikh because today you went out and you put your life on the line so that these people's desert wouldn't be abused by arms dealers. You followed your instincts and you were right. You've earned your sheikhdom now. After all, they say that nobility is not a birthright. In England you can buy a title if you want but that gives you nothing. You're a natural, Faisal.'

'Thanks.'

'I don't think you believe me but you should.'

'Brave words from a girl who'll chuck in her career but not her safe cotton-wool world. What's the point in your stopping being a supermodel if you're going back to live in the place where you won't be allowed to stop?'

'What?'

'Why go back to New York when you'll be surrounded by people paid to make you stay in front of the camera because every single one of them has a vested interest in your being a model. You're not the only one who makes a lot of money out of you. Even your beloved Uncle Rory, who obviously has a good heart even though he's never looked further than the end of the nearest catwalk to see what's going on in the world, won't let you give up modelling. I bet when you try to talk to him about this he tells you not to fuss your pretty little head about it because you'll only give yourself wrinkles and then goes on to remind you that your job is to look pretty and his is to worry about the rest of it.'

'You've been listening through tent walls, you have.'

'Isn't it time you started making choices for yourself?'

'But it's hard.'

'Says the girl who's just lectured me about setting out and trying to achieve something on my own merits! I know it's hard. I'm in the same position. I'm surrounded by people whose actions are precipitated entirely by what I do first; everyone from Ahmed to Ali to Faraj to . . . I don't know, Attallah. What is it you really want, Pandora?'

'I don't know.'

'You must have some longing, ambition . . . something.' Pandora looked up through her magical eyelashes and for the first time during this conversation their eyes met. The closely shorn hair stood up on the back of Pandora's neck. Faisal shivered. Pandora looked at his pool-black, moon-glinting eyes. She looked at his questioning eyebrows, at the fine lines of his cheekbones. She tried to think. Faisal watched her. He thought her so perfect that he couldn't quite believe she was real. Now that the mane of her hair was gone he could see something finer in her make-up, a curiosity which he wondered if she would ever dare to satisfy.

Moon time stood still.

'I know what I want now.' Pandora's voice was barely audible.

'Do you?' Faisal reached out and traced the fine curve of her cheek from her eyebrow to her chin. She held her breath. His fingers moved on, down her neck, along to the point of her shoulder. She let her pashmina fall away and his hand carried on along the porcelain perfection of her arm until it reached her hand, which he took and held. He examined her palm, the lines of her life in clear relief against the pale pearl skin in the moonlight. Bent over her, Faisal held stone still, the unruly curls falling away from the crown of his head like a mass of unwoven silk. It was her turn to reach out and touch him, to feel the stillness of him, the contained energy of him; she kissed his head to thank him; she kissed him again because he believed that she could be more than just an image produced by a photographer. And she kissed him a third time because his belief in her was such that he hadn't tried to tell her what to do; all he'd done was help untie the silken chains which bound her.

'I want to jump free,' she said, taking his shoulders in both her hands. She pulled her head back from his and looked him straight in the eyes. 'But I want you to jump with me.'

'Are you prepared for anything?' He kissed her lips for the first time.

'Anything,' she whispered.

'No regrets?' Her answer was to kiss him back.

Chapter 16

Pictikhov shovelled his wounded men into the jeep in which Faisal had planned that the Russians should effect their escape. Filled with jerry cans of petrol, water and enough food to last for a week, the jeep was ready for anything Pictikhov might like to do with it. Faisal and Pandora watched his departure while lying next to each other, high above the camp, flat on their stomachs, their bodies just touching all the way down one side.

The jeep left in a plume of dust, cutting north across raw desert.

'That's the end of that lot then. It's their funeral if they insist on going that way.' He kissed Pandora who nuzzled up to the warm breadth of his chest and breathed in deeply.

'How did you like the jump?' he asked.

'We haven't landed yet, have we?'

'Nope.' Faisal sat up and pulled the discarded pink pashmina round his shoulders. 'But we will soon.'

'I wish we didn't have to. I want this minute to last forever. I never want the sun to get hot, I never want Rory or Mimi to wake up and start asking questions. I just want to lie here with you and with nobody else.' Pandora still lay flat on her stomach watching the camp below them begin to come to life.

'I should stop dreaming and prepare to land. Today's going to be manic: you lot are going home, I've got to work out how I'm going to make a living. This is it. Real life begins as soon as the first person down there sees us.'

'I wish it didn't.' Pandora curled round and rested her head in Faisal's lap. He stroked her tousled hair. She pulled the sarong she'd been wearing the night before over her shoulders and rubbed the sleep out of her eyes before turning onto her back and watching a desert hawk hover over his breakfast, high in the pale azure of the early-morning sky. 'Don't talk about going home yet. I don't know what I'm going to do.'

Rory hummed the 'Laudamus Te' from the Mozart C Minor Mass while he joyfully packed his things. As the tempo picked up so did the speed with which he threw his belongings into his case, and he ended up slinging his bottles of Eau de Hadrien gaily across the room and for once actually seeing the fine glass bottles make perfect landings in the cut-velvet shelter of his dressing gown.

Mimi hummed too, snatches of 'I wanna be in America', as she picked up her trusty notepad filled with lists and headed off to the wardrobe tent to supervise George's packing of the quarter of a million dollars' worth of clothes which she hoped were still in her possession. Courteney had been seconded to work for Flash; she loathed the job but Joey had been drinking camel milk while paying scant attention to the warnings he'd been given of its purgative qualities. He was in no fit state even to sit in on a packing session with Flash, let alone help.

Mimi arrived to find George still bravely sporting his last-season Nikes which, after a few days in the desert, felt to him more like souvenirs of battle than ordinary trainers. Thin-lipped and determined, shattered but invincible, he stood once more before the coffins for the clothes and began to pack, ticking, labelling, sticking; precision was his only defence against totally losing control in this desert environment. He didn't realise that he was talking to himself.

'Get the sand out of the slingbacks and the other shoes can look after themselves,' he said as he carefully wiped the perspex heels of Pandora's favourite Manolo's, only a little melted after being left in the sun at Crac des Chevaliers.

Across the tent Courteney was packing for Flash, who sat in the canvas wardrobe chair emblazoned with Pandora's name while he directed operations.

'No, not like that,' he snapped, not getting up, not helping, not showing how things should be done. 'Come on, babe, didn't you learn anything from that old pouf Saul Smytheson?'

'Only manners,' Courteney snapped in self-righteous indignation. 'Flash, with respect, I do not work for you and I'd be grateful if you remembered that. I'm only doing your packing because your fuckwit of an assistant seems to lost control of his bowels in his desperation to get away from you. So I should just shut up or you'll have to sort out your kit yourself. And for your information, if you call me babe once more I won't be responsible for my actions.'

'Glad to see we're all so cheery this morning.' Mimi stood, hands on hips, at the entrance to the tents.

'Mimi, can't you tell Flash to either help or get out of here?'

'Darling, he is a famous photographer, we do have to treat him with a certain amount of due deference. Can we just bury the hatchet until we get back to New York?' Mimi grinned pacifically at Flash and took Courteney by the elbow, dragging her outside. 'Darling one, I know he's hell on earth, and I give you my word that I'll never ask you to work with him again, but just for the sake of a peaceful journey, can't you force yourself to ignore the babeing.'

'And the rest.'

'And the rest . . . And just do your bit to get us all back to Manhattan in peace. Think about it, in a little over twenty-four hours we'll be home.' Tears sprang into Courteney's eyes at the thought. 'That's my girl. Not long now and I'll try and make sure that you never have to speak to that odious excuse for a man again.'

'Hello, my lovelies. Isn't it the most glorious morning?' Rory appeared from his tent all crisp ecru linen, battered panama and freshly shining patent leather Birkenstocks; he'd even painted his toenails deep Chanel red to celebrate the fact that they were finally going home. The sight of him couldn't help but make Mimi and Courteney feel better. 'Oh, tears of joy because we're going home I see. Well, darling, I quite understand. I'm a little overwhelmed at the idea myself. Now then, where's that Georgie boy who's so clever with the phone system? I think we should call the lovely Nina Charles and tell her that we're alive and well and finally have an estimated time of arrival. George!' He called and George appeared, blushing like a child being congratulated for brilliance after a performance as a bumble-bee at a kindergarten concert.

'Oh God,' groaned Mimi. 'Looks like I really am losing that assistant. Where's Pandora?'

'Here.'

'Where've you been, precious?' Rory, holding George firmly by the hand, turned to quiz his niece.

'Are you packed?' asked Mimi.

Pandora smiled nervously. 'I'm not sure I'm coming back with you.'

'What?' The fashion team chorused universal outrage.

'Don't go all mad on us again, Pandora. Not now. We've got a plane to catch.' Mimi refused to countenance Pandora's leaving the fashion cavalcade.

Pandora registered the horror in Rory's face: he was her uncle and he'd looked after her all her life and in spite of his many and various failings she couldn't bear to hurt him. 'I'm not mad.'

'In that case you'll see sense.' Rory looked as if he was about to internally combust again, high points of colour rising up his pale, pinched cheeks. 'You know the shows start in London next week, Pandora, and you'll need some rest before you start prancing about a catwalk for that Alexander McQueen. And then there's Milan and then there's Paris and then there's New York.' Pandora's future life as a model flashed before her, a ragged-edged passport belonging to someone who seldom saw more of a country than the airport, a couple of five-star hotels, a catwalk and maybe a photographer's studio or the park of a famous house artificially glammed up for her to pose in; she forced herself to breathe normally and to smile, if only with her well-worn dentistry. She dragged herself away to her tent where she sat on the edge of the bed she had never yet slept in and didn't do

308

anything about the small scattering of belongings which lay sparsely sown all over the carpet-covered floor.

'Nina, it's me.'

'When do you get home?'

'Darling, if all goes well and we get back to Damascus tonight then we'll jump on a little plane tomorrow and be back with you in no time.'

'And tell me, Rory, truthfully, has everyone really survived intact?'

'Darling, they're all fine. Even Pandora seems to have calmed down a bit. And her hair looks fabulous, though I say so . . .' George was making frantic 'no, don't tell her she doesn't know' faces at Rory.

'Her hair! What's happened to her hair?' Rory kicked himself. He'd forgotten that they'd decided that Nina had enough to worry about without the knowledge that the world's favourite supermodel, with her princess hair, had chopped it all off in a moment of complete madness.

'Nina, even I nearly lost the plot when she did it.' Rory knew that now he'd started he was just going to have to finish. 'She's chopped it all off. Short. Fortunately she looks about fifty million dollars in it but I'm afraid she's lost the Revlon contract.'

'She's chopped her hair off?' Nina, in her pristine New York office, surrounded by the trappings of her success, couldn't believe what she was hearing. 'But how dare she? Is this the thanks we get for a lifetime of nurturing and caring for and loving her?'

'Darling, I know precisely what you're trying to say. But if I'm perfectly honest then I think it's a miracle it was only her hair.'

'What on earth are you talking abut, what else is she keen to get rid of? Does she want to lose a hand too?'

'Nina calm yourself. Listen, we're coming home. Everything's going to be back to normal and in spite of every-thing I think we'll probably have some truly fabulous pictures.'

*

The fashion cavalcade set off back for Damascus. In the bus Pandora sat alone, staring out of the window at the desert as they passed. She ignored other people's attempts at conversation. She chewed her fingernails and tore at dry skin on her thumbs until they were raw. In her backpack was one of Faisal's keffiyehs and on her wrist a little silver bracelet set with turquoise which he'd given her. That night, lying in the sandalwood-scented room at the al Mez'al House in Damascus, she watched the desert moon rise one more time. It hung beside the Umayyad crescent, already losing its fullness; soon a new moon would hang again next to the man-made example, and Pandora wouldn't be there to see it.

And in the desert, Faisal sat alone on a flat stone still warm from the sun, facing west, Damascus, Pandora. She had to make this decision on her own, he knew he mustn't try and influence her; but perhaps if he held his breath for long enough, saw nothing but her moon for long enough, then she would feel him willing her through the thickness of the night and agree to come with him. He held his breath and stared out into the great dome of the night, focusing until the stars around the moon began to dance in a kaleidoscope of shooting diamonds.

Epilogue

A POSTCARD arrived on Nina's desk. She grabbed it and ran to the art department, where she hoped she'd find Rory. It was post-marked Stamford, California, and was dated 31st October. It read:

Darling boths,

Faisal's business school's teaching him how to count up columns and do complicated maths on a spreadsheet, and he's finding it so difficult he's making me work too by forcing me to read nineteenth-century French novelists so I needn't be frightened of people who are educated and know all about them. Can't see what's so scary so far. Isn't Madame Bovary just the ultimate trashy novel? F. says I'm going to have to learn French next so I can really see what all the fuss is about and keeps saying 'Germinal' to me while sharking about singing the soundtrack to Jaws. Sometimes I think he's a bit mad! Hope you're all behaving yourselves and nobody died of heart failure at the shows.

Love P.

Nina looked at Rory with tears in her eyes.

'We've lost her, Rory, haven't we?'

'Oh darling, she had to fly the nest some time. If the nest hadn't been so comfortable we might have encouraged her to go long ago.'

'But what's she going to do with her life?'

Rory shrugged. 'That's for her to decide. Look where forcing her's got us.'

'But that grotty little apartment . . .'
'She's happy!'
'I hope so. Why don't we send her a care package?'
'Sacks or Barney's?'
'Oh darling, both don't you think?'
'We could go down and see her at the weekend . . .'
'Do you think she'd have us?'
'Do they have hotels in Palo Alto?'